C000296059

Real Gone Kid

Kate Fridriks

Steel Thistle Press Ltd

This paperback edition first published in 2022 by Steel Thistle Press Ltd, Cheshire, England.

ISBN   978-1-915847-00-3

A CIP catalogue record for this book is available from the British Library.

*Dedicated to the memory of my late father, Peter,
the best storyteller I've ever known.*

Chapter 1

Friday, 15 June 1984

There's something unnatural when lassies fight each other.

Since time began, guys have traded insults, thrown punches, and started wars. That's the natural order. Lassies, on the other hand, are supposed to conduct themselves like ladies when resolving issues – at least in the opinion of Gran and Mammie.

It's after school, and here I am, standing in a crowd, reluctantly watching two sixteen-year-old girls scrap with each other. Why did I agree to come? Fights aren't a favourite thing of mine, but as Trisha Gallagher personally invited me, I didn't feel like I could refuse.

I keep my eyes locked on the mud and grass of the playing field in front of me, the blur of Trisha Gallagher and Heather Sneddon's feet in my eye line while they fight. There's a great deal of excitement and speculation about who's going to win. I plunge my hands deep into my blazer pockets to stop myself from trembling. My heart pounds in my ears and I think I'm going to faint.

The crowd cheers as Trisha Gallagher throws Heather Sneddon to the ground in a wrestling move that would make Big Daddy proud. Gripping Heather's long, greasy hair with one hand, Trisha punches and slaps Heather with the other. Both lassies are covered in mud. Blood leaks from Heather's nose.

'Come on, Trisha, stop,' I say, willing Heather to start crying, but she remains defiantly silent.

Trisha glares at me and lands another blow to the side of Heather's face.

Some of the guys lean in, clearly enjoying the fight, and call out useful tips like they're boxing trainers standing ringside, urging on their fighter. 'Stop slapping! Punch her!'

I don't share their excitement, but still, I'm standing here, complicit, in allowing a bully like Trisha make an example of poor Heather. All because Heather won't submit to Trisha's supposed superiority over her. In my head, I'm looking for an explanation for what else the fight might be about, but when it all boils down, I think it's just about being different. Aren't all fights caused by being different? Trisha is tall, pretty, popular – lives in one of the 'bought' houses. Heather's shorter, dumpier, with pale, lumpy skin like porridge and comes from a council estate – rougher than the one I'm from and that's saying something.

The fight continues, the wind picks up, and it starts to rain hard – that special kind of Scottish rain that comes at you sideways with such a speed it stings your cheeks and any other exposed areas, even in June.

Some of the crowd dash towards the main school building. My pal, Geraldine, tugs on my sleeve, her head bent against the driving rain. 'Aileen, sod this! My hair's not getting ruined to watch some stupid fight!'

I shake my head, stand where I am.

'And mind that you're having dinner at my house later!' My other pal, Marie, calls over her shoulder as they sprint away.

I don't admit to my pals that I'm so scared of Trisha Gallagher that I'd rather get soaked than have her pull me up for leaving her fight. I stay with the die-hards on the muddy playing field.

Despite the beating she's taking, I'm sensing that Heather isn't about to surrender any time soon. Perhaps desperate for the fight to finish herself, Trisha times her slaps with screaming insults, 'You stink! You're thick! Ugly! Fat! *You had scabies last year!*' The crowd gasps at this last revelation. Heather reacts by swiping at Trisha's face, leaving scratch marks bleeding across one cheek. Quick as a flash, Trisha slaps Heather so hard that she knocks her pink National Health glasses off her face. The crowd holds its breath. Slowly, Heather turns her face up to Trisha and smirks.

Oh, dear God, Heather, relent! Let Trisha get the glory, and you'll stop getting battered.

I look away. My throat tightens, and I want to vomit. I know I should leave, but I'm afraid to.

'You make my skin crawl!' Trisha pants as she towers over Heather and boots her prostrate figure. Heather grunts with each blow. Trisha's going too far now, and I sense the rest of the crowd feels the same.

Watching the scene unfold before me, I'm transported back to when the bullying started towards me ten years ago when we moved to South Africa. There, I was picked on by older Afrikaner children for being European, and then when we returned home to Scotland, I soon discovered that what religion you follow also flags you for a battering.

I live a double life but not in a slick, secret spy sort of way. By day, I'll go to school, then come home to help my da and gran and do my homework. By night, I plot the best streets to safely get me to my pals' houses on the other side of town. I do this because I'm bullied – not at school – but in my home town. Ever since we moved back to Scotland four years ago, I've been getting beaten by lassies and guys, usually older – because I come from one of the few Catholic families living in a predominately Protestant area.

For a long time, I didn't know what 'Fenian' meant when it was being shouted at me in the streets. I knew it was an insult of some sort, and when I asked Gran, she explained that Fenian is a slang word for Catholics. She chuckled when she told me: 'They don't realise that Fenian comes from Irish Gaelic and means something like "brave young warrior." So, when they're shouting 'Fenian' at you – you just smile, hen – cos you know what it really means. Sticks and stones and all that.'

When you're about to be battered, though, smiling doesn't help. I'm still figuring out this religious difference stuff. Surely, we're all the same? Teenagers together, just wanting to have fun before all the serious adulting begins.

I'm jolted back into the present as two sixth-year laddies put a stop to the fight by yanking Trisha off Heather, to the relief of the group of onlookers. Trisha's still screaming at Heather as she's being dragged away. Heather's staggered back onto her feet, hair sticking up, covered in mud, but still standing her ground, jutting her chin out, shouting defiant responses. No one won this fight, and no one lost, either.

The sodden audience disperses. Heather's still rooted to the spot, squinting at the departing figure of her assailant. I'm stood, now alone in a non-existent crowd, blinking the rain out of my eyes, staring at Heather, a girl I only know of, through cruel jokes about how clatty she is and how bad her home life is. I know she can't help the start she's had in life, but she can certainly stand up for herself.

Heather stoops to retrieve her glasses, and when she puts them on, one of the lenses is cracked. Her eyes rest on me. *Why didn't I stop this fight?* Despite the cool rain, my face burns. Guilt and shame seep into my pores as the answer is obvious: because I'm the same as Heather, living my life in fear. Unlike Heather, though, I don't fight back – I avoid confrontation in the first place.

We're the only two left on the playing field now. Stupidly, I half-smile at Heather, who scowls back as she turns to run for the school gate.

With a sour taste in my mouth and a heavy heart, I head for the bus, hoping there won't be anyone on it who doesn't like me.

⊷ ·•· ⊶

Using my sleeve to wipe condensation off the bus window, I'm thinking about how brave Heather was at the fight – I could never have taken the public humiliation of what she went through. No, I'd rather dodge the fight in the first place, or run away as fast as I can when confronted. Granted, there's also the shame of running away, but at least there's no physical pain involved.

I've always been a great runner – taking after my mammie, God rest her soul. I began my running career early on when we moved to a steel town near Pretoria, South Africa, running away from older Afrikaner kids who picked on me at every opportunity. 'Piss off slimy limey! Get back to your own country!'

One day, when Mammie was making breakfast, I found the courage to ask her what a 'slimy limey' was. Mammie had looked sad as she explained: 'Some of the Afrikaners call anyone from Europe, "limeys". Some are mad at us for coming to South Africa – they think we're taking their houses and jobs, but it was their government that recruited us. "Come and work in the sun!" the ads said – when it was grey and freezing in Scotland, how could we resist?

'I'm so sorry that you've been having a hard time.' She had hugged me and had even put my little sister, wee Mary, back into her pram so that she could cuddle me on her knee while we ate toast and jam. I didn't mention that the Afrikaner children also hit me. I endured the torment for six more years until my parents finally moved us back to Scotland: tired of apartheid, racism, and sunshine.

I had hoped that my new life in Scotland would be different, but no, my running-away-from-bullies world would continue. This time not due to my nationality – but due to my family's religion. Now there were people called Protestants who wanted to beat me – because my family is Catholic. The red colour of my school uniform informs the world which religion I follow. Every kid in my town and surrounding towns wears a school uniform, so we're branded from a young age.

Cathy cats eat the rats!
Proddy dogs eat the frogs!

If I thought the Afrikaner kids were cruel, the Scottish ones had a whole new level of nasty waiting for me.

⟫ ⋅ ⋅ ⋅ ⋅ ⟪

Lost in a daydream, walking home after dinner at Marie's house, I realise too late that, still dressed in my Catholic school uniform, I've turned into a street which has a gang of Protestant lassies congregating on the corner. I gulp. While my underage pals are getting ready to head into pubs, I'm about to get my head kicked in.

My heart sinks deeper when I spot the frizzy red hair of Lorraine Pollock as she steps out from the gang. With a flourish, she hands her bottle of Buckfast Tonic Wine to another lassie and rolls her sleeves as she swaggers towards me.

'Haw, you! Fenian boot! Miss Snooty Drawers! Ah heard ye called me a cow!' She comes to a halt not far from me, eyes glaring, chubby-fisted hands by her side.

Sensing the crowd's anticipation and already knowing the drill, I try desperately to reason with her: 'I would never call you a cow, Lorraine.'

She pulls herself taller and takes another step towards me. 'Ur ye callin' me a liar?' Her voice rises, and the lassies edge in closer, giggling.

Oh. Oh. Lorraine takes a few slow steps towards me; the lassies form a half-circle around us. She clenches and unclenches her fists, all the while edging nearer. I step backwards. Any moment now, she'll pounce for me – probably reach for my hair to swing me to the ground like she's done on countless other occasions. I plan to bolt before she does this, but only when Lorraine and her gang are least expecting it. Clutching my arms around my stomach to stop myself from shaking, I focus on calming the waves of terror washing through my body.

I steady my voice. 'I'd never call you a liar, Lorraine.' I hate this whole charade of her pretending to be affronted by something I've supposedly said so that she can batter me to look hard in front of her pals.

Most of all, I hate myself for not being able to stand up to her.

As I take another tentative step backwards, Lorraine lunges for me, but not before I've spun around to take off running, pumping my arms and legs as hard as I can. She tries to give chase, but I'm too fast for her and her gang, seeing as they're already half-cut.

The laughter of her gang fades as I take the corner into the next street. I keep running.

Chapter 2

Friday, 15 June 1984

'I'm home!' I call, pushing the back door open into the kitchen. Bruno, our boxer dog, bounds over to greet me.

Gran's sitting at the kitchen table, pen in one hand, specs perched on the end of her nose, poring over the *Daily Record* crossword spread out before her. 'Hello, Aileen. I've just got one more clue to get – it's stumped me all day!' she says, wrinkling her nose. 'I'm ready to ask you now.'

It's a little joke between Gran and me that I'm her last resort for finishing crosswords. She hates that she's wracked her brains all day on a tough clue, and then I just come in and tell her the answer. She'd never admit this, but occasionally, I know she cheats by looking in the dictionary.

Smiling, I lean over Gran's shoulder to read the clue. '"Raw doc who runs away". That's a toughie.' I read and re-read the clue until it dawns on me. 'Is it an anagram?' I grab Gran's pen, write the letters of 'raw doc' across the top of the newspaper and swap them around. Immediately, I spot it: 'Coward!'

Gran chuckles as she scribbles 'coward' into the last empty boxes of the crossword and makes a big tick beside it. She fixes me with her bright blue eyes, made even more brilliant by the shock of black curls tumbling around her face. Gran swears that she doesn't dye her hair, but we think she secretly does because there isn't a single grey hair on her head. 'How's your day been?'

I'm tempted to reply: 'Well, I nearly got battered again.' But as I don't tell Gran and Da about the bullying, I reply: 'School was fine. Geraldine and I met at Marie's house for dinner – Mrs Donnelly made Irish stew – not as good as yours, but it comes a close second.' I wink at her. 'Then we listened to my Top 40 tape and Geraldine showed us the new clothes she bought from the market. She bought a red tutu and tartan beret like Cyndi Lauper has on my poster, and she's wearing them out tonight.'

Gran looks thoughtful: 'You should speak to your Da about going out to pubs seeing as you'll be seventeen this year. I know he's been against it, but your pals are underage and doing it. And you're a sensible lassie. Your mammie would want you to enjoy yourself too, today of all days …'

Normally, I would have been open to speaking to Da again for permission to go to the pub, but the last thing I want to do tonight is to go out. It's a big thing – going out to the pub for the first time – but the anniversary of my mammie's passing is not the right time.

The emotions I've been damming all day start to push over the top. My throat tightens, and hot tears prick my eyes: 'I ... just want to be home ... tonight ...' I'm about to sob uncontrollably, but I want to be strong in front of Gran. Other words I want to say become stuck in my throat. Tears brim over, and I can't stop them. I gesture that I'm going to my bedroom, and I run upstairs, past Da and my little sister watching TV in the living room.

I lurch through my bedroom door and close it behind me. I'm safe. Tears spill down my cheeks. I can't breathe. My body shudders as each new wave of grief washes over me. It's four years today since Mammie died, and I miss her so much. She always knew how to make me feel better.

On display on my windowsill, I have three photos of Mammie. I examine each one in turn. There's a black and white photo of her holding me as a baby, smiling proudly at the camera. Beside this sits a colour photo of Mammie, Da, wee Mary and I cuddled together on a tartan blanket in the garden in South Africa.

After the sunshine, colour, and beauty of South Africa, it took me a long time to become used to my new home town. Craigburn is nestled amongst other towns and villages which form a circle around a giant steelwork called the Ravenscraig, or the 'Craig' as it's known locally. Rising above the council house rooftops, no matter where you are in my home town and surrounding areas, you can usually spot the bold white letters of 'Ravenscraig' spelt along the massive circumference of the blue tower inside the steelwork and the giant concrete chimneys which sit alongside. White smoke belches from these chimneys, and in the night-time, huge yellow flames issue from these to light the sky.

The last picture is of Mammie and me from my twelfth birthday – when we knew she was sick. She's cuddled into me, doing our 'squishy cheeks' thing, when we'd press our cheeks together while we grinned at the camera. Everyone says that I look like her, that we have the same smile, dark hair and light green eyes. I hope so. By the time this photo was taken, though, Mammie had lost her lovely dark hair, and she'd taken to covering her balding head with scarves. Even when sick, Mammie still looked beautiful to me.

At first, wee Mary and I were told that Mammie was a little unwell and there was nothing to worry about. I became suspicious as whispered conversations became more frequent, and Mammie had to go into hospital for an operation. Understanding more than wee Mary, I asked more questions until finally, Mammie admitted that she had breast cancer. I burst into tears. The word 'cancer' has always been spoken with fear, and everyone I know of, who's had cancer, has died with it. I couldn't lose my mother. She was quick to reassure me that there were all sorts of new cancer treatments, so there was hope. She said she had already had her breast removed and was now undergoing courses of radiation. Knowing she was being treated, I believed she'd win her fight. I was wrong. As I stare at the photos, fresh grief clings to me like a cold, wet blanket.

In the corner of my bedroom, opposite the door, I kneel to run my fingers along the rough edge of the carpet where it meets the skirting board and tug it gently. Hidden there is a thin stack of one-pound notes, and some of my most treasured possessions: a blue velvet pouch and a pink envelope. Tracing my fingers around my name written on the front of the envelope, I wipe my hands to remove the letter Mammie left for me to read after she died. Even though I know this off by heart, I re-read every precious word of her note to me. *My special girl ... know that I love you, and I always will ... follow your heart. I know you'll find strength and courage ... stick in at school. I am always with you ....*

'I wish you were here, Mammie,' I whisper, as I slip the well-worn letter carefully back into its envelope.

Ignoring the hot tears rolling down my cheeks, I reach next for the blue velvet pouch. I tug on the drawstring of the little bag and tip its contents into my hand. My tears distort the glinting of the clear crystal rosary beads. Transfixed, I gently close my hand, enjoying the gentle, comforting pressure of these against my palm. Mammie gave me these beautiful rosary beads on my First Communion. I had felt like I was a princess being given treasure and I had felt loved. Squeezing the rosary beads one more time, I kiss them and pour them back into the pouch. I return my letter and the pouch back under the carpet.

It's time to pull myself together. I don't want my family to know I'm crying. I want to go back downstairs in control. I want to appear fine to help them, especially Da, but I can't. Not yet. I cross over to my bed to sob quietly into my pillow.

When I was singing and dancing to the Top 40 with Marie and Geraldine earlier, I didn't remind them that today's the anniversary of Mammie's death. It's my grief, not theirs, and I just don't cry in front of anyone. Instead, I hide my sadness behind fake smiles.

I turn onto my back and use my sleeve to wipe my tears. To help distract me, I scan the pop posters on my lilac-painted bedroom walls. I have a crush on Bono from U2, and sometimes Jim Kerr from Simple Minds. I don't wear make-up, but I'm still jealous of how well Boy George can do his hair and face. The pretty boys of Spandau Ballet and Duran Duran wear make-up. I can see from their posters – a bit of eyeliner here, a touch of lipstick there. I can't see any on the Scottish guys in Simple Minds and Big Country, nor on my beloved Bono.

I dream about my future constantly. Gran's doing her best to persuade me to stay in Craigburn – get married to a nice Catholic guy, raise a family. The more she tries to sell the idea to me, the more I find myself resisting. As he ticks all her boxes, Gran's already got her mind set on me settling down with my boyfriend, Paul O'Sullivan. I'm not so sure, though.

As my eyes cast around my bedroom, they fall on another treasured possession of Mammie's. Her silver hairbrush sits on top of my chest of drawers. I smile as I remember how in the evenings, Mammie liked to brush my hair and I would almost fall asleep, it was so relaxing.

One night she asked me how I was getting along in Craigburn. I didn't want to worry her or lie, so I didn't answer. Mammie's voice had grown quiet when she said: 'I know the move hasn't been easy.' I had said nothing as she continued to run the brush over the top of my head. 'What are your dreams, Aileen?'

She had chuckled when I replied: 'I just want to be happy.'

'And what will make you happy?'

'To live in a fancy house in a lovely area. And I want a career, and lots of adventures, like I read about.'

Mammie had beamed at me. 'I believe that you'll achieve your dreams.'

I didn't tell her that my main dream was just to safely walk the streets of my home town without getting beaten up.

And, as I know there's a whole new world out there, I'm planning to experience places, peoples, and cultures I've only ever read about. The ticket to my dreams is to do well at school and to keep studying hard to get the best marks I can in my Higher Grade exams so that I can go to a university far from here. This hope of freedom is what gets me through the misery and fear of my everyday existence in Craigburn.

The faint sound of *Coronation Street*'s opening credits music drifts up from the living room; it's time to be with my family. I look at my face in the mirror: the puffiness and redness around my eyes aren't too bad now. I grab a bobble to tie back my hair. I'm ready.

When I walk into the living room, Gran's sitting in her usual armchair by the mantelpiece. Da and wee Mary are sitting on the couch watching the TV.

Da glances at me and asks in a low soothing tone: 'Are you alright, kid?' He reaches for my hand and gently pulls me onto the couch beside him.

'Yes,' I reply. What else can I say? We all miss Mammie terribly. We're all carrying our private heartaches, and we're done crying in front of each other. On top of the display cabinet in the corner of the living room is a statue of Our Lady borrowed from Gran's bedroom. There's also a small vase of flowers and a beautiful pink candle that flickers its light across two photos of Mammie – one of her on her wedding day, posing proudly with Da, and the other, a family photo of the five of us taken at Ayr beach.

Gran notices where I'm looking and smiles back at me with a sad little twinkle in her eye.

Chapter 3

Thursday, 21 June 1984

The sky is blue and cloudless on this, the last day of school before the summer holidays. I'm standing at the bus stop with my pals, Geraldine and Marie.

Geraldine yawns and stretches. She's the shortest of our group and has a shoulder-length, mousey-brown, bobbed hairstyle.

'Are you still waking at the crack of dawn to get ready, Geraldine?' Marie teases, stooping a little because she's so tall. She has brown eyes, and short, strawberry blonde hair in a pixie cut style. Marie's a calm soul who rarely gets irritated except when someone describes her hair as 'ginger', which she says is so wrong, as her hair is closer to blonde than it is to the orange colour of carrots.

'Yip. This perfect look doesn't happen by magic! If I don't get up early, I have to fight my stupid siblings for the mirror, and the kettle to make tea!'

We giggle, having had plenty of experience of the chaos in Geraldine's home with five sisters and two brothers. Geraldine loves testing the new hair and make-up looks and wants to be a beautician.

'I've heard we're supposed to be signing each other's shirts and blouses today.' Marie adjusts the tie around her neck. 'I'll be glad not to have to wear a uniform for six weeks.'

'Well, I know that no one's coming near me with a pen! My gran would kill me – I need this blouse for fifth year!' I shoot mock warning looks at Marie and Geraldine, who grin back at me.

'Aye, me too.' With her compact mirror open, Geraldine dabs at some invisible blemishes on her face.

'I think the shirt-signing is mainly for those who're leaving school today, and not coming back.'

Marie flicks her short hair from her eyes and tugs at the cuffs of her school blouse. Everything's just a tad short on her because of her height.

Before we've had a chance to digest the shirt-signing, Geraldine trills, 'Here comes lover boy!' Opposite us, my boyfriend, Paul, waits to cross the busy main road.

My cheeks flame. 'I've told you – we're just boyfriend and girlfriend.'

Geraldine tucks her hair behind her ears and purses her lips in that pout I see her make whenever she's in the presence of a guy she likes. 'Come on. Are you telling me that in two years of seeing each other, you've still not done it?'

'Not that it's your business – but the answer's still no.' I kick a stone. I'm annoyed that, yet again, we're having this conversation about my love life, and Geraldine making it clear that she fancies my boyfriend.

'What a waste.' Geraldine murmurs and then, licking her lips, turns to me, 'If you're not going to sleep with him, sling him. Then, I'll make a move on the Italian Stallion – show him what he's missing.'

I splutter.

Geraldine's been using the Italian Stallion nickname for my boyfriend ever since she watched Rocky with her big brother. Paul isn't a boxer, but his grandparents are Italian. The nickname was funny at first, but the joke's worn off now. A knot forms in my stomach.

'Now, now, ladies.' Ever the peacemaker, Marie steps between us.

Geraldine's not giving up, though. 'I know we're Catholics and supposed to save ourselves until we're married. But we could get knocked down by the 240 bus tomorrow, and it'll be too late to realise what all the fuss is about – and it's fun!'

'It's fun until you get pregnant!' I retort.

'You just need to be careful. That's what the pill and condoms are for.' Geraldine sends Paul a little wave.

Lost for words, I shake my head at her. She usually shocks Marie and me with tales of her sexual exploits with guys, but this is the first time she's flat-out warned me that she will sleep with my boyfriend if I don't. Paul grins and waves at us as he waits for a safe moment to cross the road.

'Come on.' Geraldine nudges me. 'You know I'm only kidding.'

'You better be.'

'Of course I am! It's just banter.' Geraldine smiles. 'Think about it, though. If you're both such good Catholics – when you finally do 'it' – it's not really a sin, is it?'

Geraldine's logic sometimes confuses me, but she's so charming with it that I smile back at her.

I've known Paul since our first year at high school when we sat beside each other in the same registration class. I loved his goofy sense of humour, and he used to tease me endlessly about my half-Afrikaner, half-Scottish accent. Over the years, Paul, along with Geraldine and Marie, has helped coach me to lose the Afrikaner accent, but it still comes back when I'm stressed.

Back in first year, Paul was all legs and awkwardness – so skinny that he wore fully elasticated-waist trousers for high school. Admittedly, he's gotten taller and broader, and he has a lovely deep voice now. Over the years, we shared other classes until we finally became boyfriend and girlfriend after we kept choosing each other in a game of postman's knock at a pal's party. We meet in school through the week, sometimes at each other's house, and always, on Sundays, for mass.

Finally, there's a break in the traffic and Paul bounds over to us. 'Morning, ladies! Are we ready for the last day of fourth year?' He chuckles as he offers each of us a Rolo. He saves the last one for me. Marie and Geraldine sigh at this romantic gesture. I grin at him as I accept the chocolate and drop it into my blazer pocket.

Her Rolo eaten, Marie quickly licks the melted chocolate from her fingertips and leans into our group. 'I don't know about you, but I think it's going to be so sad coming into fifth year, and lots of our pals will have left. Did you hear about Heather Sneddon?'

We shake our heads.

'She hasn't come back to school since the fight with Trisha Gallagher – rumour is that she's not coming back at all.'

I bite my lip.

'Fighting's a mug's game, and two lassies fighting each other is even worse. Still can't believe you three went to watch it.' Paul runs his hand through his wavy dark hair.

'Sometimes lassies have to fight.' Geraldine applies some gloss to her lips.

'Well, it's not ladylike.' Paul reaches to take my hand, but I move away. He knows that I don't want to be touchy-feely around my pals but seems to have forgotten – yet again. I half-smile at Paul to make it better, but he scowls in response.

Oblivious, Geraldine tousles Paul's hair, 'And you don't fight in case you get messed up.'

Paul fixes his hair back into place. 'I haven't fought since I was a wee boy, and that was just play-fighting. I've never needed to fight.'

I envy my boyfriend and my pals for this –
none of them seems to have to fight anyone
– only me. Wanting to divert the conversation
away from fighting, I ask Geraldine: 'Was
Heather in your art class?'

'Yes, and she's great at it. Our teacher told
her she's good enough to apply to the Glasgow
School of Art. It'd be such a shame if she didn't
come back.' Leaning into her compact mirror,
Geraldine runs her pinkie finger around the
outline of her lips and flicks her gaze to Paul.

Even though I've spotted this blatant flirting
move from Geraldine, I say nothing, keeping
instead to the topic of Heather. 'And it's tough
to get into the Glasgow School of Art. I hope
she changes her mind and comes back to do her
Highers.'

'I don't think so. I've heard she's been
accepted onto a Youth Training Scheme for
hairdressing. I suppose it's still artistic.' Marie
twiddles with one of her gold hooped earrings
as the bus approaches. I show the driver my
school pass and stagger along the packed bus
with my pals and Paul behind me.

Searching for a free seat, my breath catches
as my eyes fall on the most handsome face I've
ever seen. The sight of him makes me lose my
step. I stumble but don't fall. I swing into a seat
opposite him but a few places up on the bus's
right-hand side. My mind reels. I've never been
struck by lightning, but this must be what it
feels like.

Sitting amongst scruffy-haired laddies
heading to school or work, the guy with the
handsome face stands out with his deep tan and

short, spiky blonde hair. He was staring back at me, too, his high cheekbones angled just above his full lips, in a neutral expression.

A delicious duo of excitement and wonder courses through my body, making me tremble. My mouth has gone dry as I work to compose myself. Everyone's chattering around me, but I'm on my own as Geraldine has plonked herself beside Paul nearer to the front of the bus, and Marie's seated behind them.

Facing forward and in front of him, I'm wondering if he's looking at me now, or staring out of the bus window? As we reach each stop, other passengers come and go, but not him. He's still sitting somewhere behind me. I daren't turn around. I must keep calm. I'm thinking of things to do. Then I remember the Rolo in my pocket.

I clear my throat slightly and, with a flourish, flick out my left hand and reach into my pocket for my Rolo. For reasons I can't explain, I'm hoping he's watching me as I casually but carefully slip the chocolate into my mouth.

My teeth clamp onto something hard with a bit of an odd shape. Puzzled, I pull the Rolo out of my mouth to discover it's a green pencil sharpener!

My cheeks flame. *Who saw me – the idiot – just try to eat a sodding sharpener?* I just know that the guy must have seen what happened. I'm doing my best to resist, but my head turns around anyway. He's looking straight at me, biting his lip, presumably trying not to laugh, as are the passengers sitting around him.

'I thought it was a Rolo.' I giggle, as I hold the sharpener and the chocolate as exhibits. Feeling sheepish but curious, I brave another look at him and am rewarded with one of the most brilliant smiles I have ever seen.

⋙ ⋯✦⋯ ⋘

In our living room, I'm telling Gran and wee Mary the tale of the last Rolo, the green sharpener, and the cute guy. The longer I relate the story, the more I embellish it to make them chuckle. As I reach the climax, I can't breathe out the last words for laughing. Finally, I manage to wheeze out the punchline, and we collapse in a heap of giggles.

Gran ruffles my hair, her eyes moist with tears. 'You're some lassie! I take it you didn't tell Paul this story?'

'Nope. I don't think he'd have seen the funny side. I've never been as embarrassed! Serves me right, though, for trying to show off! Lord knows what the blonde guy thought of me!'

Da strides into the living room, clutching a mug of tea. 'It doesn't matter what he thought of you. You're still too young to be going out with anyone – including that Paul O'Sullivan.'

'Aidan!' Gran reproaches Da, a slight scowl now replacing her smile. 'I know you don't like it, but Aileen's a young woman now.'

Da's eyebrows knit together, and I shuffle on my feet, equally uncomfortable.

'She'll be leaving school in the next year or two – and home. The sooner you come to terms with that, the better.' Gran waves her finger at her son, but we both spot the little smile which has returned to her lips.

I watch them together – such a bond between them. Just behind them, sitting on the glass display cabinet, are the photos of Mammie and the one of the five of us at Ayr beach.

I don't know what we'd have done without Gran these last years. She moved in to take care of us when Mammie's health deteriorated. When she was first diagnosed, Mammie tried to keep our home life as normal as possible, but as the disease took a grip, her strength failed her, and she became confined to bed. I'd go in and sit with her whenever I could. Mammie enjoyed listening to the stories from my day, and my descriptions of the flowers in the neighbours' gardens, especially if they had tulips on display. Tulips were her favourite, in any colour. She also loved to listen to the gossip from Gran: who was going out with who now, who was pregnant, and who was working on the side. Gran was the glue that kept us together and functioning while looking after Mammie.

I've never felt such fear as I did the day I was called out of my school class by Gran. My heart had plunged when she uttered the words, 'It's time, Aileen.' When we got home, there was a large gathering around Mammie's bed, and the priest was giving her the last rites. The day before, I had given Mammie my crystal rosary beads to keep her safe; these were now threaded through her clasped hands. She was unconscious, and while she looked so pale and thin lying in her bed, I'd also never seen her look so beautiful, so at peace, like Gran's statue of Our Lady.

The extended family had filed out of the room to leave us, the immediate family, with Mammie. Standing by her bed, we held hands, as we chanted the prayers of the Rosary in hushed voices. Da moved one of his hands to rest on Mammie's, and I swore I saw a slight smile flicker on her face.

As we prayed, her body trembled with each breath which rattled in and out of her frail frame.

Then, Mammie's chest became still.

Not daring to move, I held my own breath. My ears strained to hear something – anything – in the sorrowful silence which followed. But Mammie lay still. Stunned, I scrutinised her, convinced that her chest would rise again. But she had taken her last breath.

Da cried out – a long awful sound – like I'd never heard before, or since. He kissed Mammie, wetting her sweet face with his tears. 'Goodbye, my darling Angel.'

I took wee Mary in my arms, and she leaned against me, as silent and limp as a ragdoll. I struggled to find any words to say to her. How do you express that plunging disbelief or the dark grief which has taken hold of you? I couldn't tell her that everything was going to be all right because it wasn't going to be. Our lives had changed forever. We'd never see our mammie again, or receive a hug or a kiss from her, ever again.

We stayed there in the room with Mammie, weeping and telling her how much we loved her and were going to miss her. I don't know how long we were there, or when the family began to come back in to pay their last respects.

In the weeks and months following Mammie's death, Da didn't do well. He started drinking heavily, kept sleeping in for work, lost his job, and almost lost our home. Gran observed Da from a distance, giving him some time to work through his grief. I remember after us girls had gone to bed one night, hearing Gran shouting at Da, telling him to get his act together, if not for his, then at least for our sake. The shock of a telling-off from Gran must have done the trick because Da did ease off on the drinking, started taking better care of himself and got a new job in the Craig steelwork.

'Aileen! Time to help me to make dinner!' Gran snaps me out of my thoughts.

When we're in the kitchen, Gran tells me not to pay any attention to Da, that he's just overprotective since Mammie died. Compared to my pals' fathers, my da's super strict with curfews and where I can go and with whom. And he has made it plain that he doesn't approve of my relationship with Paul.

Gran hands me some tatties to peel at the sink while she adds salt to the mince, stirring it carefully. And just like she's reading my mind: 'So, hen. Are you and Paul getting serious yet?' She tries to sound casual, but I know her too well.

'I'm not sure what you're asking me.'

'You know.' Gran winks at me. 'Are you talking of engagement yet?'

'Jeez! No!' I take myself by surprise.

Gran's not giving up. 'You've been winching a couple of years now. He's a great catch – a former altar boy, still attends mass and supports Celtic Football Club. Your granddad and I married at eighteen, you know.'

I pretend to concentrate on slicing a tattie into halves and then into quarters. 'Times are different now. We don't need to get married so young nowadays – because we've got longer life expectancies – they taught us that in geography. I want to go to university, Gran, then have a career and travel, before I will ever settle down.'

Gran comes around to the side of me, a coy smile on her face. 'I don't believe you. Every young lassie wants to meet their true love. And you've already found yours.'

'You mean, you've decided that that's Paul. How do you know when you're in love?'

'You just know, hen. You know as soon as you look at each other. The first time I laid eyes on your granddad – ' she pauses to bless herself, 'God rest his soul – I just knew. I felt it.' Gran's eyes twinkle.

'It's not like that with me and Paul. I like him, but there are no fireworks or anything.'

Gran frowns, stepping back to the cooker to stir the mince some more. 'Aw, poor Paul. Does he know that's how you feel?'

Guilt tightens my stomach, and I realise that this is the first time I've voiced that thought – that I don't think Paul and I are right for each other anymore – despite how much others wish it to be so. It may also be the reason why I don't want to go any further with Paul in our relationship. If I'm totally honest, he feels more like a brother to me now.

'Have you got a wee crush on someone else, perhaps?'

'No.' A smile forms across my lips. I drop the last tattie I'm peeling into the sink, pick it up again and rinse it off.

'Aha! So, who is he, then? I hope he's a Catholic.'

Do I admit that the first person to pop into my head is the guy from the bus who I'll probably never see again? Gran cocks her well-plucked eyebrows at me. She's not going to let me get away with not answering. 'Well, I don't know his name, but he's tall, taller than Da. He has short, blonde, spiky hair and an amazing smile.'

Gran's cottoned on. 'The cute guy on the bus?'

'Aye.' I dip my head, picking some black spots out of the tattie I'm peeling.

'I hope he's a Catholic because you know what I say ... '

'"*Never marry a Protestant,*"' I mimic in a high voice, '"*Cos they'll be nice to you until you marry them and then they'll turn nasty!*"'

Gran nods satisfied that the message she's been working hard to drum into me for years has sunk in. I'm not comfortable with this idea of marrying for religion – I'd rather marry for love. Still, if my future husband, whoever he is, happens to be a Catholic, it'll make my life a whole lot easier, especially with Gran.

Now that the dinner's been prepared and is being cooked, I stroll over to the kitchen table to read the *Daily Record*. On the front page is a photo of striking miners clashing with police while picketing outside the Ravenscraig steelwork. Gran notices me reading the article and comes to sit beside me. 'Terrible business!' she mutters. 'At least there were no arrests yesterday. Over three hundred miners were arrested last month trying to stop the lorries driving the coal into the Craig, trying to protect their jobs. That Maggie Thatcher's got them over a barrel.'

Margaret Thatcher is the UK's first female prime minister and the one controlling us Scots from 600 miles away in Westminster. I see her on TV with her coiffed hair, fancy suits and words. But along with her Conservative Party, the policies she's introduced have hit us, and everyone we know, hard. Times are tough, and money's scarce for my family and for most of my pals' families.

Da strides to the kettle to refill his mug of tea. 'That Thatcher will not be happy until she's destroyed the unions, decimated Scotland's industry, and took away everyone's jobs! She's definitely not for the ordinary working man.' Da screws his face as he turns to us. 'And that's everyone we know.'

'It must be rough on the families too.' I look at the anguish marked on the miners' faces in the photo as they tussle with grim-faced police officers. All they're trying to do is to keep their jobs, be able to feed their families. The coal mines round here closed years ago, but to help the miners put more pressure on the government, the railway unions have refused to bring coal into the Craig on trains. So the miners now picket the gates of the Craig to make it difficult for the lorries to bring in the coal needed to keep the Craig's production of steel going. Most of my pals' fathers, uncles, and brothers were badly affected by the steel strike a few years ago, and while sympathetic to the miners now, they haven't gone on strike themselves.

Gran snaps the newspaper shut. 'Can't believe that Thatcher and her lot got voted back in again. That's all them down south for you. They're making loads of money while we're all skint!'

Da nods, grim-faced, as he strides back into the living room to read his book.

Leaning across Gran, I flick the *Daily Record* open a few more pages. "Rapist strikes again!" screams the headline. Quickly scanning the story, I learn that this is the second rape attack in as many months in the Glasgow area, about ten miles from here.

'You watch yourself, hen. Hopefully, they'll catch this guy quicker than they did with that Yorkshire Ripper! Keep on the busy streets, make sure you get home before it gets dark, and don't trust anyone.'

'Aye, Gran. You don't need to worry about me. I bet I can run faster than him anyway!' I joke a little to lighten the atmosphere.

'It's no laughing matter, young lady! It's not about speed! Your tiny frame is no match for a man!' Gran wrings her hands, a worried look on her face.

'Sorry. I'll be careful, I promise. I'll carry my door key in my hand. If someone tries to attack me, I'll just stick my key up their nose or in their eye or something.'

Gran narrows her eyes. 'A good hard kick to the balls does the same job, hen. Just go for the balls!'

I do have some strange conversations with Gran. If they're not about the dangers of romantic liaisons with Protestants, they're about kicking rapists in the balls.

Chapter 4

Saturday, 30 June 1984

It's ten past eleven, and I'm stood outside Round Sounds record store on a busy Woodburn High Street. I'm waiting on my best friend, Doll, to arrive. My best pal's real name is Dora Alice McLintock, a title that I've only ever heard her parents use. Doll's older than me at seventeen, is a Protestant and a member of the Women's Orange Lodge. Coming from different religions, we wouldn't usually have become such great friends had we not met at running training. For three years, we trained together as part of the local county running team, winning lots of championships. But I was forced to stop training with the County when they moved the training ground to a town with no direct bus routes from Craigburn. I was disappointed, but Doll and I still go running together locally and have kept our friendship.

Cooler than buying records from Woolworths across the road, Round Sounds is the place to be and to be seen. It might be more expensive, but my pals like that it stocks records from up-and-coming bands and not just the usual chart music.

To avoid being noticed, my favourite game is to pretend to be deep in thought, staring at the ground – or here – I pass the time reading the notices in the Round Sounds window. These are a mix of adverts for band line-ups in local pubs and clubs, music equipment for sale, and adverts for musicians to join bands. The bell above the door tinkles non-stop as customers enter and leave, their liberally applied perfumes and aftershaves catching the back of my throat, making me cough.

When my ponytail's tugged, I look up, expecting to see that Doll has sneaked up on me. Instead, I'm startled by a skinhead guy, leering back at me, carrying a music case. 'You were stood in ma way.' He wipes his nose, which curls his lip to expose gappy, grey teeth strung out like well-worn nappies on a washing line. He also has a 'Glasgow Smile' – a scar from being slashed with a double-edged flick knife from the corner of his mouth, across and up his left cheek to his ear.

Ducking my head, I shrink back against the record store window and motion for him to pass me. As he opens the door of the record store, I notice that the bottom of his skinny jeans have been rolled up so that they end just above his maroon-coloured Doc Marten boots.

'Sorry I'm late!' Another tug on my ponytail and I'm relieved to see Doll's smiley face.

'You've met Billy McIntyre, then.' Doll's smile turns to a scowl as she tosses her long blonde hair out of her eyes. She takes one last puff of her cigarette and stubs it out on the pavement with her stiletto shoe.

'Billy McIntyre?' Peering into the gloom of Round Sounds, I'm trying to place the name.

'He started the Clyde Alloys with Sandy when they were at school.' Doll's boyfriend, Sandy, plays drums in this band. Now I remember that Billy is the lead singer and guitarist with the band.

'It's funny. The times you've mentioned Billy – I imagined him to look different – maybe have long hair like Sandy?'

'Nah, he's been a skinhead and a pain the arse as long as I've known him!' Doll takes my arm and leads me into Round Sounds which is packed with teens and twenty-somethings, browsing through shelves of vinyl records and cassettes.

It's been a few weeks since I've been in here. I dare to raise my head, my heart skipping a beat as I absorb the buzzing atmosphere. Along the walls on both sides and in units in the centre of the shop are box shelves which house record albums, singles, and cassette tapes. Artists and bands are divided alphabetically and by music category.

Adorning the walls and the ceiling, and artfully papered over older posters of David Bowie, Talking Heads, The Clash, Iggy Pop, New York Dolls, Sex Pistols, and The Ramones, are newer posters for A Flock of Seagulls, Joy Division, U2, Simple Minds, Ultravox, The Jam, OMD, and The Police. Towards the back of the record store, there's a flashing pink neon arrow sign hanging above the cash desk. Arranged on the wall behind this are the display shelves for the record sleeves of the Top 40 chart singles. Next to the cash desk are glass double doors above which someone has artfully handwritten *The Music Room* in black paint.

The throbbing beat of "Relax" by Frankie Goes to Hollywood begins to pulse through the speakers. Banned from being played on Radio 1, this record still went to number one in the charts earlier this year, and I like the edgy, catchy feel to it. I love loud music and can't stop grinning as I follow Doll through the laughing, chatting crowds.

Doll heads straight for the 'P' section of the record store, shouting over her shoulder to me. 'Prince has just released *Purple Rain.*' Her red-painted fingernails flip through the album covers.

I flick through Bruce Springsteen albums next to her. 'I don't get Prince myself. He's very ... out there.'

Doll laughs. 'You mean that he expresses himself freely! I just love his music, the way he dresses – the way he's so unafraid of what anyone thinks.'

This strikes a chord with me. It must be great to just be yourself, not to give a toss what anyone else thinks and not be feart of anything.

'Oh, ya dancer! Gas has got it in stock!' Doll squeals, fishing the new Prince album out and heads straight for the cash desk.

I only get a little pocket money from Da as things are so tight at home, so it's fun for me to vicariously enjoy Doll's purchases of records and clothes. 'I'd buy Bruce's *Born in the USA* myself, but I guess I'll be able to force myself to listen to Prince instead.' I take Doll's arm and cuddle into her as we wait her turn in the queue to pay.

'Any news?' Doll slides her fingers across the plastic sleeve of *Purple Rain.*

'Nope. School's finished like it is for you.' Then I remember about the cute guy on the bus. 'Except, I shouldn't say this because of Paul, but I did see the most gorgeous guy on the bus the other day .... '

Doll screams so loudly she makes me and the goth guy with the dyed black, spiky hairdo standing behind us jump. She urges me to tell all, squeezing my arm hard as she listens to every detail and snorts at the part where I munched down on my sharpener instead of the Rolo. The goth guy has been listening too – his face hidden behind his Echo and the Bunnymen album, shoulders shaking.

Still giggling at my story, Doll hands cash to the sales assistant. He flips the black vinyl album record this way and that, checking for scratches, before popping it into its sleeve. Doll chuckles as she accepts her bagged album and receipt. 'Sandy says Prince is a wee nyaff, but I know that's just because he's jealous that Prince is so talented and gorgeous. A lot to compete with, I guess.'

A skinhead nudges past me and reminds me of Billy McIntyre, who I can't see in the shop. 'I'm guessing Billy must have gone into *The Music Room?*'

'No, he'll be upstairs, somewhere. I forgot to tell you, the Clyde Alloys are using one of the upstairs rooms to rehearse. They're not allowed to practice in any of their houses now – the noise is too loud – I can vouch for that.' Doll winces. 'Billy can't sing or play at the best of times. I feel sorry for Sandy because he thinks the other band members have improved at playing together, but Billy just wastes the band now. But they're good pals. Sandy doesn't know how to ask him to leave.'

Doll nudges me, a slow smile spreading across her face. 'You've never heard the band play. Why don't we surprise them?' Ignoring my protests, she leads me through the record shoppers towards the glass doors at the back. Using both hands, she shoves the doors wide open to *The Music Room.*

The thin, bent figure of Gas Marshall looks up in surprise as he places a red guitar back on its display stand. Here, the walls are filled with all sorts of brass and string instruments and music books, while the floor has larger musical equipment such as drum kits, amps, one treble bass, and even more guitars propped on stands. Some genteel classical music plays over the speakers, and the room feels cooler and calmer.

Gas is the manager of Round Sounds, and because of this, I thought he would be like thirty years old or something, but Doll told me that he's only twenty-one. I rarely see him as he seems to prefer to work in *The Music Room* and leave his younger staff on the busier cash desk out front. The only other person in the room is a tall laddie wearing a red baseball hat. He has his back to us, pinging out notes on an electric guitar that isn't connected to an amp.

'Where are the boys?' Doll gushes. I stand behind her.

I've noticed that Gas doesn't like to look people in the eye. This is strange because he wears lots of eyeliner and has a Mohican hairstyle which must surely draw attention to him. Gas mumbles, 'Sandy told me no chicks – that means you too.'

Doll stands with her hands on her hips and tuts. 'Sandy can say what he likes! Come on, where are they?'

Gas shakes his head and glances at the guy with the baseball hat. 'Back in a minute, pal.'

The guy grunts, not turning around, engrossed in testing out the new guitar he's playing. Gas shows us to a door behind the cash desk. 'Up the stairs. Follow the racket!'

Doll grins at Gas. 'See you at McCoy's.'

'You coming soon, Aileen?' Gas half-smiles, his eyes cast downward.

'I'm not allowed in pubs yet.'

'Well, when you do come, I'll play some of your favourite records. You just let me know.' Gas raises his hand to us as he heads for the doors to *The Music Room*. I smile at Gas's offer. When he's not managing Round Sounds, Gas is the DJ in the local pub, McCoy's. I've been dreaming of going to McCoy's for a long time. Gran's already warm to the idea. I just need to work on Da.

The skishing sound of cymbals and the deep boom of the bass drum gets louder as we reach the top of the stairs. Doll and I giggle as we tiptoe to the room furthest down the hallway. The distorted noise of guitars and keyboards played out of time jars on my ears. 'What a din! I was expecting the band to sound ... more professional?'

As we near the closed door, the racket gets louder, and Sandy shouts, 'Fuck sake, Billy! Turn your amp down – and your mike and distortion pedals are set too loud! You're drowning us all out, and you're not in time!'

The music stops abruptly. The squeal of an amp pierces through the sudden silence causing Doll and me to wince at the same time.

'Wir a punk rock band. Wir no' supposed to be oan time or in tune!' A gruff voice, I'm presuming to be Billy's, replies.

'You're wrong, and I think the Sex Pistols would disagree with you too. Punk might sound chaotic to some people, but there's also an order! Besides, we're a post-punk band – something a bit more modern to fit with these times.'

'Whit? Yir jokin' me! When did yeez decide this?' Billy's voice rises.

Another male voice, quieter, speaks: 'The Clyde Alloys doesn't just consist of you, Billy. We've been thinking of changing direction – playing more of the music *we* listen to now.'

'Er – wait a wee minute! Yous've been talking behind ma back? Makin' plans withoot me? Cheeky bastards! I'm the lead singer!' Some bangs and crashes follow. 'Yeez kin shove yir band right up yir arse!'

Doll and I leap back from the door just as it's swung open by Billy, who storms past us down the hallway, thumping his guitar case off the walls.

'Going well?' Doll jokes as she steps into the room.

Sandy shakes his head and ties his hair back. 'He'll just not listen. We keep giving him chances, but he doesn't practice – and let's be honest – he can't sing or play!' The other lads nod in agreement, silent for a moment. The band members are older than me, a mix of eighteen and nineteen-year-olds. Gripped by shyness, I hang back by the door.

'We've not been introduced. I'm Tommy.' Wearing sunglasses, the guy behind the keyboard strides forward and shakes my hand. I've never come across anyone in real life who wears sunglasses indoors. Sometimes, I've seen pop stars wear sunglasses when they're performing on TV, maybe to look cool and mysterious. Or, Geraldine told me that it's because some of them are still signing on for unemployment benefits, so they're in disguise from the staff of the Benefits Office. There are no TV cameras in here, or Benefits Office staff, so I figure that maybe Tommy has a hangover or a black eye.

'Him over there is Frankie Fingers – so-called cos of his sausage fingers – perfect for playing bass.' Frankie grins at me, waving his thick fingers in the air as evidence.

'Second guitarist and backing singer over there is Rab – who's apparently the shyest guy

in the world but one of the best guitar players.'
Rab doesn't move but nods at me instead.

Sandy comes out from behind his drum kit,
makes his way over to Doll, and they kiss for
the longest time. I shuffle on my feet, waiting
for them to finish. The band members look
amused.

Tommy clears his throat. 'Don't mind us!' The
couple break from their embrace, laughing. I
sigh – they make such a great couple.

Sandy hitches his jeans. 'It looks like Billy's
finally left us.' The other band members nod.
'Rab, will you not play lead guitar and sing for
us? We can get another second guitarist?'

Rab swishes his long fringe across his face. 'I
told you. I prefer to be in the background.'

Sandy shakes his head, 'Guess we better find
a new band member then, guys?'

Chapter 5

Thursday, 5 July 1984

B lood oozes from my index finger, and a sharp pain shoots through my hand. Cursing as quietly as possible, I crouch by the garden fence to take a better look at my finger. I must have caught it on a nail or something jagged while I was climbing the fence. Normally, I'd wipe blood on my dark-coloured leggings, but tonight, I decided to wear white jeans. Gasping, I hold my finger out to let the blood drip away from me and grab a leaf from a nearby plant to staunch the blood flow.

It's half-past five in the evening, and it's a breezy, overcast day. I'm on my way to see Paul. He lives in a 'bought' house in a posh area about half a mile from the school bus stop we meet at. He presumes I walk the streets like any normal person to get to his house. The reality is that to visit him without being battered by some gang, and especially by Lorraine Pollock, I recce which streets are safest to walk first. Even then, the streets aren't always clear. So, I'll turn back the way I came to avoid a beating. Or I'll nip through a stranger's front gate, down their path, and into their back garden. I'll climb over the dividing fences between the houses to circumvent any gang gatherings. This is my regular stealth operation to get myself safely from A to B.

In Craigburn, each council house garden is divided from the others by spiked, grey wooden pailing fences, around three-foot-high. Paul's remarked that I only seem to wear nice dresses or skirts when he comes to visit me or when he meets me in town. If only he and my pals knew the real reason why I deliberately only wear leggings or jeans when I visit them. Over these past few years, I've turned the climbing of fences into an art form. As deftly as I can, I stick my left foot into the bottom strut of the fence. Gripping the top strut with both hands, I swing my right leg over. Wedging my right foot on the other side, my left leg swings over to follow. I drop down into the new garden. Scanning the windows, I check if I've been spotted. I'm practised at it now, only wobbling if someone opens their back door. Thankfully, most Craigburn residents are too busy watching telly or nosing out of their front living room windows to catch me skulking across their back-garden vegetable patches and flower displays. I feel ridiculous jumping people's back gardens – the shame of being caught trespassing like this would melt me, but it's preferable to the alternative of the humiliation and pain of a public battering.

My home life and Paul's couldn't be more different. His parents each have a car parked on the driveway of their big house, which is on a tree-lined street. Paul's parents own and run an Italian restaurant and can afford to buy him private tutoring, musical instruments, and ski and beach holidays. Paul regularly buys himself the latest clothes and records with the generous pocket money he receives. I don't feel poor in my home town, but when I visit Paul's home and the area he lives in, I can't help but feel a little envious of how pretty and safe it all looks.

As I head onto the last row of gardens, the blood seems to have stopped now, and my finger throbs like it has its own painful heartbeat. The sound of a man's raspy cough catches my attention, and I spot him pass his kitchen window. I crouch further on my shaking limbs and work to bring my breathing under control. Another cough and the back door is yanked open. As I curl up, I catch sight of the man, in his stained vest and underpants, coming down the stairs with a bin bag in his hand.

'Oi! What you doin'?' The man yells as he dumps the bin bag to chase me.

Heart hammering, I freeze for a panicked moment, but then spring to my feet to race across the grass and vault over the fence into the adjoining garden. Out of the side of my eye, as I head for the front gate of this house, the man gallops along the other side of the fence from me, roaring that he'll have me arrested. I hope he doesn't catch the attention of the neighbours. What if one of them calls the police? I keep running, intent on escaping by whichever means I can. I rush past the side of the council house and run headlong to the waist-high front gate. I can't seem to unlock the latch. I cry in frustration as I batter and shake it, but it won't open. In desperation, I clamber over the gate, catching myself painfully in the crotch.

I squeeze my eyes closed with the shock, and lurch forward.

Pain erupts across my face. Horrified, I realise that Lorraine Pollock has just slapped me. She's stood on the pavement, her wispy red hair flying around her face in the breeze. Leering, she takes a tight grip of my hair. 'There ye ur! I thought I saw you skulkin' aboot earlier like a wee rat. Ah've been walking these streets looking for yir wee scrawny arse!'

'Do you know her?' The man shouts and swears as he, too, struggles to open his own front gate. Then, he seems to realise that he's only in his underwear and stays behind his gate as the ghostly, curious faces of the neighbours begin to appear in the windows all around us. My mind races to plan how I'm going to escape. Lorraine bares her teeth and lunges at me, punching me hard in the face. My eyes water, and instinctively, I snap them closed to steady my blurred vision. White-hot pain sears from my jaw to the back of my skull.

Vest man gasps. 'There's no need for that! Leave her alone!'

'Fuck off!' Lorraine growls, and the man's protests disappear as he presumably heads back into his house. I open my eyes as Lorraine draws her arm back to hit me again. I scream and, twisting my head around, sink my teeth into the hand clutching my hair. She cries out, instantly releasing the grip she has on me. Seizing this chance, I sprint for freedom. Lorraine gives chase, shouting threats and swearing at me, but soon only the sound of blood pumping in my ears replaces the thud of her footsteps and heavy panting behind me.

⇒⇒⸱⸱◆⸱⸱⇐⇐

As Paul's parents are out for the night, we're nestled on the brown leather sofa in his living room. Paul asked me what happened to my finger when he put a plaster on it earlier, and I explained that I caught it on something, which is the truth. My jaw still throbs, and my scalp aches from having my hair yanked, but otherwise, the beating could have been a lot worse, and more noticeable on me.

We've just watched the film *Rocky,* and now I get where Geraldine's Italian Stallion nickname for Paul comes from. And while I don't know much about boxing, I still enjoyed the story of down-on-his-luck Rocky Balboa, overcoming tough obstacles to rise to become a world-class fighter and how hard he fought to win the affection of his love, Adrian. I was practically off the sofa, cheering Rocky on in that final boxing match, and in tears when he called for Adrian at the end of his fight.

Paul was bemused by my reaction earlier when he popped the *Rocky* tape into their new VHS video cassette recorder. I think it's amazing that people can play films through the TV which were shown in the cinema only a year or so ago. I'd love for us to have one in our house, but Da says they're too expensive.

We have our dinner plates and glasses of red wine on wooden trays, balanced on our knees. Normally, when I have dinner at Paul's house when his parents are out, he'll make something easy like chicken and mushroom Findus Crispy Pancakes with crinkle-cut chips. But tonight, he's cooked me an Italian meal from scratch, using some family recipes to make garlic bread and this spaghetti dish.

'Dig your fork into the spaghetti and then twirl it around your fork using your spoon. What would my granddad say?' Paul chuckles as he demonstrates for me. I've never eaten real spaghetti before, only out of a tin. It's the trickiest thing to get into my mouth, especially because I've only recently been smacked in the jaw.

Paul's grandfather, Gino, was an Italian prisoner of war held in a camp in Perthshire during World War Two. When the war ended, Gino stayed on in Scotland, moving to Motherwell to find work in the steel mills. He met and married Paul's grandmother, Nina, and they have three daughters, one of whom is Paul's mother.

Gino will always give me the time of day, telling me his stories from the home country, but Paul's parents have always been a bit sniffy with me, and they've made a few jokes about what a rough council estate I come from. Gran's stated her suspicions that they think I'm not good enough for their Paul, pointing out that I only seem to be asked to Paul's when his parents are out, and they've never invited me to eat at their fancy restaurant.

Paul shakes his head as he turns to me, making a bad job of eating the spaghetti. 'You're the girlfriend of the Italian Stallion.' He grins as he takes my hand holding the fork and places his other arm behind me to take the hand holding the spoon to demonstrate what he means. 'Catch the spaghetti like this.'

I pretend not to notice the little somersault sensation in my stomach while I focus on what Paul's showing me. I giggle as Paul helps me to put spaghetti in my mouth, forkful after forkful. He twirls some more spaghetti and dips it in the sauce but misses my mouth, smearing it across one cheek, with some dripping down my neck. 'Oops, I've got some sauce on your crucifix.' He dabs at the sauce on my cheek and on my chest around the crucifix. 'Do you still like your Christmas present?'

'Yes! For the one-hundredth time!' I laugh.

'And you promise to never take the crucifix off? It'll protect you.' He brings his face around to mine. He pauses, his brown eyes staring into mine. His lips part slightly.

I stare back, trying to take in what's happening. Something feels different tonight.

The crucifix now lies heavy against my chest. Perhaps it's guilt because I do take Paul's crucifix off before I meet Doll or visit her home and friends. Doll and her family know that I'm a Catholic, but I don't want to advertise it by wearing something traditionally worn by Catholics.

When Paul takes my tray, I compliment him on the dinner, and when he beams at me, my stomach flutters again. Maybe it's the wine making me react this way as I'm not used to drinking.

Paul disappears into the kitchen and returns with dessert. 'Tiramisu! A special Italian dessert. Granddad made this one for us.'

The pudding is creamy and delicious, with a soft sponge base. 'Oh my – what's in this?'

'Secret family recipe.' Paul grins, taking my empty plate.

Surprising myself, I tease, 'So what do I have to do to get it out of you?'

He winks at me, and I follow him out of the living room into the kitchen. He pops the dessert plates into the soapy sink water along with the other dishes, and I grab a tea towel and join him.

The radio plays in the kitchen, and Paul and I chit-chat as we stand side by side, cleaning and drying the dishes. When the Beatles song, "Ticket to Ride", comes on the radio, I tell him that that song was one of my mammie's favourites.

Paul smiles at me as he starts singing the song, and I join in. Feeling mischievous, I nudge the side of my hip against his, and we sway and bump like that, laughing and passing the dishes. This is how we used to carry on, having fun when we were younger.

'I miss us like this.' I sigh, placing the dish I've just dried onto a stacked pile.

Paul stops singing too, and a puzzled look passes over his face. 'Me too. Everything's so serious now – exams, university, career choices, miners' strikes ... '

I giggle. 'Jeez. It really is serious ...'

He grins at me as he offers me a wet plate to dry. Our hands touch as they have done hundreds of times, but for some reason, this time, the shock of his hand on mine makes me drop the plate, which smashes onto the floor. Before I've even had time to react, Paul is bent down, sweeping the broken plate into a dustpan and into the bin. He casts aside my apologies, and he retakes his position standing beside me at the sink. We carry on doing the dishes in silence. Only the radio is playing.

Paul's hand brushes my hand again as he passes me a dish. Again, that flip-floppy sensation in my stomach. *What is happening?* I sneak a sideward glance at him, and he turns towards me. He slides the dish he's been washing back into the soapy water and places both of his hands on my hips to draw me towards him. The tea towel slips from my hand onto the floor. Now his arms are entirely around my waist, and his head inclines towards mine. I close my eyes.

His kisses are gentle at first, then become more urgent. It must be the red wine, but I don't stop his hands, like I would normally, from tugging up my T-shirt to stroke my back and my stomach. Enjoying his touch, I caress his warm back. The wine has obviously loosened me up. Paul pants. He kisses me harder. I'm finding it difficult to breathe, and I freeze. I stop kissing him and step back.

'What's wrong?'

I turn away from Paul's confused face. 'You know I can't.'

'You mean you won't.' Paul's voice sounds bitter.

'I can't. I won't. Not with you or anyone. I'm just not ready for ... '

'Sex. Sex. Just say it.'

'Yes, for that.' I mumble, staring at the floor.

Paul touches my face and speaks in a soothing tone. 'We're allowed to do "it", you know. It's perfectly natural. We've been seeing each other for two years now. We're not kids. You're nearly seventeen, and I'm your toy boy.'

I look up. I know this is Paul's attempt to lighten the mood, but I don't like it when he reminds me that I'm four months older than him. When we came back from South Africa, because the education system is different there to Scotland, it was decided to put me in the year below so that I could start fresh with the rest of the kids in their first year in high school.

'Do you not fancy me?' It's Paul's turn to hang his head.

My stomach twists. I hate hurting him.

'Of course.'

'Do you love me?'

'Of course, but ... '

'But what?'

'I don't love you in that way.'

'Enough to sleep with me, you mean?'

'I don't know what that kind of love is supposed to feel like. I like you. We have good fun together.' I shuffle on my feet.

Leading me over to the kitchen table, Paul sits me down. 'Aileen, I don't know how much longer I can wait. I want my first time to be with you.' He squeezes my hand, watches my face.

'Maybe we should break up then.'

'No! I don't want that. I love you. I'm sorry.'

'I'm scared, Paul. And confused. This is too important to mess up. I want to wait until I'm older, maybe after university, when I get married.'

He scoffs. 'Jeez! I don't think I can wait that long!'

My stomach twists as I search for a way to make the situation better. Then it comes to me, from a long-forgotten conversation with Mammie, just before she died. 'I promised my mammie I'd wait until I was married.'

Snatching his hands back from me, Paul grimaces. 'So that's it then. If you've promised your dead mother, there's no compromising!' He runs his hands through his hair. 'I love you, but it's so hard to be near you and not be able to go further than a kiss and a cuddle. Do you understand that?'

I nod, but I don't really understand. I'm happy just being in Paul's company. I don't need the other stuff, and although I felt a bit more amorous earlier, I don't feel a spark like I imagine love or lust should feel.

Paul folds his arms and sighs. 'And another thing. I don't see enough of you.'

'But we're with each other practically every day! Are you not bored of me?'

'No.' Paul whispers, taking my hand again. 'I can't get enough of you. I miss you when you're not with me.'

'I don't know how I could see you more.'

'Maybe don't meet with your pals as often? Especially Doll?'

'I hardly see Doll as it is!'

'I'd like you to spend more time with me.'

'I also want to spend time with my pals, especially Doll.'

'Why? Why do you like Doll so much when she's in the Orange Lodge and marches and sings against our religion?'

'You don't know that.'

'Do the words, *"and we'll be up to the knees in Fenian blood – surrender or you'll die"* ring any bells with you?'

'Of course, it's the Billy Boys song that they sing at Orange marches.'

'Exactly. A song about hating Catholics. Doll's not our kind.'

'I'm not giving up seeing my best friend!' Tears prick my eyes as I rush to grab my jacket. 'You think you know what's best for me, Paul? You have no idea!'

Chapter 6

Saturday, 7 July 1984

Completely engrossed in watching a boxing match on the telly, Da has his back to us and doesn't notice Gran and I enter the living room. He ducks and dives with the boxers, punching as though he's actually in the match.

'Aidan, you left the Navy and the boxing a long time ago.' Gran chuckles, then, in a more serious tone, continues, 'I'm so glad you gave it up. All that blood, broken noses, and ribs.'

'The point is to defend yourself, so you don't get injured.' Da swigs his beer, eyes on the telly, still parrying with whichever boxer he's supporting.

Gran steps in front of the screen. Da protests. 'Aileen has something to ask you.'

He glances round at me. 'If it's to go out to the pub, the answer's no!'

'Da, please.'

'No.' Da turns back to the telly and cranes his neck around Gran to continue watching.

'It's to go with Doll to watch Sandy's band audition – '

'No!' Da's back stiffens. 'You're too young!'

'Aidan, she's nearly seventeen. You were sneaking into pubs when you were fifteen – maybe even younger.'

'I'm a guy, and I can handle myself. A pub full of drunk blokes is no place for a young girl!'

The commentator's voice rises as one of the boxers launches a series of punches on the other.

I join Gran and stand between him and the TV. 'Da, please. I promise to be careful.'

Da reaches to move my body away from his view of the screen. I stand my ground. 'I'll be home by eleven.'

'Come on. I want to see this match!' Da scowls, crushing his beer can.

Gran tosses a curl out of her eye. 'We're not moving until you agree to this reasonable request.'

'It's not a reasonable request, Ma!'

'It is.'

'I promised her mother I'd take care of her!'

'And you've been doing that! But she also needs to live a little – have some fun. She's been stuck in for months studying hard for her exams. Come on. Give her some freedom, son. Like I gave you.'

Behind us, the cries from the television audience grow louder, and the pace of the commentary picks up. A loud bell clangs to signal the end of the round.

'Can I go, please?'

Da slumps forward, his head in his hands. He looks up at Gran and bites his lip. Turning to me, he sighs. 'I can see that I'm not going to win this fight. Fine. You can go.'

Shrieking, I launch myself at him on the couch. Chuckling, he takes my arms from around his neck, sits me back to look at my face. 'Back no later than eleven.'

I nod, grinning.

'No alcohol.' Clutching his empty beer can, Da tugs my ponytail as he rises from his chair. 'Don't trust anyone. Promise me you'll keep your wits about you!'

'Promise.'

⇥ ·•◆•· ⇤

Doll had looked horrified when I turned up at her door in a hand-me-down, powder pink dress with a ruffle collar, the type that Princess Diana wore a few years ago. It was the best outfit I had, but she told me I looked about fifty in it.

She'd done my hair and make-up and chose some fashionable clothes of hers for me to wear. When she led me to a full-length mirror, I was pleasantly surprised by my reflection. Although I thought that the make-up was a little heavy, I liked how she had styled me overall.

Now, as Doll and I get off the bus to make our way to the entrance of McCoy's, I tremble with a mixture of excitement and terror. My first time going to a pub, I try to walk tall, act confident, look like I walk into pubs every day. What if the bouncers turn me away? How embarrassing would that be? I now wish that

I'd typed some fake identity card in Secretarial Studies class, in case the bouncers ask how old I am. I needn't have worried, though. As we approach the door, one of the bouncers, who is nearly as tall as he's wide, greets us. 'Welcome, wee Doll!' He booms. 'I've reserved you a table inside.' The bouncer has his long hair tied back from a face mostly obscured by a shaggy beard. 'Who's this?'

'This, Shakey, is my best pal, Aileen, who you've heard me talking about.'

Heat rises in my cheeks. As I stare at the floor and Shakey's red socks tucked into black tucker boots, his hand cuts across my vision to shake my hand. 'I'm Sandy's brother, in case you're wondering!' He has a pleasant, deep-throated laugh.

'Why are you called Shakey? Do you like Shakin' Stevens?'

He chuckles. 'Do I *look* like I do?'

'No. So, why the name?'

Shakey puts his hand on my shoulder and gently moves me inside the pub, 'I'll tell you later, kid.'

'My name's Aileen.'

'I know. Move along now, before I ask for ID.' He grins as Doll leads me inside the smoky bar. The strobing disco lights dazzle my eyes, the deep bass of the speakers pulse in time with my hammering heart. I study the floor as I pass people, convinced there's a neon arrow sign, like the one in Round Sounds, flashing above my head with the word 'underage' on it. My eyes sting from the cigarettes, and underneath the smell of smoke, the whiff of stale beer and deep-fried food sticks to my nostrils.

As we move through the bar, Doll calls to Gas Marshall in his DJ booth. He smiles at us and bends back over his decks to spin records. Doll turns to me. 'I don't know if it's all the eyeliner he wears, but he looks tired. I would be as well, right enough – working in Round Sounds in the day and then deejaying here at night.' Doll leads me to the only empty table, on the edge of the dance floor to the right of the stage. Wedged between red salt and pepper shakers is a crumpled 'VIP reserved' sign. Seated, I carefully remove Doll's thin jacket and drape it around the chair. The trembling in my body subsides, and I begin to take sneaky peeks at my surroundings.

So, this is it. I'm finally inside a pub. This is what everyone in the school common room talks about. A real pub, with great music playing and lots of what look like twenty-somethings enjoying themselves, drinking and smoking. The entrance to McCoy's is behind me, and opposite this is the bar. The mirrored walls reflect the customers as they push against each other at the bar, desperate to buy their drinks and get their evening started. The stage sits at the back of the pub, on the far wall from the entrance door to the left of where we're sitting. It's already set up with band equipment.

'Here we are, ladies!' I jump at the sound of the deep voice behind me. It's Shakey, setting some drinks on the table for us. 'Compliments of the house! A long vodka for you, Doll, and for you, Aileen – I took a guess and got you a wee Irn Bru.' Shakey mock bows, grinning as he takes his leave.

'What's a long vodka?'

Doll's blue eyes widen. 'It's a local speciality. It's got vodka, as you'd imagine, lemonade with lime cordial and Angostura bitters.'

'What?'

'Angostura bitters.' Doll repeats. 'The barman must start with this first. He can only roll a few drops of this in a tall glass as it's a poison.'

'Sounds dangerous.'

'Oh, it is. When my head hurts tomorrow, I'll know it was the Angostura bitters that did it.' Doll chuckles.

'I'll stick with my Irn Bru then.'

Doll grins, 'So, what do you think of McCoy's?'

'I love it!'

'How's Paul? I thought you might bring him along tonight. I wouldn't have minded.' Doll leans back, watches me.

'No, I wanted my first night out to a pub to be with you. He wasn't happy when I told him.' I shrug. 'We're not getting on so well. I just want to enjoy myself tonight, no pressure about anything. He's still going on about you-know-what, too.'

'That laddie deserves a medal for trying!' Doll tosses her blonde hair from her face to light a cigarette.

'I'm thinking of breaking up with him.'

Doll chokes a little on her smoke. 'Are you?'

'Aye. We were weans when we met, and we've both changed. I won't give him what he wants, and he's just miserable.'

'You know best.' Doll pats me on the arm. Then, with a mischievous look, she asks me if I can see anyone I like in McCoy's. I scan the room, trying not to look too obvious. Everyone looks so much older than me, more worldly and knowledgeable. I must stand out here as being underage.

There's a group of guys near the dance floor, carefully keeping an eye on the lassies swaying and posing on the dance floor. The guys are dressed in a mix of New Romantic and city trader fashion styles. Many flick their floppy, wedge, or mullet hairstyles to one side or another, and some sport moustaches. Some wear puffy shirts tucked into high-waisted baggy trousers, while others have their jumpers tucked into jeans.

All the laddies seem to be keeping a careful eye on a gang of skinheads near us. I've never seen a group of skinheads on a night out together – they're all dressed in black or red Harrington jackets, blue jeans with turn-ups, and Doc Marten boots. One of them catches me looking at him and winks. Embarrassed, I immediately lean behind Doll so he can't see me anymore.

'So, anyone you like?' Doll giggles, watching my expression as I keek out from behind her shoulder.

In a different section of the large room, a set of guys with long hair, rock T-shirts, and ripped jeans, stand opposite some goths who manage to look depressed and cool at the same time.

Leaning over to Doll, I flick my hand across the crowd. 'Everyone looks great in here – wish

I had money to buy new clothes – get my hair done. I'd love to ask Da for money to shop in Wrygges or Chelsea Girl for a new outfit,'

Doll throws her head back and laughs. 'When you get any money, you spend it on maths tutoring – I'm not surprised you appeared earlier dressed like my mum!'

I can't deny it. When I'm given any money, I'll spend it on private maths tuition because I find it so challenging. I get A grades in my other subjects, but I have to work hard at maths. I think of it as a worthwhile sacrifice, though, as I really want to go to university. Meanwhile, I'll just have to walk about like a scruffy scarecrow.

As tonight's DJ, Gas has already played a few of my favourite songs, and I tap my feet, singing the words. I'd love to dance, but I'd be too embarrassed as I hate people looking at me. Some of the older lassies bop and laugh on the dance floor, all confident, while the guys watch on, holding their pints. The excitement in the air is palpable – the anticipation of the night to come.

The Clyde Alloys is the opening act for a mixed bill of bands auditioning for a slot at McCoy's, and I'm really looking forward to it.

'So, I can't wait to see how the band plays and what the new singer is like!' Doll's eyes are bright with excitement, 'Sandy says that the new guy can play a proper lead guitar too! Bye, bye, Billy!' Doll laughs and swigs some more of her drink.

Doll's glee is infectious, making the butterflies in my stomach swirl faster. As well as this being my first time at a pub, it's also my first proper gig. 'Are the band here now?'

'No, they're all in Tam Parks.'

'They're in *Tampax*? Is that a place?'

'Yeah.' Doll blows out some cigarette smoke and coughs a little. 'Have you not heard of Tam Parks? It's a men-only pub, tucked up the High Street – absolutely no women allowed!'

I'm puzzled. 'They've called a men-only pub after a *women's sanitary product*?'

Doll stares at me, mid inhale of her cigarette, and chokes the smoke out, laughing. 'Tam Parks! The pub's called Tam Parks!'

Now we're both crying with laughter, catching the attention of people around us and work to calm down again.

The distraction comes when an older man hops onto the stage to take hold of the microphone. Gas lowers the music, and the crowd quietens. Doll tells me that the man on the stage is called Alan McCoy, the owner of the pub. With a flourish, Alan says a few words and raises his voice to announce the Clyde Alloys.

There's a smattering of applause and some feedback from one of the speakers as the band files onto the stage. Sandy leads the way, twirling his drumsticks through his fingers as he takes his seat behind the drumkit. He searches for Doll and flashes her a big smile. I like Sandy. He and Doll make such a lovely couple – and we get on well. I notice he's been growing his hair into more of a rock god look. Tonight, he has a red bandana tied across his hair, like Axel Rose wears in *Smash Hits* magazine.

Doll spins around to me: 'Doesn't he look gorgeous?' She turns back to the stage to continue gazing at her beloved.

Next, the keyboard player, Tommy, sporting his sunglasses, struts onto the stage and waves to the crowd. Doll hisses, 'If that guy was chocolate – he'd eat himself! He loves himself so much!'

I bite my lip and giggle with her. So that's why he wears sunglasses – because he thinks it looks cool. He's followed by Frankie Fingers, the bass player, and then Rab, the second guitarist, quickly limps on stage. Doll leans across to me to explain: 'Rab's got one leg slightly shorter than the other.'

Now that the rest of the band is assembled, I'm curious about what the new lead singer will look like, and I'm on the edge of my seat as a guy with a red baseball hat strolls onto the stage. He's wearing black jeans with a tight black T-shirt, which shows off his broad chest, slim waist, and tanned, muscly arms.

Doll's face lights up as Sandy taps his drumsticks together, and the band launches into a cover of U2's "New Year's Day". The new lead singer oozes confidence as he belts out the songs and plays his guitar. He struts around the stage, singing into the mike, and all the while, I, along with the rest of the girls in the pub, are watching his every move, mesmerised.

Doll distracts me when she leans in to tell me, 'U2's coming to play the Glasgow Barrowlands in November. The tickets are like gold dust, but if we can get a spare ticket, would you like to come?'

I'm in a pub, listening to a live band play for the first time, and now I've been invited to a real concert – a U2 one, no less. I grin, thrilled at the prospect of travelling into the city to see one of my favourite rock groups perform.

Catching me off guard, Doll grabs my hand to drag me onto the dance floor. I resist until the band starts playing Bruce Springsteen's "Born to Run", and lots of people get up to dance. We wriggle into free space and dance there until the Clyde Alloys finish playing.

As we come off the floor, the band exit off the stage and Sandy makes a beeline for Doll. They kiss and hug like they haven't seen each other in a year. Sandy beams: I'm guessing he's pleased with how the audition went. I take my leave to visit the loo.

When I return to our table, the next band to play is setting up their equipment on the stage. The band members have skinheads and look like some of the guys standing at the bar earlier.

Doll and Sandy are still wrapped in each other's arms, kissing. I cough pointedly and sit. They break away from each other, giggling.

'Lovin' the new look!' I tap the bandana on Sandy's head. 'You did well, too. The music sounds completely different to what I heard when you were practising in Round Sounds.'

'Thanks,' Sandy smiles broadly as he lights a cigarette, 'That'll be getting rid of Billy and bringing in a proper lead guitarist and singer. What did you think of him?'

'Smashing! He sounds like Bono or Jim Kerr. What's his name?'

'Ask him yourself, Aileen. He's just behind you.'

I spit out the Irn Bru I'm drinking when the lead singer places his hand lightly on my shoulder. 'Hiya, I'm Steve.'

Spluttering, I wipe at my mouth as he takes a seat beside me. My jaw drops as he removes his red baseball hat. It's my guy from the bus! Now my heart is thumping inside my rib cage, and a goofy grin spreads across my face. I know I'm about to say something I'll regret, especially as I've just realised something else. 'Wait a minute – were you in *The Music Room* last Saturday?'

He smiles slowly, revealing a set of the whitest, straightest teeth I've ever seen. 'Yes, I was. I thought I recognised you! You're the girl from the bus who likes to eat pencil sharpeners!'

My face flushes. Doll kicks me under the table as she's presumably just realised the connection. Then, if it's possible to feel how a firework does when it explodes into a million happy pieces, this is what is happening to me right now. He remembers me! Not for any cool reason, but still ... beggars can't be choosers.

He's even better looking than I remembered. I realise I must be staring as he's waiting for me to say something. Thinking quickly, I ask him where he's from, as he has an English accent.

'Liverpool – you know – where the Beatles are from?'

I nod recognition of the Beatles as my mammie used to play their albums on the record player. Before I know it, I've blurted out something else I've thought of, 'You sound like the actors on *Brookside*. I love that show!' I kick myself as soon as the words leave my mouth. Guys don't watch soap shows, do they?

'Well, we are from the same neck of the woods, so yes, I will sound like them.' Steve frowns.

Scared that he might have been offended by my last remark, I babble, desperate to let him know anything else I know about Liverpool. 'And you've got a football club too - Kenny Dalglish left Celtic to play for you.'

He twirls a beer mat over and under his fingers. 'He didn't come to play for my team – my team's Everton – the other team from Liverpool. How come you know about football?' He waits for me to respond, but suddenly paralysed by shyness, I can't speak or hardly look at him. I'm so nervous I'll say or do something else stupid; I've frozen up.

'Hello! Hello! We are the Billy Boys!' The opening words of this sectarian song startle me, and I'm even more surprised to find that it's Billy McIntyre, who's belting out the song and pulling up a chair to our table. 'That wis some gig, boys!'

Doll and Sandy straighten up. Steve looks confused. I find myself touching the empty space below the centre of my clavicle, where my crucifix normally sits. Thank goodness I thought not to wear it tonight.

Sandy tugs on his bandana, leans back in his chair. 'Steve – meet Billy, the former lead guitarist and singer of the Clyde Alloys.'

Steve's eyes widen, presumably in recognition of the name, and they nod at each other. Billy flips the chair backwards, straddles the seat, and leans his arms across the backrest. One of the pub lights shines directly onto the scar on Billy's face, making him look more menacing.

Billy's eyes dart between Steve and Sandy. He clears his throat and addresses Sandy. 'I thought you might have come to see me through the week. Thought you might have needed me the night?' He drums his fingers on the backrest of the chair, waiting for Sandy to reply.

'Sorry, pal,' Sandy says, not sounding very sorry. 'You made it clear that you'd quit. Gas let us know about Stevie boy here and that not only had he bought a new guitar, but he'd also put an ad in Round Sounds window to join a band.'

Billy shakes his head. 'Fuck's sake, man. Whit ir the chances, eh?'

Steve takes a sip from his pint: 'Right place, right time, mate. I was in a band in Liverpool, but the travelling got too much. So, I put the ad in the window, and Gas introduced me that same day.'

'Aye, well, yiz irnae bad.' Billy bites his nail.

'Not bad?' Sandy scoffs. 'That's the best our band's ever sounded! We were in tune, we were on time, and we've practised every single day and night to get ready for this audition.' Sandy stubs his cigarette out and leans back with his hands behind his head.

Billy's eye twitches. 'Well, I kin see that ah'm no needed in the band. Kin I be the manager of the band, then?'

Sandy snorts but seems to recover himself when he notices that Billy's serious. 'What about you joining that skinhead band up there?' Sandy waves his hand toward the group playing on stage, which has also not received the memo that their music should be in tune and in time.

Billy shakes his head. 'How long huv we been pals fir?'

'Must be coming on for seven years, Billy.'

'Aye, and dae ye mind that it wis me that introduced ye to Big Boab, so you could go robbin' the coal to save fir yir first set of drums?'

Sandy nods.

'And it wis me that pit ye in touch wi Gas to git a guid deal on that second-hand drum kit? It wis also in ma hoose where ah let ye hide yir drum kit fae yir Maw, and it was ma hoose where wi practised when wi first started oot.'

Sandy squirms in his chair.

'We go back a long way, Sandy boy. We've been in the Orange Lodge band fir the same length of time, too.' Billy places his palms on his knees. The laddies eyeball each other, and Doll and I exchange nervous glances.

Perhaps feeling guilty, Sandy breaks his silence to mumble: 'I'd need to speak to the rest of the band ... we don't need a manager but if that's what you want to call yourself if they agree ....'

Billy slaps his thighs and leers, revealing those grey teeth of his. 'That's ma boy!'

'But no musical direction, please.' Sandy laughs. Billy joins in. Steve, Doll, and I smile at each other, uncertain but bemused by what we've just witnessed.

The initial tension broken, the conversation centres around what Billy, Doll, and Sandy have planned for this year's 12th of July celebrations – a big day in the Protestant calendar but a sometimes dangerous day for Catholics. On this date, the Protestants taking part in the Orange Walks can drink a lot of alcohol. Hatred of Catholics is stirred amongst the beating of the drums and the swirling of the flutes. Nasty fights can break out. I've seen enough of this before.

As the folk round our table carry on chattering about their plans, I notice that Steve doesn't join in. He sips quietly on his pint. I wonder if he's a Protestant or a Catholic. I hope he's a Catholic, maybe, so I'm not the odd one out. The subject doesn't come up. Both of us nod and smile at the appropriate times of the conversation. After a while, I make my excuses to go home. Da has me on a curfew, and I wisely don't mention that I'm planning to attend the early morning mass at the chapel.

Sandy palms his face. 'Aileen. Sorry, we went on a bit.'

I tap his bandana again and smile. 'No bother. I'm just tired.'

Billy practically knocks his chair over in his rush to stand. 'I'm knackered too – need to be up for work. I'll come out with you; make sure you get in a taxi okay.'

Surprised by his offer, I hesitate but do the polite thing and allow him to escort me outside. I say bye to Sandy. Steve stares at his pint.

Doll walks out with us and hugs me goodbye. 'So I'll drop by your house at nine tomorrow morning for our run to the Country Park.'

'Are you sure you'll make it?' I tease her, pointing to the drink in her hand.

'Course I will! You know me – don't get hangovers!' Doll hugs me one more time and scowls at Billy. 'No funny business!'

'Whit dae ye mean?' Billy raises his hand to draw an imaginary circle above his head.

'I know you're no angel, Billy McIntyre! That's my best pal. Take good care of her.' The lecture given, Doll hugs me one last time before disappearing back into McCoy's.

After the heat generated by the crowd in the pub, I wrap my jacket closer to ward off the chill outside. There's a small queue at the taxi rank and one couple drunk-fighting. Billy tells me this is precisely why he had come out with me, to protect me. He assures me that this isn't bad for ten o'clock on a Saturday night – that there are usually a lot more fights going on.

When it's my turn to get in a taxi, Billy insists that he get in too, share the ride and the fare home. Then, to my dismay, instead of leaving the taxi when we arrive at his home village, Billy insists that he must escort me all the way home.

A knot forms in my stomach when we pull into my street. I'm hoping Billy doesn't think he's coming in. I nod at him in the darkness of the taxi as I take a hold of the door handle.

'Actually, taxi driver, I think ah'm goanna puke.' Billy groans and lurches forward.

'Not in my taxi, son! Out you go!' The driver pulls over to the kerb, not far from my home.

My heart sinks as we stand on the pavement, watching the taxi disappear into the night.

'Kin ah come in?' Billy clutches his stomach. 'I'm not queasy anymore, but I could do with some water.'

My head thumps. I don't want this. And Da would kill me.

Chapter 7

Saturday 7 July 1984

I curse the fact that I'm too polite for my own good, that I find it hard to say 'no'. Across from me is Billy McIntyre, eagerly perched on my living room couch. He cradles a mug of coffee in his pale hands, which bear the tracings of gang tattoos.

Doll's told me before that Billy's been going steady with a lassie who she knows in the Orange Lodge. Billy doesn't know I know this, and I have a good idea that he will not admit this either. It's now becoming apparent that he's here with only one thing on his mind, and it isn't to drink some water or sample a cup of Nescafé instant coffee. 'So, whit did ye say yir name wis?'

Fidgeting in my chair, I figure out the nearest truth to my name, which won't give me away as a Catholic. 'It's Ally, like Ally McCoist.' I'm thinking he'll approve of the link with the football player, who plays for Rangers Football

Club, a club which is famous for only signing Protestants.

Billy shuffles further forward. 'Ally, eh? Pretty name to suit a pretty lassie.'

I wince as he says this. I'm lying to hide my Catholic background from a skinhead laddie whom I don't know, or even want in my home in the first place. My heart races, my hands clammy. I've made an awful mistake in ever allowing this intimidating guy into my home.

Feeling like quarried prey, I run various options through my head on how to politely persuade him to leave. How long does it take to drink a cup of coffee anyway? My heartbeat steadies as Bruno sleepily pads into the living room and settles himself at my feet. I will handle this situation, somehow.

Billy peers around the living room, checking out the family photos and ornaments placed at strategic points. What light there is in this room is provided by a few small lamps. He looks like he's searching for something else to say when finally: 'Cool dug!'

'His name's Bruno – after Frank - the boxer?'

'Ah git it! Boxer dug – named after the boxer, Frank Bruno!' Billy's chuffed he's made the connection.

Bruno nuzzles my hand as I pet him. Billy watches, then adds, 'Yir hoose is smashin'. Nice furniture ... curtains ....'

Bemused by the skinhead's unexpected comments, I smile. Perhaps encouraged by my reaction, Billy continues: 'Ah mean, it's so *clean*. Ah kin *smell* it's clean. Catholic hooses are filthy, man!' Billy shakes his head and grimaces.

I'm so taken aback by his remark, that at first, I'm sure I've misheard, but Billy goes on: 'They don't huv carpets oan the flair, they have the clattiest furniture and don't get me started oan the state of thur toilets or kitchens ... urgh!'

My stomach tightens. *Oh my god! He knows I'm a Catholic! He's just toying with me until he decides to knock me around – or worse – and in my own home!* I've been too soft, too careless. *Stupid, stupid girl!* As Da's on nightshift at the Craig, I had hoped that Gran might have been waiting up for me, but she must be upstairs with wee Mary, fast asleep, oblivious to the drama which may be about to unfold here.

Billy scowls: 'They dae aw that confession shit, tellin' thur secrets to durty old men who're all paedophiles anyway. Following what a poncy guy in a white robe in Rome says, who's probably at it with all the nuns in the Vatican. It's pure hypocrisy! And their hooses ir full i' aw that religious guff, like crucifixes and pictures i' the Pope and aw that!'

I steal a glance at the only religious item in the room: a small picture card of the Sacred Heart of Jesus, about four inches square above the living room door, put there by the parish priest after he blessed the house. My heart stops as Billy follows my gaze but doesn't seem to recognise what's on the small image.

Da stopped going to mass after Mammie died and hates having any religious items in the house because he points out that religions have caused too much hatred and division in the world. Only the house blessing card is allowed to stay in the living room. Meanwhile,

Gran's a dyed-through Irish Catholic and prays at the wee altar she's made in the corner of her bedroom. I like to visit her wee altar because she has it looking nice with a bible, some candles, and her statue of Our Lady. I'm thanking my lucky stars right now that Gran moved her wee altar back into her bedroom after Mammie's anniversary.

Billy's on a roll, 'And they don't use contraception, so there's loadsa thum.. Suddenly he stops speaking: 'Ur ye OK, darlin'?'

I manage to recover myself once I realise that Billy's assumed that I'm a Protestant. I relax a little more. I'm no longer feeling afraid – in fact – I feel like laughing. This guy is real, and so is the guff he's talking. 'Why are you talking about Catholics?'

'It was us talkin' aboot the 12th of July, earlier.'

I'm intrigued. I've never heard Doll or Sandy talk like this. 'What else do you know about Catholics?'

Billy seems pleased with the question: 'Catholic lassies gie oot that *I'm a Virgin* shit, but they're the biggest cows of all, riding any dicks that'll have thum! And man, they're pot ugly! No' like you, yir beautiful. For them, you'd need to put a bag o'er their heid when they're geein' a gammy!'

Baffled, I ask: 'What's a gammy?'

He laughs: 'See! Yir that innocent, ye don't know whit ah'm talkin' aboot! A blow job!'

Heat rises in my cheeks. I squirm in my chair. We sit quietly as Billy sets his mug of coffee on the carpet. Sensing that he might be about to make a move on me, I spring to my feet. 'Listen, you should go. My da'll be back from his shift soon, and he'll not be pleased to find a stranger in his living room ....'

'Aw darlin'. The night's just getting started.' He eyes the HiFi unit in the corner. 'Let's put oan some music – set the mood.'

'Set the mood for what?'

Billy winks and moves across the floor towards me. He places his hands on my shoulders: 'Ye know whit fir, darlin'...' He sets some strands of my hair aside and inches his face closer to mine. I lean back from him, pushing both my hands against his chest. His breath, a mixture of coffee, beer and cigarettes, wafts across my face.

I turn my face away from his. 'No, I don't want this. I have a boyfriend.'

'He doesn't have to know. Besides, you invited me in.' Billy leers, the smiling scar on his face also seeming to mock me.

Then it hits me. I'm so bloody stupid sometimes! 'You tricked me, you mean? Kidded on you were sick?'

Billy's not listening. He digs his bony fingers in harder to pull my shoulders towards him. I resist with all my might, pushing my hands against him, leaning my head back as far as it will go. His gaunt face looms closer to me. He will kiss me any second and who knows what after that.

Jeez, what am I supposed to do here? There is no polite way to handle this. This has gone beyond being polite. *Oh, bollocks! That's it – bollocks!* Suddenly, Gran's advice about men's balls pops into my head.

His arms trembling, Billy's face twists as he works harder to pull me in for a kiss. My last hope, I swing my leg back to drive my right knee as hard as I can into his groin. He cries out and drops to the ground like they do in fight scenes on TV. But I mustn't have kneed him hard enough, as he soon springs to his feet. Sneering, he draws his arm back and slaps me so hard across the face that he knocks me to the couch.

Billy stands over me, his eyes bulging, his fists clenched. As he lunges for me, Bruno pounces, knocking him to the floor. The skinhead reaches around, trying to scrabble to his feet but Bruno circles him, snarling and snapping his teeth, warning him to stay where he is. Billy cowers on the floor, his arms over his face.

My cheek throbs, my hand trembles as I point in the direction of the back door: 'Leave!'

Pale-faced, Billy eyes me, then Bruno.

'Heel!' My voice quivers as I command Bruno to my side. He complies with a low growl, keeping Billy in his sights.

The skinhead carefully uncurls himself from the floor, and as he stands, he holds his hands aloft like he's in a holdup. Billy stumbles to our back door, fumbling to open it.

My jaw drops, and I'm sure I've not heard right when he turns to me to say: 'Ur ye sure ye don't wanna gie me a wee kiss then?'

The guy is unbelievable! I skirt around him, careful to keep my distance. 'Good night, Billy!' Shaking, I yank the back door open and point the way to him; it's already starting to get light outside. Bruno takes up position beside me, still snarling and baring his teeth at Billy.

Finally, seeming to accept defeat, Billy descends the steps and starts walking along the garden path, past Da's tattie plants, towards the back gate. I guess being ever the optimist, or just plain stupid, he turns and calls: 'Kin ah I take ye oot some other time darlin'?'

At first, I'm gobsmacked. I don't know how to respond. Then I find the courage to voice what I've been thinking: 'You don't want that, Billy! Oh, no! You see – this clean, well-kept house with no religious items in it – and this pure, gorgeous female living in it – are Catholic! The house is Catholic! Even the fecking dog's a Catholic!'

Billy visibly flinches every time I spit out the word, 'Catholic'.

'So, I'm afraid my answer will have to be – no – feck off! You ignorant bastard! And God, forgive me, but I'll need to go to confession now – with one of those dirty old men!' With that, I slam the door, my heart pumping, my cheek throbbing.

Chapter 8

Sunday, 8 July 1984

'Jesus, Mary and Joseph! What was all that racket?' Gran ambles into the kitchen, sleepy-eyed, wrapping the cord of her dressing gown around her waist.

Thinking quickly, I turn away from her so that she doesn't notice me trembling or my red cheek from when Billy slapped me. 'Sorry – Bruno wanted out for a pee – a gust of wind caught the back door and slammed it before I could stop it.'

Gran blinks and yawns. 'Sorry I didn't wait up. There was nothing on the telly, so I had a wee nip of whisky to help me sleep. Did you enjoy yourself?'

I nod, reluctant to say anything more.

Her eyes half closed, she hugs me. 'Glad to see you're home safe.' Gran shuffles back upstairs.

Alone, the enormity of what just happened, and what nearly happened, washes over me. I slump into a chair, gulping back tears as I grip the kitchen table to quell my trembling.

Gran would have a fit if she knew that not only had a guy just been in the house but that he was a Protestant who had tried to force himself on me. Once I've calmed, I stagger around the living room, switching off the lamps and stop to give Bruno a nuzzle for being my hero of the hour.

Upstairs in bed, my mind races. Why, oh why, did I not see that Billy McIntyre was just lying to get into my house? I keep imagining how I could have played the evening differently. I think of even better questions and smarter answers for Billy. Round and round it all goes in my mind. It'll soon be time for Da to come home from his night shift. With an exasperated sigh, I abandon trying to sleep and tiptoe into the bathroom to have a quick wash.

A little later, Da comes in from work, and blinks, taken aback to see me fully dressed in the kitchen. 'How come you're awake at this time? Have they changed the time of the mass?'

'Couldn't sleep.' I search his face for any sign that he might know someone like Billy McIntyre had not only been in his home just a few hours previously but also tried to force himself on his daughter. Da just looks his usual tired self after a long shift. 'Up this early, I take it that you got home before your curfew?'

'Yes. Gran saw me.' Two truths.

'Did you get any bother?'

'No, no bother.' One lie.

My mood lightens as I stroll the mile to chapel in the early morning sunlight. A happy habit from when Mammie was alive, I distract myself from last night by admiring the colourful flowers and shrubs in people's front gardens. I'm also looking forward to my run with Doll later as it'll also help to clear my head more.

I attend the first mass at seven o'clock, mainly because it's a peaceful half-hour long – especially shortened for the men coming off nightshift at the Craig, and the women on their way to their day shifts. No crying babies or kids are in mass then, and there are no bullies out of their beds, roaming the streets to cause trouble.

At the chapel entrance, I bless my forehead with the cool holy water from the font. After our argument on Thursday and what happened with Billy last night, I'm extra glad to see Paul sitting in our usual pew, looking happy to see me. I walk up the aisle, genuflect in front of the altar, and seat myself beside him. He takes my hand, and we whisper 'sorry' to each other just before the soft bells signify the start of mass. My Sunday's getting off to a better start.

Against the monotone voice of the priest, I pray for Mammie as usual but also find myself saying quiet prayers to God and the angels to bless and protect wee Mary, to keep her safe from the bullies. I don't want her to suffer the way I have over these years. She's too gentle and kind. I've also noticed that her eczema seems to be getting worse, with painful-looking scabs on her legs and arms, and she seems to be wheezing more with her asthma. I pray that she gets better soon.

Next, a little guilt creeps in as I pray for myself.

Please, God, I know I'm supposed to pray for other people, but this one's for me.

Please help me get good exam results so I can go to University and leave Craigburn. Please don't let that Billy McIntyre tell anyone what happened last night.

Please also help me with Lorraine Pollock — make her disappear or move or something.

Please help me get through this next year in one piece.

When the mass is finished, I walk to the front of the chapel with Paul, and we light our candles in memory of the family we've lost. My candles are for Mammie, my two granddads and my nana. God rest their souls. Paul puts his arm around me as we walk down the aisle to exit from the chapel door.

Outside, as we're chatting, heat flowers in my cheeks at the memory of Billy trying to force himself on me last night, and, seeking comfort, I pull Paul in for a hug.

'Hey.' Paul whispers, stroking my hair. 'I'm so sorry about the other night. I won't mention 'it' again.'

Mixed emotions swirl through me as I lean back from his chest to look up at him. Paul doesn't realise that Thursday night isn't the reason I hugged him. Even though I wasn't at fault with the Billy incident last night, guilt churns my stomach. I feel like I've cheated on Paul because I stupidly allowed a stranger into my home. Now, more than ever, I want the safety and security of what I have with Paul.

·»·····•···««·

It's just past eight o'clock when I get home. I enjoy the quiet as my family sleeps and happily munch on some toast and sip tea while flicking through the *Sunday Mail*. I change into my running kit, lace my gutties, and do a few warm-up exercises in the back garden, just as Doll arrives to go on our run together.

'I'm pretty rough!' Doll confesses as we begin to jog out onto the empty main road.

'Thought you didn't get hangovers?' As this is a steady run, our breathing soon relaxes, so we can chat as usual while running.

'It's the Angostura bitters in those long vodkas! Anyway, I take it you got home, okay?'

Now would be a good time to admit what happened with Billy, but I just can't. Even with my best friend, I just can't admit to my stupidity and guilt about allowing a cretin like Billy trick his way into my home. I decide not to tell.

'Yes, no drama.' I try to sound light, grateful that Doll's too busy looking forward to see the lie which must surely be written all over my face. 'Is Sandy rough, too?'

Doll snorts. 'Nope. You know guys – they just bounce back after a heavy night of drinking! He's away robbing coal from the Craig, with Big Boab.'

'Is that not dangerous? I mean, crossing the railway line, and he might get caught by the police?'

'Oh, it's a real danger – I'm constantly begging him to find a proper job – but he just points out how much more money he can make by humping coal over the railway line and selling it on the side with Big Boab and his gang.'

'Does your Dad know?'

'Jeez, no! Could you imagine how embarrassed he'd be? His daughter's boyfriend stealing coal, and him a policeman and all! Doll stumbles, almost losing her balance.

'You, okay? Shall we stop running?'

'No. I'm a bit queasy, but I'll run it off.'

'Speaking of the police – are you still thinking of joining?' I slow my pace as I notice Doll's running slower than usual.

'I'd love to, but there are a few things stopping me – Sandy stealing coal is a big one, and another is that my dad's not keen.'

'Why?'

'He doesn't want me in danger – female police officers get more aggro. He'd prefer that I go into nursing – says that will stand me in good stead until I get married. Then I can stay at home or work part-time as a nurse when my kids go to school.'

'Is that what you want? To go into nursing?'

'I'd prefer policing, but if my dad's against it, and my boyfriend breaks the law, I'd say I'd best stick with the nursing plan.'

'And kids?'

'Not for a few years yet.' Doll groans, clutching her stomach, and we stop running. She bends over to vomit into a bush, close to a busy bus stop. She wails, wiping her mouth, 'I'll never drink long vodkas again! Angostura bitters really are poison!'

'You're not fit to run, Doll. Go home. There's a bus due any minute.'

'I don't want to let you down.'

'You're not. I'll carry on with my run. You go home to bed.' I fish out the one pound note I keep in my sock for emergencies and hand it to Doll.

She smiles weakly. 'Thanks, it's normally me looking after you.'

'Well, it's my turn now.' A bus approaches, and I usher Doll on and wave her off.

Worried about my best friend, I jog on, the morning sunshine lightening my mood as I break into a faster run. Deep rumbles sound in the distance to signal that some important element of steel production is happening in the Craig as I run away from my home town and on to the next. The miles melt under my feet until, at last, I enter the Country Park and head into the forest.

As I run along a path, through sun-dappled shadows, my breathing is rhythmic, in time to my soft footsteps. Squirrels skitter away from me, darting through old leaves – my ponytail swishes across my back.

My mind often wanders when I'm running. I force myself to put thoughts of Billy McIntyre aside, and I tell myself that Doll will be fine. Perhaps because it was played in McCoy's last night, Bruce Springsteen's song "Born to Run" pops into my head. When I'm rich, I'll buy one of those Sony Walkman portable cassette players I see on American TV shows so that I can combine my love for music and running. Then, I'd get better at remembering song lyrics, and I might even run further.

I turn onto the path which leads me to the river bank in the forest. A little way along the river is the bird watchers' hut, set back against the trees, but in a high enough position where twitchers can view the birds, including the grey herons who come to breed. Wooden benches fringe a little wildflower meadow which looks onto a jetty perched in the water. This is my refuge, where I've come with my family for picnics over the years. In the last two years, it's also become the place where Paul and I have met to be alone and chat. The tree canopies are filled with different bird calls, and I relax more into my run.

As I head deeper into the forest, footsteps thud somewhere behind me. The footsteps speed up, the heavy panting getting nearer. My heart quickens, and my breath catches. I daren't turn around. What if they attack me? I'm not carrying anything to protect myself. The only possible weapon I have is the back-door key, which I've threaded through my laces. I could stop, pretend to tie my shoelace but secretly untie my key, ready to stick it up the attacker's nose or through his eye.

As the footsteps hammer closer, I quickly hunker to release my key. A grunt sounds as a heavy force, which I presume to be a man, knocks me sideways into some ferns.

Dazed, I stagger onto my feet. A man lies spread-eagled, face-down on the path in front of me. He mutters something as he finds his feet.

Brandishing my door key, I rapidly assess my options. I can run back the way I've just come, or I could stick my key up his nose. Or, remembering Billy's reaction from last night, I could try for a kick to the balls, which might buy me a bit more time to run away. As I'm not exactly sure how I'm supposed to use a key for defence, I've decided to heed Gran's advice, kick the man where it hurts and then scarper.

Before he's turned fully around, I run to boot him as hard as I can, squarely, where I believe his balls are. He drops to his knees, groaning and falls sideways, curling into the foetal position. As I'm stood rooted to the spot, I realise that maybe he doesn't look like a rapist. He seems to be dressed for a run. And, as he rolls over to another, presumably, more comfortable position, I stare in horror at the jagged pain etched across the most handsome face I've ever admired. Steve!

My would-be attacker squints at me. 'You! Why did you stop without warning? And why on earth did you kick me in the nuts?' His voice rises, his eyes water.

'I thought you were going to attack me!'

Steve writhes in fresh pain, his hands cupping his private parts. He puffs and sits up, wincing as he does so. Dusting the dirt off his palms, he stands gingerly, then staggers to sit on a nearby log. He folds his arms across his stomach and bends over. 'I'm going to throw up. Leave, please!'

Panicked, I run away as fast as I can.

Chapter 9

Monday, 9 July 1984

'Y ou wouldn't think it's summer out there,' I remark, peering through the kitchen window. 'Those dark clouds are heading our way!'

Gran joins me by the sink to look out of the window. 'That'll be a storm coming.' She wrings her hands. 'Your Da should finish work soon ... and wee Mary should be home from her pal's house any minute.' Gran glances at the clock: 'Wonder what's keeping her? She's normally home by five.'

We both jump as jagged edges of lightning streak across the darkened sky, followed by distant rumbles of thunder. Fat raindrops plop onto the paving stones in the back garden, then fall with such intensity that it's difficult to see out of the window. The sky is lit more frequently by lightning bolts, and the rain and the wind picks up yet more speed.

Gran shouts above the deafening noise of hailstones battering against the window. 'Jesus,

Mary and Joseph! I hope wee Mary and your Da are not out in this!' She holds her face with her hands, her eyes wide as she peers out into the storm. 'I keep saying to your Da that we should get a phone in the house, then we could just call wee Mary's pal, find out where she is.'

Having a phone costs money, though, so we Murphys are not likely to have one installed any time soon. I wrap my arms around myself, to help soothe the unease I feel. Trying to lighten the mood, I take Gran's arm and lead her to the kitchen table: 'Let's not worry ourselves. And, who needs a phone when we could do what that Peggy Fisher does with her sisters? We could just hang out of our front window and shout at the top of our voice for wee Mary!'

Gran smiles a little. 'It's so unladylike how those women do that – bawling out of their windows for their kids to come in for dinner, or gossip across the street to each other. You'd think they'd get off their fat arses and walk across the street to have their conversations in private!' Gran chuckles. 'Aye, those ladies are classy! Just last week that Peggy broadcast to the street that her man's got piles! Why would you broadcast that?'

Some of our neighbours provide endless sources of amusement and, sometimes, despair. Gran and I agree that there are plenty of self-respecting, law-abiding residents of Craigburn – decent folk who're great neighbours and take great pride in the area and the community. Then, there are the pockets containing the 'roughie-toughies' – as Gran calls them – the problem families, both Catholic and Protestant, that Glasgow City Council decanted out to areas like Craigburn when they demolished the inner-city tenement buildings. Gran swears that it's these families that have been bringing parts of Craigburn down.

We're startled as wee Mary bursts in through the back door, at the same time as lightning crackles across the sky, shortly followed by a peal of thunder. Wee Mary's soaked from head to toe. She splutters and wheezes as she stumbles into the kitchen.

'Aw, hen, are you alright? We were hoping that you didn't get caught in the storm! How come you're a bit later coming home?' Gran fusses over wee Mary and helps her to remove her soaking cardigan. 'Hey, what's this? Your sleeve's torn. How'd that happen, hen?'

Wee Mary looks guilty. 'That's why I'm late. Margaret and I were messing about in the swing park earlier. She grabbed my sleeve – and it tore.' She lowers her eyes.

'Ah, never mind. I'll get this mended for you tonight, hen.' Gran takes the cardigan and drapes it from the top of the kitchen door to drip dry. 'Let's get you out of these wet clothes and into a warm bath.'

'Your asthma seems bad.' I fetch wee Mary's brown medicine bottle from the cupboard, give it a good shake and tip the smelly, yellow syrup onto a spoon. Wee Mary makes her usual reluctant face, holds her nose, and swallows the medicine. She shudders and smiles weakly: 'I'm fine, honest.'

'Hiya, ma lassies!' It's Da's turn to come rushing in the back door. Shaking the rain from his hair, he slings his wet donkey jacket onto the kitchen table before sitting to remove his work boots. He comes around each of us to give us a big, damp hello hug. He pauses by wee Mary. 'You look like you've seen a ghost.'

As if on cue, flashes of lightning illuminate our dark kitchen, and the deep boom of thunder makes us jump. Wee Mary's chin wobbles, and tears brim in her eyes. Da holds her. 'There. There. My angel. There's nothing to worry about. Storms always pass.' Wee Mary sobs, her body quivering. Da raises his eyebrows at Gran and me.

'You really did get a scare! Never mind, let's get you in that bath.' Gran reaches to put her arm around wee Mary's shoulder. She flinches away.

'I can go in the bath myself, Gran. You don't need to come into the bathroom.'

Gran opens her mouth to say something but shakes her head instead. As she's leading wee Mary away, she calls over her shoulder to Da: 'Aye, mister, get that jacket put away properly, please!' Da skulks into the hall, the storm overhead almost drowning out his muttering that he's henpecked.

Later, when the storm had passed, wee Mary's sat on the living room rug in a long-sleeved nightie. Her head is bent, her damp hair hanging over her face. I know wee Mary too well. 'How are you?'

Wee Mary sniffles. She won't look at me.

Seating myself beside her, I tilt her chin so that I can look at her face. Her eyes are red and puffy. She turns away from me.

'Mary, what's wrong?'

'Nothing. I just got a fright from the storm, and Gran's bath soap got in my eyes.' This time she looks up. 'I'm fine, honest. Stop fussing.'

Wee Mary gives me a watery smile and squirms past me to retrieve the photo albums which are tucked underneath the display cabinet, from Da's time in the Navy. As we're leafing through the first album, Da strolls into the living room, spots what we're looking at, and lays on his belly beside us on the rug. He tries to look nonchalant as we coo and giggle, pointing at black and white pictures of him, looking handsome in his Navy uniform and sharp suits. Some of the photos are of him in his boxing matches, representing the Navy, and some are of his travels around the world. The travel photos are my favourite ones. Da grins in every picture, standing beside exotic animals like elephants and with snakes around his neck, playing beach volleyball with his Navy pals; on the steps of mystical temples and eating street food from market stalls.

Wee Mary and I love it when Da spins his yarns as we flick through his photos. As well as being a great storyteller, Da's funny with it and has the most infectious laugh. He's bright as a button, too, my da – always winning the pub quizzes. Gran said he did well at school, but he wasn't interested in any fancy jobs; he just wanted to travel the world. And that's what he did before he met Mammie. He joined the Royal Navy and sailed all over the world.

'Have I ever told you about the first time I saw your mammie?' He has, countless times, but he tells us again anyway with an impish grin. He met Mammie at the dancing when he was home on leave. As much as Da tries to make the story funny, he can never hide the soft glaze in his eyes as he recalls the first time he ever saw her.

Da flicks to the end of the second photo album to gaze at the last photo of him standing in front of his ship in his smart Navy uniform, his arm wrapped around Mammie's waist. Without thinking, the three of us have laid a forefinger on the side of the photo with Mammie in it.

With a sad sigh, he slowly closes the album. 'That's enough reminiscing for tonight.'

I meet wee Mary's tear-filled eyes. We love talking about Mammie, looking at her photos, remembering her. It makes us feel just that bit better. Mary takes both our hands and whispers, wide-eyed, 'I've stopped dreaming about her.'

Da gathers wee Mary into his arms. 'Ma darlin'. Just because you don't dream about Mammie doesn't mean you'll forget her. She's always with you, watching over you.'

Tears stream down wee Mary's face, and she swallows hard. 'Do you think so? It doesn't feel like anyone's watching over me.'

'What story did Mammie tell us before she died?' Using my sleeve, I dab the tears away from wee Mary's face.

'The story about her at Ayr beach as a wee girl, when she was waving at the biggest and shiniest ship she'd ever seen. How she had run along the beach, waving, and waving at it, and how she sobbed when it disappeared over the horizon because she was waving hello, not goodbye.' Wee Mary falls silent.

'What else?'

'And how Nana told her not to be sad because the ship was supposed to disappear from her view. And although she couldn't see the ship anymore, someone else could, on the other side of the horizon, so there would be another wee girl waiting to welcome the ship there.'

'What was Mammie meaning when she told us that story?'

'That when you can no longer see something, it doesn't mean that it's not there anymore.' A lone tear weaves down wee Mary's cheek.

'Exactly. Just like Mammie. She's never left us – she's just on the other side of the horizon. You can still talk to her, you know. In your head, or out loud. She'll hear you.' I squeeze wee Mary's hand.

We sit in silence for a moment.

'I still speak with your mammie in my dreams.' Da's voice breaks.

Wee Mary leans back to stare at Da. 'Tell us about them.'

'Well, you know how much Mammie loved her flowers. In my dreams, I usually find her in the most beautiful gardens, bending to admire some tulips. She looks so serene and happy.' Tears glisten in Da's eyes. 'She tells me not to worry about her because she's not in pain anymore.

'I know I'm dreaming, but I don't ever want to leave her. I watch her face as she talks and the way she moves.' Da's body shudders, and he gulps. 'I can smell her perfume. And I can still sense her touch, and how I feel when she's in my arms.'

I take Da's hand and squeeze it. 'I'm glad that you still dream of her.'

Every single night for the first two years or so, Mammie visited me in my dreams, but I haven't dreamt of her for a while now. Instead, I talk to her in my prayers, and sometimes in my head when I'm running.

'Could we have flowers in the garden again, please?' Wee Mary gazes up at Da.

He clears his throat, wipes the tears from his face. 'I could never take care of the garden like Mammie. That's why I haven't tried.'

'Please, Da, it would help us remember Mammie, and cheer us up. Tattie plants just don't look as pretty.'

'Aye, but you can eat tatties, not flowers!' Da chuckles. 'I suppose I could dig the borders again. Maybe plant a few bulbs and shrubs.'

As wee Mary snuggles into Da, the sense of foreboding brought on by the storm seeps back into my pores.

Chapter 10

Tuesday, 10 July 1984

Wee Mary didn't seem herself this morning, saying she wasn't feeling very well. Despite being July, she had sat with her dressing gown wrapped tightly around herself at breakfast, just staring at her untouched bowl of cornflakes. Gran sent her to bed, where she's stayed. She was still sleeping when I looked in on her after lunch.

Speed walking my way to Doll's home, I shake off my worries about her. Soon my mind drifts to Steve. Daydreaming, I replay the scenes from the bus, the pub and even our encounter in the Country Park and admit that I'm becoming more curious about him. I might even be developing a crush and this thought's confirmed when a lovely, warm feeling gushes through me, just thinking about seeing him again. Then, I bring myself back to reality when I remind myself that Paul's still my boyfriend. And that even if I was single, someone as good-looking as Steve will have a girlfriend, and not be interested in me anyway.

With one of my hands plunged into my jacket pocket, I cradle the familiar blue velvet pouch containing the crystal rosary beads that Mammie gave me. I crunch the velvet bag in my palm, turning it over and over, enjoying the comforting sensation of the little sharp edges of the rosary beads inside the soft bag. My mind wanders back to Steve again, and I'm so lost in my daydream that I don't spot Margaret, wee Mary's pal. She's running a message to the shop for her mum.

'Is Mary alright after last night? Did she get into trouble about her cardigan? That was terrible what that big lassie did to her, and with a gang too. I couldn't believe she hit Mary.' Margaret shakes her head, regarding me with eyes made bigger by her thick glasses.

'What big lassie?' I grip my rosary beads tighter.

'Did Mary not tell you? After she left my house, this older lassie punched and kicked her. Mary said that she was scary-looking – fat, with bad skin and red hair. The lassie told Mary you called her a cow and that she was hitting her to get you back. Poor Mary, she put up a bit of a fight and managed to get away – that's why her sleeve ripped. She ran back to my house; she was all white and shaking, Aileen. We had a wee glass of ginger together while Mary told me all about it.'

I can't believe that anyone would harm poor wee Mary. The knot of fear in my stomach twists into anger. I'm hoping that it isn't, but it sounds like the lassie who battered my wee sister is Lorraine Pollock. How dare she! How horrible is she picking on a wee lassie who doesn't keep very well? The more I think about it, the angrier I become. And then I'm hit with a realisation. Why didn't wee Mary tell us? Why did she lie? And in that instant, the answer comes to me: *for the same reason that you've never said anything. She feels ashamed. She doesn't want to worry us. She's hoping it doesn't happen again.*

My mind reels, trying to take in what Margaret's just told me. I scurry away from her towards Doll's home. I've been running away from trouble my whole life, but now that trouble has come to my front door. I can't let that fat cow hit wee Mary again – I'm going to have to take a stand. The thought fills me with terror.

Doll's smiley face is a welcome sight as she greets me at her front door. Grateful for the distraction, I tuck Lorraine to the back of my mind and follow Doll into the kitchen to make tea. When I ask how she is, she confesses that she's still a bit peely-wally, so it must be some sort of tummy bug, and not the Angostura bitters in the long vodkas after all. She makes a face when I offer her some biscuits, so I take enough just for me, then we head to Doll's bedroom, which is a lot fancier and bigger than mine. Everything in her bedroom matches and is pastel-coloured. *Pierrot the Clown* posters hang on the walls, and she has throws and cushions on her double bed. I've only got a single bed with a holey candlewick bedspread, and my walls have mismatched posters torn from magazines. Doll also has her own HiFi unit in her bedroom. I love that we can put on records and sing and dance in peace there.

Once we've settled onto Doll's bed, a shadow passes over her face. 'I need to ask you something, and you might not like it.'

I shuffle, dread creeping through me at the sudden serious change in Doll. I munch on my custard cream biscuit.

'Billy told Sandy that he got all the way with you, that you were gagging for it.'

I choke on my biscuit, spluttering crumbs in all directions. For a minute, I can't speak. This on top of the story about wee Mary. 'He said that he *shagged* me?'

'He's got a psycho girlfriend, you know. She'd rip your face off if she found out about you.' Doll narrows her eyes, tapping her cigarette against the ashtray on her bedside table.

'Nothing happened! Come on! *Billy McIntyre?*'

Doll scans my face. 'I said to Sandy that I couldn't believe it. I told him that you're saving yourself. Billy went into a lot of detail. He could describe your house and your living room well.'

Of course. Billy being able to describe where I live would help add colour to his black lie. 'I didn't tell you because I was embarrassed that I'd been stupid enough to believe his lies. He pretended he was sick, then asked to come in for some water. Then he asked for a coffee.' When I'm saying the story out loud, it sounds even more obvious that Billy tricked his way into my home.

'I tried to get rid of him. He tried to kiss me, but I refused. Then he slapped me hard. It was only our Bruno snarling at him that persuaded him to leave. I knew he wasn't happy that I said no, but I can't believe he's telling these *lies*!' I thump the mattress, mentally kicking myself for ever having allowed the guy in my house. I'm too angry even to cry.

Doll sighs. 'I knew he was lying! And he slapped you too! I'll tell Sandy what you've told me. His girlfriend should know what a snake he is as well!'

There's a part of me that's itching to tell Doll about my crazy conversation with Billy, about how he spent most of the time slagging off Catholics and how his jaw dropped when I told him that I was a Catholic. Still, even with my best friend, I'm not comfortable talking about the religious stuff. The story's also not so funny since Billy decided to lie about what happened, to get revenge on me for knocking him back.

Doll stubs out her cigarette. 'Well, I like him even less if that's possible! I think Sandy's regretting saying that Billy could still hang around the band. He's grating on Sandy's nerves. Does Paul know what happened with Billy?'

'Are you kidding? Me letting a strange guy into my house who then tried to force himself on me. Paul was jealous enough as it was that I was going out with you instead of him.' I roll onto my back. 'Can I ask you a question?'

'Sure.'

'Do you think about other guys?'

'Yes, I notice other guys, but Sandy's the only one for me. Why?'

'No reason.' The image of Steve's smile from when I first saw him on the bus dances before my eyes.

Almost as though she's reading my mind, Doll remarks, 'I forgot to tell you. Steve's officially the lead singer of the Clyde Alloys. They've done a few more practice sessions, and the band are pleased with him. Sandy likes him, says he's dead funny. Steve was asking about you after you left that night at McCoy's. He thought Billy was your boyfriend! If only he knew how much you hate Billy!'

My heart leaps at the scary but thrilling news that Steve was asking about me – it'll just be friendly interest but still I'm pleased. Not wanting to be obvious about Steve, I change the subject to Tommy, the keyboard player of the Clyde Alloys, and my amusement that he wears cheap sunglasses bought from the market, even when he's indoors.

Doll chortles. 'Yip, Tommy seems to have taken over the 'arsehole' category in the group from Billy. The guy's so up himself – he's convinced that he's going to make it to the big time. Sandy says that Tommy's dropping big hints that he might be looking at other bands because he doesn't think that the Clyde Alloys will make it.'

'Do you think they'll make it?'

'I hope so. Or my dad will make me split up with Sandy. He says he's too much of a dreamer.'

Chapter 11

Tuesday, 10 July 1984

The orange glow reflection of a street lamp ripples across the puddle in front of me. Skittering footsteps sound somewhere nearby. My heart thunders as I flatten my back against the wall, gasping for breath. Perhaps Lorraine and her gang won't think to search for me here behind the chapel? I'm ready to bolt like a greyhound as soon as I suspect they're too close.

Silence.

Has Lorraine given up, bored with the hunt? Hope flowers inside of me, but only for a moment, as between the gravestones, the blur of running figures catches my eye. I bolt off in the opposite direction, pumping my arms and legs hard.

'Git her!' Lorraine roars.

The high-pitched squeals of the gang almost drown out the clattering of their heels as they give chase. I sprint as fast as I can, eventually aware of only one set of running footsteps behind me. I'm expecting my last pursuer to tire as they normally do, but no, this person gains on me. I scream, as my hair's yanked and I'm whirled around to face a pale, blonde girl.

She whoops as she drags me in the direction of Lorraine and her gang.

'Meet ma new secret weapon.' Lorraine crows. 'Ah wis delighted when ah heard JoJo wis movin' back hame. *Champion sprinter. Champion fighter.'*

The blond girl, called JoJo, kicks my legs from under me, landing me on the rough pavement, into a puddle. Spluttering, the rank taste of the filthy rainwater fills my mouth as my face is plunged into its chilly depths.

Umpteen hands and arms launch me back onto my feet, and the breath's knocked out of me as I'm shoved backwards and pinned against a wall. I try to lash out with my arms and legs, but it's no use. I'm outnumbered, with no way to escape this time.

'No' so smart at running away the night, then?' Lorraine Pollock guffaws, poking me in the shoulder. 'Yir so ugly that every time ah see you, ah just want to heave. You. Annoy. Me.' I cry out as she slaps me hard. The smell of drink on her breath nips at my nostrils.

I try to appeal to her better nature, 'Lorraine, I don't want any trouble ...' She slaps me again. Even some members of her gang gasp. She scowls, clenching and unclenching her fists.

She mimics me, *'Lorraine, I don't want any trouble...'*, exaggerating the half Scottish, half Afrikaans mix of my accent. 'Yir so fucking *up* yirsel!'

She leers. 'It's bad enough there being one i' ye to annoy me – noo there's two i yeez! Yir wee scabby, breathless sister is something else to behold! She's nae eyebrows, aw covered in sores – I'm feart to touch her in case ah catch somethin'! She screams and whines louder than ye, and that's saying somethin'!'

I strain forward, but the gang members yank me back, pulling my shoulders so hard that I cry out.

'Ye goat any money?' Lorraine leans inches away from my face.

I shake my head no, fighting off tears and trying to sound broad Scottish. 'That's why I'm walking hame – ah've no bus fare.'

'Don't believe ye. Haud her there!' Lorraine commands, 'Ah'm goanna give her a wee search, see if she's anything worth taking.'

She rifles through my pockets, tossing tissues and old bus tickets aside. A smile creeps across her face, and my heart sinks as she discovers the blue velvet pouch in my jacket pocket. 'Ah, whit do we hiv here?' Lorraine points the pouch towards a nearby streetlight and loosens the drawstring. She pulls out the rosary beads with a puzzled look on her face.

Icy fear grips me. Why, oh why, did I bring my precious rosary beads out tonight with me? I compose my face into what I hope is a look of calm. Lorraine watches me with a glint in her eye.

'Whit's these? Aw, a sparkly necklace,' Lorraine crows as she twirls the beads to catch the light from the streetlamp. Suddenly, she stops and with a look of disgust, 'No, wait –

there's a guy hinging aff a cross there – ugh –
pape beads!' She promptly releases the rosary
beads onto the pavement like they're on fire.

I curse myself as I try to lurch forward again.
Now, I've given away that the rosary beads
mean something to me. With a cruel laugh,
Lorraine bends to snatch up the crystal beads.
She tugs the hanging section, which has the
crucifix on it. It won't budge. 'Ah suppose ah
could snip it aff wae a pair i' pliers but ah cannae
be bothered!' She yanks at the rosary beads
harder and harder. The other gang members
sneer and giggle.

Panicked, I begin to cry and plead. 'Please,
don't. My mammie gave them to me!' I wriggle
to twist my arms free from the women who
hold on to me tighter. I scream in frustration.

'Whit? These are fae yir wee baldy, pathetic
Maw?' Lorraine looks across at me knowingly.
'Ye can shout and greet all ye want. I'm keeping
these. They're kinda cool.' The beads twinkle in
her fingers as she turns them over to catch the
light. She tugs again at the crucifix section and
then yanks it hard.

Spluttering, I gawp in disbelief as my
precious rosary beads are viciously snapped
apart – a thousand prayers and dreams
scattered into the night sky like broken rain.

'Oops!' Lorraine mocks. She traps as many
crystal beads as she can under her Doc Marten
boots and kicks them and the crucifix section
into a nearby drain. 'Guess ye won't be needing
these noo.'

My shoulders drop. I sob so hard that the
gang members struggle to keep a tight hold on

my arms. Lorraine grins as she boots the last crystal bead into the drain. 'Let the pathetic cow go! Ah'm bored.' As she leaves, Lorraine tosses the velvet bag like a piece of rubbish over her shoulder for it to land in a puddle. The gang joins Lorraine's side. The girl called JoJo, hands her a half bottle of something, which she swigs from as she swaggers away.

Stunned, I stare at their departing figures, waiting for my body to react to the murderous thoughts exploding in my head. A whirlpool of hatred, anger and grief gathers in the pit of my stomach and cascades from me. I scream with all my strength, 'Fucking Bitch!'

Lorraine and her pals stop in their tracks and pivot back to face me. 'Ur ye wanting me to gie ye a severe doin'? Cos if you ur, let me tell ye, ah'm back in the mood.'

I hang my head immediately, noting how badly I'm shaking. I bite my lip to stop myself from saying anything else.

'Thought so.' Lorraine cackles and turns to walk away with her cronies again. Despite my best efforts, I can't let her go without a last word from me. Perhaps too scared to say it in English, I yell what I'm thinking in Afrikaans so that I've made the promise out loud to Lorraine Pollock: '*Ek sal jou pimpel en pers slaan, jou teef!*'

I am going to beat you black and blue, you bitch!

She doesn't know and doesn't care what I've just said. 'Quit gibberin' all that voodoo shite.' She flaps her hand to indicate that she's done with me. Lorraine, JoJo, and the rest of the gang disappear into the darkness.

Weeping, I drop to my knees. Just as I shake the muddy water from the blue velvet pouch, a glint catches my eye. Slightly buried in the mud surrounding the puddle is a solitary crystal bead.

Back home, I drop the precious crystal bead into its pouch and carefully place it back under the carpet.

I hate Lorraine Pollock.

I hate my life.

Chapter 12

Thursday, 12 July 1984

It's the day of the Orange Walks and the celebration of the victory of the Protestant King, William of Orange, over the Catholic King, James II, at the Battle of the Boyne, on the east coast of Ireland in 1690. It's been almost 300 years since this battle and everyone involved in it is long since dead, yet it's still celebrated today.

I know from reading the *Daily Record* and watching the news that the troubles are bad in Northern Ireland, with Protestants and Catholics dying in the name of religion and politics. Both sides think they're right, and so they keep fighting. I guess hundreds of years of sectarianism are hard to snap apart, and so remain alive and well in my part of Scotland. For me, though, I want to live in a town where it doesn't matter which school you go to, where and how you worship God, or if your first or last name has a religious clue in it.

It's eleven in the morning. I'm standing at the bus stop at the bottom of the hill on Woodburn High Street, waiting to go home after getting some messages at *Wullie Low*, the supermarket. I'm clutching the brown paper bag containing a few bits that Gran needs for tonight's dinner. The faint shrill of flutes playing and the dull thuds of drums drift in the air. *Of course – it'll be the Orange Parade marching through the local towns and villages on their way to meet other bands in some park.*

Excitement pulses through me. I know I'm not supposed to, but I enjoy watching the spectacle of the Orange bands marching past in strict formation, the flashy banners of their various lodges held proudly aloft. Following the lodge banners, there is the twirling and tossing of a substantial wooden stick into the air, decorated in the red, white, and blue of the Union Jack, in time to the band's music. Each lodge band wears a different coloured uniform, with the flautists at the front and the drummers following behind. Then the men in dark suits come marching past, arms and legs swinging in unison, wearing bowler hats, coloured sashes, and white gloves. The women march behind them in pretty dresses, sashes, and white gloves.

And sometimes, in amongst the women, there is a gap where a little boy is dressed as King William, proudly holding the arm of a little girl dressed as his wife, Queen Mary. I imagine their parents must be proud that they've been chosen to be their lodge's King and Queen for that year's Orange Parade. No more cars have come down the hill, so I'm guessing that the police must have stopped the traffic to allow the Orange Parade to march freely through Woodburn. Coming over the crest of the hill, I spot some banners and the rhythmic white flashes of the gloves of the marchers. The music gets louder and louder, and my heart quickens as I crane my neck to enjoy the parade. I get lost in the music and even tap my feet as a passing band plays, "Billy Boys". I hardly flinch as the marchers chant: *We're up to our knees in Fenian blood, surrender or you'll die...* Then the next tune begins as another band marches past. The noise is thunderous and thrilling.

Taking a break from viewing the bands marching past, I watch the people coming down the hill. Some hold their loved ones' hands while others swing carrier bags that bulge with food or clink with alcohol. Their faces are bright as they sing the lyrics and walk to the music.

Then, my eyes happen to fall upon a guy about my age, who swaggers towards me. He gives me a great big smile, which I return. A second later, I'm puzzled as he frowns. He's staring at my chest. I realise, too late, that I've forgotten to hide my crucifix necklace. I falter backwards to get as close as possible to the shop window behind me.

He spits in my face.

At first, I try to work out if what I think happened has happened, but then some of his thick green and white spittle slides off my cheek and onto my cardigan. Some of the people leer and laugh at me as they march past. Using an old tissue I've found in my pocket, I desperately wipe the guy's gobber off my face and cardigan. Humiliated, I hang my head and snap the chain and crucifix from my neck.

•》›·•◆·•‹《•

I've changed into a summer dress and, feeling brave, have also put on a pair of white heels instead of my usual flat shoes. I'm heading to Marie's house, where I'm also meeting Geraldine. Doll has been marching today and is partying tonight with her pals from the Women's Orange Lodge. I'm still thinking about the guy who spat on me earlier. What I'm most shocked by is not the fact that he did that but by the change in his face from happiness and admiration to disgust and hatred when he saw that I was wearing a crucifix necklace. I love my family, but I know I will need to leave them to escape this vile place. My mind's now definitely made up to move to somewhere where no one cares what religion I am. I'm going to choose a university far away from here.

As I'm walking along a street, I'm distracted by the number of Union Jacks and Red Hand of Ulster flags fluttering in the breeze and jammed into the window frames of the houses. A group of guys appear ahead, and they're walking on the same side of the street as me. The guys swig from beer cans, shouting and roughhousing with each other as they approach me. My breath catches as I notice that one of the gang members has the same swaggery walk as the guy who spat on me this morning.

Despite my fear, I'm curious if it's the same guy. It's too late to turn around or even cross the road, so I take a deep breath, my heart leaping in my chest and look him in the eye as we're about to pass.

Oh no, it is him! I steel myself.

He looks right at me and winks, 'Awright, darlin'?' His friends tease him loudly as we pass each other. And that is that. He's gone. He doesn't remember me, nor my offensive crucifix from earlier. I'm only a girl to him now, not a Catholic.

A little while later, I'm glad to walk into the chaos of Marie's house. She's one of nine kids from one of those Irish Catholic families that Billy McIntyre was talking about that don't believe in contraception. It's always busy in her house with children coming and going, and it constantly smells of food – sometimes Irish stew, sometimes roast chicken, mostly potatoes.

Marie shares a room with two of her older sisters, and luckily tonight, both her sisters are out with their boyfriends. Her and Geraldine slouch on Marie's single bed. I sit opposite, not far from them, against the wall where the cassette player's plugged in. I pop my most recent recording of the Top 40 into Marie's cassette player.

The girls live close to each other, and so they meet regularly. Meanwhile, I've been busy seeing Doll and Paul and haven't seen Geraldine and Marie for over two weeks, and they're eager to hear my news. They ask how Doll is and love listening to my stories about my first visit to a pub, about the band gossip and that the cute, blond guy from the bus is now the lead singer of the Clyde Alloys.

We're chatting away, listening to my tape of the Top 40 countdown. There are a lot of good slow songs this week. I love Lionel Richie's "Stuck on You" and Cyndi Lauper's "Time after Time".

As Marie and Geraldine gossip, my mind wanders from thinking about what to do about Paul to getting lost in images and memories of Steve, and after the day I've had, my heart lightens at the thought of him. A small smile flickers across my face.

'Who are you thinking about?' Geraldine's voice cuts through my daydreaming, 'Spill the beans!'

I know I can't admit who I'm really thinking about it, so I shrug.

Marie teases, 'She's thinking of Paul.'

'And when she's finally going to sleep with him.' Geraldine nudges my foot with hers.

'I've told you. One, it's none of your business; two, it's none of your business.' I kick Geraldine's foot back.

'Such a shame you two are still virgins. Let me know when you split up. I know I'd teach him a thing or two.' Geraldine purrs, pouting her lips.

'Geraldine Byrne!' Marie digs her in the ribs, shaking her head.

Geraldine grins, enjoying the shock factor.

'Don't you dare think about it!' I chuck one of Marie's teddies at her, which she easily catches and launches right back at me.

Frankie Goes to Hollywood come on next. The group has the number one single with "Two Tribes" and the number two song, the controversial "Relax". The record is banned from being played on Radio 1, but Radio Clyde's still playing it.

'That band's from Liverpool, just like that guy, Steve.' I say, and the girls laugh at the not-so-subtle way I've changed the subject back to him.

Trying to look as nonplussed as I can, and having reminded Marie and Geraldine of the first time we saw Steve on the bus, I tell the lassies more about the next time I met him, singing in the band and how the girls in the pub seemed to like him. I tell them about how he recognised me and touched my shoulder when he pulled a chair up to my side of the table.

I describe how well the night was going until Billy McIntyre turned up. They listen, dumbfounded, as I tell them what happened later in my living room and that eventually, I kicked him out, announcing that I was one of those Catholics he'd just been slagging off. Geraldine and Marie love this last detail.

'That'll serve the dickhead right!' Geraldine laughs.

'He meant you harm, Aileen. You need to be more careful.' Always the voice of reason, Marie's statement stirs the guilt I'm still feeling about being hoodwinked by Billy McIntyre.

I bite my lip. 'I learned a lesson, that's for sure.' We fall quiet for a moment, and then I add: 'Thing is, he's telling everyone he slept with me! Apparently, I loved it ....'

'Well, we know that isn't true!' Geraldine shouts, and I'm surprised by how angry she is on my behalf.

Marie frowns as she sits forward on the edge of her bed, 'Can you not prove he's lying?'

I shake my head. 'No. It's my word against his. And, a guy spat on me today.'

The girls listen as I tell them about watching the Orange Walk earlier.

'I just don't get Prods sometimes.' Geraldine screws her face. 'Is Doll out at the Walk?'

I nod.

'Is it not strange having a best pal in the Orange Lodge?' Marie regards me with her big brown eyes.

'No. Our religions have never come between us. And we don't discuss it.'

Geraldine presses. 'But she'll be singing with all her pals about driving out Catholics and all that.'

Shrugging my shoulders, I admit that for me, my friendship with Doll means more than the sum of the differences in our religions. Buried deep down, I'm also aware of the fear that our friendship may be tested one day and that makes me sad.

Marie knocks her foot against mine. 'Forget about all the Orange Walk stuff and Billy the dickhead. Tell us more about that Steve.' She winks at me, and I work hard to suppress the smile spreading across my face. I tell them the story of my run and how I thought the rapist was chasing me, how he fell over me, and then I kicked him in the balls, but it turned out to be Steve. The girls hang on to my every word.

When I finish, Geraldine joins Marie on the edge of the bed: 'Poor guy!'

'I know. It'll be a little awkward next time I see him play in the band.'

'Let us know when the Clyde Alloys play next, and we'll come along too.' Geraldine grins at Marie.

I agree to let them know, but I'm uneasy. Geraldine's teased me too many times about getting her hands on Paul. Now, when I imagine Geraldine turning her charms on Steve, anxiety mixed with jealousy creeps into my heart. And it's a surprise, even to me, that I'm thinking mainly about Steve.

Chapter 13

Thursday, 12 July 1984

Alone, I thread my way through the dark streets. I mentally kick myself because I should have left Marie's house a lot earlier, especially as it's the night of the twelfth of July. The muffled noise of drunken parties in the houses filters through open windows to drift on the air. Occasionally a door opens, and the chatter, music and singing briefly interrupt the quiet out here.

Speed marching through the streets, it seems everyone is inside; I relax. I'm soon lost in my guilty pleasure of thinking about Steve and replaying images of him in my mind.

I've been so caught up in my dreaming that I've not noticed a couple seemingly disagreeing under a streetlight just ahead. The clicking sound of my heels on the pavement slows as I consider what to do next. It's too late, though.

As they turn to look at me, I swallow hard as I recognise Billy McIntyre and the plump red-haired lassie in his arms.

'*You shagged ma man!*' In an instant, Lorraine Pollock has shoved Billy's arms away and runs full tilt at me.

Dear God, no! Is Lorraine Pollock Billy McIntyre's girlfriend?

I turn to bolt in the opposite direction, but one of my heels buckles under me, sending me flying onto the pavement. I twist onto my back, ready to scramble to my feet, but Lorraine has other ideas. She towers above me as she plants her heavy boot on my chest, pinning me down. She's had most of her hair shaved off, leaving only a frizzy red fringe at the front, which makes her look even scarier.

'Ye threw yirsel' at ma boyfriend, used your voodoo ways to trick him into sleeping with ye!'

Billy approaches us, leering.

I laugh as theatrically as I can. 'No offence, but Billy's *definitely* not my type!'

'Yir such a liar! Ma Billy's gorgeous!'

Billy wipes his nose, clearly pleased that two women are fighting about him. 'Noo, noo, ladies, calm doon! Form a queue.'

'In your dreams!' I spit at Billy.

Lorraine rolls her sleeves. 'Likely story. His pal telt me that ye gave ma Billy a blow job, and ye let him shag ye. Ah knew ye wur a durty hoor!'

'I kicked Billy out of my house when he tried to force himself on me!'

Lorraine scowls and shakes her head. She's not having my version of events.

Thinking quickly, 'Okay, prove you're telling the truth, Billy! I have a large birthmark on my body that you wouldn't have missed. Where is it?'

'Dunno, ah wis too busy enjoying masel.'

Lorraine releases her boot from my chest and steps over to slap Billy.

'Ah mean, that ah wis distracted.' Billy holds his face, his lips curling over his grey teeth.

'Stop lying.' I stagger back onto my feet. 'I don't have any birthmarks. We both know you didn't sleep with me. I'm still a virgin, and you're still a wanker.'

Billy ignores the insult. 'Whit ye talking aboot? Ye gave me a gammy – pretty shite at it too – and then when ah wis trying to get away, ye sat on ma dick!'

Disgusted, I shake my head. 'You've been reading too many porn magazines!'

'Durty hoor!' Lorraine lunges for me.

Before I can twist to run away, I'm rugby-tackled, face-first back onto the ground – I realise, by Billy. He scratches my left cheek on the pavement as he forces my face down. 'Ah've goat her, Lorraine. Whit ye gaunna dae noo?' He's panting heavily, pinning my arms behind my back, his full weight on me.

Trapped. I kick backwards with my legs, switching my body from side to side, trying to escape. Threading his fingers through my hair, Billy yanks my head back. His voice cracks with what sounds like excitement. 'How do ye know this lassie, Lorraine?'

'We go back a long way, Billy Boy! Ah've knocked fuck oot her fur years, but shaggin' ma man – that's the lowest of the low!'

'He's lying!' I scream.

'Naw, you're lyin'! Lassies throw themselves at ma Billy aw the time, and sometimes, he cannae seem to say naw.' Lorraine's voice drips with sarcasm.

I watch her boots pace in front of my face. 'Bit ah've seen you use your voodoo ways. You tricked him!'

Billy's breathing quickens just above my ear.

'No! He tricked me! He lied to get into my house – '

He tightens his grip on my hair. 'She wis cryin', said she wis feart and could ah make sure she goat in the hoose okay.'

'Ah fuckin' knew it! *Hoor!*'

Punches rain on my face, head, and body. Pinned to the pavement, I'm at eye level with Lorraine's Doc Marten boots. They're the kind that probably have steel toe protectors in them, and when she kicks me with them, I know it's going to hurt so bad. And it does.

The booting and punching continue, and the taste of blood seeps into my mouth. I scream as loudly as I can. As my head's being yanked back again – ahead of me – I see the fingers of neighbours prising open the slats of their Venetian blinds to get a better look. Surely, someone will come to help. At least call the police. But the blinds are snapped back into place. The beating continues. No one is coming. Tears mix with the blood running into my eyes, stinging them.

'No' so snooty noo, are ye, ya cow!' Lorraine shrieks triumphantly, booting me some more in the side. My screams subside into whimpers.

Now, I just want it to be over. All of it, finished. I'm so tired of living in fear and pain.

Billy's still astride my back when he hisses into my ear: 'This is whit ye git for no' gie'in' me ma hole, ya ugly Fenian hoor!' He reeks of drink.

Beyond caring now, I hiss, 'Say it louder so that she can hear!'

'Hear whit?' Lorraine pauses. I watch her boots freeze mid-step.

'He's lying!'

'Naw, ah'm no'. I wis pissed, you took advantage i' me.'

'What?' I laugh bitterly, spitting blood out of my mouth. I know that it's hopeless. Billy's so far into his lie, and Lorraine is not going to believe me. Part death wish, part just wanting it all to be over, I yell, 'You have the toatiest wullie I've ever seen!'

Billy's body tenses against mine, and he slaps me so hard that the other side of my head bounces off the pavement with a painful crack. 'You fuckin' cheeky slag!'

Dazed, I lie still and register that Lorraine has hauled Billy from me. They boot me as hard as they can. I wail uselessly into the otherwise now silent night.

Spent, a strange sensation slithers around me. My fear turns to calm as I understand that it's all about damage limitation now. I curl into a foetal position, bringing my hands and arms over my head and face. I screw my eyes shut to try to take myself to a different place in my mind.

Then, the sound of a man's angry voice pierces through my pain. 'Get the fuck off her!'

Billy protests – he sounds scared. There's a scuffle and a couple of loud smacking sounds. I sense somebody land on the pavement beside me, followed by a loud crack.

'And you! Do one before I do something I regret!' The man sounds enraged.

Lorraine protests: 'Billy, ur ye alright?' He moans somewhere behind me.

'Ya bastard!' I cringe as Lorraine screams like a banshee. Then there's another dull thud.

'I'm telling ya! Fuck off home, bitch, or you'll regret it!' The man growls.

Too scared to open my eyes, I lie as still as I can.

'You're safe now. I've got you.' The man's soft voice is soothing as his arms cradle me towards him. My body shudders, and I begin to sob. Not just from the pain but also from relief and joy that someone has come to rescue me, finally. The more comforting his voice is, the harder I cry, white-hot pain wracking through my body.

Now the neighbours begin to come out of their houses. 'Is she alright? What was the fight about?'

'She's fine! No thanks to any of you!' The man shouts. 'Has anyone phoned the police? Rang for an ambulance?' The neighbours mutter, quietly protesting that they didn't want to get involved.

Gates squeak open. Doors close.

Silence.

I'm startled when the man lifts me up from the pavement into his arms. Fresh waves of pain radiate across my body. I bite my lip to stop from crying out. I can't open my eyes. I feel so *ashamed*. Then, whispering, he says, 'Come on, let's get you away from here.' He takes a few strides and then his body lurches. Billy screams out in pain - I think the man has kicked him as he's walked past.

God forgive me, but despite the pain, I'm smiling now. Take that – you lying, skinhead bastard!

It's only when the man says, 'Now *that* was a proper kick to the nuts!' that I realise the man carrying me is Steve.

⊶ ⋅⋅+⋅⋅ ⊷

Having driven me to the hospital, I lean against Steve as I hobble into the too-bright Accident and Emergency building. At this time of night, the waiting room is busy with people here for some drunk-fighting injury or other. Even through my pain, the sight of all these formerly well-dressed people, their clothes now dishevelled and bloody, does look funny. I'm also grateful they're here because they'll help to take the spotlight off me, one of the youngest patients in the room.

I suggest to Steve that he sits while I limp over to the desk to register. The receptionist looks exhausted; it must have been a busy night here already. As I give her my details, her eyes keep flicking to where Steve's sitting. She asks me how I got my injuries. I tell her the same reason as most of the people here. She draws herself higher in her chair and says in a low voice: 'Aye, but I'm guessing from your name that you weren't out celebrating at the Orange Walk! Did he do this to you?' The receptionist draws daggers at Steve.

'What? No! He saved me. I was getting a kicking on the street; he got them off me, helped me here.' I start to cry and shake again, remembering what happened to me.

The receptionist nods. 'I'll put you higher on the waiting list. These pissheads can wait a bit longer.' She winks at me, and it's then that I notice her name tag, 'Angela O'Connell'. She's probably a Catholic. 'You know when you get seen, they're probably going to suggest that you report what happened to you to the police. Think about it. It's not right for a young lassie to be attacked like this.'

As I shuffle back to Steve, he stands to help me lower myself back onto the waiting room chair. 'Did she think I did this to you?'

'Aye, she thinks you're a wife-beater.'

Steve looks around, passes his hand through his blond hair. 'Well, it does go on ....'

The waiting room is packed full. Assembled around me are other injured people, some holding rags to their bloody noses and faces, some with homemade bandages on their arms, legs and heads, and others using upside-down broomsticks as makeshift crutches. It must have been a good celebration today. Some of the former party people look sad and thoughtful, but there's a bigger section tonight who are still full of drink. They are by far the noisiest and are either arguing loudly with one another or breaking into singing Orange songs. Angela rings a bell to get their attention.

'There are very sick people in here! If you can't be quiet, I'm phoning the police! That means a doctor won't see you!' Angela's announcement gets their attention and keeps the noise down for a while. She glances over at me with a smirk.

I send her a little knowing smile in return and turning my head, I gasp as I catch my reflection in the glass-panelled door in front of me. The sight shocks me because I'm covered in blood, my hair sticking out in all directions. What will Da and Gran say when they see me? I need to tidy myself as best as I can before I go home. Da won't let me out the door again, never mind to a pub.

'I look like an extra from *Night of the Living Dead,* would that be right?'

'Well, I've seen better-looking zombies, to be honest!' Steve takes my hand and picks at some dried blood which flakes off. 'Look. You're falling apart.' We both have a little chuckle. 'Once they clean you up, you won't look so bad.'

He searches my face, lifting sections of my hair, scanning the bits of skin he can see on my arms and legs. 'It's amazing, but I don't believe you'll need any stitches. It looks mostly like minor cuts and bruises. Where do you hurt?'

'My head, my back, my sides – all over. This thigh's sore.' Without thinking, I've hitched my dress to look at the side of my leg. A massive red lump has appeared, the length of the side of my thigh. Then I gingerly touch my head and am stunned when my fingertips stick to a warm, wet patch on my scalp. Shaking, I bring my hand to my face to behold a loose clump of bloody hair in it. 'Oh my God. My hair's falling out too!' I laugh dryly. 'I really am a zombie, aren't I?'

I hobble over to a bin to dispose of the hair and return to lower myself to sit next to Steve. 'How come you know about injuries? Are you a nurse or something?'

Steve looks at his hands, flexes his fingers. 'No. Nothing like that. I'm a boxer. I've had a fair few cuts and bruises over the years – and a broken nose.' I'd never noticed his nose before, but now I'm looking, there is a little bump on top of it, and it bends slightly to the left.

I say: 'Cannae notice your nose unless you look closely.' I'm thinking: *Your face is so gorgeous that no one's going to notice your slightly wonky but still perfect nose.* 'Is that why you were out running the other week? Boxing training?'

'Yeah. I run most days and usually in the Country Park. First time I saw you there, though. Mind you, I was out running later than I normally do. I believe my balls have just about recovered! For a while, I didn't think I'd be able to claim Family Allowance.' His eyes flicker to his groin area, and we smile at his joke.

'I'm so sorry.'

Steve pulls a face. 'Don't worry about it! I've been kicked in the balls a lot harder before. I survived. Anyway, the main point is about you. Why were Fatty and that Billy beating you up?'

'For the same reason as always. I'm a Catholic!' My voice rises a little higher than I mean it to when I say 'Catholic', and a few Orange Day parade people turn around to gawk at me, the enemy in their midst.

'You get beaten because you're a *Catholic*?'

Before I know it, I begin to describe to Steve what it's been like for me ever since we came back from South Africa. How the bullying started with name-calling until it became more physical, how it could be one individual or several, and how there were no rules about how much older than me the bullies were, or what sex.

'So, you're saying that guys hit you too?' Steve's eyes widen.

'Aye.'

'Have you tried sticking up for yourself?'

'In the beginning, yes, but they're scarier than me and better at fighting. I usually get battered twice as bad because I had a go. Now, I run away.'

Steve shakes his head. 'I never knew this went on. *You're a girl!*'

When I glance at Steve's shocked face, it dawns on me that this is the first time I've trusted anyone with my secret. He was there earlier, he saw what happened, so there's no point in lying.

He shuffles in his chair. 'I've never liked that no-mark, Billy. And that girl – if you can call her that ... looks more like Buster Bloodvessel!'

I don't mean to go into detail, but now that Steve knows my secret, I trust him to learn more.

'She's been picking on me for years – calls me a 'Fenian cow'. Turns out that my biggest bully is Billy McIntyre's girlfriend, and she believes his lies about sleeping with me. Tonight's the worst beating she's given me. She's too fat to catch me normally, but I tripped over, and then that Billy held me down so she could hit me.'

'*That bastard held you down?*' Steve's face pinches. 'Did he hit you?'

I shrug. Now, I tell Steve the story of how Billy tried to force himself on me last weekend and how it was only my dog who saved me.

Steve twists his right fist inside his left palm. 'The fucking liar!' He must have read something in my face because his voice softens. 'You're one tough cookie, aren't you?'

I start to cry again, and then I can't stop. Maybe it's the relief of finally sharing my secret, or maybe it's because someone believes me. Steve leans over and holds me gently in his arms. We sit like that for a while. The smell of him is comforting, and eventually, I stop crying. Resting against Steve's chest, I close my eyes.

Very softly, Steve hums a gentle song. I enjoy the vibrations of his chest against my cheek as he sings the sad notes. The soothing sound of Steve's singing, plus the comfort of being held, of feeling safe, helps to take my mind off the pain. Exhausted, I want to stay here forever.

Steve breaks the spell: 'Should we call your parents, let them know what's happened to you?'

I lift my head and croak matter-of-factly: 'My da's at work, and my gran'll be in her bed by now. Plus, we don't have a phone.'

'I'll just give me Ma a quick ring, cos I know she worries.' Steve carefully peels me off his chest and sits me back against my seat. He's over by the payphone now, feeding it with coins. As I note how tall and muscular he is, I wonder what my own mammie would have made of what happened tonight. I know she would have been heartbroken, but, like me, would be eternally grateful to Steve for rescuing me.

Angela calls my name and directs me along a corridor to a room. Steve nods as I walk past him, talking on the payphone. A nurse carefully cleans me up, dabbing around my face and hairline. Her hands flutter to her face when I tell her what happened to me, and she gasps when I take off my dress so that she can attend to the cuts and bruises on my body. Before she has a chance to suggest it, I tell her that there's no point in calling the police because I don't know who attacked me. She shoots me a dubious look as the doctor comes in. He examines me a little more, flashing a light into my eyes, moving parts of my body around, prodding me here and there.

'You've taken a nasty beating, young lady. Nothing appears to be broken, although you may have cracked some ribs. You have some cuts which don't need stitches, and bruises, which will heal with time. I can't find any signs of concussion, but if you feel sick or your headache gets worse, come back. You need to rest over the next few weeks. Whoever did this to you needs locking up! Will you be making a report to the police?'

I shake my head, tears well in my eyes.

'Ah, *snitches get stitches*, eh? Very well, young lady. All we can do now is manage your pain.'

When I limp back out to the waiting room, clutching my prescription, Steve takes my arm. 'What did the doc say? Have you broken anything?'

'I'll be fine, just need to rest. The doc gave me some painkillers.' A wave of tiredness washes over me.

Steve guides me carefully to his car and I give him directions to my home. All I want to do is crawl into bed.

And right now, I don't care if I wake up tomorrow.

Chapter 14

Friday, 13 July 1984

The sound of gentle knocking on my bedroom door awakens me, and for a moment, I've forgotten what's happened the night before. That is until I try to move. I cry out in pain.

Gran scurries into my bedroom, freezes. She cups her mouth to her hands. Then she screams. 'Jesus, Mary and Joseph! What's happened to you?'

The shock registered on her face sets me off sobbing.

Da comes bounding in. 'What the ? Aileen!'

Before they can reach me, I wail: 'Don't touch me!' The physical act of crying causes my body more pain. I do my best to stop, but I can't. My dirty secret's about to be exposed, and somewhere deep inside me, a valve has opened. The torment caused by years of emotional and physical abuse issues forth in a slow trickle then gathers such momentum that it becomes a tidal wave.

The harder I cry, the more the pain ratchets. Finally, spent, my body shudders to a stop, and my tears dry. Exhausted, I open my eyes. Gran and Da are stood in front of my bed, faces pale, both trembling.

Da speaks first. 'Aileen, kid. What happened?'

Gran sobs, which starts me off crying again. Wave after wave of shame, guilt, and sadness wash over me.

Da disappears to come back with some toilet roll sheets. I wipe my tears, blow my nose, blinking at the sight of scarlet blood on the tissues and my blood-stained pillow and sheets. I have no idea what I look like, but I'm guessing from what I glimpsed last night it isn't pretty.

I motion to the open box of painkillers by my bed, and Gran comes back with a glass of water. She pops two painkillers out of their packaging and helps support me while I take the tablets. Every inch of my body throbs with pain.

'I'm sorry.' I croak.

'For what, kid?' Da kneels beside my bed, carefully takes my hand, and searches my face. 'How did you get in this state?' Different emotions flicker across his face: fear, concern, disbelief, anger. I glance at Gran, who looks similar.

My chin wobbles. I take a deep breath. 'I don't know. I was on the wrong street, at the wrong time. Unlucky, I guess.'

Gran gasps and begins to cry again. I fight back tears too, but a stronger urge to tell Da and Gran at least a little of what happened takes over. 'The neighbours just watched me get beaten through their blinds, Da, and no one came to help at first ... eventually, a guy rescued me.' I swipe at the tears pooling in my eyes again.

'Do you remember me telling you about the guy on the bus? It was him – Steve. He lives in the next street to where I was beaten up. He was out for a walk, could see what was happening and stopped them. He drove me to the hospital, brought me home. I'll be okay, just cuts and bruises.' I do my best to sound light-hearted, but my voice cracks to betray me.

Da and Gran take it in turns to ask me more questions, and I answer each as best as I can but leave out the part where I know who the attackers are and that I've been getting bullied for a long time. I also skip the fact that one of the attackers was a guy who had tried to force himself on me only a few days ago. Something tells me it would not be wise to let Da know all of what happened. His growing fury is evident as he paces the room, scowling as I recount each new censored detail from last night.

'I want you to go to the police, Aileen! You need to report these bastards!' Da's face has flushed a deep red, his jaw set.

Before I get a chance to reject Da's idea, Gran throws her hands in the air: 'The police are all Orange – they won't do a thing about a young Catholic girl being attacked!'

Da shoots Gran a warning look. 'There are Catholic police officers, you know, and some Protestant ones who are not in the Orange Lodge.' He turns back to me. 'Kid, we can't just let this go. Look at the state of you ....' His voice trails off, tears glisten in his eyes.

I shake my head. 'Gran's right. There's no point going to the police because I can't tell them who did this to me or give a good description.'

I resist telling Da and Gran that I think that my little sister's being picked on too. Then another thought occurs to me. 'We can't let wee Mary see me. I don't want to frighten her. She can't know about this beating. What can we say to her?'

Da runs his hand through his hair. 'We'll tell her that you're not well, that you've got something that's catching, and so she can't see you. Then we'll say you've tripped running to explain how your face looks when you do see her.'

An image of Lorraine battering wee Mary flashes across my mind. I cannot allow that to happen ever again. I shudder.

A deadly expression passes over Da's face. He turns to Gran first, and then he looks at me. 'Nobody's harming my wean. I'm not letting this go. There were witnesses. Somebody must be bragging. They'll be sorry when I find out who they are!'

Chapter 15

Sunday, 15 July 1984

S itting on my bedside table, when I open my eyes, is a crystal vase with some pink carnations in it. There's also a folded piece of paper. I wince as I reach across for some painkillers.

'I'll help you.' Gran rises from the chair she's positioned beside my bed to hand me two painkillers and a glass of water.

'We had quite a few knocks at the door yesterday. We're not letting Paul or any of your pals in to visit, of course. I told them that you were sleeping. Folks have heard what's happened to you.'

This is the news I have dreaded. Shame washes over me, and the icy fingers of fear tap me on the shoulder, reminding me that the beatings will never stop. I am so sick and tired of all of this. I tremble.

Gran takes my hand: 'It's going to be alright. It was Paul who left the flowers. He looked white as a sheet when I was telling him the details.

And then a tall, blond guy – Steve – came to the door.'

'Steve was here?'

'Yes, he came to ask how you were. Such a good-looking fella. I wouldn't mind him rescuing me! Do you know if he's a Catholic or a Protestant yet?' Gran tosses some curls from her eyes.

Another bizarre conversation with Gran. 'No, it's not come up! Anyway, I thought you had me earmarked for engagement to Paul?'

'Always good to keep your options open.' Gran chuckles, handing me the folded piece of paper to read.

My heart leaps when I see the swirly signature on the bottom of the note:

Aileen

I've been worrying about you all night, so had to call by.

I'm made up to hear that you're getting better - thinking of you.

Steve

PS My phone number's 78809 - call me!

He's been worrying about me all night; he's been thinking about me. He's left his phone number and asked me to call him! A huge smile slides across my face. I don't know if it's the effects of the painkillers or Steve's note, but I'm feeling just a little bit better.

❧

I have no idea how long I've been sleeping, but when I wake up, it's dark. While I'm certain that there's someone else in my bedroom, I'm not sure if I'm dreaming. Or, maybe it could be the tablets I'm taking or the knocks to the head that I took.

Reluctantly, I open my eyes and adjust my focus so that I can see a little better in the darkness.

'Aileen.' A small voice whispers.

I moan. I'm so exhausted. Much as I'm trying to rouse my mind and body to full consciousness, I want to remain in that soft, safe sleep space. But the thought that someone is in my room keeps tugging at my mind. *Wake up, Aileen! Wake up!*

A bolt of fear shoots through me, and I cry out as I struggle to sit upright in bed. 'Who's there?' I hiss.

'Sorry, Aileen. Only me. I didn't mean to frighten you. Can you come? I want to show you something in my room?' It's wee Mary's voice.

'Show me what? It's the middle of the night.'

'Please. It's special, and I'm afraid it'll disappear. I want you to see it.'

Her small hand tugs on my arm. As my eyes adjust more to the darkness, I can make out wee Mary's silhouette, but I can't see her face. 'Please.' She pleads again. 'Come into my room. I know you'll be amazed.'

I've no idea what wee Mary wants to show me, but it's obviously important to her. And despite the pain I'm in, I can't deny my wee sister, so I carefully shuffle myself out of bed and do my best not to groan too much as I hobble behind her.

The quiet snores of Da and Gran drift towards us in the darkness as we tiptoe past their bedrooms. *Like Mother, like son,* I smile to myself.

Wee Mary leads me around the open door of her bedroom. 'Look.' I follow the direction of her hand in the gloom. She's pointing at something in front of the window. Her bedroom curtains are open.

'What? Something about Cornflake?' I believe wee Mary's pointing to her giant teddy bear in the corner, named after her favourite cereal.

'No, silly. Look over there.'

I can vaguely make out the shape of the object that wee Mary has her attention on in front of the window. 'What am I supposed to see?'

'Wait.' Wee Mary urges. 'She'll light up soon.'

I've no idea what's possessed wee Mary, and for a fleeting moment, I wonder if this is one of those dreams where you think that you're awake, moving about and talking, but you're actually fast asleep. 'I can't see anything.'

Just then, wee Mary's bedroom brightens as a beautiful white light is cast into the room – I realise from a full moon. The light falls onto the object in the window.

'Look.' Wee Mary urges.

I desperately want to see what my little sister wants me to see.

Wee Mary blesses herself. 'It's Our Lady. She's appearing to us.'

I scrutinise the object in the window again, and it really does look like Our Lady. It's a side view of her kneeling, head bent in prayer. The moonlight frames her figure with a white glow. I can see the drape of her robes around her face and body, her hands in the prayer position, just under her lips.

'Oh my.' I whisper, transfixed by the vision.

'I'm so glad you can see her too.' I hear wee Mary's smile in the darkness.

My logical mind is doing battle with itself. 'Why's she appearing to us?'

'Why not?' Wee Mary counters. 'Our Lady hasn't appeared to anyone for a long time. Why not to us? I've been good – only ever stolen some custard creams from the biscuit tin.'

Wee Mary gazes straight ahead at Our Lady; her face also brightened by the moonlight. 'I'm so pleased that she's appearing to us. I wish we had one of those Polaroid cameras to take a picture to prove she was here. What do you think it means?'

I study the vision of Our Lady. 'I think she's saying that you're a good lassie, Mary, and to keep up the good work. You share the same first name too. Maybe that's why? The Marys sticking together?'

'Aileen! That isn't funny! Show some respect! That's Our Lady over there. Should we say a *Hail Mary*?' As I join in the prayer with wee Mary, the moonlight gently fades, and the vision of Our Lady gradually disappears with it.

'Oh, she's gone again.' I feel a similar sadness and disappointment that I can hear in wee Mary's voice. Only the vague shape is left in the window now that the clouds have hidden the moon.

Taking wee Mary's hand, I lead her over to her bed. 'We both saw her. No one can take that away from us.'

Wee Mary frowns. 'Maybe she was appearing to let us know that our mammie's looking over us? Keeping us safe?'

The thought warms my heart, especially after being attacked by Billy and Lorraine. Thinking of her makes me realise that now is also a good time to raise the subject of Lorraine. 'Has a big lassie been picking on you?'

Wee Mary gulps, eyes still locked on the shadowed shape in the window.

'I know who she is. Don't worry. I'm your big sister. She's not going to touch you again.' With my body and spirit broken, I have no idea how I'll stop Lorraine, but I know I must try. I hug wee Mary into me, careful not to lean her into any tender parts of my body.

'She's big, Aileen, and tough. She's going to really hurt me next time she sees me.' Wee Mary quivers against me.

'She's not going to hurt you. If you see her – you run away. She can't run fast; you can. And besides – you have Our Lady on your side – and she's got a son who'd doof that nasty lassie right up!'

Wee Mary nods against my chest. 'Aye, I hope you're right. Our Lady must have gone back to heaven.' She pauses, then says, 'Do you think they'll build a shrine here like they did in Lourdes?'

As I give her another gentle squeeze, I giggle softly as, from the perspective of wee Mary's bed, I can now make out that the shape by the window is a crumpled brown paper bag bearing the familiar logo of *Wullie Low's* supermarkets. 'Well, we do have Carfin Grotto not far away, so I don't think so. Plus, I'm pretty sure Our Lady appeared to Saint Bernadette every day for a fortnight – and she asked Saint Bernadette to build the shrine. Did Our Lady ask you anything?'

'No. She didn't say anything – she just appeared.'

'In that case, then, Our Lady was just stopping by to let you know that she was taking care of you.'

Wee Mary smiles and yawns.

'Right, it's late. Let's get you back to bed.' I tuck her in and kiss her head.

'Remember that I've got something which is catching – so don't come back into my bedroom – I know it was for something important this time – but I don't want you to fall sick with what I have. Promise?'

'Promise.' She mumbles into her pillow, already sounding very sleepy.

Knowing that I'll miss her, I add: 'But you can speak to me through my bedroom door any time.'

'Aileen?'

'Yes?'

'Can you take care of that blonde-haired lassie too? She's the one who's been catching me for the fat lassie to batter.'

Chapter 16

Thursday, 19 July 1984

It's been a week since the attack, and my cuts and bruises are slowly healing. I'm not ready to see anyone yet, but I'm glad to know that Paul and my pals have called round several times, but not Steve. Each day I've hoped against hope that he would visit again. I've fantasised about sneaking out to phone him: what he would say, what I would say. The phone box is too far away, though. I'd be scared and bound to be spotted by someone.

The day after the attack, Gran had persuaded me to get in the bath and wash the blood from my hair and body. As soon as I had poured the first jug of water over my head, the water ran scarlet, and by the time I'd finished bathing, the water was pink. Gran also took the opportunity to change my bedsheets. The bath and the change of bedclothes helped me feel fresher, although the stain of what happened will probably never leave me.

Could I have done anything differently a week ago? The image of Venetian blinds being snapped open and closed replays over and over in my mind. I still can't believe that no one in those houses came out to help, or at least call the police. If Steve hadn't come when he had, I shudder to think what state I would have been left in, especially as Lorraine was hell-bent on avenging something which didn't happen, and Billy seemed to be getting off on how violent Lorraine was towards me.

Today, I'm on my own in the house for the first time since the attack. Wee Mary's away with her pal, Margaret, and her family, on a day trip to Ayr beach. After asking my permission about a hundred times, Gran's finally left to go to Wullie Low's for a few messages, and Da's gone to work. She and Da seem to have eased up on cross-examining me about the attack, but I sense they both suspect that there's more.

Padding downstairs in my slippers and pyjamas, it feels good to be out of bed. Curled up on his blanket in the kitchen, Bruno snoozes while I make a cup of tea and some toast. The sun's shining, and, on a whim, I open the back door. There's a gentle heat outside. I poke my head out, squinting against the sunlight. There seem to be no neighbours around. I carry my tea and my plate of toast outside and carefully lower myself onto the top step to sit.

I miss running. On a day like today, I would normally have been out on an early morning run to the Country Park. Still, I know I need to give my body a chance to heal. Although the throbbing pains and achiness over my body have lessened: many parts of me are still too tender to touch. Black, blue, and purple bruises cover my body. I abandoned pulling on a pair of jeans yesterday; the bruises on my calves and thighs are still too painful. I can't wear a bra either; the straps cut into tender areas around my back and shoulders. I'll be wearing loose dresses, or jogging pants and T-shirts, over the next few weeks until the swelling subsides.

There's a faint knocking at the front door. I freeze, straining to hear, but not daring to move. I wait for another knock, but there isn't one. I relax but almost jump out of my skin as someone comes around the corner. Too late. Busted. I can't turn and run.

'Aileen! There you are! It's such a nice day; I thought when no one answered the front door that someone might be in your back garden. You don't mind me calling round, do you?' It's Doll. She looks concerned and relieved to have found me.

'How are you?' she asks as she slowly climbs the back stairs to hand me copies of the *Jackie* and *Just Seventeen* magazines. I set the magazines to one side.

Unable to speak yet, I shrug my shoulders, unsure of what my next move is going to be.

'Is it okay if I stay a little? Maybe make some tea and toast too?' Doll touches my hand.

I nod.

She edges past me, and I hear her moving around my kitchen, fixing herself something to eat and drink, a place as familiar to her as her kitchen is to me. I sit completely still as Doll settles herself on a step further down and turns sideways to look at me. She takes a bite of her toast and sips some tea, regarding me all the while. I nibble at my toast again.

Finally, Doll breaks the silence. 'How are you, Aileen?'

'I've been better.' I manage a weak smile. I remember this feeling; it's called trust. I've always trusted Doll. That's not completely true, and I correct myself. I haven't trusted her enough to tell her about the beatings I've taken all these years. Is that a lack of trust or just a stronger impulse not to burden a single soul with a problem which I think I'm supposed to sort out myself?

Even if it is serious looking, it's so good to see Doll's sweet face again.

I try a little joke to lighten things. 'The last time I saw you, you hurled into a bush. I take it you've stayed away from long vodkas since?'

Doll frowns, pecks at her toast. 'The thing is that I don't think it was the drinks now because I'm still being sick. I'm thinking it's some sort of tummy bug.'

'Is it not coming on for two weeks now? Maybe make an appointment with the doctor.'

'Maybe. I just don't want to waste anyone's time if I feel better tomorrow.'

'Make the appointment. You might need some antibiotics or something.'

Doll shuffles on her step. 'Anyway, we're not here to talk about me. How are you? You look ...'

'Bloody awful?' I offer.

'Well ...' Doll bites her lip. 'Yes. What did they do to you? Your face ...'

I lift my pyjama top to show her my bruised torso and hitch my pyjama bottoms to show her my equally marbled legs.

'Fuck sake!' I'm surprised by Doll's response, as she doesn't usually swear. She squirms, mouth open, shaking her head like she can't quite comprehend what she's seeing.

'This is it better, believe me.' I look again at my best friend. I know I should trust her more. 'Thanks for calling around before. Sorry I wasn't taking visitors. Nothing personal against you – I just couldn't face anyone – I was in too much pain.' I decide against adding that shame, misplaced pride, and humiliation have also prevented me from receiving any visitors. I can't bear to think of the gossiping which must have been going on.

'You don't have to apologise to me for a single thing, Aileen Murphy. You're my best pal, always will be. I'm here for you when you need me.' She fixes me with her lovely blue eyes, her long blonde hair shining in the sun.

I decide to go for it. I choose to trust Doll. 'What have you heard?'

'Only that you took a good beating – I can see that's true – and you ended up in A&E. I've been so worried about you! And the fact that your gran and da wouldn't let me visit you only made me think the worst.

'I know it was Steve who found you and took you to A&E. He told me. He took me aside when the guys were taking a break during band practice on Tuesday gone. He's so worried about you.'

'What did he say?' I'm eager for any news about him.

'That he was heading home when he saw someone getting beaten by two people. When Steve realised the screams were coming from a girl, he said he just had to get involved.'

Doll's eyes tear up. 'Is that true, Aileen?'

I nod, fighting back my own tears.

'Who was it? Who did this to you?'

I shake my head.

'Steve wouldn't tell me either. But I believe he knows – just like you do. Tell me, Aileen. Who did this?'

'I don't want to say.'

'Do I know them? Aileen – do I know them?' Doll sounds shocked at this thought.

Raising my head, I look her straight in the eye. 'You must promise to keep this to yourself.'

'To the grave.'

'The lassie's called Lorraine Pollock.'

Doll gasps. 'I know her! She's in my lodge!'

'And the guy – well – it was Billy McIntyre.'

Doll's eyes widen. 'Her boyfriend, of course!' Doll drops her toast onto her plate. 'Sandy wasn't supposed to tell me.'

'Tell you what?'

'I noticed Billy hadn't been hanging out with the band this past week – when I asked Sandy why, he told me that Steve punched Billy when he turned up for band practice. The rest of the band didn't know why, just that Steve seemed to be raging about something. He shouted at Billy to admit the truth about you. Billy kept saying that he'd slept with you. Steve punched Billy in the face, landed him right on his backside!' Doll grins as she pats my arm.

'It was only then that Billy confessed that he'd lied about what you did. Finally, we got the truth about that night in your house! Sandy said that Steve was trying his best not to batter Billy out of the window. He just got him by the shoulders and slung him out of the door. Billy hasn't been seen since.'

Inside, my heart rejoices. Billy got a taste of his own medicine! And Steve stuck up for me.

Doll cuts through my thoughts. 'And just wait till I get my hands on that Lorraine Pollock!'

'Doll – you promised!'

While a part of me is enjoying hearing talk of revenge, I'm not comfortable about arranging real revenge. Revenge that I know about – that I've orchestrated. Lord knows I have been running all sorts of fantasies through my head this last week where I bounce that Lorraine's thick skull off the pavement and cut out a new Glasgow kiss on the other side of Billy McIntyre's ugly face. And usually with Steve by my side. That's always the best part of these get-my-own-back fantasies, having Steve on my team. And it turns out Steve is sort of on my team.

Then Doll seems to read my mind: 'Can I tell Steve that I saw you? He keeps asking for news of you.'

My cheeks flush, and I bite my lip to stop myself from smiling.

Doll examines my face. 'Oh, oh. I know that look! Do you *like* Steve?'

I nod. Then I laugh. 'Oh, I like him, Doll, so much it hurts. It's warped – what about Paul, I keep thinking? Steve's on my mind a lot, though! Maybe there's a psychological reason for it – you know – because he rescued me?'

Doll chuckles, setting her plate of toast on the step. 'He's not exactly ugly, either. Don't tell Sandy I said that!'

'Anyway, forget I said anything like that about Steve. He's my hero, whatever.'

'He's mine too, for saving you.' Doll sips her tea. 'Have you seen Paul or the girls yet?'

'No. They've called round lots, but I haven't been ready to see anyone.'

Doll looks thoughtful. 'What are we going to do about getting you justice?'

'Nothing, Doll. We're not going to do a thing.'

'We have to do something!' Doll takes a chunk out of her slice of toast.

'No, let's not do anything. And this happened to me, not you. So, I'll decide what to do.' I remind Doll.

'Does your Da know who did it?'

'Are you kidding? If my da knew, he'd be behind bars by now! He's that angry there's no telling what he'd do! That Lorraine's also been hitting wee Mary.'

Doll stops chewing. 'She's hitting the wee one too? She's going to get a bad doing when I next see her.'

'No, Doll. It's my fight. I will sort it, somehow. I can't run away anymore.' As much as I daydream about revenge, I know I'm also aiming for damage limitation. Another fantasy of mine is to carry on as though nothing has happened – this is pure make-believe. Lorraine's not going to stop. Billy's not going to stop.

'Why?' Doll asks quietly. 'Why did that cow, Lorraine, attack you? Why was Billy holding you down?' She frowns, watching my face carefully.

I'm like a deer frozen in the headlights being asked this question. I could simply tell Doll the partial truth – that Lorraine wanted to batter me because she'd believed the lie about Billy and me. Or I could tell the whole truth. And so I decide to trust Doll with my biggest secret. So, I talk about the elephant in the room, the one that we've dodged around all these years.

We've never discussed our different religions in detail. Yes, I'll briefly mention going to chapel and confession as part of what I've been doing, and Doll will talk about her part in the church and the Women's Orange Lodge. I've never told Doll about the beatings or the sectarian taunts I get on the streets where I live. Or, told her about the petrol bombs hurled against our front door and the cries of "*Fenian Fuckers!*" as the culprits ran away into the night. I've also never let on about what happens every July 12th, when the local Orange Lodge members march on my street to pick up their Grand Master who lives nearby. How they play "The Sash My Father Wore" on their flutes and drums and as they approach our house, pause their playing to shout "*Fuck the Pope!*" as though he lives with us. And how they then resume playing "The Sash" with renewed vigour as they march victoriously past.

Clearing my throat, I tell Doll that although this is the worst beating I've ever taken, it's not the first time. The other times she'd spotted cuts and bruises on me, those weren't from me tripping when I was running. I describe what it's like to be me, one of the few Catholics around my part of town and the living hell I exist in. I tell her about the awful names I've been called – and the beatings – all in the name of religion. I describe the daily terror and anxieties that haunt me whenever I walk out my front or back gate. I tell her about skulking in people's back gardens like a criminal, just to get from A to B in one piece. Finally, I tell her how sick and tired I am of being picked on for my religion, and I burst into tears.

Doll sits in stunned silence. Then she rises to hug me, and she holds me for the longest time while we both cry.

'I had no idea.' Doll whispers.

'No one did. It took two deranged people to beat the truth out of me.' I laugh dryly. 'It's been a week of confessions for me, and absolutely no priests were harmed during the making of these.'

'Would it surprise you to know that I've been bullied too because I'm a Protestant?'

'You've been bullied too?'

'Aye. At primary school, some Catholic kids would call me names, chase after me and hit me. I used to only walk certain streets, too.'

'How did the bullying stop?'

'I started meeting my pals, and we'd walk to school together. Some of my pals came from tough families – I mean, like some of their Dads were in prison – and the Catholic kids knew of that, so they stopped bothering me.'

I'm shocked by this news. There are Catholics out there, bullying? I always thought that only the 'Proddies' were the baddies – at least, that's what my gran's tried to drum into me.

'So, I know a little of what's been happening to you,' Doll continues, 'but not on this level.

'We've never talked about this because it's never mattered in our friendship, but let's talk about it now. I'm proud to be in the Women's Orange Lodge, not because we love to hate Catholics. That's not what we're about. We're there to defend our Protestant faith. We worship God at church, and we raise money for charity. It means a lot to my mum that I'm in the lodge as her Dad was high up in it, and after he died, Mum gave me his sash.' Doll pauses.

I nod for her to carry on.

'It's the social life too – the club at the Orange Lodge is brilliant – cheap drinks, great atmosphere. I can go with Mum and Dad and meet friends my age there too. It's where I met Sandy, remember?

'Yes.'

Doll's on a roll. 'Sure, there are bitter people in the lodge – Lorraine and Billy are two of them. They are just small-minded people who need any excuse to make their lives seem more dramatic, more meaningful. They cling to the past instead of looking to the future. They're losers.'

I listen in wonder to my best pal. 'I just thought it was black or white. Protestant or Catholic. Love or hate.'

'There's shades of everything, Aileen. Just as we have loyalist bands, you Catholics have your bands, playing rebel songs, singing about hating Protestants.'

I've heard about our bands and seen one march – I think it was on St Patrick's Day. They looked and sounded much like an Orange band, except that their signature colours weren't the red, white, and blue of the Union flag; they were the Irish flag's green, white, and gold. Their songs are about driving out the Protestants.

I think about Gran's warnings of the perils of marrying Protestants, and I think of Billy's views of Catholics. Stories and suspicions have been handed down from generation to generation on both sides. It's hard to break from our family histories; they are so powerful. But each generation has a choice. I set my plate and mug on the step and straighten to look Doll in the eye. 'I'm tired of the religious differences stuff. I can't run away anymore. I'm ready to be something different.'

Doll smiles. 'You and I have already broken the mould. You were my something different. You are my absolute best, and so lovely, Catholic pal!'

Chapter 17

Wednesday, 25 July 1984

A lone fly totters across my dog-eared copy of *Romeo and Juliet*. It buzzes, flaps its little silvery wings and takes off to land on my bookshelf on the other side of my bedroom. Books have been my refuge over these last few weeks, a welcome escape from the awful reality that I'm in. I miss visiting my local library, wandering around the hush of its sweet-smelling rooms, and the promise of wonder on its bookshelves. But, as I'm too ashamed of my appearance, Gran's been great in borrowing library books for me.

Still in my pyjamas, I pick up the second book of the trilogy, *The Lord of the Rings*. I've meant to read these books ever since I read *The Hobbit*. I'm loving learning all about the alliances being forged against the forces of evil in Mordor. Things are looking bleak for Frodo the Hobbit on his quest to save Middle Earth, but he has friends in the Elves, the Dwarves, and men. He also has a vest made of mithril chain mail to protect him from attack and a ring that makes him invisible when placed on the finger; how I'd love to have that ring! It really would be amazing to stride along any street unafraid.

'Aileen! You've got a visitor!' Gran calls upstairs.

Who on earth is it? I catch a glimpse of myself in the mirror. Although a lot of the swelling has gone on my face – some cuts and bruises are still visible. I quickly change into a navy sweatshirt and jogging pants and tie my unruly hair back. At least I look a little neater if still a bit damaged. I will have to do for whoever is downstairs.

When I hobble into the living room, the only thing I can see is Steve. Trying to disguise my shock, I compose myself as I sit on Gran's chair opposite the couch Steve is on. I tug on the sleeves of my sweatshirt to cover myself a little more. It's full daylight, and I know I don't look pretty. Gran's clattering some crockery in the kitchen.

'Hope you don't mind me dropping by? I was hoping you'd ring me.'

'We don't have a phone. The nearest phone box is a few streets away, and I haven't been outside since ... you know.'

'Of course, I forgot. Sorry.'

'I'm glad you called in.' I glance at him, so gorgeous, I could stare at his face all day and never be bored. 'Really glad.' I add unnecessarily.

'How are you?'

Gran comes in with a tray of tea and biscuits and sets this on a side table beside Steve. 'Sit beside Steve so you can reach everything okay.'

While I'm too shy to sit beside Steve, the idea of sitting close by him fills me with happiness. 'Come on. Skootch over to the couch.' Gran commands.

I shake my head. I'd rather be at a distance from Steve. Gran sighs but leaves a mug of tea on the carpet in front of my chair. I can get a better view of Steve from here: his expressions, his every move, and those are sights I wish to savour. He doesn't know I have an ulterior motive for sitting where I am – as far as he's concerned, he's just visiting a poor, beaten lassie he helped save.

Gran leaves the room and returns with some yellow roses in a vase which she sets on top of the display cabinet. 'Steve brought you these.'

When I turn to smile at him, he drops his head, seemingly fascinated by the action of dipping his biscuit into his tea. If I didn't know better, I'd say he's blushing. 'Just wanted to say how sorry I was about what happened to you.'

'Awful business.' Gran mutters, leaving the living room again.

Wee Mary passes through and trips over her feet as she gawps at Steve. He calls out 'hello' to her before she disappears upstairs.

'That's my wee sister, Mary. Lorraine's been beating her, too.'

Steve's face twists. 'It's bad enough she battered you, but hitting your little sister?'

My hands tremble. 'I know. I feel helpless. How can I protect my sister if I can't even protect myself? It seems so hopeless.'

Steve pauses, shoots me a look I can't quite fathom. He leans forward. 'I kind of know what you're going through. My little brother, Nathan, was bullied when we lived in Liverpool.'

'Is he bullied now?'

'No.'

'So you took care of it then?'

'Not exactly.' Steve clears his throat and slumps his shoulders. Then he straightens up and changes his tone. 'Doll told me she'd stopped by, but I wanted to come to see you myself. Sorry I haven't come sooner – we were in Liverpool last week.'

He continues: 'You don't look as bad as I was expecting.' He laughs a little. 'I mean that you seem to be healing well. How are you? And I don't mean physically.'

I open my mouth and close it again. That's the first time anyone has asked me that, and not meant how I am in my body. Lowering my eyes, I search for the words. 'I feel ashamed. Guilty. I'm terrified that it's going to happen again. Well, I *know* it's going to happen again ....' My voice breaks as I confirm my worst fear aloud.

Steve lowers his voice and wrings his hands. 'But what if I could help you?'

'Help me, how?'

'Well, let's just say I know girls – really tough girls – who are more than happy to be paid to take revenge on another girl.'

I'm appalled and fascinated at the same time, but I know that my conscience would haunt me. I shake my head. 'I can't knowingly commission someone to get hurt. It wouldn't be right.'

'You wouldn't be involved.'

'I can't, Steve. No matter the pain I've suffered, I can't knowingly ask someone else to give Lorraine Pollock a beating. Besides, what happens when I leave home next year for university? Who's going to protect wee Mary then? I need to make my own stand. I've no idea how, but there it is.'

A smile tugs at Steve's perfect mouth. 'In that case, I might have another idea.'

'What do you mean?'

'You deserve more of a fighting chance. That Lorraine's much taller and wider than you – she has those advantages. But what if you had a surprising superpower?' Steve's eyes twinkle.

I scoff, gesturing to my face and my body. 'What like Wonder Woman? Boomeranging tiaras and bullet-repelling bangles only exist in comics and on the telly. What superpower could I have anyway?'

'The ability to properly defend yourself. Learn how to fight with confidence.'

'In case you haven't noticed – I'm pretty rubbish at fighting!'

'I know. I know.' Steve raises his palms. 'But what if I taught you *how* to defend yourself? What if I taught you how to – let's say – box?'

'*Box*? I'm a lassie!' Images of boxing matches I've watched on TV with Da spring to mind. I see the men slugging at each other, eyebrows split open, burst noses. I shake my head and laugh at the ludicrous idea.

'Why not? You've already got aerobic fitness. I can teach you the technical skill of boxing – how to block blows and throw a right good punch. At someone like that Lorraine, for instance?'

He has my attention now. Could I really learn how to fight? The idea of being able to defend me and wee Mary against Lorraine, and other lassies (and laddies) like her, does sound tempting. Imagine if I gained a reputation of being a local 'hard woman' where no one messes with me because they're too scared? I continue this fantasy of me strolling along the streets, up to any tough gang, the members parting in fear as I walk through them. My mood plummets, though, when an image enters my mind of Lorraine's Doc Marten boots lifting in slow motion to boot me hard. Now, I just want to hide forever so that I won't get hurt ever again.

'What do you think?' Steve stares at me intently.

'Sounds interesting, but terrifying. I can't imagine hurting anyone. Plus, I know I'll get beaten twice as bad if I fight back.' I point to the bruises on my face.

At first, Steve looks disappointed but then gradually, his face changes, and he flashes his bewitching smile at me. Oh. Oh. He's about to persuade me to change my mind. 'That's the beauty, Aileen. I'm not going to train you to go looking for fights. I'm going to teach you to defend yourself first, you know, to guard yourself against anyone who tries to hit you.' He edges closer to me.

'At the same time, you'll also learn how to punch and to put together a sequence of punches that can take your opponent by surprise. I'll teach you strength, confidence, and about mental and physical agility – like Mohammed Ali. You know – *float like a butterfly, sting like a bee?* How you think about yourself is key. More importantly, what you *believe* about yourself is going to make the difference. What do you believe about yourself?'

His words and his passion enthral me. 'I believe that I should feel safe.'

Steve nods, and I continue.

'Be able to walk any street, unafraid. I believe I deserve not to be hurt, and that I'm a good person who doesn't intentionally harm anyone else. I deserve peace and respect.'

'There you go!' Steve beams.

'I also believe that I'd be rubbish at boxing.'

'Nah.' Steve counters. 'You're going to surprise yourself.' He sends me a knowing look that makes my insides melt. Hope flowers inside me, and I think something else – I really am developing an almighty crush on Steve. If I accept his offer, I'll get to see him regularly.

I bury my head in my hands and speak through my fingers. 'Alright. I'll give it a go. On one condition, though.'

'What's that?'

'That we keep it a secret. I'm a girl, and I might be really rubbish at boxing, and I don't want people to laugh at me.'

'Sure, I'll work something out. Mum's the word.'

'When do we start?'

'We'll leave it for another few weeks; give your body more time to heal.' When I look up, Steve's grinning at me.

The logical side of my brain screams: *'Have you just signed up to learn boxing?'* The other side of my mind is drinking in the image of this amazing guy sitting across from me. Even if it's just to teach me boxing, I'll get to spend some glorious time with him, and right now, that's the only thought that cheers me amidst the misery.

'Any sign of that Billy or Lorraine?' I'm holding on to a ridiculous hope that maybe the police have arrested them for another crime they've committed, or perhaps they've had a nasty accident or something.

'I did see Billy the day after he attacked you. Let's just say he's not been near me or the band since.' Steve fists his right hand inside his left palm and twists it around. He catches me watching him do this and reaches instead for his mug of tea.

'What about Lorraine?'

Steve hesitates. 'Doll's hinted to her pals at the Women's Orange Lodge that Lorraine was the attacker of the Catholic lassie they heard about. The women there aren't pleased with Lorraine and have made this clear to her.'

A burning question bubbles out of me: 'Why are you helping me?'

Steve looks surprised. 'Because it's not right what's been happening to you.'

The sound of the letterbox snapping closed catches our attention. Gran strolls into the living room, clutching some post and hands me a brown envelope. I stare at it and whisper, 'I think these are my exam results.' A duo of awe and anticipation wash over me. Nervous, I trace my finger along the gummed seal. Inside the envelope is the key to unlocking my future life.

Great Ordinary Grade results should indicate good Higher Grade exam results next year and a stronger likelihood of going to university. I'm torn. Do I wait until after Steve leaves, or open the envelope now? Gran and Steve watch me expectantly, and I realise I must know right now. I rip open the envelope and unfold the sheets of paper. My eyes quickly scan through the letter, seeking out the letter 'A'. My heart bursts with joy as I count seven A grades out of seven! The relief is overwhelming. I burst into tears.

Gran's worried: 'Aw, hen. Did you not get what you wanted?' I can't speak for crying, and she comes over to remove the sheets of paper from my hand. She touches my shoulder. 'I'm so proud of you! Well done! Your Da's going to be delighted.' She gives me a gentle squeeze and dabs at the tears on my face with a tissue.

I glance over at Steve, who's looking bemused. I laugh self-consciously. 'Sorry, practically every time you see me, I'm greeting my eyes out!'

'This time, I'm glad it's for good news. Congratulations.' As he shakes my hand, a jolt of electricity runs through me. Stunned, I wonder if he felt what I just felt. I can't read any surprise in his twinkling eyes, but just looking at him makes my heart soar.

After such a dark time, this other little sparkle of light and hope is also welcome. If I do well in my Higher exams too, I'll be accepted into a university and can make a fresh start. A twinge twists through me, though, as I realise that this will also mean leaving my family and leaving Steve – not that we're together – but still – that's also a sad thought. I cheer up as I remember that Steve will be training me to box at least for a while, and I'll get to see him at the Clyde Alloys gigs. Gran sniffles as she hands me a tissue box. We wipe our eyes and laugh. After the last few weeks that I've had, it's so great to cry over good news!

Am I allowed this hope? When I look at Steve, I know the world is full of possibilities, even for someone like me. That's confirmed when I walk Steve out to the front door.

'Well done again, Aileen.' I love listening to his Liverpool accent. His striking eyes sparkle as he hugs me softly. I breathe in his smell, savouring the sensation of his strong arms wrapped around me, feeling so safe, so protected. When I release my arms from him, I realise he's still holding me for what is longer than a goodbye hug should be. Shivers tinkle up and down my spine as he whispers: 'So pleased for you. See you soon, brainy box.' If the human body could melt, I'd be a puddle at the front door.

Chapter 18

Wednesday, 25 July 1984

I can't wait for Da to come home from work. I check and re-check my exam results on the paper – they haven't changed – I still have seven A grades!

I resume reading *The Lord of the Rings,* and I'm soon engrossed in Frodo and Sam's challenges as they continue their epic journey to defeat the evil Sauron and save Middle Earth. The sound of the backdoor slamming has me on my feet in no time. I carefully but quickly make my way downstairs, holding on to the walls and bannister for support. I hobble into the living room, clutching my exam results paper.

Da looks worried by the speed of my entrance. 'Everything alright, kid?'

Gran's stood behind Da, grinning. She's just as desperate as me to tell Da about my results. I hand the envelope to him, hopping from foot to foot.

'What's this?'

His lips move as he scans the papers. An enormous smile spreads across my beloved Da's face. 'Aw, kid! Wow! I couldn't be prouder!' Before I know it, he has me in a hug, crying into my ear. 'Congratulations, Aileen! And your mammie would have been so proud of you, too!' Da wipes at his eyes and gathers me in his arms to spin me around. Then my crazy, fantastic Da leads me on an impromptu waltz around the living room, careful not to knock me against any furniture. He's booming out some random song he thinks is in time to the waltz he's taking me on.

I'm laughing. I'm crying too. I trust Da when he's leading me in a dance, and I spin and dip on his direction, feeling so free and so happy.

Our merriment's interrupted by loud hammering at the front door, and Gran skips off to answer it. Da gently releases me from his dance hold, and still chuckling, we wait to hear from Gran, who's at the front door.

I stop breathing when Lorraine Pollock swaggers into our living room.

There's an older man behind her who prods her in the back to approach me. His eyebrows knit together in a scowl on his thin face. Is he a policeman? Perhaps he caught Lorraine doing something she shouldn't have been? But why are they here? My mind whirls, still trying to comprehend that the person who inflicted so much pain on me only a few weeks ago is standing right in front of me, here in my family home.

Gran, grim-faced, skirts around them and takes her position beside Da and me.

'Aidan.' The man nods at Da.

'Tony.' Da acknowledges in return, placing his arm around my trembling shoulders. I lean against Da, afraid that my legs may give way underneath me.

'Dear God, Lorraine! What have you done to this poor lassie?' The man called Tony steps beside Lorraine and shoves her.

Lorraine's silent. She cocks her head to one side and sneers at me.

Without warning, Tony skelps her across her ear, the sharp noise making me cringe. 'What have you got to say?'

Lorraine makes no move other than to cross her arms and clench her jaw.

The colour rises in Tony's face. He visibly shakes. This time he cracks Lorraine so hard across her face that she stumbles and lands on the carpet. 'Apologise, ya bitch!'

Da steps forward. 'Tony, there's no need for that, pal.'

Tony glares at him, so many emotions flashing across his face. 'I can't believe she's done this to you, Aileen!' I'm surprised that he knows my name.

Da offers his hand out to Lorraine to help her up. She spits on Da's hand. Tony boots her hard.

Gran's so incensed that she grabs Lorraine by the arm like a seasoned pub bouncer and yanks her to her feet. She puts her other hand behind Lorraine's back and shoves her hard out into the hall, 'You – feck off!'

She turns to Tony, who's side-stepping around Da and comes to a full stop in front of me. I stare, stunned, as Tony lifts his hand towards my face. I flinch, instinctively turning my head away. Tony cups my cheek in his hand and says softly: 'I'm so sorry. I promise she won't touch you again.'

Da steps forward: 'That's enough, Tony. You've brought your lassie to apologise. Which she hasn't done.' Da shoots a look of disdain at Lorraine out in the hall, who gives him a two-fingered salute.

Tony repeats. 'I promise she'll not hurt you again, kid, I'll make sure of that.'

Da escorts him out to the hall and towards the front door. I remain standing, locked into a position I can't seem to move from. I stare in horror as Lorraine swivels her head to make sure that no one is watching, then draws her finger across her throat, mouthing to me, 'You're dead.'

Oblivious to what Lorraine's just done, Gran grasps my arm, tugs me away to close the living room door, but I can still hear the raised voices of Da and Tony on the other side.

Gran turns to me. 'Come on. Let's go into the kitchen, leave them to it.'

Once we're seated at the table, Gran shakes her head: 'She's dead gallus – a right wee bitch, eh? It took all my strength not to slap her myself! Tony'll leather her when they get home. She'll regret not saying sorry.'

'Is that man, Tony, her Dad?'

'Aye. Well, her stepfather, anyway.'

'How come they turned up today? I'm confused. How do they know where I live?'

Pursing her lips, Gran regards me with those bright blue eyes of hers. 'You've no idea how furious your Da was when you got jumped! We both were. It was a shock to see our wee lassie in such a state. There was no way your Da was going to let what happened to you slide. Let's just say your Da knows people ... knows how to persuade people ... He went to see Tony – he knows him from way back.'

Gran's eyes narrow. 'I don't know how your Da thought it would happen, but it was certainly a surprise the two of them appearing here today.'

We jump as Da throws open the kitchen door and heads to the kettle to make himself a drink.

'What about the guy?' Gran rises and walks over to Da.

Da's back stiffens. 'He's being taken care of.'

I gasp. 'Billy? How did you know?'

Da shrugs. 'It wasn't difficult to work out. Once I had the woman's name, it didn't take a genius to work out who the laddie might be. I've got my guys looking for him. He's in hiding. He's going to get kicked into next week when I get a hold of him!'

'Don't you do anything daft, Aidan Murphy! We need you here, not in Barlinnie Prison!'

Da stirs his tea and frowns. 'Give me some credit, Mum. Let's just say a few of the guys owe me a favour ....'

'Don't get into trouble for me, Da.' I say, though secretly, there's a part of me that's glad he's looking out for me. I also have Steve's offer to train me to box, too. I pray Lorraine's stepfather will somehow keep his promise. I want to believe that I won't have to worry about Lorraine again. But I can still picture her scowling face mouthing, 'You're dead.'

And I believe that she could kill me. A chill sweeps into the kitchen.

Chapter 19

Saturday, 4 August 1984

Paul sits next to me on the edge of the couch. 'Why wouldn't you let me visit before?'

It's been just over three weeks since the attack, and I've been dreading this question as I know I must lie. 'I wasn't well enough to see anyone.'

'But you saw Doll, and that Steve.'

'She sneaked up on me in the back garden, and Gran let Steve in because she knew he was the one who rescued me.'

'Rescued you?'

'Yes. You know. Pulled my attackers off me, took me to hospital.'

'What were you doing walking home by yourself late at night and on July the twelfth of all nights?'

I'm not in the mood for a lecture from Paul. 'I'd been visiting Marie and Geraldine – I just didn't think.'

'Didn't think? A young Catholic girl out on her own with all those Protestants out celebrating?' Paul places his hand on top of mine. 'Do you have any idea how worried I've been about you?'

'I'm sorry.' I'm not, and Paul's narrow-minded, anti-Protestant attitude is beginning to irritate me more than usual. I withdraw my hand from his, noticing the relief when I do this. If I didn't know better, I'd say that Paul is almost saying that I brought the beating upon myself just by walking the streets of my home town, which I should be able to walk without being harmed anyway.

'Were you wearing your crucifix?'

'What? No! I took it off earlier that day.'

'Why? It might have protected you.'

'Paul, they're Protestants, not vampires.'

'I meant God would be looking after you.'

'Crucifixes haven't protected me in the past!' He shifts away from me, looking offended by my acerbic response.

I sigh. 'I really appreciate your gift of the crucifix necklace – I know it's an important symbol to you and your family – but I don't think I can wear it anymore. I'm not comfortable labelling myself like that.'

'It's not labelling yourself – it's just a symbol of your religion.'

'I don't need to remind myself, or anyone else, of my religion. I'm sick of religion! Look what it's done to me!'

It's still early morning, but I'm relieved and grateful when a knock at the front door interrupts our disagreement. Standing on the doorstep are Geraldine and Marie, clutching the standard gifts people bring to a sick person: an orange crinkle-papered bottle of Lucozade and a bag of grapes. I think even they are taken by how warmly I welcome them in. The girls sit on the couch next to Paul, and I perch myself on Gran's chair.

'I would have hated to have seen you just after you got beat up!' Geraldine openly gawps at me.

Marie digs Geraldine in her side. 'What she means is, you're looking not too bad after what happened to you. How are you keeping?'

I tell them I'm much better, although I'm still sore and tired. My pals listen intently as I fight hard not to cry while describing the detail of the attack on me. Marie cries anyway, Geraldine sits silent, looking sombre, and Paul, pale-faced, comes over to perch on the edge of the armchair and puts his arm around me.

My pals sit quietly as I describe how Steve rescued me and took me to the hospital. Paul shuffles by my side while the girls give me knowing smiles which I carefully ignore, as I sense Paul's still smarting after our earlier disagreement.

Feeling brave after having divulged the details of the 12th of July beating, I explain the rest of the bullying I've been suffering over the years. To my surprise, Paul, Marie, and Geraldine admit that they have also been bullied – but not to the same extent as I have been, and not necessarily because they're Catholic. They also tell me off for not confiding in them about my troubles, and, having admitted mostly everything to them, I understand now that they wouldn't have judged me.

Consciously diverting the subject away from bullying and beatings, I ask the question I've been wanting to pose to them. 'How did you all do in your exams?' Paul immediately perks up – he got straight As like me. I give him a big hug. He wants to be a doctor, so he must get great Higher results next year to study medicine. After her favourable exam results, Marie's also hopeful of pursuing her dream of becoming a social worker. Only Geraldine's disappointed as she failed some exams. She made us laugh when she declared that as fewer exam qualifications are required to become a beautician, she's not planning on becoming a nun over the next year just to do well in exams she doesn't need.

'Don't you think that nuns look creepy?' Geraldine shudders. 'Their skin's like see-through and, well, they don't have sex. Can you imagine that?' She tucks a strand of hair behind her ear. We giggle. The usual Geraldine logic.

'Speaking of school, I've met a new pal.' Paul sits forward. 'You'll meet him next week. His name's Ruaridh. His family's moved close to my house, and it turns out that our mothers know each other from way back.'

'Roo-rey ...' Geraldine deliberately rolls out the 'r' sounds of his name. 'Is he good-looking or a fud?' There's Geraldine, straight to the point again.

Paul shrugs his shoulders and grins. 'I'm not qualified to comment on another guy's looks.'

'Interesting.' Geraldine purrs.

We laugh. Poor guy when he meets Geraldine. She already has her sights set on him.

It feels good to talk to my pals about school and the future. After the rocky start with Paul, the rest of the visit with him, Geraldine, and Marie cheers me up.

'Is there anything we can do to help you now? Or will you just stay in for the rest of your life?' Geraldine half-jokes as she helps herself to the bag of grapes they've brought me.

'Nothing I can think of right now, but thanks for listening.' I beam at them, so grateful to have such great friends. 'As for going out again ... well, I've planned to visit Doll after lunch today, so I'll start with that.'

Paul's body stiffens beside me, and a line from an old record that Gran plays comes to mind: *There May Be Trouble Ahead...*

•➤➤•••◆•••◄◄•

It's been a few hours since Paul, Geraldine and Marie left, and I've spent the time watching some of the athletics footage of the Olympic Games on TV. Feeling inspired, I'm itching to go out for a run, but I know that a walk is the best I can do for now.

Proud that I've finally plucked up the courage to venture outside; I speed march to Doll's home. Wearing loose clothes, I've also put on my gutties in case I need to run. I've safely navigated myself through the streets of my home town and, on the way, two red phone boxes, which were occupied with queues formed outside. I'd love to phone Steve, but I'm too shy. Another time, maybe. I march on, focussed on seeing my best friend.

When I arrive at Doll's home, she's opened her front door before I've even walked up the path. 'Well, look at you!'

'I did it. I've finally left the house, and I've walked it all the way here. And I was only a little bit scared. That's something, isn't it?'

'It certainly is. Come on in.' Doll's parents ask how I am as I pass them in the living room to follow her into the kitchen.

Sandy's sitting at the table, tucking into a fry-up. He looks as though he's wearing eyeliner or mascara or something. And his eyes are red. He wipes his hands and stands to give me an awkward hug. 'I was awful sorry to hear what happened to you. We'll hopefully catch the bastards soon.'

I'm impressed. Doll's not told Sandy about Billy and Lorraine.

Doll notices me staring at Sandy's eyes and laughs. 'He's been robbing coal all morning at the Craig.'

Sandy lowers his voice, presumably so that Doll's parents won't hear next door in the living room. 'One of the bags of coal split while I was carrying it. The coal and dust spilt all over me. I've had two showers, but I still can't get the coal dust out of my eyelashes.'

'Are you not scared of getting caught?' I've heard of people stealing coal and scrap metal from the Craig, but Sandy's the first person I know who's actually doing it.

'No, we have a good system. We jump over the railway line and nick the coal from the piles on the other side. Big Boab lives by the railway line, and he's cut a hole in his wire fence, just big enough for us to crawl through, but small enough that he can clip it back together again. It's hard work, but it supplements the dole.'

'Is it not dangerous, being on the railway?'

Sandy flicks his hair out of his eyes as he concentrates on making swirly patterns with tomato ketchup on his plate. 'Nah. We know not to step on the metal tracks or touch the overhead railway lines. We're sensible. The biggest danger is getting caught – either by the security guards – or by the police. One of us acts as a lookout like they do in the war movies. We have a special whistle if something's not right.'

Doll watches Sandy, a look of satisfaction on her face that her guy is enjoying the fry-up she's cooked for him. 'Shall we tell Aileen our news?'

Sandy's eyes glow with pride. He pauses, then, 'Doll's pregnant.'

I splutter; I don't mean to.

Doll thinks it's with excitement, but it's with shock. 'I know!' She squeals excitedly. 'And – Sandy's asked me to marry him – I said yes!'

Two shocks in as many minutes. I quickly recover myself and offer congratulations like I'm supposed to do.

The couple beam, their happiness evident.

'When? When are you due?'

'March, for the baby.' Doll's face shines. 'Our wedding will be on Saturday, 27th October at four o'clock!'

Sandy takes Doll's left hand and gently kisses it. 'You're going to be my beautiful wife, Mrs Ross.'

Doll giggles. 'I can't wait! Sandy's saving for an engagement ring – we're going into Glasgow to choose it!'

Sandy leans over to plant a soft kiss on Doll's cheek. 'And you can have any ring you want, as long as it's not over £100 – cos we need to save for the baby, too.'

Doll stares dreamily at Sandy. 'I can't wait to be Mrs Ross! And we're going to have a baby together. I couldn't be happier. Oh – and I have something special I want to ask you, Aileen. Will you be my chief bridesmaid? Well, my only bridesmaid, in fact.'

I pause, trying to process everything I've just been told. A pregnancy, an engagement and now a wedding. I'm not yet seventeen, and I've been asked to be the chief bridesmaid at my best friend's wedding! Doll and Sandy wait for me to answer.

'I'd love to. You'll need to let me know what I'm supposed to do, though. I don't have a clue.'

'Me neither!' Doll chuckles.

'How have your parents taken the news?' Sandy and Doll exchange frowns.

'Not great. Sandy's mum and dad took the news better than mine.' Doll glances across to Sandy and lowers her voice. 'His parents were shocked at first but seemed to be more accepting of the idea than mine. His mum's now talking about knitting baby clothes and such, while his Dad's more concerned about the practical things – you know, where we're going to live and so on. We've put our name on the council housing list.'

Doll whispers now, Sandy rolls his eyes. 'My dad shouted at Sandy, and my mum was crying. They thought we weren't using contraception, but I'm on the pill, so we're not sure how it's happened. They think I've wasted my life, and what about my nursing plans? I told them we can't change what's happened – a wee baby is on the way – so they best get used to it.

'I know it must be a massive shock for your teenage daughter to stroll in and announce that she's pregnant, but I was hurt that they reacted that way. I dunno – I suppose I was hoping they'd be more understanding.'

I'm nodding at Doll as she tells their story. Inside, I'm still trying to get over the shock that Doll and Sandy are having a baby and getting married soon. Personally, I wouldn't want to be married and a mother at Doll's age. I have so much I want to do before settling down. But they're right for each other, and happy, so I'm pleased for them.

Doll continues: 'My mum's worried about how we're going to cope. But we are going to be fine. I love Sandy, and he loves me. And we couldn't be happier. And I think if we love each other, yes, it'll be difficult, but there is no reason why this can't work!' Doll pats her tummy and looks at me with tears in her eyes, now with an uncertain smile on her face.

Just then, Doll's mum bursts in through the kitchen door.

'So, they've told you their news then?' Mrs McLintock has a high-pitched, nasal tone to her voice, which sounds like she has a peg on her nose. She wrings her hands. 'I can't believe I'm going to be a Gran at thirty-six years old! And you, young lady, are too young to be a mother!'

Sandy mops the last of his egg yolk with a piece of toast, sets down his cutlery and takes Doll's hand.

Doll laughs nervously. 'I'm eighteen. I can take care of myself, and I can take care of a baby.'

'Thank goodness you're at least getting married. I don't know what we're going to tell our friends at the Church and the lodge.'

'The truth, Mum. Sandy and I are in love, we're expecting a baby, and we're going to be married.'

'You have no idea what's ahead, Dora Alice.' Only Doll's parents address her by her full name, and it's usually when they're telling her off for something.

'What do you think, Aileen?' Mrs McLintock folds her arms across her thin waist, her face pinched.

I gulp. A serious adult question addressed to me. 'Just as Doll says, Mrs McLintock. They're made for each other, and they'll be great parents. Weren't you around the same age when you had Doll?' I immediately regret saying this as Mrs McLintock visibly stiffens.

'I was already married; it wasn't a shotgun wedding, thank you very much.'

Mr McLintock joins his wife at the kitchen door. 'We had so many dreams for you, Doll. We were just watching the Olympics and saying that if you hadn't stopped your running training, you could have been good enough to compete for your country. And then there's the nursing. I've been asking around about getting you into Law Hospital.'

'Dad, I'm pregnant. Not dying. We've been through this – I can go into nursing later.'

Mr McLintock tugs on his bushy moustache. 'How are you going to get by? How are you going to support your wife and family, Sandy? You can't seem to get a job, and let's face it, son, playing in a band isn't going to pay the bills.' Mr McLintock puts his arm across his wife's shoulder. She rests her head against him.

'We'll be fine.' Doll folds her arms and leans back in her chair.

Doll's Dad shakes his head and leads his wife back into the living room, closing the door behind them.

'They'll come round to the idea.' Doll sighs. Sandy looks dubious.

Chapter 20

Tuesday, 7 August 1984

Switching from foot to foot, I'm mesmerised by the rain falling in sheets outside the living room window – the noise is almost deafening as huge puddles form on the empty road beyond. Today would be a good day for a run, just a little leg loosener. Gran would be annoyed with me running in the wet especially the day before school starts, but I must. Running's another therapy for me. And a steady run in the rain with no one around will help sort out my head.

Although I'll get soaked, I like to keep the rain off my face, especially out of my eyes. I flip on Da's old Navy baseball cap and grin at myself in the hall mirror. I'm looking forward to the run and the hot shower after.

Stepping out of the front door, I'm drenched immediately. I gasp, tingling all over, mentally preparing to do my run. A car door slams as I'm hunched over, threading my door key through the lace of my gutty.

As I stand up, a hooded figure wearing a black rain jacket suddenly appears. I pause, uncertain of what to do. I'm trapped outside my house, and the figure is between me and the front gate. So I vault over the fence dividing our house from our neighbour's and run over to open their gate. The next-door neighbour's dog barks as it watches me from their living room window. From inside my house, Bruno joins in with the barking.

'Aileen! Where are you going?' The dark figure is Steve.

Feeling foolish, I tell him I'm going for a run, as though it's normal regular part of my routine to jump my neighbour's fence. The dogs are still barking as I manage to open the neighbour's gate. I pull my hat down against the rain and jog over to Steve.

'Running in this weather? Want to come with me instead?' The vibrant red of his car stands out against the greyness of the day. He holds the car door open for me, blinking the rain out of his eyes. I'm about to protest that I'd rather run, but what's better? A run in the rain which, yes, I would enjoy? Or sitting in a dry car with this guy who fascinates me more and more. No contest. I get into the car.

Steve pops his hood down as he hops into the driver's side. 'I dropped by to fix a time for us to go boxing training. I was going to suggest in a few weeks, but you look like you're ready now. How about you skip the run and come training with me instead?'

Being this close, I can smell his aftershave, and the thought of reaching over to touch him occurs to me – what a delicious idea. However, I quickly shove that ridiculous thought to the back of my mind and remind myself that I am still seeing Paul and that Steve must also have a girlfriend.

I nod, a little too vigorously, sprinkling rainwater from my baseball cap onto my lap.

'Great! Well, we best swing by my house, so I can change too.'

'Go to your house? Will your parents be in?'

'Dad's working his shift at the Craig, but me Ma will be at home. It's cool. You're only popping in to wait while I get changed – or you can stay in the car?'

I look around. 'Cool car,' I say, 'Is it your Dad's? What kind is it?'

Steve laughs. 'You obviously don't remember asking me the same questions the night I took you to A&E? It's my car – a Ford Capri RS – six years old.' He pats the dashboard and smiles as he fires the engine. The window wipers switch rapidly across the windscreen, barely improving the visibility from the beating rain.

'Bet you're glad you're not going for a run now!' Steve chuckles, as the car pulls away from the kerb.

Oh, my goodnight. Just the sight of him. Just being so close to him in such an intimate space. The guy is so gorgeous; he takes my breath away I need to control myself; I don't want to feel foolish. Before I know it, we arrive at Steve's home. 'So, will you wait in the car, or come in?'

I hesitate, but I believe I can trust Steve – he's no Billy McIntyre – so allowing my curiosity to take over, I agree to come in with him. It'll be interesting to see where he lives, what his mum's like.

Steve lives at the end of a block of four terraced houses. Before Steve's front door sits a yellow rose bush that has had some stems removed. I smile at Steve, who looks a little sheepish. A shiny brass nameplate on the front door reads *Mr and Mrs R Henderson*. 'Steve Henderson ... nice.'

'That's my name, don't wear it out!'

I'm usually a little anxious and awkward when I enter someone's house for the first time, like I'm intruding or something. When I walk through Steve's front door, though, I feel immediately at home. The hallway is bright and welcoming. The house smells of baking, reminding me of Mammie.

'Ma!' Steve roars from the hallway. 'I'm just fetching my training stuff and heading back out again!'

'Alright, lad! No need to shout! I was only in the kitchen.' Steve's mum strolls into the hall, wiping her hands on a dishtowel. 'Ooh, hello!' Steve's mum is dressed in blue jeans and a pink satin blouse. She has curly hair, in a modern hairstyle I would love. I'm sure I look quite tatty standing opposite her.

'This is Aileen – the girl I was telling you about – that I'm going to train how to box. Remember, it's a secret, though.' Steve takes off his rain jacket and kicks off his shoes.

Steve's been talking to his mum about me. 'Pleased to meet you, Mrs Henderson.'

She grins. 'Likewise – and please – none of this Mrs Henderson stuff – makes me feel old!

I'm Queenie.' She takes my hand and leads me into the kitchen while Steve heads upstairs.

'I was so sorry to hear what happened to you. How are you?' Queenie has put the kettle on and lined up some mugs and the teapot ready.

In between my update on how I am, Queenie expertly weaves other fact-finding questions about me. As I'm stating my age, where I live and which school I go to, I do my best to dismiss thoughts in my mind of Steve changing, maybe even just above our heads. I wonder what his body looks like, and I blush. Queenie sends me an odd look. I bite my lip as I forget how I was going to end the sentence I was on.

Steve bounces in through the kitchen door. 'Ready! Ma, we don't have time for tea, sorry.'

Queenie's face falls. 'No time to sample my fresh scones. Another time eh, Aileen?'

'Definitely. Lovely to meet you.'

'She would have had you there all day chatting! She can talk for England, me Ma!' Steve calls to me as we rush back out into the rain towards his car.

On our way to the gym, Radio Clyde plays one of my favourite Cyndi Lauper songs, "Time After Time". Steve sings the words, and I join in while the windscreen wipers work hard to keep the heavy rain off the windscreen. Cars on the other side of the road have their headlights on even though it's daytime. Their tyres slew through deep puddles. I'm the most content I've felt in a long time.

I ask Steve how he's enjoying being in the band.

'Love it. Lads are great. I think Sandy has a few gigs arranged for us, too.' Steve smiles. 'Oh, but you know Tommy – the keyboard player? He claims that he's been recruited by another band who are going places, apparently. The Clyde Alloys are 'too small town' for him now – he wants to be famous.'

'So, you're looking for a new keyboard player, then?'

'Yeah, we're asking around for one now.'

Next thing, we've arrived outside a shabby, square-shaped building that stands on its own in the middle of a housing scheme. The yellowing paint on its exterior walls peels off in sections. Hanging above the faded wooden entrance door is the red T of a yellow and rusted Tennents Lager sign which creaks in the wind. 'Used to be a pub. Now it's a gym.' Steve explains.

Steve fishes some keys out of his pocket and unlocks the door. As I step in, the smell of stale sweat, beer and cigarettes hit me.

'Sorry, it's a bit whiffy. That's why I'm here. I clean the place in return for getting to train at the gym.'

'You've brought me here to clean?'

'No!' Steve looks offended. 'You're here to train. The gym opens later than usual to the other boxers for three weeks because Mr Mackenzie, the gaffer, is in Benidorm, so we can get the run of the place.'

A jolt of joy jumps through me as he takes my hand to lead me through to the gym.

'Right! Here we are!' Steve flicks on some light switches. In front of us is a large rectangular room with a boxing ring set towards the bottom left-hand corner, and along the mirrored left-hand side wall, a few battered punching bags hang from the ceiling. The mirrors reflect the opposite wall of the gym where there is a small bar – presumably retained from its old days as a pub. High stools with wooden seats well worn by many bottoms sit in perfect order against the bar. Three shiny beer taps sit on the bar top; spirit optics hang from the wall behind, and underneath these are fridges filled with various alcohol and soft drinks.

I stroll over to the bar to take a closer look at some old black and white boxing photos on the wall behind the bar.

'That's the boss of this place – Colin Mackenzie – or Mister Mac as we call him. Heavyweight champion boxer. Amazing guy.' Steve joins me as I gaze around the photos of Colin Mackenzie fighting in boxing matches or proudly holding his belts and trophies. Steve points to two pictures in the centre of the wall, 'That's him at an awards evening with Jim Watt – you know – the Scottish champion boxer? And that's him with Frank Bruno.' I recognise the boxers as Da's a big fan, and of course, he named our dog after Frank Bruno.

'Is that his family?' I point at a photo of Colin Mackenzie with his arm around a woman who looks like a model. Colin has his other hand resting on the shoulder of a wee girl with pigtails standing in front of them.

'Yeah, that's his wife and his daughter, Karen. She's about twenty now.'

'He's done well, eh?' I marvel at the photos of accomplishment and triumph placed in neat rows and, for a fleeting moment, imagine myself standing over Lorraine Pollock grinning, one foot pinning her to the floor, my arms held aloft after successfully knocking her out.

'Really well. He started boxing as a twelve-year-old. When he joined the Royal Navy, he represented them in boxing matches. He went on to win the combined forces championship to beat the boxing champions of the Army, Royal Air Force, and Marines. That's some feat, eh? When he left the Navy, he turned professional to be the best heavyweight champion boxer of his time.

'Boxing's his passion, so after he retired, he started this gym to give the local guys something to aim for, to provide them with a purpose. He keeps the training fees low, and he doesn't accept excuses for not coming to training.'

'Is boxing your passion?'

'It used to be. When I was a lad in Liverpool, I used to count down the time until my next boxing session; I loved the training and the fights that much. In the last few years, though, music's taken over as my main interest. I still enjoy the discipline of boxing training, but I don't compete in matches anymore.'

Listening to Steve's soft tone as he tells me about Mr Mac's boxing achievements and reminisces about *his* boxing, a surge of anticipation courses through me. I shiver, excited by the sight, sound, and smell of where

I am, what I'm about to do, and who I am with. I'm in a secret place, about to do a secret thing, with my best-kept secret. I grin at Steve. 'Let's get started.'

'First things, first. Jackets off, then we need to get you warmed up.' Steve searches in his sports bag. 'I've brought you a dry T-shirt.' He flicks it at me. 'Put it on – you're soaking!'

Clutching Steve's T-shirt, I bite my lip. 'Well, look away then.' Steve tuts but turns away as I peel off my wet top to pull on his dry one. Even washed, it smells of him. 'Ready.'

'I'm not a coach, but I can teach you what I know about boxing, so that you can defend yourself in a fight. I never want you to be beaten ever again.' Steve scowls as he hands me a rope.

I giggle. 'I haven't skipped since I was ten! Are you sure this is boxing?'

'Definitely.' Steve nods, his brow furrowing. 'But the skipping is different from how I imagine you did it. There are no big arm movements. Instead, I want you to hold your hands by your hips as you twirl the rope around your body. Jump a tiny bit as the rope comes towards your feet.'

Steve takes his rope and demonstrates. He skips faster and faster. The rope whirs and slaps the ground in a blur. Now he's crossing his arms, still skipping rapidly. 'Your turn!'

Struck by how serious Steve has become, I grip the handles of my rope and concentrate on skipping, cautiously at first, as my brain tries to remember what the arms and feet coordination should be. I skip a little faster, but I'm quickly out of breath, my heart beating out of its ribcage. 'I can't anymore – need a rest!' I almost trip over my rope.

Steve frowns and continues to skip. 'Come on. You can do this. You're fit. You just need to train your body to this particular exercise.'

I take the rope again and start to skip.

'You focus on your breathing when you're running, right?'

I nod, amazed at how even his voice is, even though he appears to be skipping at 90 miles an hour.

'Well, it's the same with skipping – and boxing in general. Time your breaths with your feet. Control your breathing, consciously slow it down.'

Listening to his instructions, I count how many times I jump and start to control the inhales and exhales of my breath in time to these. Now my heart begins to settle. I grin. *I'm doing it!*

Next, Steve shows me how to do the warm-up stretches for my upper body, and includes a few back and leg stretches, which I'm already familiar with as a runner. My body buzzes all over. I'm ready!

With his hand on my shoulder, Steve leads me over to the mirrored wall and points to a cross shape on the wooden floor, marked out by white tape. 'First, we focus on your footwork. How you stand and move around is the foundation of how well you will box. Which hand do you write with?'

'My right.'

'Ok, so you're what they call an *orthodox* boxer. You'll lead with your left hand – but always deliver your strongest punches with your right hand. Left-handed boxers are called 'south paws' – like Stallone in *Rocky* – have you seen it?'

'Great film. *Adrian!*' I mimic the ending of the film where a bashed-up Rocky, with swollen eyes, cries out for his girlfriend. My impersonation of Stallone was obviously rotten as Steve only nods, a serious look still etched on his face.

I'm a little unnerved by how formal he's become since we stepped inside the gym, like he's a teacher at school. Although, I suppose that's what he is. He's here to teach me boxing which can be a dangerous sport. I must work harder at suppressing how girly and giggly I am when he's around. He's giving up his time to train me, so I should 'knuckle' down.

Steve takes his position on the white cross. 'Straddle the line. Stand with your feet shoulder-width apart. Put your right leg back and twist your left shoulder.' I copy what he's showing me.

'Hold your hands naturally to each side of your face. Clench your fists, thumb over the top over your closed fingers. Bend your back leg slightly and lift your back heel off the floor. Relax, centre your body weight. Do not lean forward.'

As Steve bends to re-position my feet, I notice the soft, blonde hairs on the back of his tanned neck. With my hands now hanging loosely by my side, I resist the urge to brush my fingertips across the back of his neck. Thankfully, before

I can entertain any more of these thoughts, he straightens up.

'Footwork drills now.' Steve demonstrates, moving his feet around the white cross on the floor. 'Step forward for three, back for three. Then step to the right for three, left for three. Then diagonally. Watch yourself move in the mirror, correct anything that needs correcting.'

And that's what I do for the rest of the session – as per Steve's instructions, I step my feet forward, back and around the white cross like I'm in a slow-motion Scottish country dancing class. Using all my will, I keep my face straight while I work hard to ignore the thrills each time Steve touches me to adjust my body and foot positioning.

Dear Lord. Please stop me from falling for this guy. Or maybe, it's too late.

Chapter 21

Wednesday, 8 August 1984

First day back at school, and I had another training session with Steve earlier this morning. My arms, shoulders and legs ache, and as the footwork didn't seem too taxing, I'm guessing it's the skipping that's gotten my muscles so stiff.

I'm stood in the school quadrangle with Marie and Geraldine, surrounded by a red haze of chattering schoolies. You can spot the first-year pupils by a mile because, without exception, their blazers are oversized, with only their fingertips dangling below their sleeves.

'They look so cute!' The girls follow my gaze to two little first-year girls with plaited hair playing a hand-clapping game close to us. They look so innocent in this sunshine.

'Remember our first day here?' Marie smiles, a wistful look in her eyes as she twirls one of her gold hoop earrings.

'I was dreading it,' I admit. 'Freshly back from South Africa. No friends. Brand new school.'

Marie cocks her head to one side. 'I noticed you because you were standing alone, looking so sad. I felt sorry for you because everyone was stood with pals from their primary schools.'

'And you were dressed, ready for a snowstorm, with boots and a duffle coat in August!' Geraldine laughs.

'That was my mammie! She couldn't remember how cold it'd be when we came back from South Africa, so she opted for warm clothes. I was sweltered that day!'

Geraldine snickers. 'You had a great tan, too. I remember being jealous and thinking you must come from a rich family.'

'Ha, well, that was wrong! I was so happy and nervous that you two approached me. Thanks for kind of adopting me, though, taking me under your wing.' I beam at them. 'And here we are now. Starting our fifth year here. Time flies, eh?'

Geraldine flips her compact mirror open, checking on her make-up. 'Please, God, let a mysterious, handsome new hunk join our year today and fall in love with me.' She looks up from her mirror and surveys the school crowd. 'Fat chance of that. It's been slim pickings here since I was twelve.'

We laugh. I don't realise that I've been stretching out my arms and shoulders until Marie shoots me a look. 'What are you doing?'

I'm not ready yet to tell my pals about the boxing training with Steve. 'I must have slept in a strange position.' I drop my arms by my sides. If I want to keep the boxing secret from my family and pals, I need to be more careful.

A familiar voice pipes up behind us. 'Morning! How are we all?' It's Paul, and standing beside him is a good-looking, red-headed laddie. He's taller than Paul and broader. 'This is Ruaridh, the guy I was telling you about. The only thing wrong with him is that he plays rugby – too posh to play footie, apparently!' Paul puts Ruaridh in a pretend headlock, and they wrestle.

'Roo-rey ...' Geraldine's already sidled over to the new guy, deliberately rolling out the 'r' sounds of his name. 'Roo-rey ... that sounds like a name from up north.' She jerks her head to the left like she knows where north is.

Ruaridh seems to understand, though. 'From Inverness.'

'How come you ended up here?' Geraldine simpers.

Marie and I exchange puzzled looks. Ruaridh, with his short, red hair, pale face, and freckles, doesn't look like Geraldine's usual type of mean and moody bad boy.

'Dad got a job in Glasgow on the nuclear submarines, and my mum originally comes from here.' Ruaridh smiles.

Geraldine offers out her hand to him, '*Enchanté.*' Ruaridh looks a little flummoxed. 'It means *pleased to meet you* in French.'

Marie and I giggle as Geraldine blatantly bats her eyelashes at the new guy. She's gone for a full gothic look for the start of fifth year. Over the summer, she's perfected the make-up with a pale face, dark eye make-up and black or purple lipstick. She's also had her hair dyed jet black and had it cut into a shoulder-length spikey style like Siouxsie Sioux, from Siouxsie and the Banshees pop group.

Paul then introduces Marie and me to Ruaridh.

'Nice to meet you all.' Ruaridh looks relieved as the headteacher calls us to form our registration lines ready for the morning assembly announcements. For fifth year some of us are sharing registration classes – I guess because the year is smaller, due to many of our friends leaving school to look for work or join Youth Training Schemes. Ruaridh has been put in my registration class, while Paul's assigned to the same registration class as Geraldine and Marie.

After the morning announcements, and before we head off to find our new registration classes, Geraldine makes a beeline for me and hisses into my ear. 'Can you work on Ruaridh for me, please? I think he's dead cute. Tell him how wonderful I am!'

Geraldine is as subtle as a flying mallet. I promise her that I will and smile as she sashays off with Marie and Paul, pausing briefly to send a coy smile over to Ruaridh, who's watching her, open-mouthed. Marie rolls her eyes behind Geraldine's back, making me laugh.

'Geraldine's quite a lady, eh?' I take Ruaridh's arm to lead him to our new registration class.

'Well, she's certainly different to the girls in Inverness!' Ruaridh's still watching Geraldine as she teeters off in her high heels. I grin as I think they may be mutually interested in each other. I ask Ruaridh some questions as we walk.

I love that he has that soft Highlander accent that I've heard on the TV programmes at New Year time.

It turns out that we're allowed to sit where we like in our new class, so I decide to adopt Ruaridh as my desk mate for this year. Mr Duddy, our new registration teacher, is well known for being relaxed. He welcomes us briefly to fifth year and takes the register. He sits, snaps open *The Glasgow Herald* newspaper and leaves us to chat.

After introductions to the others in our registration class, I ask Ruaridh if he has a girlfriend. He replies, no, he split with her before he moved. I'm fascinated as he describes what it was like to live in a little village close to Inverness, and the beautiful scenery surrounding it. He tells me he misses walking in the glens and mountains and swimming and fishing in the lochs.

I confess that I've always wanted to visit the Highlands and other pretty parts of Scotland, but I've only ever been on day trips to seaside towns. Living here, I remind him, we only get to gaze upon a smoky steelwork instead of a beautiful mountain. I also tell him that I don't feel like a true Scot because my accent is a bit mixed up sometimes, having lived in South Africa for six years. Ruaridh laughs when I say that.

'I like the way people talk here. It's more Scottish, more sincere. And Billy Connolly wouldn't be funny without his accent, which sounds very similar to yours. As for scenery, a fifteen-minute drive in any direction, and you can be in the hills.'

By the time the bell signals the end of registration and the start of morning classes, I've decided that not only do I like Ruaridh but that he is a very suitable, if different, match for Geraldine. With his red hair and stocky build, he couldn't look more different to her usual type of guy.

At lunchtime, I meet with the girls in the fifth-year common room. Geraldine pounces on me as soon as I walk in. 'So, what's he like? Does he have a girlfriend?'

The girls huddle around me as I tell them everything I've learned about Ruaridh. I finish by telling Geraldine that I believe she has an admirer in Ruaridh. She squeals in delight so loudly that she catches the other pupils' attention in the room, including Paul and Ruaridh, sitting in the opposite corner with the guys. She immediately pulls a composed face but leans in to ask more questions about her new love interest.

'Keep putting a good word in for me.' Geraldine urges as we split for our afternoon classes.

The next morning, as instructed by Geraldine, I ask Ruaridh more questions about his home life and interests. I learn that he has a big sister and little brother, likes bands like The Cure and The Smiths, and loves punk. He confesses his crushes on Debbie Harry from Blondie and Siouxsie Sioux. This gives me the confidence to ask him what he thinks of Geraldine. I see him blush for the first time, and he evades my question. I gleefully make a mental note to record his response later to the girls as confirmation that he may well have a crush on Geraldine.

Ruaridh tells me about his rugby playing and laughs about how he'll have to take up an interest in football as nobody around here knows about rugby. When I'm confident I have enough information to take to the girls, Ruaridh mentions that he misses playing in his band in Inverness. He has my full attention again. 'Like a pop band? What do you play?'

'Mainly keyboards, but I can play a couple of other instruments too.'

'No way! Are you looking for a band to join? I know one that needs a new keyboard player!'

He grins as I tell him what I know about the Clyde Alloys, including that they have a few short gigs lined up in local pubs. It's not my band, but I can't help but feel pleased when Ruaridh tells me that he's interested in meeting them.

At the lunchtime debrief session, the girls listen enthralled as I provide the latest updates on Ruaridh. Geraldine is especially excited to learn that he has a crush on Siouxsie Sioux and what that might mean for her future love life prospects. As for me, I'm excited to tell Steve and the band about the keyboard player.

Chapter 22

Saturday, 18 August 1984

S teve's picked me up at around six most mornings, and we're about to finish my second full week of boxing training. I think Da and Gran are a little suspicious but seem to have accepted my reason that I'm going out running with Steve, as Doll is no longer able to.

When I first told them that Doll was pregnant and soon to be married, they were shocked. I think Da was also afraid that I might have designs along a similar path, but I reassured him that I was still going to uni and settling down could wait. She'd never admit it, but I think Gran's a little sniffy because Doll's fallen pregnant out of wedlock. She says things like Doll will make a great mother and how she's looking forward to the wedding, but I also sense what she's not saying.

This morning, I've already skipped, done my warm-up exercises and am now practising my footwork drills using the white cross on the floor, being careful to watch my foot positions and keeping my weight centred. My breath puffs out in little clouds as the sun hasn't yet come around to the windowed side of the building.

Steve presents me with two objects wrapped in plastic. 'I bought these from the chemist not long after you agreed to come training with me.'

I stop my footwork drills to watch, fascinated, while Steve unwraps the crackly packages. 'Crepe bandages?'

'Yip. Six feet in length. Some people use crepe bandages to cover an injury. You'll use them to cover your hands. The more you box, the more grateful you'll be for the protection that these bandages offer. Keep them safe now – they're one of the most important pieces of your kit. As you use them, they'll mould to the shape of your knuckles.'

Using a small pair of scissors, Steve snips a hole at the top of the crepe bandage, hooks my right thumb through this, and begins to painstakingly wrap the cream-coloured bandage around my knuckles, palm, and wrist. When he nears the end of the bandage, he cuts through the middle to split it into two and ties the ends around my wrist. To finish, he uses tape to secure it in place.

Keeping my face neutral on the outside, inside, I'm relishing the sensation of Steve's strong hands on mine. I flex my bound right hand as he repeats the same process for my left hand. When my fists are wrapped, Steve steps back to survey his work. 'There. You look like a boxer now.'

I turn to look at myself in the mirror behind us. I do look like a boxer, but I don't feel like one. In my mind, I ask the figure staring back at me in the mirror. *Can I really learn how to box?* One glimpse of Steve standing not far behind me has the little voice inside my head agreeing that I would give anything a go with him by my side. It's a crazy, crazy idea – a lassie learning to box – it breaks so many rules – but I'm ready to be a rule-breaker now. I really am. I've followed the rules all my life, but now I'm willing to try something radical, something that will work.

Steve talks to me in the mirror. 'It's time to teach you how to throw a punch. Today, you're going to learn how to jab. You know your stance by now, and you've been practising how to move around.' Steve demonstrates stepping back with his right leg and twisting his left shoulder. He curls his hands into fists and places them on either side of his jaw. 'Put your weight on your back foot, lean forward onto your left, and jab. Give it a go.' I copy how Steve's standing.

Satisfied that my stance is correct, Steve takes my hands. 'Now, this is how you make a fist. Tuck in your fingers. Always close your thumb over the top of your clenched fist. When you punch, you hit with the flat side of your middle two knuckles.' He stands behind me and reaches around me with his arm to hold my fist closed. 'This is how to jab.'

God forgive me, but I can hardly concentrate on what Steve's saying or doing, for being so deliciously distracted by the closeness of his body to mine. *Concentrate, Aileen!* With some effort, I zone back into the drill.

Steve towers behind me in the mirror's reflection. He reminds me how to stand correctly when facing an opponent: my knees slightly bent, my weight forward on my feet. He adjusts the positions of my hands. 'Place your right fist by the right side of your jaw. Keep your left fist also by your jaw but slightly out so that you can see above your knuckles. Keep your chin down, elbows tucked in, always. They're there to protect your ribs and chest. And another little secret – you're not punching with your fists.'

'I'm not?' I stare, confused, at my bandaged hands.

Steve concedes: 'Ok, yes, you're using your hands. But the power comes from your feet and legs and drives up through your body, across your shoulders and arms and into your hands.'

As I concentrate on my feet and fists being in the correct positions, Steve stands alongside me and demonstrates with each hand what a jab punch should look like. I copy what he's just shown me. He makes me practice each jab over and over and corrects my body when I move out of line.

'I want you to imagine your opponent in front of you – let's say it's Lorraine. Now, with each jab, aim for the middle of her face.'

'Her fat, ugly face, you mean.' He ignores my joke. Deflated, I tell myself off for trying to be too friendly with him and resign myself to focussing instead on practising jabbing in slow motion.

I use a different tack to get Steve's attention. 'She came to my house a few weeks back.'

Steve turns to me. 'How did that go?'

'Not very well. I think she was supposed to apologise. My da had had a word with her stepfather – and he'd forced her to come. She didn't apologise. Just scowled and sneered a lot, and he clipped her a few times. Gran asked them to leave.'

In the mirror, as I practice my jabs, I notice that my face has turned pale. 'On her way out, she mouthed, *you're dead* to me.

Steve whistles. 'She's a right nasty one, eh?'

'Think she means it, too.' The familiar knot tightens in my stomach.

'Well, she might try to have a go, but you're going to be a female *Rocky* by then – the 'sassy lassie' – who's not going to take any shit from anyone.'

'*Sassy lassie* – I like the sound of that!' I grin at him, grateful for his support and faith in me. I continue practising jabs.

A slight smile plays on Steve's lips. 'I've never seen a girl box before.'

'Do I look weird?'

'No, the mean girl look suits you.'

My cheeks flame. I'm unsure if this is a compliment or not.

'I take it no one knows?'

'Only you, your parents, Doll and Sandy.'

'So, you haven't told your dad, then?'

'Jeez, no! Da would string me up if he knew! He used to be an amateur boxer, but he didn't fight much, as he says it could get really brutal. He did it mainly because he enjoyed the training. No, he wouldn't be pleased if he knew. He's mentioned women boxing abroad – let's just say he's not a fan.'

Steve nods and, with a sly smile, says, 'I'm guessing your gran wouldn't be a fan either?'

Chuckling, I gesture with my bandaged hands down the length of my body and throw out some jabs. 'I'm guessing that she would say that this is *unladylike?*'

I continue jabbing, trying to ignore how red and blotchy my cheeks and neck have become in the mirror. I think about who I have and haven't told. I haven't said anything to Geraldine and Marie because they would gossip, and it'd get back to Da and Gran. I haven't told Paul as I suspect he would be jealous of the time I've been spending with Steve. Paul's never met Steve, but I think he's guessed from the reactions of Geraldine and Marie when Steve's mentioned that he might be good looking.

Keen to change the subject, as casually as I can, I ask, 'Any news about Billy?'

'Nah. I've been asking around again. No one's seen or heard from him in a few weeks. Some reckon he's headed over to Belfast.' A shadow passes over Steve's face, which makes me uneasy. But his face brightens again when he resumes his position beside me to watch my jab. 'That's it. Now, you can speed up, just a little, mind. Flick your arm out straight – but snap it back before it's fully extended. The jab's short and sharp.'

Steve makes me practice over and over until my arms and shoulders ache, but on I go jabbing, fascinated by my reflection, my worries beginning to dissolve. Maybe, just maybe, I can pull this off. I smile at the sassy lassie in the mirror, and the guy beside me grins back.

Chapter 23

Saturday, 25 August 1984

So many excited teenagers and early twenty-somethings are packed into McCoy's this Saturday night. The lassies are done up to the nines with perfectly coiffed hairstyles and carefully chosen clothes and make-up. Similarly, the guys sport hairstyles like pop stars and footballers, many dressed in shirts and ties, teamed with belted baggy trousers.

The thrum of chatter and laughter vibrates just below the music being played. Gas Marshall is well underway with his rock and pop music set; red telephone clamped between his ear and shoulder as he spins the next record, ready to play on seamlessly from the last one. Gas is a music magician who really knows how to fill a dance floor.

Paul's been begging to take me out to a pub, but I've managed to fob him off by saying I want to enjoy as many nights out as possible with my best pal before the baby arrives. The chasm is widening between Paul and me.

Doll and I are sitting at our now regular table in McCoy's, ready for the night ahead, which includes the first proper gig from the Clyde Alloys with Steve as their lead singer and guitarist. They are the warm-up act for a local band. Even though I see Steve most days, I'm really looking forward to seeing him tonight, when I suspect that he'll be in his element, doing the thing he loves most.

Not put off by the legend of Angostura bitters, I sip on a long vodka. I remember that Doll has some big news to tell me. I'm so excited that when I nudge her, I almost tip her glass of Irn Bru over her. 'Oops! So, come on. What do you have to tell me?'

'Not tell – show you!' Doll waves her left hand in front of me.

Lights sparkle, and I grab her hand to gaze at the new diamond engagement ring sitting on her dainty finger. 'It's beautiful!' I hug her.

'I know!' Doll squeals. 'We bought it yesterday in Glasgow – made a day of it – pub lunch and everything.' She stares into space as she recalls the day. 'It was so romantic, strolling around the Jewellery Quarter, arm in arm, looking in the windows of all the shops. I tried on a lot of rings – this was my favourite, though.' Doll lightly taps her new engagement ring.

She leans into me. 'We also bought our wedding rings! Well, we thought, seeing as we're getting married soon, we may as well buy those too!' She smiles so broadly, her happiness evident, that I must admit to a stab of envy as I look at her. It must be fantastic to have already found the man of your dreams and know how your future will look.

'Can I make a wish on your ring?'

'Of course.' Doll carefully slips off her engagement ring and hands it to me. I slide the delicate ring onto my finger. Doll's fingers are much smaller than mine, so it only reaches a third of the way. As is the superstition, I turn the ring three times towards my heart and make my wish. As no one else will find out, guilty pleasure bubbles inside me as I wish for Steve to be my boyfriend, not Paul.

'What did you wish for?'

I laugh good-naturedly. 'You know, I can't tell if I want my wish to come true!'

Doll's eyes twinkle mischievously. 'Aye, but you can tell me. Let me guess. Did you wish, perhaps, to replace your Scottish boyfriend with an English one?' I hold my best poker face. Doll scrutinises me. 'Ah, I can see that I was right. When are you going to do something about it?'

My heart sinks. I know Doll's right, but I really don't know how to break up with Paul. The more I distance myself, the more he seems to cling to me. I'm waiting for the right time, but deep down, I know there'll never be a right time. I just have to find the courage to tell him I don't feel the same way about him anymore. And it's nothing to do with Steve. Well, not much, anyway.

Tommy, the keyboard player from the Clyde Alloys, distracts us as he hops onto the stage to plug in some equipment. He waves his hand

and shakes his head as though he's found something not to his liking with the equipment.

Doll giggles as she watches him. 'Sandy and the rest of the band are pleased with Steve. He says he's like a breath of fresh air, with really good ideas. Steve's introduced them to songs from Liverpool bands and is helping them to experiment more and write their own music.'

It's nothing to do with me, but this endorsement of Steve warms my heart.

'Steve's told Sandy that you're picking up the boxing well. Are you enjoying it?'

'I suppose so. I'm not sure how I'm going to use it, but I'm enjoying the training for sure.' A grin slides across my face.

Doll swats my arm. 'You need to split up with Paul!'

'I know. Just wondering, though – does Steve have a girlfriend?

'Yes. She's in Liverpool – that's why he goes down there regularly.'

'That makes sense.' I roll the ice cubes around in my long vodka glass, doing a bad job of hiding my disappointment from my best friend. 'I bet she's drop-dead gorgeous, too. Not like me.'

Doll watches me carefully. 'You're the most amazing lassie I know, and the best looking!'

I laugh, grateful for Doll's compliments and hand her sparkly ring back to her. 'So, soon-to-be Mrs Ross – what are you doing about school?'

'I've not gone back - I don't want to be the girl who got herself up the duff, waddling between English and Biology classes, folks talking and staring at me. No, I want to enjoy my pregnancy. I'm signing on, and Sandy's able to earn some extra cash.' Doll stares off into the distance, then returns her gaze to me. 'Once I've had the baby, I'm hoping Mum will babysit so that I can find a part-time job, and then we can save to buy stuff for a new house. I can't wait for the three of us to be in our home as a family.'

'How are you keeping?'

'I'm still nauseous, and I'd really like a pint of cider, but I'm sure I can wait until March for my next drink!' Doll grins and grabs my hand. 'Come on. Let's go see them!'

Horrified, I pull my hand back.

It's no use, though, pregnant or not; Doll now has a firm grip on my wrist and yanks me through the crowds over to a faded green door in the back corner of the room, close to the stage.

She twists the handle and shoves the door wide open. The guys are in various stages of undress and freeze as they realise that everyone on the dance floor can see them.

Doll tugs my arm hard one last time so that I come flying into the room and almost crash against Steve. He catches me just before I'm about to fall against him. My cheeks burn; I don't think I've ever felt so embarrassed. This is a private inner guy sanctum of the band, and two lassies have just gate-crashed the atmosphere.

I don't know where to look or what to do next. Luckily, Steve senses my unease and directs me to sit on an empty chair.

Tommy bursts in the door. 'Equipment's checked!' He takes his place in the corner. Most of the band are standing up, getting changed into something or other.

We really shouldn't be in here. I squirm in my chair. Searching for something to say, I remember about Ruaridh. I announce, a little more loudly than I'd planned: 'I know a guy who plays keyboards and is looking for a band.'

The noise in the room stops. Everyone turns to look at me, including Tommy. He clears his throat, hurriedly ties his long hair back and puts on his sunglasses.

'Is he any good?' Sandy asks.

'Don't know, haven't heard him play.'

The band look around at each other. Tommy speaks first. 'If you hold auditions, I can help tell you if they're any good or not?'

Both Doll and Sandy rise from their chairs. Sandy looks thoughtful, 'We best audition soon. We should put an advert in the Round Sounds window. Does anyone know of anyone else who might be interested in joining us?'

The band members shake their heads.

Through the brief silence which follows, Tommy roars: 'Stevie, git that shirt aff! The folks oot there are gaunna think we're trying to be Big Country!' Steve is tucking a red tartan shirt into his blue Levi jeans. My breath catches. He's so handsome, like a model – the guy would look great dressed in a tattie sack.

'Ah lads. Me Ma bought me this – said it'd make me fit in better with all you Jocks!'

The guys laugh, and Sandy tosses a black Jack Daniel's T-shirt at Steve. 'Here, ya Sassenach!

Put that on! We might play a bit of Big Country, but it's not a fancy dress party!'

'Alright. Alright.' Steve has his hands up, grinning. 'Me Ma'll be heartbroken when I tell her that you didn't like the shirt she bought me.' As quick as a flash, Steve's loosened a few buttons at the top of his shirt and yanks it up and out of his jeans and over his head. My breath catches as I catch sight of Steve's half-naked, lean, and muscled torso. All composure I had managed to muster since being yanked into this room leaves my body as I drink in the sight of his lightly tanned and rippled stomach, chest, and arms. As Steve tosses his shirt into his bag, he catches me gawping at him and winks back at me. My cheeks burn hotter as he whips the black T-shirt over his head and body.

I can tell from Doll's expression that she was equally impressed with the back view she got of Steve. She recovers to give Sandy another long, lingering kiss and turns back to the room. 'Right, guys, we're off. Break a leg!' And with that, Doll ushers me back out of the changing room and into the crowd.

'I'm so excited! Have I mentioned that before?' Doll beams as she claps her hands together. I know what she means as butterflies collide in my stomach. Tonight will be a great night and the crowd's mood adds to the atmosphere. Doll and I find space on the dance floor to sing and dance along to Gas's records.

Not long after, the Clyde Alloys begin to file out of the dressing room. Steve is head and shoulders above the rest of the band and smiles as he catches my eye. Thrills course through me, and I wave shyly back at him. Oh God, it's going to be so tough for me to play it cool in any shape or form in his presence. Doll blows Sandy a kiss as he makes his way through the crowd to hop on the stage.

Once assembled, the band begins to ready their equipment. Steve tunes his guitar, connects it to the amp and sets up his pedals. Almost like a well-rehearsed dance, the band members work around each other, twisting and bending and plugging things in. Gas continues to play the tunes, with the crowd bouncing and singing in unison.

I don't think I could be any happier. I'm chatting and dancing with my best friend, and the guy I like is at least being friendly to me. Every inch of me feels alive.

Gas fades out the dance music, which tells the audience that the band's about to start. Each band member is gathered in front of their instruments, and Steve is behind his microphone. 'Good evening, folks!'

Once he has everyone's attention, he clears his throat and roars into the microphone: 'We're the boys from the Clyde Alloys!' The crowd cheers as Frankie Fingers strikes the opening bass chords of "Waterfront" by Simple Minds. At the same time, Sandy plays the drums, and Steve joins in with the lead guitar.

For the next song, Steve announces: 'This is by a legendary band from Liverpool. No, you can 'relax'. It's not by Frankie Goes to Hollywood or the Beatles. This next song is by A Flock of Seagulls, called," I Ran".

The atmosphere intensifies as the opening bars cascade from the speakers. As Tommy's keyboard is a lead instrument in this song, he pulls as many poses as he can, hands raised dramatically off the keyboards, looking like a pop star off the telly. Doll and I giggle.

'The band's playing great!' I call into Doll's ear as we dance along to each song. The rest of the crowd seems to be enjoying the set, too.

Sandy's arms and feet sound out the opening beats to the next song. Recognising the tune, so excited, I squeal into Doll's ear, '"It's Should I Stay or Should I Go?"'

Doll laughs. 'It's your song for Paul!' It certainly is.

Sandy distracts me as he grins at Doll, moving his head in time to the music and throwing his hair around. He and Doll look so happy. I want that kind of relationship.

Too soon, the band finish their set and come off the stage to make their way to their various family and friends. Sandy makes a beeline straight for Doll, and they kiss and hug passionately. It seems they cannot be apart for an hour, even if they are in the same room.

As I'm stood awkwardly beside them, watching the crowd, a strong arm wraps itself across my shoulders. When I turn around, I'm looking into Steve's bright eyes. He smiles down at me. 'Did you enjoy the gig?'

Hypnotised by his presence, all I can do is nod. As he slowly drops his arm from me, I stare at it, longing for him to wrap it back around me again. What a feeling that is.

Utterly oblivious to the effect he has on me, he asks: 'How are you after the training?'

I cough to find my voice. 'Pretty stiff. I keep pulling muscles in places I didn't know I had them! All along my arms, my shoulders, and my back. Even my stomach muscles ache when I laugh.'

'That's what happens when you're training your body to learn a new skill – you'll get used to it. The training's obviously working. Speaking of which, what do you think about meeting tomorrow to take your boxing to the next level?' A combination of a smile and a knowing wink is enough to persuade me.

I do my best not to look too enthusiastic, although all I do between training sessions is dream about the next one. 'I'm free. Could we start with a morning run in the woods for the warm-up?'

Steve looks pleased with the idea. Another thought occurs to me, one which makes me grin. 'And can I be the trainer for that session? Seeing as I know more about running than you.'

He laughs. 'Okay, I'm not sure what I'm letting myself in for. I'll pick you up at 8:30.' Steve flashes me that brilliant smile of his, touching my arm briefly as he heads off to the bar. A group of girls immediately surrounds him.

I stare after him. I much prefer this Steve, the one who's so relaxed, who smiles. The Steve in the gym is too stern. But I'm in the gym with him for a serious reason, I remind myself, and we're both in relationships.

Chapter 24

Sunday, 26 August 1984

'We seem to be hitting all the red lights,' Steve sighs as he slows the car.

'Did you know that in South Africa, they call traffic lights, robots?'

'Really?' Steve chuckles, 'How do you know that?'

'I used to live in South Africa.'

'Did you?' Steve whistles softly, his eyes on the road ahead as the traffic lights change, and we move off. 'I thought I could sometimes hear an accent when you speak. What was it like?'

'It was different.' I'm not sure how much detail he'd like to know, so add, 'Like the sun shone almost every day – and the life was about being outside – not being cooped in the house.'

'What about apartheid?'

'I hated that I couldn't have any Black or Coloured friends – the whole segregation thing felt wrong.' I turn to Steve to gauge his reaction. He nods, looking thoughtful. 'I gave up talking to my Afrikaner pals about it. They couldn't see past it – said that the place would fall apart without this discipline of dividing the people – so I didn't have that many friends.'

Steve's eyes are soft. 'It's mad how apartheid seems reasonable to them. South Africa's slapped with economic sanctions, its athletes aren't allowed to compete on the world stage, yet still, they carry on with it. Or their athletes have to change their citizenship so they can run for Great Britain if they're Zola Budd.' Steve's eyebrows knit together. 'My dad's black.'

He glances at me, obviously amused by the surprise which must be registered across my face. 'Well, my stepfather. My birth father's Danish – hence the blonde hair and blue eyes. Ritchie's been my dad since I can remember. So, as a family, we take great interest in what's happening in South Africa.'

I quickly gather my thoughts. 'So was your family pleased when Glasgow was the first city in the world to award Nelson Mandela the Freedom of the City because it refused to accept the legitimacy of the apartheid system?'

'For sure. My dad was impressed with that. Helped persuade him and me Ma to move here. Hopefully, he'll be freed soon. Nelson Mandela, not my dad.'

I laugh.

'The world's a mess, eh? With all these racial, religious and political divides.' I'm enjoying this conversation with Steve, about something as important to me as it is to him. Paul's never really been interested in my life in South Africa beyond the language and the sunshine.

'Is that why your family came back ? Because of apartheid?' Steve grips the steering wheel as a car brakes in front of us.

'Yes, my mammie and da struggled with it so we knew that we weren't going to stay, but we came home sooner than planned when we found out my mammie was sick and needed treatment.'

Steve looks at me. I'm sensing that there's a question he can't ask.

'She's dead, yes.'

'I'm sorry.' Steve murmurs and falls into a thoughtful silence, which I sense I shouldn't disturb.

◦◦ ◦◦

My heart lifts as we turn into the car park of the Country Park. It's a beautifully crisp morning; it won't be long now until the leaves begin to change colour.

Nerves flutter in my stomach as I take Steve through the warm-up routine. I'm worried that my running might not be good enough. At the same time, I decide that I'm going to enjoy every precious moment with him today.

'Right.' I say, trying to sound like my old running coach. 'We'll start with a jog, and then I've got a route planned through the woods, which will allow us to get some hill and speed work in.'

Steve cocks an eyebrow at me. 'Hill and speed work?'

Ah, maybe he's not as good a runner as I think he is. This is going to be fun. I can get him back for beasting me at our boxing training sessions. I set off running at a steady pace, and Steve falls in easily beside me. Soon, we enter the woods and run under the sun-dappled tree canopy. It doesn't take me long to settle my breathing into a steady rhythm, and I notice that Steve's breathing also sounds relaxed.

I spy the hill section ahead. 'Okay, there's a tree about a quarter of the way up the hill?'

'Yeah.'

'We'll run – not sprint – about 70 per cent effort – up to that tree, jog back and then run back up the hill to the tree further up, and then jog back down. Got that?'

Steve nods. He gathers himself to pick up his speed. We reach the first part of the incline, and he pulls away from me but falls back to be level. 'Run at your own pace; you'll naturally be fitter and stronger than me.'

He runs ahead again, easily reaching the first tree, looping around, and passes me as he lightly runs back to the start of the hill. We repeat the hard run up the inclines, and the recovery runs on the way back to the bottom to four trees that stand almost evenly up the hill.

We're both lightly sweating and out of breath, and I can tell from the grin on Steve's face that he's enjoying it. Having done all the trees on the hill, we gather again at the bottom and, this time run steadily back to the top of the hill. My thigh muscles sing as we near the top, but I keep pushing as I can't lose face in front of Steve. I lean forward into the incline, arms swinging, lifting my knees, and driving my feet into the ground. Finally, we crest the hill. I ease off to recover my breath.

'You're not a bad runner - not bad for a girl anyway!' Steve ducks out of my way as I throw a mock jab at him. He gasps as he works to bring his breathing back under control.

'Doesn't sound like you found it too easy?'

'Well, it was different, that's for sure! And enjoyable!' He chuckles as we fall back into step with each other. I enjoy this smiling Steve. Just the sight of him has me catching my breath again, just when I was almost breathing normally. His hair looks particularly blonde today, highlighted by the sunshine, which contrasts nicely with the tan on his face and neck, glistening with sweat. I think if he just flashed that smile of his at anyone, he would receive anything he desired.

We continue running for another mile, and then it's time for the flat speed section – this time using lamp posts that are spaced apart at even distances on the path next to the loch. We sprint for the distance between three lamp posts, jog between the next four and repeat this four times.

'Okay, ease off! Recovery run now.'

Steve laughs breathlessly. 'I was struggling for a bit there at the end, girl! Thought you had me.' We both slow so that we run lightly on our toes to gradually come to a stop.

It's time for our cool down, to stretch our muscles out, and I have to say that it's the best view I've ever had doing this. Yes, there was the loch, and the hills and the trees, but, oh my – nothing can beat the sight of Steve stretching

– bending over from his waist, touching the ground, leaning one way, then the other. He has the best pair of legs I've ever seen on a guy and the most fantastic arm and shoulder muscles.

'For a laddie with your fitness, I thought you would find that workout a pure skoosh.' I tease him.

'A what?' Steve jerks his head towards me mid leg stretch.

'If something is a skoosh, or you skooshed it – it means 'dead easy'.

Steve smiles, shakes his head, and changes to stretch his other leg out. 'Is that Jockenese, or Afrikaans?'

'It's Scottish slang, yes. As well as meaning that something's easy, it can also be used as a general word for a bottle of Coke or Irn Bru – you ask for a bottle of 'skoosh' in the shop, and they'll ask you what kind.'

Steve's straightened up, chuckling. We've both finished our stretches now.

I continue, 'Or you can use it in a phrase like, "That will be skoosh!", which means, "Aye, that'll be right!"'

I'm laughing, glad that he seems to be enjoying the banter.

'The gig went well last night, eh?' I ask Steve as we stroll back to the car.

'Definitely. Think Sandy's fixing us some more warm-up gigs with the local pubs. Good practice for us, beer money and a laugh.'

Hearing Sandy's name makes me smile. 'He and Doll make such a great couple – they have some exciting times ahead, eh?'

'They sure do, but it wouldn't be for me, settling down so young. I am jealous of him, though.'

'Why?'

'He's found the girl he loves.'

'Have you not found that?'

'No, not like Sandy and Doll have.' Steve screws his face up. 'Some girlfriends have wanted to hear the big L-word, but I've no idea what love is – what it's supposed to mean. I've never gotten butterflies in my stomach or anything ....'

So, not like how I feel when I'm with you, then? How I wish I dared to say that out loud!

'How about you? Do you know what love is?'

This is turning into a deep conversation. 'Not yet, it seems.' My cheeks flame. The more I get to know Steve, the more I'm falling for him, which I know I shouldn't be.

Some swans stretch their wings as they emerge from the loch and waddle across our path. We smile as we wait for them to pass in front of us.

'Do you mind if we drop off at my house on our way to the gym? This workout you've just given me certainly wasn't a skoosh! I want to have a quick shower before we start the training.'

I bat him on the arm, trying not to stare, as I notice that Steve's T-shirt is so wet with sweat that it's stuck to every ripple and muscle on his torso.

'I'm happy for you not to shower,' I joke as a few ladies walking their dogs pass us by, casting appreciative glances at Steve.

'Actually, I'm really hot. Excuse me.' Steve takes off his top, and once again, I'm looking at his naked upper body, this time glistening with sweat in the cool sunshine. He strolls to the edge of the loch and leans over, scooping water over his back, chest, neck, and face.

The ladies who passed us have stopped a little further ahead and are unashamedly gawking back at Steve. One of them calls, 'It's not often we see a laddie get his kit off in this park.' Her friends grin. 'Thanks for making our Sunday!'

Steve twists his head from side to side, shaking off the last of the water. He runs his fingers through his hair, smiles and waves at the ladies as he makes his way back to me.

I can't resist asking: 'Do you know the effect you have on lassies?'

Steve gives me a shy smile. 'What do you mean?'

I struggle to put into words the effect that he has on me and obviously has on other women. 'You know – lassies just falling at your feet like that,' I say weakly, waving at the ladies ahead. 'You can have anyone. You must have constant queues of girls at your front door.'

'Nope, no queues.'

I'm waiting for him to mention his girlfriend, but he doesn't. And I'm glad because I don't want to know about her.

Walking towards the car, I cast sideward glances at Steve as he walks beside me. He must be a little chilly as goosebumps have appeared on his arms and chest, and the fine blonde hairs lining his arms and chest stand up. He looks so attractive. *Sexy is the word you're looking for*, a little voice chimes inside my head. *Sexy. That's what he is.* I realise I've never really understood what that word means until now. And another word pops into my head, which I now fully understand: *desire.*

→→ ·•• ·•←

In the hall, we meet Queenie, carrying a stack of folded towels.

'Hello, love. Is it hot out there?'

'Yip, not helped by a hard training session from Aileen. I'm going to shower, get changed.'

Queenie tosses him a couple of towels. 'Dad's just in the living room. Come on in, Aileen. Cuppa?'

Sitting by their red phone in the hall, we pass a photo of Steve with his arm around a gorgeous blonde girl. Queenie catches me looking. 'That's Caroline. The last time she came, she left that photo there to remind our Steve to call her more often.' Queenie giggles. 'Steve's never been good at taking hints.' Suppressing the pangs of envy radiating within me, I smile like I'm supposed to.

She leads me into the kitchen and puts on the kettle. Steve's followed behind us to grab an apple and a banana. Queenie makes the tea and sets the cups and biscuits on a tray, saying, 'Come into the lounge, meet Steve's dad.'

I follow her into the hall towards the homely lounge. I hesitate by the door as she sets the tray on the coffee table. A large cream sofa and two armchairs face the TV. A silver HiFi music centre sits in one corner of the room, some records neatly piled beside it. A picture frame hangs above the fireplace, and photos are dotted around the room. The back of Steve's dad's head rests against his chair as he watches something on the TV.

Queenie ushers me to sit by her on the couch. Steve's dad stands to greet me. 'Call me Ritchie.'

'You must be hungry after your run – would you like a cheese sandwich or a piece of fruit?' Usually, I'd politely decline, but I am hungry and having an idea of what Steve might have in mind for me at the boxing, I accept Queenie's offer. She disappears into the kitchen and returns with a tray of food which she sits on my knee.

I thought I'd be self-conscious eating in front of Steve's parents, but the conversation flows smoothly, with them doing most of the talking while I wolf down a cheese sandwich, demolish a banana and drink my tea. They tell me about their lives in Liverpool, what it's like to live there and how they miss their families and friends.

'So, how come you moved to Scotland, then?'

Ritchie sits forward in his armchair. 'Times were tough in Liverpool – still are – under Thatcher's rule. Have you heard of Toxteth?'

I nod, recalling the TV images of burnt-out cars, and ranks of police officers in riot gear facing off against the protesters hurling petrol bombs and missiles.

'We lived near there. There were no jobs, not for someone like me. Queenie and I were also getting aggro because we're mixed-race. We decided to get out. One of my friends knew a gaffer in the Craig looking for a welder. I got the job; we got this house, and the rest is history.'

'How do you like Craigburn?'

'We like it, though Queenie's still getting to grips with when to hang her washing out.' Ritchie grins, nudging his wife.

'I have to check which way the wind's blowing in case any of the Craig's smoke and stuff spoils my clean washing!' Queenie giggles.

Ritchie leans back in his armchair. 'And up here, Thatcher's still got a tight grip, but at least there are still some jobs if you have a trade.' He chuckles. 'It's also amazing to be somewhere where no one cares about my skin colour. Sure, some are shocked when they first meet me, and I do get second looks when I'm walking about. Up here, though, they're more concerned about whether I'm a Protestant or a Catholic!'

'It's a big thing here – what religion you are. I just wish that it didn't matter – that everything was about how you are as a person, not what religion you follow – or what colour your skin is.' I nibble on the last bite of my sandwich, trying to look ladylike, just as my gran has taught me.

A slow smile spreads across Ritchie's face. 'Do you know that Liverpool has two cathedrals – a Catholic one and a Protestant one? And guess what else, girl? The two cathedrals sit at either end of a street called Hope Street!'

'*Hope Street*. I love that.' I smile back at Ritchie and drain the rest of my tea. 'I don't think Catholics and Protestants will ever stop fighting here, though. Your Steve's teaching me to box, so maybe I can protect myself better if I get jumped again.'

'There's no 'maybe' about it!' Steve's just walked into the living room, and I catch a whiff of his aftershave as he grabs the last remaining mug of tea and sits in the other armchair.

It's just then that I notice that the picture above the fireplace isn't a picture, but a photograph of a schoolboy, smiling across at the camera.

Queenie follows my gaze. 'That's our Nathan. God rest his soul. The main reason why we left Liverpool.'

I'm trying to process what Queenie's just said. Steve hangs his head and Ritchie gazes sadly at the photo. He reaches across to Queenie and squeezes her knee. 'Hey there, girl.'

'I'm so sorry. I didn't mean to ... remind you.' I bite my lip.

Tears well in Queenie's eyes. She shakes her head and gives a little laugh. 'Don't mind me!' She glances at the clock on the mantlepiece and rises to her feet: 'I best get ready – got a client in a minute!'

Steve spots the look of confusion on my face. 'Me ma's a hairdresser,' he explains.

'Ah, that's why you always look so glamorous.' I set my tray on the coffee table.

Queenie smiles at me. 'I can do your hair if you like. With your length, you'd suit a spiral perm.'

I smile back, uncertain what a spiral perm is but knowing it means curls of some description. 'I'd like that. I've never had my hair done in a hairdresser – my gran trims it.'

Queenie looks a little shocked. 'We can't have untrained grans cutting hair! I'll do it for you. Let me know when you're free. In fact – Sandy and Doll are coming to the salon to get their hair done before their wedding – why don't you come at the same time?' She's more relaxed now that the subject's been changed from Nathan. I don't want her to be sad, so I agree to 'get my hair done'.

Steve takes one last slurp of his tea and stands. 'Come on, you. Time to get back to training.' Even though I don't need help getting off the couch, he extends his hand out to me, which I take, thrilling inside at the strength of his touch.

Chapter 25

Friday, 31 August 1984

A perky pop song plays on the ghetto blaster in the gym. Sunshine beams in from small square windows placed high along the wall at even intervals, and shafts of light stream along the middle of the floor. It's here that Steve has led me to do our now regular body conditioning exercises. For the past few weeks, I've learned that while I have strong legs, I have little upper body strength. And, no matter how much Steve tells me I'm improving at shadow boxing, my arms still ache after doing press-ups, even though I've been practising. Also, I'm not too fond of burpees, but I don't mind star jumps. I groan as Steve orders me to do more knuckle press-ups.

Next, I'm standing beside Steve, facing the mirror, shadow boxing. Peeking over my bandaged fists, I practise jabbing with my left and right hands, stepping this way and that, over the white taped cross on the floor. I focus on each step and each jab, adjusting my stance when Steve reminds me to protect my jaw, my chest, and my ribs.

'How did you start boxing?'

'It was my dad – Ritchie – he encouraged me to come with him to boxing training. I think he just wanted to keep me off the streets – there wasn't much to do when I was growing up. Plus, then my dad knew that I could protect myself.'

'So, we both have dads who used to box, then?'

Steve smiles. 'Yeah, that's true.' He takes position beside me, his face serious again. 'Next, I'm going to show you how to deliver powerful body and head hook punches.'

He turns me around to watch him as he curls his fists and places them by the side of his face. He fixes me with those blue eyes of his just above his knuckles, about to demonstrate the new punches.

'Your jabs are like your set up punches to test your opponent, but you can also use them strategically to distract them. If your opponent has their hands up defending their head because you're throwing jab shots there – then their body's exposed. Nice and ready for your hook punch combinations. And when they drop their arms back down to defend their body, that's when you come in with your head hooks.' He throws some shadow jabs in the space between us and follows with some shadow hooks.

My stomach lurches. My throat tightens. It's all beginning to feel too real now. 'I'm scared.'

'Scared?' Steve drops his hands, steps towards the ghetto blaster, and switches it off.

I shake my head. 'I don't think I can do this.'

'Why not?'

'It's too much to remember – guarding this and guarding that, and then getting ready to throw punches hard ... which will hurt someone. I don't think I can hurt anyone.'

'Even if they're hurting you?'

'Even then.' I bow my head and press my bandaged palm over my lips to stop myself from crying. Failed again. I'm such a coward. 'So sorry to waste your time. Somehow, I thought I could do this.'

Steve puts his hand on my shoulder. 'You're just having a wobble. Everyone gets scared. All the best boxers do. Maybe Mohammed Ali and Mike Tyson would never admit it – but Frank Bruno, Jim Watt – all of them – they get nervous.'

'Yeah, but that's their job, and they're guys, and they've been boxing for years! And I'm just a lassie who only wants to feel safe. I shouldn't have to learn how to box so that I can be safe!'

'Aileen. You can do this. You're already better than some of our younger lads because you listen, and you practice over and over.' His kind words make me cry, and I scold myself for not being strong right now. I stumble when he gently gathers me in for a hug.

Once I've registered that he's holding me and I'm resting against his chest, I'm immediately transported back to the beating on the 12th of July. The pain and confusion of that night come flooding back. More tears flow as I realise that Lorraine won't ever stop terrorising me, or wee Mary. Not unless I stand up to her. But I was a fool to think I could do that.

As if reading my mind, Steve murmurs, 'You can't keep running away. That woman's never going to stop battering you. She's bigger than you and is usually with a gang.'

He leans back from me slightly and tilts my head up to his. 'Nobody has to get hurt. You never know – the surprise of you learning to box – to defend yourself and attack – might help persuade her to leave you alone.'

I shake my head slowly. 'I'll never beat her.'

'Do you know what Mister Mac's number one rule is?' Steve doesn't wait for me to answer. 'All disputes are to be resolved in the ring, like gentlemen. No street fighting is allowed.'

I'm puzzled why Steve's telling me this.

He leans back from me. 'The only way to stop Lorraine is to stand up to her. You'll never fight in a ring – your fights have always been on the streets. Let's take the fight to her.'

Steve steps back and throws some shadow punches. 'Let's knock her off her feet, literally. Show her your strength and your courage, and your will. You've still a lot to learn about boxing, but you're showing so much promise.' He puts both his hands on my shoulders.

Looking into his eyes, I believe he means what he's saying. 'Why are you helping me?'

Steve lifts his chin, flexing his fists. 'I told you. I hate bullies. I felt sick when I saw how badly they'd beaten you when you were lying, bleeding, on the pavement. I wanted to damage that Billy and his slag of a girlfriend so badly. It took all my strength not to beat him to a pulp.'

'I'll always be grateful that you were there. God knows what state I would have been left in.

They weren't for finishing any time soon when you arrived. I honestly thought I was a goner – that that would be it.'

Steve's face twists. 'Never on my watch.' He takes my hands and drops his head towards me. 'Come on now. Please don't give up.'

I rub the back of my neck. I honestly don't know what to do. I'm scared to go forward. I'm terrified to turn back.

'Please. Just say yes.' As Steve holds my gaze, my resolve and excuses, crumble.

'How can I say no when you're guilt-tripping me?' I jab him lightly on the chest.

Steve exhales, a slow smile forming on his face. 'Right! Back to learning how to throw hook punches.' He demonstrates the left and right body hooks and head hooks, and I spend the next half an hour practising these in various combinations while stepping over the white cross.

While I'm shadow boxing in the mirror, the reflection of a large photo of Colin Mackenzie catches my attention. It reminds me of the photo of Steve's brother hanging above the fireplace. I'm curious. 'What happened to Nathan?'

Steve crosses his arms and turns from me but not before I catch his expression so full of sadness. I immediately regret asking the question. 'It's okay. I don't need to know. I didn't mean to intrude ….'

'No, I want to tell you.' Steve leads me to sit on a nearby bench.

A heavy atmosphere hangs in the gym. Steve clears his throat, pauses, and then, 'My brother was murdered. He was ten.'

My hand flutters to my throat. I stifle a sob. Why, oh why, did I ask this question? Still, morbid curiosity creeps through me. 'What happened?'

'He'd been playing footie with his mates and took a shortcut on his own through a park. A gang of skinhead lads jumped him – beat him to death.'

'So, they didn't know Nathan?"

I'm unable to comprehend the magnitude of what he is saying. My mind immediately leaps to Wee Mary, and panic rises and burns like acid in my throat. To lose a sibling in any circumstances would be heart-breaking, but to lose one like that?

Steve nods, tears glistening in his eyes. 'They believe it was because he was black. A woman whose house backs onto the park said she thought it was just some young lads messing. Then she heard shouts of 'coon' and 'nigger' and our Nathan screaming. She looked through the gap in her fence. Nathan was on the ground, being kicked and beaten. She called the police – but it was too late.'

'God, I'm so sorry.' I take his hand. 'Did they catch them?'

'Eventually. The lady provided a good description of the ringleader, and the police were able to arrest him and his mates. The lads were much older than Nathan – picking on a little lad – defies belief! The local lads wanted to take revenge, but my parents persuaded everyone not to do anything rash. Everyone except me.'

'What did you do?'

Steve bows his head and whispers. 'I lost it. I broke the boxing rules. I found the ringleader, took out all my anger and grief on him. I was twelve; he was sixteen.'

'What happened?'

'Nothing. The lad didn't report me. Everyone understood why I beat him. We had the funeral for Nathan, and I can't remember much about that. Ma was destroyed. Dad was in pieces. The lad that killed him only got twenty-five years! The other lads just got three each – they're out now - can you believe it? Nathan would have turned sixteen on July 12th.'

My mouth falls open. 'The night you found me.'

'Yeah, I was out walking to clear my head. Didn't have any particular plan of where I was going. I turned up the street you were on ...' Steve sighs. 'There was no way I could walk away. Billy was lucky I only punched him the once.'

I squeeze Steve's hand.

He uses his T-shirt sleeve to wipe his face and clears his throat. 'Anyway, look at me. Don't tell anyone – you'll ruin my hard man reputation.'

It's my turn to reach across and hug him to me. 'I know what senseless loss feels like. The hardest time in my life was losing my mammie. No one or no thing can ever replace her.'

Steve squeezes me a little tighter and laughs, 'Bloody hell, girl. I wasn't expecting this confession session! We'd better get back to work, eh?' He pulls back from me, smiling through fresh tears. He wipes his eyes again. 'On your feet! Let's get you ready to rumble with that Lorraine!'

He leads me back to the mirror, his face back to being solemn, thoughtful, 'Same rules as before. When you're throwing your punches, imagine Lorraine in front of you, jeering. And throw those punches *hard* to her body and her face!'

Thinking that I've connected with him a little better, I tease: 'You're so bossy!'

'That's what my girlfriend says.'

With my bubble burst, it's back to the business of boxing.

Chapter 26

Friday, 14 September 1984

It's audition day for the new keyboard player for the Clyde Alloys and Paul, Marie, Geraldine and I have nipped home after school to change our clothes in time for Ruaridh's tryout for the band. We're seated on rows of wooden chairs in a loose semi-circle in the upstairs rehearsal room in Round Sounds.

In one half of the front row of the semi-circle, Doll sits with the band members. Tommy isn't wearing sunglasses today, perhaps so that he can get a better look at the people auditioning. Steve seems to avoid looking at me, concentrating on chatting and laughing with Doll and the band.

I'm guessing that this unusual behaviour may be explained by the fact that I'm sat beside Paul, in the other half of the front row, who's making it obvious that he's my boyfriend. I wriggle out from under his arm, using the excuse of making myself more comfortable so that I can turn sideways to talk with Geraldine and Marie.

About a dozen various people belonging to the auditionees sit behind us.

As we wait for the first up, I do my best to appear fascinated by the banter between Paul, Geraldine, and Marie. Meanwhile, out of the side of my eye, I keep a close watch on Steve. These last few weeks of early morning training with him have felt so precious and exciting. I've worked so hard in these sessions, training and practising as Steve has taught me, to please him, to please me. I must work harder, though, to keep my thoughts and growing feelings about him under control. In the gym, I force myself to look serious so that he doesn't guess I'm having stupid thoughts about him, and when I have a boyfriend already.

As I talk with my pals, my heartbeat quickens every time I catch Geraldine making eyes and pouting her lips over in Steve's direction. I'm pretty sure he's absorbed in conversation, oblivious to her blatant attempts to catch his attention. Still, I squash the envy and frustration bubbling inside of me.

I'm sorely tested when Geraldine purrs while gazing at Steve: 'I can't believe that you were in the arms of that total dreamboat, Aileen.' At this moment, I could honestly throttle her. Paul's body stiffens beside me.

'Would you like a wooden spoon, Geraldine? See if you can stir some more?' Marie quips – I'm guessing to lighten the mood.

None of us is smiling.

Summoning the coldest tone I can in my voice, I mutter: 'There was nothing romantic about our encounter. You seem to forget that he saved me from a brutal battering.'

Geraldine examines her new false fingernails. Paul's body relaxes against me, and he drapes his arm back across my shoulder again. Great. And Steve still isn't looking over in my direction.

In the front of the room, the Clyde Alloys' instruments sit ready, from their practice earlier, with Tommy's keyboard equipment set up in the centre.

First to enter the room is a man wearing round tortoiseshell glasses, a pink bow tie and a paisley-patterned waistcoat. Clearing his throat, his hands tremble as he fusses over the keyboard and opens his music book. Sandy leans over to the lads. 'He can read music. That's a plus.' The Clyde Alloys nod, but I'm guessing by their faces that they're not so impressed by how the man is dressed. I suppress a grin as Tommy mutters, 'Fuck sake, I thought Stevie's dress sense was bad.'

Sandy indicates to the man in the bow tie to begin.

Some dramatic swirling notes fill the room, and it takes me a moment to register that he's playing a hymn. I pinch my lips together to stop myself from laughing. The band members are Protestants, with at least two of them in the Orange Lodge.

The keyboard player, engrossed in the music, moves his hands across the keys, fixing his specs as he turns each page of his music book.

After a few minutes, Sandy coughs and raises his hand in a stop motion. The man lifts his fingers from the keyboard, looking puzzled.

'Is that religious music you're playing?'

The man blinks, his eyes like saucers behind his glasses. 'Yes, I play the organ at the chapel.'

Tommy mutters again, 'He's a fuckin' Fenian. Bet his name's "Tim"!'

Paul shifts beside me, and I sense Geraldine and Marie's unease.

Sandy tries to be diplomatic. 'Eh, we're more into rock and pop music. Can you play anything else?'

'Not really. But if you give me the sheet music for your songs, I'll be able to learn them.'

Sandy huddles the Clyde Alloys around him for a confab. After a minute, Sandy sits back on his chair and shakes his head. 'Sorry, pal. You can play, but you're far too good for us. We're not a good fit for you.'

The man opens his mouth, perhaps to protest, but recognises it's a no. His head down, his people come to help him pack away his equipment, and they shuffle out of the room.

'Next!' Sandy roars. A wiry boy of about fourteen or fifteen pokes his head around the door and saunters into the room. 'This for the audition?'

'Certainly is, pal. Come on in.' Tommy stands to show the boy where to go.

With his hands clenched by his side, the laddie swaggers to a chair in front of the room. He takes a seat, facing us.

'So, are you not going to play for us?' Frankie Fingers, the bass player, asks.

'Play?' The laddie scowls.

'Yip!' Tommy points to his keyboard. 'Show us what you got, then.'

The boy hops off his chair to stand in front of the keyboard and presses some keys, apparently in random order. We exchange puzzled glances.

'Can you play a song?' Sandy prompts, frowning.

'Aw, I can't play, mister. I want to be in a band – I thought youz could teach me.'

After him, there are another half a dozen who can't play, or the band didn't think they'd fit in. As each auditionee leaves the room, the chairs behind us empty. Only Ruaridh is left to audition, and Paul, Geraldine, Marie, and I, are his support squad.

Tommy leans back on his chair, his hands behind his head, a satisfied look on his face. 'Seems like there's no one better than me. Looks like you're going to have to scrape the barrel and get back in touch with "Tim".'

Frankie Fingers sits forward. 'I don't care if he's a Catholic, but we'd need to rattle some dress sense into him! Anyway, we've still got one more.' He gestures with his hand in our direction, a smile tugging at his lips. 'Last one's with them. I guess he's a "Tim", too. Isn't that right, Aileen?'

I smile back at him. Steve still faces straight ahead.

Paul makes a show of pecking me on the cheek as he leaves the room to fetch Ruaridh. As they enter, Geraldine perks up, pouting her lips, tucking her hair behind her ears, now trying to get Ruaridh's attention. Marie and I roll our eyes at each other, smirking. I turn to Doll, who's also trying not to grin. I know she's been keeping an eye on Geraldine. Steve's watching Paul and Ruaridh set up. Apart from a quick nod when we first arrived, he hasn't acknowledged me.

It's so strange for me to have Paul and Steve in the same room. As Paul works alongside Ruaridh, I spot him stealing glances at Steve. When Paul's finished helping Ruaridh, he rubs my arm as he takes his seat beside me. I sense Steve watching us.

'How do you want to do this?' Ruaridh calls.

Sandy tosses his hair. 'Just play. Whatever comes to mind.'

'As long as it's not a hymn!' Frankie Fingers adds, chuckling. Paul bristles beside me.

Ruaridh pauses for a moment, hovers his hands over the keyboards and plays "Dream On" by Aerosmith. Everyone smiles, except Tommy, who flops his hand in the air like he's waving away a half-cooked dinner in a restaurant. 'Maybe something a little more recent?'

The electric notes of "Jump" by Van Halen soon have Steve and Rab singing along, playing outrageous air guitar and Sandy drumming out the beat with the sides of his hand on his knees.

As Ruaridh nears the end of the tune, Tommy frowns. 'What about something British that we might play?'

Tommy shakes his head impatiently as Ruaridh plays the piano introduction to "Bohemian Rhapsody". 'Okay, old tune again, pal.' Ruaridh begins to play again, twisting between keyboards, and I recognise that he's created a medley of tracks by Howard Jones and Nik Kershaw.

Sandy claps his hands loudly. 'Impressive! Can you play anything else?'

'I can play a few other instruments, and I sing a bit too. Would you like me to sing?' Sandy nods, and Ruaridh moves the microphone across to his mouth while he picks out a tune on the keyboard. I melt when he performs my da's favourite, John Lennon's "Imagine".

Sandy stands, hitching his jeans. 'Come on, boys, grab your instruments. I think we've found our new member; let's hear how we sound together.' The Clyde Alloys join Ruaridh in a huddle and exchange a few words, slapping each other on the back.

With the band re-assembled at the front of the room, Sandy taps his sticks together, Ruaridh plays the opening bars of U2's "New Year's Day", and the rest of the band joins in. The hairs on the back of my neck bristle. When I look around, everyone, apart from Tommy, is grinning at each other. The band works with Ruaridh, and he suits the Clyde Alloys.

We chair dance to the song, tapping out the beat with our feet and singing the song – all, except Tommy. He pulls his hair back and puts his sunglasses on. 'Okay, guys. You've got your keyboard player.' He leaps to his feet, salutes us and turns to walk out – straight into the door jamb. Tommy's back stiffens. He whips his sunglasses off and barrels down the hall.

There's a pause, and then everyone erupts into laughter.

Frankie Fingers chuckles, 'I bet that wasn't the dramatic exit he was planning!' Fresh peals of laughter fill the room. It takes us a few more minutes to compose ourselves.

'He thought we'd be devastated when he left, and now he knows we've found a better keyboard player, and one who can sing too. We'll be on Radio Clyde with our own music before his new band is!' Sandy grins, his arms wide.

The Clyde Alloys gather around Ruaridh to shake his hand. I grin at the girls and turn to Paul, who leans over to give me a celebratory hug. My chin on Paul's shoulder, I look up to find Steve finally watching me. I smile at him; he frowns in return.

Chapter 27

Friday, 14 September 1984

To celebrate Ruaridh joining the Clyde Alloys, Geraldine and Marie take him and Paul to their favourite pub Jinkie's, down a side street off Woodburn High Street. I've made plans to go with Doll to our favourite fish and chip shop first, to have a catch up.

Normally, Doll gives me half of her chips, but as she's expecting a baby, I only take one from her now and again. We sit on the library wall beside the bus stop, swinging our legs and chatting.

'The audition was a bit awkward for you, eh?' Doll's eyes twinkle mischievously.

'What with having Paul there?' I could pretend that I don't know what Doll's talking about, but she knows me too well.

'And Steve.' Doll prompts. 'I felt like Paul was making a deliberate show of being touchy-feely with you in front of him. He kept taking sneaky looks at Steve.'

I dig a chip out of the wrapping paper. 'I thought Paul was over the top, too. It made me uncomfortable.'

'Are you going to break up with him soon?'

'I've tried.' I mumble as I gulp down some chips. 'He threatens me with splitting up, then changes his mind once I start agreeing.' I confess some more. 'I'm also a bit scared of not being with him, you know?'

Doll crunches on a chip. 'What? *Can't live with him, can't live without him*, type of idea?'

'Something like that. Paul, Marie, and Geraldine were my very first pals when I came back from South Africa. Paul's been there for me before and after my mammie died. He held me. He listened to me. He was there to pick up the pieces.' I shake my head. 'Breaking up with him is letting go of a piece of my past. It would change everything – yet it's feeling more right to me.'

Doll offers me some chips, which she snatches away at the last moment to stuff in her mouth.

This makes me laugh and breaks the tension. And for good measure, Doll watches my face as she adds: 'That Geraldine isn't very subtle. She's a right man-eater, eh? I was keeping my eye on her to make sure she wasn't going to throw any of those pouty lips in my Sandy's direction!'

'Couldn't even imagine your reaction!'

Doll splutters. 'I'd rip they false nails right off her and stick them where the sun don't shine! She wouldn't be pouting at anyone else's man after that, I can tell you!'

I giggle, pleased to have an opportunity to express what I've been thinking about Geraldine. 'Aye, she was *ripping my knitting*, as my gran would say. I've heard her tell stories of what she gets up to in pubs and clubs, but today was an eye-opener, seeing her in action. She was working three guys!'

'Yip. She's definitely well-practised at it. Keep your eye on her.' Doll burps loudly as she takes a swig from a bottle of Irn Bru. An old lady draws her a dirty look as she shuffles past. Doll grins at her.

Wishing to change the subject, I remind Doll that tomorrow we'll be having our fittings done for the dresses. 'I can't get my head around the fact that in six weeks you'll be a married woman!'

'I know. Married and up the duff at eighteen!'

'Your mum and dad coming round to the idea more?'

'Slowly. They aren't happy with the order that things are happening. Mum says that we can't live on love alone, not with a kid – says that Sandy needs to find a proper job.'

I find a crunchy chip that I pop into my mouth. 'Are you worried about the future?'

'Nah. It wasn't what I planned, but a baby with Sandy was what I wanted eventually. It's just come a bit sooner. Mum and Dad just need to get used to it!' Doll's face tightens.

'They're just worried about you.'

'It's getting me down. All couples start with nothing and then work their way up to a place of their own. They forget that's how it was for them when they were first married.'

'What about Sandy's parents?'

Doll's brow furrows as she scoffs the last of her chips. 'Well, after the good initial reaction, the truth is coming out more. Apparently, they think I've deliberately set out to trap Sandy by getting pregnant! I gave them a piece of my mind – I wouldn't normally disrespect them like that, but the hormones make me brave and, frankly, not give a toss!'

She hands me the chip paper to hold and hops off the wall, surprisingly nimble for being four months pregnant. 'I'd best stop eating chips, or Mammie's dressmaker pal will have to let my dress out!' She wipes her greasy fingers on the outside of the chip paper, crumples it and fires it into a nearby bin like a pro basketball player.

'You're hardly showing.'

'I know, but six weeks can make a big difference – apparently, my stomach can just suddenly pop out before the wedding. Mrs Hooper says she'll build a special panel into the tummy area and design the dress so that the attention is on my bust. I've finally got one!' Doll nudges up her new, fuller breasts to make an impressive cleavage. She winks at me, 'Check these puppies out!'

A man passing us whistles at Doll, who gives him the V sign in return.

She turns her attention back to me. 'Do you know where the wedding dress shop is?

I shake my head.

'It's up from the train station, not far from Jinkie's. It's called Dreams Do Come True.'

'Seriously?'

'Seriously. Mrs Hooper thinks that it's every young lassie's dream to be married.'

'Is it yours?'

'Aye. I can't think of anything better than being married to Sandy and with our baby on the way.' Doll cradles her slight bump, smiling. 'What about you? Do you want to be married?'

'When I'm thirty or something.'

'Thirty! You'll be an old woman by then!'

'No, I won't!'

As I'm about to tell Doll more of my plans for the future, she interrupts me. 'Oh, and I almost forgot – the Council's offered us a flat.'

'A place of your own? That's quick!'

'I wouldn't get too excited. It's in Bonny View housing estate.'

'Concrete Jungle?'

'The very same. Bandit Country. Shit Tip. Land of Reprobates and Junkies.'

'Someone at the Council had a sense of humour when they named the place *Bonny View!*' I chuckle.

Doll wrinkles her nose. 'We've still to view the flat. We can refuse it, but that'll put us at the bottom of the list. Sandy's dad wouldn't be pleased cos he had to pull a few strings with some pals of his from the lodge to get us the offer.'

'You never know. It could be decent?'

Doll mock whistles, gazing upwards. 'Did you see that pig fly across the sky?' When she presses her lips together and a shadow of a smile begins to appear, I know she's doing her best to look on the bright side.

She pinches my arm as her bus pulls alongside us. 'See you tomorrow at Dreams Do Come True! Come prepared for petticoats, frills, and veils!' Doll skips onto the bus and waves at me like a big kid from the back window.

I wave back, grinning. My heart lifts at the sight of her, but the more I wave, the heavier the shroud of sadness descends on me. My best pal is changing before my eyes.

⋅⋙⋅⋅◆⋅⋅⋘⋅

As I step forward to enter the gloom and smoke of Jinkie's, my left foot slides out of its shoe and gets stuck to the carpet. Ducking my head, I'm hoping that no one saw my entrance. I plant my sticky foot back into its shoe and bend my toes to stop them from being sucked off my feet again as I make my way through the crowd.

The dress code in here seems to be black, perhaps because the place is so dingy. I spot Geraldine and Marie waving at me from the booth they are sitting in with Paul and Ruaridh. Although they're wearing different dark-coloured tops, I notice that Geraldine and Marie are wearing short black skirts, fishnet tights and silver-buckled army-type boots, which I think would make light work of the sticky carpet. I'm regretting wearing my white skirt and pink top and I wonder why Geraldine and Marie didn't warn me.

I thought McCoy's was loud and smoky inside, but Jinkie's takes the biscuit. Heavy metal music blares from the jukebox, and the smoke hangs so heavy around the light suspended over the pool table that I'm surprised that the players can see each other never mind the balls on the table. Jinkie's has seen better days, I decide, but it's still packed because the drink's cheap and the bouncers aren't so bothered about how old you are.

Marie stands to usher me closer to their booth. The table brims with half-empty drinks glasses, crumpled crisp packets and a full ashtray. Yellowed stuffing bursts through the faded red velvet and cigarette-burned seat coverings, reminding me of the inside of a Crunchie bar. Paul and Ruaridh grin at me as I approach, swaying slightly in their seats – both tipsy. They totter to the well-lit bar to buy the next round, screwing their eyes like moles against the bright lights of the bar.

Geraldine plops across one of the low stools around the table to make space, and Marie and I sit in the booth. Geraldine yells: 'I'm so glad we went to Ruaridh's audition! The band are so good, aren't they?'

Marie nods by my side. 'I got shivers when they started playing "New Year's Day". I'm definitely going to their gigs!' She ruffles her short red hair to make it spikier.

'And, oh my God! Steve! Aileen – he's a total dreamboat!' Geraldine reaches to take my arm, and I pretend not to notice that she misses. 'Promise you'll let us know the next time they play?'

I nod, knowing that I won't be going out of my way to do this.

Geraldine's on a roll. 'I can't believe how drunk the laddies are! Have you ever seen Paul that drunk, Aileen?'

I admit that I haven't. A heavy unease settles on me.

'We've had a few vodkas since we got here, so we're ready for a party!' Geraldine throws her arms in the air and, with a sly grin, leans over and winks at us. 'Maybe I can make a move on Ruaridh tonight?' Marie squirms in her seat. Before I can ask her if she's okay, the laddies return to the table with drinks trays. They've bought double rounds for everyone and included double whisky chasers for themselves to go with their pints.

'They don't serve long vodkas here.' Paul informs me. 'So I got you a couple of vodkas and Irn Bru.'

Accepting the drinks with a forced smile, I consider downing at least one of them to try and catch up with my pals. I decide against that, though, because I want to be clear-headed tomorrow when I meet Doll and her mother for the dress fitting. I'm also in training – I don't quite know what for yet – but it's with Steve, and the thought of that always makes me happy. I miss Steve. It was difficult to be ignored by him in Round Sounds earlier. I'm guessing he did that to protect me because my pals and Paul don't know that I see him practically every day for boxing training. Still, that was hard to have him so close to me yet be so distant. What is happening to me? I need to stop thinking this way – Steve is just my trainer. I have a boyfriend. He has a girlfriend.

We settle into our night, the guys giggling as they tell stories, and Geraldine and Marie hanging on to their every word. Ruaridh talks of his plans with the Clyde Alloys and how excited he is to have found a decent band. He mentions how cool the guys were with him, especially Steve. As soon as Steve's name is mentioned, there is a noticeable change around the table. Paul pulls me in tighter to him, his arm weighing heavy on my shoulder. I shuffle out from under his arm and lean against him instead.

'Steve can play too, and with someone as gorgeous as him as the lead singer, the band's going to pull in crowds of lassies.' Geraldine taps her cigarette against the ashtray. She's only recently started smoking. I think she's taken it up because she thinks it looks sexy or something. She just looks like a gothic Puff the Magic Dragon to me.

'And Aileen was the lucky girl who was rescued by him.' Geraldine continues, smirking. She's deliberately trying to cause trouble, but I'm too scared to call her out on it because I don't want to lose her friendship. Even if she's the one in the wrong, like I always do, I will choose a different moment to speak up.

'Do you fancy Steve?' Paul slurs into my ear.

I shift away from him. 'No!'

'Don't deny it, Aileen. I've seen how you look at him – and I've caught how he looks at you.'

Unable to resist, 'How does he look at me?'

Paul's face twists like I've stabbed him in the heart.

I jump to correct what I've just said. 'I mean – I'm with you.' Paul looks unconvinced, so I search for a lie to avoid hurting him. I feign disinterest. 'I don't know what the big deal is about Steve anyway. Why would I be interested in him when I have my very own Italian Stallion?'

It turns out that flattery does work, and Paul's face softens as he leans over to peck me on the cheek. 'Why do I love you, Aileen Murphy?'

'Because I'm so cute?' My stomach twists. How false am I being? But the devil in me has come out as I sense Geraldine glaring at us, so I snuggle closer into Paul to annoy her.

Drinking does strange things to people. Paul and Ruaridh have become like naughty schoolboys who've been dodging the headmaster. Geraldine becomes louder, more wide-eyed and exaggerated in her gestures, desperately trying to attract Ruaridh's attention. He seems to be more interested in talking to Marie, though, and she, to him. As the night goes on, their heads and bodies bend closer together as they become more engrossed in their private conversation.

Geraldine scowls at Ruaridh and Marie, unable to join in their intimate-looking conversation because the music's now gotten so loud. She turns her attention to Paul and me. Nodding over in Ruaridh and Marie's direction, she remarks, 'I think they'll have lots of ginger babies together.'

'You sound a little bitter, Geraldine?' By the delayed expression on her face, I can tell she's drunk.

The music gets louder, and the three of us have a shouty conversation for a while. Geraldine calls something out to Paul, and she nudges her chair closer to him to hear what he's saying. I watch the two of them in disbelief, as laughing, they lean into each other's necks as they exchange words. At one point, Geraldine nuzzles Paul's ear and places her hand high on his thigh. I'm thinking she'll move her hand soon, but she doesn't. She slides it to rest further up Paul's thigh. It appears that I'm not here.

My stomach clenches when she leans back, laughing at something Paul has said, and she pouts her lips, giving my boyfriend a blatant come-on look. I glance over to Marie and Ruaridh for moral support, but they're oblivious, too engrossed in each other. The pub's becoming more packed with very drunk people, as Jinkie's has a late licence.

Still too scared to say anything and still being that annoying, frighteningly polite person I try to be in case I'm reading too much into situations, I sit back, a silent witness. This must be what morbid fascination feels like when, as a bystander, you stand powerless, watching as a car crash unfolds before your eyes. Geraldine's face is buried against Paul's neck as she talks into his ear. They both giggle and glance across at me. Geraldine stands and sashays off to the toilet. 'What was she saying to you?' My mind explodes as a thousand thoughts collide.

Paul stops grinning and looks serious. 'Actually, she was telling me how sorry she is for me that I'm still a virgin and that my frigid girlfriend won't sleep with me.' My mouth drops open, and I'm sure I've not heard him correctly. Paul understands and repeats it to me with a nasty look on his face. He tells me he's going to the bar and disappears into the throng.

Dejected and confused, I slump deeper into the booth, struggling to process what is happening. I'm surrounded by a sea of laughing people, and Ruaridh and Marie are now cooried together, kissing. This is another surprise I didn't see coming. I was so sure that Ruaridh fancied Geraldine, but no, it turns out that he prefers the quieter and gentler Marie. I'm glad they've gotten together; they suit each other better. I sip some more of my drink and tap my fingers on the table as I wait for Paul to return. The next heavy metal song comes on, and then the next one. My ears ring from the speaker noise. Five songs later, I'm starting to worry. There's a big queue at the bar, though, so he must be somewhere near the front by now, waiting to be served.

Then my thoughts turn to Geraldine. Maybe she's being sick in the toilet, or she's reapplying her make-up and doing her hair. Disbelief, disappointment, and anger bubble inside me. I can't believe that one of my best friends would make an actual move on my boyfriend in front of me. I clench my fists. I was wrong when I told Steve I couldn't hurt somebody because now I believe I could quite happily deck Geraldine, the cheeky cow! In fact, I am going to find her right now and give her a piece of my mind. I'll even interrupt her puking if that's what she's doing.

As I march towards the toilets, my attention's caught by a plump figure, with its sleeves rolled up, as it muscles its way to the bar. Too late to turn back, Lorraine Pollock spots me and lunges through the crowd in my direction. The front door is too far to reach, so I spin on my heels to head towards the toilets to hopefully lock myself in a cubicle. The loos are off a hallway. I shove people out of the way as I sprint in search of the ladies' toilet sign. I spot a fire door ahead. Never one to break the rules – now's the time to start doing just that. In my hurry, the fluted sleeve of my blouse catches on a door handle stopping me in my tracks. I yank it free just in time to crash through the fire door as Lorraine comes flying towards me.

Outside, I slam the door behind me, my heart ricocheting inside my chest. I rapidly assess my options. It's hard to see outside, and I can hardly hear myself think. Even out here, the deep bass of the heavy metal music booms, and the laughter and chatter of the crowds inside can still be heard. *Think, Aileen. Think!* I figure if I follow the building round to the right, that should lead me back to the street. In the gloom, up against a perimeter wall, there's a skip, and some beer barrels are piled high.

For once in my life, I decide not to run. Lorraine may already be lying in wait for me out front. I dart to hide behind the skip. Hunkering in the darkness, I edge as close as I can to the cold metal. Panting, I watch the fire door, my eyes adjusting to the darkness. I wait. A piercing whistle, shouts and laughter echo in the air from what must be the front of the building – that's the direction I'll head in when I think the coast is clear.

I could do with Frodo's invisibility ring right now, and a peg for my nose. I hold my breath as I can almost taste the stink wafting from the skip and beer barrels. Is this really my life? I'm being hunted down by my arch-enemy, hiding behind a stinky skip, scared out of my wits. While I want to move, I force myself to wait some more. If Lorraine had been coming after me, she would have burst through the door by now. I bide where I am, just in case.

After about ten minutes, my breathing steadies. Maybe I can make a run for it now? I listen. In the brief silence between records being changed on the jukebox, my mind latches on to some strange sounds ahead, somewhere within my escape route. I peer in their direction.

My heart stops as a shape shifts against the wall of the building. Is it Lorraine creeping towards me? The hairs on the back of my neck stand up. I wait, a coiled spring ready to load.

The shape shifts and moans. This isn't Lorraine. My skin crawls. Is it a ghost?

Breathing rapidly, my heart jackhammers inside my chest. I grip the side of the skip, working hard to ignore the smell of my hiding spot. I know I need to run for it. And now!

Suddenly, the shape shifts to become more of a rhythmic pulse. I'm frozen to the spot, my legs trembling. The shape shrieks and pants and becomes faster in its movement. Inch by inch, I edge more around the skip, and now I can see a streetlight just around the corner of the building.

I bolt for the light.

'Aileen?'

I stare uncomprehendingly as Paul's slurred voice drifts from the shape that seems to have folded into itself and separated. Half of the shape sashays towards me, pulling its skirt down.

The grinning face of Geraldine approaches me from the darkness.

Chapter 28

Saturday, 15 September 1984

'Yes, well, they were always planning to get married. When you've found 'the one', that's it, isn't it?' I'm sitting alone in the waiting area of the Dreams Do Come True wedding dress shop listening to the high-pitched voice of Doll's mother, Mrs McLintock, drift through the closed door of the bride-to-be's changing room. She's chatting to her friend, Mrs Hooper, the dressmaker.

'Lots of young women get 'caught' nowadays, and – well, it's different from our days – people are more accepting of people having babies outside of wedlock.'

'The baby won't be *born* out of wedlock!' Mrs McLintock interrupts Mrs Hooper, sounding horrified.

'I know. I meant – '

'I know what you meant, but our Doll will be a blushing bride just like any other.'

'Will you two stop talking as though I'm not here?' Doll sounds a little irritated.

Her mother hasn't heard her, though. 'And she'll hold her head up high. She's not done anything that her friends haven't been doing – well – ' Mrs McLintock lowers her posh voice, but I can still hear her. 'Except the pal outside. She's a Catholic, you see.'

Shocked at first, I bite my lip to stop myself laughing aloud as, without missing a beat, Mrs Hooper replies, 'Catholics do it too, you know.'

Swinging my legs, I wait patiently, listening to the fussing and sighing noises coming from the bride-to-be's changing room. Suddenly, the door is unbolted, and Mrs McLintock and Mrs Hooper scurry over to where I am. We turn to watch Doll as she glides into the main reception area, a beaming vision in white.

'You look like an angel. So beautiful!' I gasp.

'Thanks!' Doll turns to admire herself in the main mirror in the reception area.

Standing in front of her daughter, Mrs McLintock tugs on both sides of Doll's veil and steps back to survey her. 'Well, no one's going to say we skimped on your wedding. Only the very best for our one and only child.' She dabs at a wee tear in her eye, and we smile at each other.

With some final tweaks and slow twirls in the mirror, Doll's ushered back into the bridal changing room.

It's my turn next. I watch in the full-length mirror as Mrs Hooper tucks and pins the bridesmaid dress onto me. It's a midnight blue silk fabric, and the sweetheart neckline sits snugly across my bust. It will be the fanciest dress I've ever worn.

'Your boyfriend's going to cry when he sees you, hen.' Mrs Hooper's remark takes me by surprise.

How prophetic those words are. 'He'll certainly cry.' It's not until you're about to break up with your boyfriend that you realise how much people talk about you being part of a couple.

Perhaps alerted by my cool tone and stony face, Mrs Hooper looks up at me and glances over to Doll and Mrs McLintock. So far, I've managed to act how I think you're supposed to act at dress fittings – all girly, secret squirrelly. To be fair, that part wasn't hard earlier when we were admiring Doll in her wedding dress. That truly was a breathtaking moment and made me so happy for her, but little by little, that happiness has leaked away as flashbacks from last night keep coming back to me.

My shoulders tense as Mrs McLintock asks: 'What are your plans for your hair, Aileen?' I've tossed and turned so much through the night that I was forced to tie back my frizzy hair into a ponytail.

Doll beams. 'Aileen's getting her hair permed at the same time as Sandy and I. Steve's mum's going to do it for us next month.'

'Your arms and shoulders are very ... toned ... like that Madonna.' Mrs Hooper observes.

'Aileen's training to be a boxer!' Doll grins, clearly enjoying the look of shock on her mother's and Mrs Hooper's faces.

I scowl at Doll. 'It's supposed to be a secret!'

'Women don't box ...' Mrs McLintock's mouth twitches into a strained smile.

'I do!' I force a cheerful note into my voice, noting the irony of what I'm declaring in a wedding dress shop.

I'm in no mood to explain or be judged right now, and definitely not by Doll's snooty mother. I don't know why, but on impulse, I brought Mammie's crystal bead with me. I have my fist clenched tightly over it, enjoying the comfort that it's bringing me right now.

Finally, pinned into my dress, I turn to face Doll and her mother.

'You look so pretty!' Doll's eyes twinkle as she sits arm-in-arm with her mother. Right now, even though I know they have their differences, this sight fills me with envy and sadness.

Forcing a smile, I crush Mammie's crystal bead deeper into my palm. A longing for my own mammie washes over me. I miss her more than ever. A lump forms in my throat. I reach deep to compose myself. I don't want to spoil this special day for Doll and Mrs McLintock.

A crazy but comforting thought occurs to me at that moment. I offer the crystal bead to Mrs Hooper. 'This was my late mammie's. Could you stitch it into the dress somewhere?'

'I know just the place.' Mrs Hooper pops my bead into a blue velvet box. Tears prick my eyes when she replies, 'Now she'll be with you on Doll's big day.'

The lump in my throat grows until it's the size of a small rock. I swallow hard, trying to make it smaller so that I can breathe, but it's no use.

Before I can stop it, the tears explode, and a strange wailing noise comes out of my mouth. I can't explain myself to the three shocked faces in front of me. I want to run straight out of the door and away down Woodburn High Street, but I have a dress half pinned onto me, so I bolt into an adjacent changing room.

Tapping on the door, Doll asks to come in. I open the door for her. The changing room is mirrored on every wall. I stand with my back to Doll but can see her in the mirror.

She takes some steps towards me and wrings her hands. 'I'm sorry. You must be missing your mum. I didn't think – of course, all this bride and mother-of-the-bride stuff will upset you.'

'I'm the one who's sorry. I didn't mean to put a dampener on your big day. Yes, I miss Mammie.' I swipe tears from my face. 'But there's something else, too. Paul and I have split up. I caught him and Geraldine at it last night.'

I tell Doll the whole sordid story. I remind her about how Geraldine's been dropping hints about fancying Paul, then Ruaridh, and was even making eyes at Steve yesterday. About how when Ruaridh and Marie got together, she then moved on to Paul.

'What a tart! What a cow!' Doll hugs me and offers me a hankie.

Wiping my tears, I notice in the mirror that my face and neck have gone red and blotchy again. 'Paul's not blameless either. He'd gotten so drunk. Think he's jealous of Steve, so he was trying to make me jealous by flirting with Geraldine, but they took it too far. I feel so hurt, humiliated, and stupid! Betrayed by two of the people closest to me. What do you do after something like this?'

'I don't know. You were thinking of leaving him. Maybe this tells you that you were right to think that.'

I nod, even as fresh tears drip from my face.

There's a tentative knocking at the door. 'So sorry to interrupt ladies, but the next bridal party's arrived for their appointment. Could we have the changing room back, please?'

As I hand the dress back to Mrs Hooper, she says, with a kind look: 'Being without your mammie is hard at any age. I'll create a wee centrepiece of your crystal bead on this dress; make it beautiful for you and her.'

Sniffing, I do my best to smile. 'Thank you.'

'You're never alone, you know.'

Why do I feel so lonely, then?

Chapter 29

Saturday, 15 September 1984

Deep in thought about Paul and Geraldine, as I walk home from the dress fitting, I'm only vaguely aware of a bus pulling alongside me and a passenger getting off. The person sways as they stumble towards me – I'm guessing because they're drunk – and it's only lunchtime. Too late, I realise that it's Lorraine Pollock. That familiar feeling of fear cascades through my body. Not that I'm ever in the mood to get battered, but today is not a good day for me to cross swords with Lorraine.

Thoughts tumble through my mind. What do I do? Do I run away as usual? Do I use my boxing? How do I start a fight anyway? Throw her a few jabs? She's not another boxer who's going to spar with me, who knows the rules of the game. What does it feel like to physically hit someone instead of just pretending? How bad will it hurt my fists when they connect with her body?

'Aw, look who it is! You were like that wee voodoo princess, Zola Budd, nippin' oot that fire exit last night.'

As she approaches, I'm trying to work out what her first move might be and how I should react. What boxing punches should I use? My skin prickles, and my fists tighten by my sides. But then, as my mind goes utterly blank, my body begins to tremble. I'm about to get battered. Again. My brain screams at me to run, but I'm frozen to the spot. Do I want to be beaten, maybe to stop the pain inside?

Lorraine steps in front of my face. My heart beats out of its rib cage. Please let this be over soon. I brace myself.

To my surprise, she sighs and steps to the side. She staggers away from me, calling over her shoulder, 'Can't be arsed! Fuck off, Fenian floozie!'

I exhale slowly. Lorraine Pollock has never missed the chance to beat or torment me, especially when she's drunk. What's changed? Has Tony Pollock kept his promise to ensure that she never touches me again? Or has Lorraine somehow heard that I'm learning to box, and she's afraid? Hope flowers inside of me.

⋅⋅⋅

When I arrive home, Da and Gran are deep in conversation in the living room but break off talking when I enter. It can't be about Paul because I haven't told them yet. It turns out that it is.

'Paul's called round a few times.' Gran scratches her lip. 'Have you two had a falling out?'

I'm about to deny it when Gran hands me an envelope and a Rolo chocolate wrapped in gold foil. 'He left these for you, said he's sorry.'

'Miserable git, not even a full packet of Rolos!'

My attempt at humour falls flat with Gran. 'He seemed really upset.' She glances at Da.

'I don't want to talk about it.' I place the Rolo and envelope on the mantlepiece to show that the subject is closed.

When I turn, Da and Gran are still watching me. 'What's the matter?' I sit beside Da on the couch. Gran perches herself forward on her armchair.

'We're worried about wee Mary. She doesn't seem very well.'

'Is it her asthma?'

'Aye,' Gran sighs. 'And her eczema is bad too, even though she tries to hide it. We've decided to take her to the doctor – find out if we can get her some extra help. She's just not herself, the wee soul.'

Da takes my hand. 'Can you maybe talk to her, kid? See if anything else is bothering her?'

My chest tightens. I've been so absorbed in my stuff that I've neglected wee Mary at a time when she's been needing me.

'She's in her room now. Gran says she's put on her nightie and gone to bed.' Da bites his lip.

'It's only lunchtime.'

'Exactly.' Da frowns and lets my hand go. 'Go see her, please.'

Upstairs, I tiptoe to wee Mary's room. She sniffles as I nudge the door open to step into the gloom of her bedroom. 'Are you okay?' Her curtains are drawn, and the room is in darkness. I pad over in the direction of the lump that is wee Mary underneath her bed covers.

The sniffles turn into sobs. Sitting on the edge of wee Mary's bed, my eyes adjust to the dimness in the room. Wee Mary's lying on her side; her dark hair spread across her pillow. Cornflake, her giant teddy bear, sits at the bottom of her bed. It looks like wee Mary's holding something in her arms.

Stroking her damp face, I ask wee Mary why she's crying. She continues to weep. Instinctively, I bend to hug her to me, but recoil when she yelps and shoves me off.

'Mary? What's wrong?' I sit back on the edge of the bed, being careful not to touch her and wait until her sobbing subsides. She wipes her face with the sleeve of her nightie and settles onto her side, turning away from me, cuddling the object. I can't quite make out what it is. It doesn't look like her teddy bear or one of her dolls. 'What's that you're holding?'

Wee Mary curls the object further into her body.

I decide to leave her alone and come back later. 'Okay, remember, I'm always here for you when you want a wee blether.' I stand.

'It's Our Lady.' Wee Mary wheezes. She faces back towards me, carefully sits up and offers me the statue.

Gran's statue of Our Lady lies warm in my hands. 'I thought you were cuddling a toy.'

'I've been praying to Mammie and Our Lady, asking them to come back to help me. If Our Lady comes back to visit me again, I know everything's going to be okay.'

'Help you with what?'

Wee Mary pauses.

'Nothing.' Wee Mary rasps, her breath becoming more rapid.

I bound over to the light switch and snap it on. Wee Mary screws her eyes, protesting as she dives under the blanket. 'Switch off the light!' Even from under the blanket, the sandpapery noise of wee Mary scratching herself can be heard. She does that when she's upset or anxious, and of course, it only makes her eczema worse.

'Stop that!' I throw back her bed covers. She burrows back inside, and as she does so, her nightie slips to reveal some marks on her skin that don't look like eczema scabs or scars. 'Stand up!'

Wee Mary curls into a sitting position on the edge of the bed and, from there, reluctantly rises.

'Lift your nightie!'

Wee Mary shakes her head. Fresh tears well in her eyes.

In one move, I whip off her nightie. I gasp. I do my best not to look too horrified at the sight of her body covered in sores. More terrifying, though, is that among the oozing scarlet scabs are purplish bruises snaking across her chest, ribs, arms, and legs.

Wee Mary snatches her nightie out of my hands and throws it back onto her body. 'Get out!'

'I'm not going anywhere until you tell me what's happened.'

'It's eczema.'

'I've never seen it this bad. How did the other marks happen?'

Her face crumples, and she wails as she steps towards me. She bends from her waist like she's bowing to me so that the only part of her which touches me is her forehead on my chest. She trembles as she whispers, 'I hurt so much.'

As I place my hand on her head, she winces, so I lighten my touch in response. My mind races. 'Tell me.'

'Only if you promise not to tell Gran or Da.'

I nod. She looks so vulnerable that I'd agree to anything to make her feel better.

'Everything hurts. My skin, my mind, my heart. I don't know what to do.'

I'm aching to hold her, to make it all better. Tears prick my eyes, but I must be strong for her sake. I gently lift her face to mine.

Wee Mary gasps, trying to speak through the wheezing. 'My skin is like paper. It itches so bad. I can't sleep. It hurts to wear clothes, and when I move, some of the sores crack, weep, and become stuck to what I'm wearing.'

She lowers her head, 'I'm so ashamed of what I look like. I've been dogging school. I hide under the old railway bridge until it's time to go home.' She steps back from me and sobs into the sleeve of her nightie.

'You poor thing. Why haven't you said anything?'

Wee Mary shakes her head and mumbles into her sleeve. 'I thought I could fix this myself.'

'We'll get you sorted with the doctor; don't you worry.' Afraid to ask, but knowing I need to know: 'How did the other marks happen?'

'That JoJo and Lorraine Pollock.'

It's not until my fingernails dig into my palms that I realise my hands have curled into fists. Deep regret grates on my heart. I heard wee Mary stir in her bedroom this morning, but I deliberately avoided her and the rest of my family because I was feeling so sorry for myself. I could have taken wee Mary to the dress fitting and saved her from being beaten.

'Why do they hate us?' Wee Mary picks up Our Lady again and holds her close.

I indicate to wee Mary to get back into bed and tug the bedclothes back over her. The blue of Our Lady's veil reminds me of a headscarf Mammie used to wear when she was ill. 'I'm not sure. Lorraine started picking on me almost as soon as we came back from South Africa. 'Her mum, Betty Pollock, didn't like Mammie, either.'

'Why? I couldn't imagine anyone not liking Mammie?'

'No idea. I always sensed tension between them when we passed on the street. One time – it was my twelfth birthday – my last one with Mammie, we were making apple tarts in the kitchen, and there was a loud hammering on our door. Lorraine was stood on our front door step with her mum, snivelling, nursing a black eye.'

Wee Mary shrinks back under her covers, but I know she's still listening.

'Betty Pollock demanded that Mammie take me out to her so that she could beat me for hitting Lorraine.'

'What? Lorraine told her mum that you'd given her a black eye?' Wee Mary keeks out from under the covers and shuffles her body back up to place her head on the pillow.

'Yes. Her mother's super scary too. She rolled up her sleeves, effin' and blinding, a really mean look on her face.' My stomach churns as I recall this memory. 'Poor Mammie was trying to stand her ground, but she was pretty ill by then. I felt so bad for her and terrified for both of us.'

Tears prick at my eyes. 'Then, Betty Pollock slapped Mammie so hard that she knocked her headscarf off. Mammie didn't have much hair left by then, and Betty Pollock laughed at her.'

Wee Mary gasps.

'I was so angry that I shoved her down the steps.' I grip wee Mary's hand. 'Before she could react, Mammie yanked me inside and put the chain on the door.'

'That must have been awful.'

'It was. Betty Pollock tried to kick the door in to get at me. She was making such a racket! All the neighbours were out, but none would get involved. Most of the Pollock family have done time in prison – including some of the women. Nobody messes with them; nobody would dare call the police on them.'

'What happened next?'

'Well, Mammie wasn't about to hand me over, but neither was Betty Pollock ready to stop trying to get her hands on me. So Mammie told her that she'd beat me, not her.'

Wee Mary's eyes widen. 'So, she thought you'd done it, too?'

'No. Mammie had to do something to get rid of the Pollocks. She told me to fetch one of Da's belts.'

Wee Mary gasps. 'She belted you – in front of everyone – for something you didn't do?'

'No. She closed the front door to everyone. She gathered the belt in her hands, pulled the ends back sharply to make a whip-crack sound, and then told me to scream and cry as though she was belting me. So, that's what I did. Mammie cracked the belt as hard as she could and walloped it off the hall stairs, and I pretended to scream and cry.'

Wee Mary giggles. 'So, you tricked them?'

'We did. For a few minutes, we put on the show they wanted, and Mammie told me off while I cried out that I was sorry. Then we tiptoed into the living room to peek through the net curtains to watch Lorraine, her mother, and the neighbours gradually leave.

'I'll never forget the sadness and hurt on Mammie's face as she re-tied her headscarf. I was, and am, still so angry at Lorraine and her mother for putting our Mammie through that. *She was dying, for Christ's sake.'*

A lone tear trails down my cheek: 'Mammie told me she was sorry that she couldn't defend me better. I reminded her that she wasn't well and she still saved me from an actual beating. She was happier when I said that.'

'Who really gave Lorraine the black eye?'

'Only she knows, Mary. And why she lied to her mother.'

'Why do these women enjoy scaring and hurting people?' Wee Mary clutches Our Lady into her chest, her eyes wide.

I shrug. 'They enjoy it? I don't know.' My fists tighten, a steely determination taking hold of me. 'What I do know, though, is that neither Lorraine nor her cronies will ever hurt either of us ever again.'

Chapter 30

Sunday, 16 September 1984

'Whoa! Steady, girl!' Steve urges as I whip myself into a frenzy, stepping and shadow boxing as quickly as I can. I increase the momentum, channelling all the rage inside me, punching harder and faster, scowling at my reflection in the gym mirror.

'Hey! What's eating you this morning?'

'I don't want to talk about it!' Huffing, I step over the white cross taped to the floor and shadow box my punching routines. As much as I want to pour my heart out about what happened between Paul and Geraldine on Friday night, I know that I'm too proud to discuss this with Steve.

I'm also trying to make sense of how I feel about everything. On the one hand, I'm gutted that I don't have my first love anymore, that it's over between Paul and me, because he betrayed me, because he allowed himself to be seduced by one of my former best friends. Anger boils inside me when I think of Geraldine and what she did. Then I wonder if I should thank her because she's done me a favour. Taken the decision about splitting up with Paul right out of my hands. Shaking my head to get rid of these thoughts, I continue punching.

'Come on, tell me.' Steve's not giving up. He steps beside me in the mirror, watching my face. 'Who's got you this riled up?'

I am, however, willing to discuss what's happening with wee Mary still getting beaten. 'Lorraine! Fucking! Pollock!'

'Thought she was staying away from you?'

I say nothing. When I've finished practising jabs, I move on to body hooks. Left, right, left, right, now a left head hook, then a right head hook. I imagine Lorraine's smirking face in front of me, and I throw my arms out even harder. 'I met her on the way home from the dress fitting yesterday.'

'And?'

'She didn't hit me, just sneered. It turns out that her and that JoJo lassie had already battered wee Mary earlier.' My face burns as my punches intensify. 'Those bitches have been knocking her about instead of me!' Tears pool in my eyes. 'And she's made me promise not to tell Da or Gran.'

Steve's face tightens. 'Something has to be done.'

'I know, and it's up to me to somehow take care of Lorraine and that JoJo for her.' I blink the tears away as I shadow box.

'What do you mean, "somehow"?' Steve catches my eye in the mirror. 'When the time comes, you can still beat them with the element of surprise. You've got some punches on you now.'

'I'm scared, though. I've never *hit* anything. I don't know what that *feels* like.'

'Well, it's a good job that you're in a boxing gym, then.' I manage a faint smile at Steve's joke, grateful for the distraction from the worry about Wee Mary. 'I've spent a fair bit of time teaching you the technical skills, but now it's time to put these into practice. I've one more punch to show you – the uppercut – and we'll use boxing gloves and pads for this.'

The uppercut punch might just be my favourite. Steve explains that in the middle of throwing jab and hook punch combinations, I can switch to an uppercut punch using the flat of my knuckles. This involves driving the punch upwards from my waist, aiming for underneath the chin. I might even knock Lorraine Pollock's spiky teeth out with this one.

When I've finished shadow boxing the uppercut punch, Steve opens a cupboard to rifle through a box. He returns with a couple of pairs of faded brown boxing gloves. My nose screws up as I catch a whiff of how badly they stink.

'That's the smell of blood, sweat, and sheer determination.' Steve chuckles as he chooses the size he thinks will fit best, pulls the gloves over my hands, and secures them. He hooks his hands through some large cushions, which he tells me are punching pads.

'Now you get to hit something. Hard! As hard as you can! You have to imagine that you're not just punching the pads – you're aiming to punch *through* the pads.'

Gloves in position by my chin, I focus.

'I'll call out the punches I want you to throw, and I'll offer you the left or right pad to punch.' Steve holds the pads up, and I begin to throw the punches as he drills me through combinations of jabs, body hooks, head hooks and uppercuts. 'Keep your elbows tucked in, chin down. Remember, you're driving the punch from your feet, up through your body, into your arms.'

I adjust my body to concentrate on the power of the punches as they leave my body and transfer into and through the boxing pads. I imagine Lorraine's face on one pad, and JoJo's on the other. Punching as hard as I can, I vent all my frustration and anger.

'Good!' Steve encourages. He lifts the pads. 'Uppercuts. Keep practising!'

Gradually the rage lessens, and the more I punch, the clearer I can think.

'Time to hit something even more substantial.' Steve leads me to one of the boxing bags suspended from the ceiling. At different points, little white pieces of tape are stuck onto the dark shape. He shoves it, and it swings. 'Don't be fooled. Although you might punch the bag away from you, it's always going to come back harder, just like an opponent. Working the bag will also teach you precision in your punches.'

Steve disappears into the cupboard again and comes back with some blue electrical tape. 'The white tape pieces on the bag have been put there by other boxers to mark their spots for where an opponent's jaw and ribs might be. You and Lorraine are smaller – I'll mark some spots lower for you to aim your jabs and hooks at.' He gets to work with the blue tape.

With my new blue crosses in place, Steve shows me how to stand in relation to the bag and encourages me as I work through the different punches. I'm relishing connecting with something substantial.

'Now we're going to learn some combinations of punches.' Steve pops his boxing gloves and demonstrates punching the bag. 'The jab can work as a warning punch and test the distance between you and your opponent so that you can get into a better position. Double jab with your left hand, and before your opponent reacts, follow through with a right cross, like this.' Steve steps forward and back and side to side of the bag as he shows me the jab and cross. 'Your turn.'

Unlike with Steve, the bag doesn't move at all when I practice my double jabs and crosses on it. I concentrate on the power of my punches as they hit the blue crosses on the bag. Steve grins at me, 'Atta girl! You've got quite a jab and cross there!'

Puffing hard, I step towards the bag to jab twice, cross punch, and step back.

Steve straps on his gloves a little tighter. 'Now, body hooks to the bag – left first, and then follow through with the power punch of your right hand. Got it?'

I nod, mimicking the punches he's just demonstrated for me.

Then, instinctively, we both freeze as keys jangle in time to the sound of heavy footsteps approaching. Frowning, Steve puts his finger to his lips, cocks his head to listen. I shrink against him as a massive figure steps out of the gloom and into a shaft of light further down the gym.

'What the feck's going on here?' The figure booms, striding towards us. Wiping sweat on my sleeve, I fumble to get my gloves off.

Steve steps in front of me. 'Hey, Mister Mac! We've just been doing a little training.'

'A little training? It looks to me like she's been boxing! A woman – in a men's boxing gym! In *my* gym!'

Colin Mackenzie is a giant of a man. He's a fair few inches taller than Steve, and he's built like a double wardrobe.

'True, I've been showing her a little boxing too.' I sense that Steve hasn't thought about how Mister Mac would react if he knew a lassie was being trained to box in his gym.

'Did you have a nice holiday?' Steve's stalling as he takes my gloves and tosses these with the pads back into the cupboard. I stuff the rest of my training gear into a bag while they talk across the floor at each other.

'You've been training someone in my gym without my permission? You've been training a *feckin' lassie* on how to box? Have you lost your marbles, son? Do you know how dangerous boxing can be? No lassie's getting trained in my gym – get her oot! And you and I are going to have words, son!'

Mister Mac's scarred face becomes more visible when he steps into the light. He has a thick sausage nose that I guess has been broken on a few occasions, and his left ear is flattened and knobbly.

'Get her oot i' here!'

Steve's finished putting everything away and approaches Mister Mac. 'I'm sorry. I didn't think you'd mind – we come before the gym opens ....'

'Mind? Of course, I mind! That there's a young lassie – she could get hurt! And it's no' happening in my gym!'

'Boss, there's a good reason why she's here. She's getting bullied!'

'Bullied? She's a lassie! That's just a catfight, and we men are best off staying out of it! Leave now!' Mister Mac throws his arms in the air. I notice that he's barely capable of looking at me. His face flushes purple. 'She can't learn how to box! She's a young lassie, for Christ's sake! It's unheard of – it's up there with women going to the moon or becoming prime minister! It shouldn't happen! You can see what happens when it does!'

The memory of wee Mary crying, having lost all hope, flashes across my mind. The flame of rage and seeking retribution reignites in my belly. More potent than the danger of Lorraine Pollock and JoJo is the fear that I'm about to lose this opportunity of learning how to box so that I can stand up to them.

Taking a deep breath, I step into the light. 'Mister Mackenzie, my name's Aileen Murphy.'

Mister Mac pauses in the middle of his tirade and turns his body to face me. 'You related to Aidan Murphy?'

'He's my dad.'

'Good boxer in his Navy days.' Mister Mac looks wistful. 'So, does he know that you're doing the boxing training?'

Caught off guard that Mister Mac knows Da, I nod. Maybe he's not convinced by my lie because he begins to turn away from me again, muttering, 'It's still not right, a lassie boxing.'

Panicking that my chance is slipping away, I blurt, 'I might not have the strength of a guy, but I have the courage and determination to train hard. And I have heart, Mister Mackenzie.' Clearing my throat, I place my hands on my hips. 'You didn't see me – how badly I got beaten – by an older, bigger lassie. And not just her, her boyfriend held me down and smacked my head off the pavement.'

Mister Mac winces. I carry on talking, aware that if I don't speak now, I will lose not only the boxing training but also the hope of finally ending the beatings for wee Mary and me.

'I've been getting beat up my whole life, Mister Mackenzie. I'm tired of it, and I'm tired of the bullies. I want to be able to defend myself. I know boxing's a man's sport, but I want to be able to hold my own against anyone – woman or man. No one needs to know.'

'Naw, kid. I'm sorry about your troubles and all that, but they're not mine, and you're not coming back to this gym. End of.'

'She's battering my wee sister. She's eleven and covered in bruises, too feart to go outside.'

Mister Mac shakes his head and turns away from me.

'I need this chance. I promise that I'll work just as hard as any laddie.' Afraid that my opportunity is slipping away, I curse as tears sting my eyes. I can't look weak at this crucial moment. I straighten up, retaking control of my voice. 'Steve tells me that you have a daughter – Karen? A little bit older than me. I'm betting that Karen doesn't get bothered on the streets ....'

It's Mister Mac's turn to straighten up. 'That's because no one would dare. They know who I am.'

'Exactly! I don't have that advantage. But if I could train here? I could make all the bullies disappear!'

Mister Mac turns back to me, folding his arms across his chest.

'If Karen was getting beaten and wasn't protected by your reputation – would you not want her to be able to defend herself?'

'There are no female boxers for a good reason! It can be a brutal sport.'

'I'm only asking to train, not to fight competitively – please? What harm would it do?'

Colin Mackenzie sighs and looks over at Steve. 'Is this how she wears you down?'

Steve laughs and gives him a look that says 'Yes, it is.'

Mister Mac wags his finger at Steve and turns to me. 'You can train when the gym's closed, but this must be kept quiet. The blokes would string me up if they knew!'

I leap, punching the air with delight.

Chapter 31

Friday, 21 September 1984

Tucked in a corner in the fifth-year common room before school begins, I sit with my fingertips pinning the pages open of the final book of *The Lord of the Rings* trilogy. Captivated by the story of Frodo and his allies, I'm oblivious to the chatter of the pupils around me.

All week, Ruaridh, Marie, Geraldine and Paul have had the good sense not to approach me after what happened at Jinkie's. Curiously, I only see Marie and Ruaridh together. Paul and Geraldine always seem to be on their own and separate.

Out of the corner of my eye, a couple approaches me. 'Is it ok if we sit down?' Marie shuffles onto the seat next to me. Ruaridh sits on the other side of her, his cheeks red. He mutters, 'The bus took ages this morning! Must be more strikers at the Craig or something.'

I nod and turn to the next page of my book while Marie and Ruaridh cast furtive glances at each other. I pretend to concentrate. I know I can't.

After my pre-school training session with Steve, my shoulders and arms ache like they haven't done in a long while. Pretending to yawn, I raise my arms over my head and out in front of me. I'm enjoying the relief in my muscles as I stretch them out. Ever since I told Steve about wee Mary, he's increased the difficulty and volume of my training. He makes me practice each boxing move and a combination of these over and over – strength and conditioning training, footwork, shadow boxing, and pad and bag work. If I didn't know better, I'd say that he also has something to prove.

Marie and Ruaridh stare at me. Maybe I looked like I was enjoying a yawn too much.

'Can we talk about what happened at Jinkie's?' Marie turns towards me.

I swallow hard and snap my book closed.

Marie's cheeks bloom a deep red. 'I've not said anything before because I had no idea what to say.' She wrings her hands together. 'I mean, it was just so awful –'

Wriggling in my chair, I'm unsure of how to react. I glance around to see if anyone is listening, but thankfully, everyone in the common room seems absorbed in their own chatter about what their weekend plans are.

I wait, and Marie falls silent, sorrow etched on her face. 'I am so sorry.'

'It wasn't your fault. It was Geraldine and Paul who hurt me.'

'I've been wanting to talk to you all week, but I didn't know how.'

'And I've wanted to speak with you, too, but I didn't want to come across Geraldine.'

'I think she's really sorry about what she did to you, Aileen.'

'I need more time to think about Geraldine.'

'That's understandable. I miss you, Aileen. Listening to the Top 40 on a Sunday isn't the same without you, and I miss our chats and laughs. Geraldine doesn't see me either.' Marie frowns.

'What's happened, happened, and can't be undone.' I whisper, daring to look Marie in the eye.

'Maybe it can't be undone. But can it be forgiven?' Marie holds my gaze, a light sweat breaking out on her forehead.

'No, I don't think so.'

Ruaridh squirms in his chair. 'Paul's asked me to speak with you, too, to ask if you'll at least talk with him?'

I guffaw. I don't mean to. 'Too scared to approach me himself?'

Marie lowers her voice. 'He's definitely too afraid to face you after what he and Geraldine did.'

Much as I'm not relishing reliving what happened last Friday night, I'm also not enjoying the look of anguish on Marie's face. 'Did you volunteer to do this?'

Ruaridh leans forward. 'We had to do something. Paul's so miserable.'

'So he should be, the low-life cheater!' Hurt, shame, and anger swirl inside of me.

'I know. And he deserves you to be pissed off at him. He really does. He's messed up big time, Aileen. He just wants to talk with you.'

'No, I can't face him. Not yet.' I squeeze my eyes to stop the tears.

Ruaridh flicks his red hair out of his eyes. 'I understand. Just know that he's mortified and so very sorry.'

'They were both so drunk!' Marie shakes her head.

'Being drunk doesn't excuse either of them!'

A shadow passes over Marie's face. 'We're also a wee bit worried about Geraldine.'

Now I find myself feeling concerned about my ex-pal who seduced my ex-boyfriend.

'Geraldine's locked herself away from everyone, including me. She's stayed home all week. I've knocked for her a few times, but her mum says she's not at home when I know that she is. She avoids us at school. We've been pals since we were five, It's really sad.'

'Poor Geraldine.' My voice drips with sarcasm. 'She knew what she was doing. She's been after Paul all along. Maybe she was only friends with me so she could be closer to him?'

Marie shakes her head, takes one of my hands. 'Everything's gone to pot since this happened. Our wee band of pals is split up. Can we find some way to sort this out?'

Shuffling in my seat, I glance around, embarrassed by the unexpected gesture. 'Paul and Geraldine should have thought about that before they decided to shag each other!' I hiss, just loud enough so only they can hear.

Marie and Ruaridh exchange looks.

It's not fair of me to vent on them. They haven't done anything wrong, so I change the subject, 'Are you seeing each other now?'

'Aye.' A smile plays on Ruaridh's lips. His eyes soften. 'We see each other every night.' He puts his arm around Marie, who leans into him, smiling.

Before I can stop myself, I say, 'But I thought you were interested in Geraldine?'

Ruaridh laughs softly. 'Nah. It's always been Marie for me. Geraldine's too ... she's just not my type.' He finishes, blushing again.

'Well, if one good thing came out of Jinkie's, it's that you two got together.' I take both their hands. 'I'm not mad at either of you – you've done nothing to upset me.' I beam at them. 'You make a lovely couple.'

'Thanks.' Marie says as she nestles against Ruaridh. 'You ok, though?'

'Don't worry about me. I can take care of myself. I've always taken care of myself, and if I'm honest, I'm not that good at it.' Tears prickle my eyes, and I force a smile as I ask, 'Have you told anyone about what happened last Friday?'

'Not a soul.'

'No one in the band?'

Ruaridh knits his eyebrows together. 'Nope.'

I breathe again.

Chapter 32

Sunday, 23 September 1984

'Good run?' Gran's eyes twinkle mischievously. I blush, Gran thinks it's with embarrassment, but it's really with guilt that I've not told her I'm learning to box. I'm showered and changed after my earlier boxing session with Steve, getting ready to leave for morning mass at a different chapel from the one I normally go to. 'It must be fun running with that Steve, eh?'

I hate lying but learning to properly defend myself and wee Mary is more important. I know Gran would throw a fit if she knew that I was learning how to box, and in a men's gym too. She'd faint at how unladylike it all is.

Gran clears her throat, a serious look crossing her face as she sits beside me on my bed. 'Hen, we need to have a wee chat.' She hands me another envelope from Paul. 'You can't keep avoiding him. Will you tell me what's going on between you two?' I take the envelope from her and toss it onto the unopened pile of envelopes on my chest of drawers.

'Paul needs an answer – he's going to wear out his shoe leather and spend his life savings on stationery from Woolworths.'

'I couldn't care less.' And I couldn't. I've anaesthetised myself. I don't think about it.

'Aileen, it's embarrassing for me and your da every time he comes to the door. You won't see him. You won't engage. And he keeps coming back; you need to talk to him. One way or the other.'

Gran takes my hand, fixes me with those bright blue eyes of hers.

'He doesn't deserve my time.' I withdraw my hand from Gran.

'What happened, hen?'

Gran and I have never talked about sex. She's so holy that I'm afraid of offending her, but I can tell from her face that she isn't going to let this drop.

I summon the courage to say the most outrageous thing I've ever said to Gran: 'Paul had sex with Geraldine.'

As soon as Gran gasps and throws her hands in the air, I immediately regret telling her. Her next response surprises me more. 'I always knew she was a floozie! As soon as she started with all those short skirts and the heavy make-up and the different hairdos, I knew she was going to be trouble!'

'Gran, Paul was there too?'

'Aye, I know, but it's the women who make the trouble.'

'What do you mean?'

Gran edges back from me on the bed, whispers, like God or the BBC might hear her: 'Men are weak. They let what's in their underpants guide their thoughts and actions.'

At first, I squirm, but then I want to laugh. This wasn't the conversation I'd imagined having with Gran. While I'm guessing it was Geraldine who instigated the sex and took advantage of Paul, to me, he'd looked and sounded like a willing participant that night.

'She knew what she was doing. Paul knew what he was doing.' And from a well deep inside of me, tears leak from my eyes. 'I wouldn't lose my virginity to him. He got frustrated. She was there, making it plain she was available.'

Gran takes my hand again. 'Never blame yourself, hen. You stuck to your principles! And there was me thinking you'd only had a tiny disagreement about something!'

Tears drip from my chin onto my hands. Gran fetches some tissues.

Blowing my nose, I splutter, 'I don't know where all these tears come from. Is life about crying?'

'Oh, you'll cry a lot, hen.'

'I wish I didn't cry. I wish I didn't feel anything.'

'You care. That's why you're so beautiful inside and out. Do you love Paul?'

'I thought I did, but I've just been so confused recently ....'

'Steve?' Gran finishes for me, smiling. 'I've noticed the change in you. I have eyes.'

I open my mouth to deny what she's just said, then close it again. 'Can you like two guys at the same time?'

Gran nods, her eyes twinkling. 'But which one sets your pulse racing, has you smiling from the inside out?'

'Steve.'

'There's your answer, hen.'

The tears have dried up. I wipe my face, blow my nose and mumble into the tissue. 'But Steve has a girlfriend, and he wouldn't be interested in me even if he was single.'

Gran hands me another tissue, a small smile on her lips. 'Oh, you'd be surprised.' She reaches for the pile of envelopes. 'Now, you need to open these and put Paul out of his misery.'

»· ·•· ·«

Perched on a wooden bench, I sit with my back against the wall of the birdwatcher's hut in the Country Park, waiting for Paul to arrive. I've deliberately arrived early to give myself time to gather my thoughts before our meeting. My mind wanders to when Mammie and Da used to bring us here as a family. We'd lay a picnic blanket out on the banks by the River Clyde and wonder at the comings and goings of the different birds and animals. This spot has been a sanctuary for me, away from the bullying and other worries – a place to come with my family, and later with Paul.

To avoid gossip, when we first started seeing each other, we used to meet here, away from curious eyes. I sigh. Those innocent days seem so long ago now. Still, this remains a magical place. I make a mental note to return to enjoy it, and not just run through it. I breathe deeply, appreciating the tranquillity of the river and forest views around me.

It's early evening, with maybe another hour or so of light left. Autumn is coming, and I wrap my cardigan around me to ward off the chill in the air as the sun begins to dip in the sky. A grey and white heron stands on one leg in the river across from me. With its long neck bent, its sharp yellow beak is poised to strike any moment at an unsuspecting fish in the water.

And I don't have to wait long on Paul as he rounds the bend ahead, waving as he makes his way towards me.

He sits beside me. We both look out to the river where the heron waits, ready to claim its reward for patience.

'So, we're back to where we began, eh?' The trace of a faint smile is etched on Paul's face as he turns to me. 'I didn't think you'd ever meet me.'

'Have you really come here every night at half-past five? I only read your letters today.'

'Yes, but what matters is that you're here right now. I am so glad to see you, and yet, I'm so frightened.'

'Try being me.' I joke half-heartedly.

Paul shifts on the bench. 'You've read my letters. You know how sorry and stupid I feel, how angry I am at myself for doing what I did and hurting you. I let you down.' Tears pool in his eyes.

'You let yourself down.'

'Can't argue with that. I love you, Aileen. Is there anything – anything at all – I can say or do to make this better?'

I search Paul's soulful brown eyes – the ones I used to love staring into – and I see the pain I'm experiencing reflected there, too. I've been on a roller coaster of emotions since the event at Jinkie's. That night, not only did I lose my childhood sweetheart and one of my best friends, but I also lost my innocence and my trust in people.

Before this moment, I didn't know if I could find the courage to break away from Paul, from the haven he represents for me. But I've never been more certain than I am now that we must split up.

The decision now taken, relief surges through me, the weight on my shoulders lightens. When I'd pictured this moment previously, when I'd summoned the courage to even think about this scenario, I had seen myself making a big speech and flouncing off. Now though, with sunset beginning to shoot oranges and golds through the clouds, sitting beside my high school sweetheart, I don't want to hurt him. I only want to be honest with him.

'Say something.' Paul's face looks ghostly white in the gathering dusk.

'I forgive you.'

Paul looks as stunned as I feel when the words leave my mouth.

He edges closer to me. 'Does that mean that you'll take me back?'

I move away, shake my head. 'We should've split up a long time ago. We've outgrown each other. And ... I don't love you.' There, I've said it.

His face twists. 'That's it, then?'

'Yes.' I stand up.

'Aileen, I'm sorry. Please give me another chance.'

I shake my head and bend to peck him on the cheek. 'It's over. But I don't bear you any grudges. I want you to be happy. I want me to be happy. Take care.'

I walk away from him crying on the bench, turn round once to wave goodbye, then break into a light run.

In the gathering dusk, swarms of swallows swoop overhead, their high-pitched cheeping growing in volume as they swirl and shift as one towards me. Gazing skywards, I grin at the swallow formations, feeling as effortless as they look in their aerial ballet spectacle, seemingly in celebration for me. Soon, I know these swallows will migrate south to warmer climes. Most of them will make it, some of them won't.

I have no idea where I'm going, but I do know that for once in my life, I'm not running away from something.

I'm finally running towards it.

Chapter 33

Friday, 28 September 1984

Wrinkling my nose at the smell of bleach and antiseptic, I scurry after Gran in the direction of the children's wards. Our shoes squeak on the linoleum as we push open double door after double door, following the signs to wee Mary's ward.

'What happened?'

Gran's grim-faced. 'When I wakened wee Mary, she was struggling for breath and felt hot. When I pulled back her covers to cool her down, that's when I saw the state of her skin and the blood on the sheets.'

She marches on, shoving the doors wide open, her heels now clickety-clacking on the floor. I trot beside her.

'Wee Mary was determined to go to school, telling me she was fine like she has done all week. I phoned the doctor anyway. As soon as he examined her – he called an ambulance. She has a bad chest infection, which isn't helping her asthma. Her skin's also become infected, and she's badly dehydrated. The doctor said if we'd left it any longer, wee Mary might have developed septicaemia.'

'Oh my God.'

'Exactly. A blood infection.'

Poor wee Mary. Guilt grips my heart. I find myself trying to outwalk Gran, even though I don't know which direction we're headed. 'How is she about being in the hospital?'

'Shocked but resigned. I don't think she realised how sick she was.' Gran's face tightens, and she shoves her bag over her shoulder, still galloping forward.

We arrive outside a door where Gran's hand hovers over the door handle. Tears glisten in her eyes. She takes a deep breath, puts on a smile, and shoves the door open into a four-bed ward with only one other patient, a pale boy, fast asleep in his bed.

Wee Mary's propped on pillows on a bed under a window with an oxygen mask over her face. Da holds her bandaged hand and nods to us.

'Look at the kafuffle you've caused.' I tease wee Mary as we approach her. Underneath the condensation of the face mask, I can see a weak smile spread across her face. 'And you sound like Darth Vader.'

This makes wee Mary laugh and splutter. She gasps, trying to catch her breath again. 'It's like ... I'm trying to breathe ... through a straw – one that's got ... something stuck in it.'

Gran nips me. 'Don't make her laugh, and don't ask her to talk. Let her rest. We can chat with her, and she can listen. Wee Mary nods and, with her other hand, indicates that I sit opposite Da on one of the chairs by her bedside.

Ointment oozes from underneath the bandages that cover her arms and appear to go all the way underneath her nightie. 'Is she bandaged everywhere?'

Gran answers. 'Aye. The doctors are using high strength steroid and antibiotic creams on the infected skin, and every wee while a nurse comes in to apply more ointment to keep her skin moist and cover her in fresh bandages.'

'Oh, Mary, I'm so sorry.' I dab at the tears in my eyes. I'd promised her that I wouldn't tell Da and Gran about the batterings but seeing how frail she looks in the hospital bed, I should have said something earlier.

Da's silent, his head hung low, tears dripping onto his donkey jacket. Gran must have gotten a message to him at work. Gran sits beside me, her knuckles still white from gripping her shoulder bag.

Wee Mary rasps, tries to sit up from her pillow stack and squeezes my hand. I know she's trying to speak but keeping her breathing manageable is more important. I lean into her. 'You promised.' She hisses into my ear and, gulping for air, rasps, 'To keep ... the secret.'

I nod, blinking the tears out of my eyes as I sit back in my chair. Hopelessness washes through me. I never dreamt that wee Mary would get bullied too, and I never imagined that she would end up so ill with it, either. Do Lorraine and JoJo even know the horror and the pain they inflict? Meanwhile, Da and

Gran have no idea that I still live in fear, the constant threat of Lorraine hanging over me. I really want to tell them what's been going on, but gentle pressure on my hand from wee Mary reminds me to keep quiet. She, like me, is desperate to protect Da and Gran from the truth. For whatever misguided reasons.

'Oh, I nearly forgot!' Gran searches in her shoulder bag. 'A bottle of Lucozade.'

A grin forms across wee Mary's face as she reaches out to crinkle the orange cellophane of the wrapped Lucozade bottle. 'Now ... I know ... I'm sick.'

We giggle softly at her attempt at a wee joke.

'And I've gotten you some comics to read, and some sweets.' Gran sets everything into the bedside cabinet beside wee Mary's bed. She rifles in her bag and produces another object which she lays beside wee Mary.

'Our Lady!' Wee Mary wheezes, her eyes lighting up as she runs her fingers across the statue. 'Thank you.'

Gran beams, but I notice that her eyes are moist again. 'I've no idea why you wanted me to bring you a cold statue when you could have cuddled into one of your teddy bears or dolls.'

'She makes me ... feel better ....' Wee Mary lifts the statue and motions Gran to stand it on her bedside cabinet.

My bruised heart breaks wide open.

⋙ ·•· ⋘

I've never been in a consultant's office before. A black leather chair sits in front of a desk piled with neat manilla folders. On the wall behind the chair are framed certificates for Mr Singh, wee Mary's consultant. Da, Gran and I sit in a semi-circle facing Mr Singh's desk. He called us away from wee Mary's bedside earlier, asking to have a private word. He escorted us into his office, then excused himself.

He enters again with a middle-aged lady who's wearing a kaftan and headscarf. She sits on a chair near Mr Singh's. They face us.

'This is Ellen Terrence. She's a social worker.'

We nod at her. I'm wondering why she's here. What does a social worker do? Make sure people are being social at their work? Perhaps she's assessing Mr Singh on his people skills?

Mr Singh presses his palms together, leans his forearms onto his desk. 'We're here to talk about Mary. As you know, she's in a pretty bad way.'

'Yes.' Da sits forward, runs his hand through his hair.

'Mary's skin is badly infected, and her chest infection is severe. Why haven't you brought her to a doctor before?'

Silence. The veiled accusation hangs in the air.

Gran shuffles. 'We didn't know it was this bad – not until this morning!'

'Mrs Murphy. Wee Mary's been ill for a while. You must have noticed her struggling to breathe?'

'Of course. We've made sure she takes her regular medicine, and we got one of those inhaler things from the doctor a few weeks ago. She told me that she was better!' I detect a growing panic underneath Gran's indignant tone,

'And you've never noticed the state of your granddaughter's skin?'

Again, the judgement. The disbelief.

'She stopped me coming in to help her at bath time. I only see her fully dressed now.'

'And you didn't think that was strange?'

'No! She's getting to that age when wee lassies become self-conscious about their bodies!'

'Something is triggering Mary's asthma and eczema. Something like dust or a pet or a new soap or shampoo, perhaps?'

'I'll have you know that our home's spotless!' Gran bristles, indignant. 'We use the same brands of toiletries we've always used. We have a dog, but he's been with us for years. So it can't be any of those.'

'I see. Is she under any stress? Maybe something she's worried about?' Mr Singh shoots a look at Ellen Terrence.

'She's eleven years old, doctor – what would she have to be stressed about?' Da passes his hand down the front of his face and rests it over his mouth and chin.

Ellen Terrence sits forward, 'Tell me about the bruises.'

'Bruises?' Da and Gran say at the same time.

'Bruises. Mary is covered in bruises.'

'I don't know anything about bruises.' Gran's hands flutter to her face in confusion, her eyes bewildered.

'How can she have bruises?' Da turns to Gran and me.

'That's why Mr Singh has called me in – to get to the bottom of why Mary appears to be getting beaten?'

Da splutters. 'I have no idea what you mean.'

'I think you do, Mr Murphy.'

'How dare you!'

Ellen Terrence's face remains impassive. 'What can you tell me about the bruises?'

'I don't know what bruises you're talking about! I don't see my daughter undressed, and she's covered in bandages now!'

'What do you say, Mrs Murphy?'

Gran lifts her head, straightens in her seat. 'I don't like your tone or your accusation. We would never hurt our girl.'

Finally, Ellen Terrence turns to me. 'Aileen?'

Trembling, I stand and motion for them to follow me. 'Only wee Mary can tell us.'

We gather around my sister's bedside. Mr Singh draws the curtains around her bed area. Wee Mary's eyes are wide; she gasps for air.

'I need you to stay calm, Mary. Everything's going to be alright.' I take one of her bandaged hands. 'The doctor, and this lady here, think that you're getting beaten.'

Wee Mary shakes her head, pulls her hand away. 'I can't tell ...' she wheezes.

Mr Singh and Ellen Terrence exchange knowing looks.

'You don't understand, Mary. These people are *investigating* why you have bruises. They think one of us, your family, is hurting you.'

Wee Mary's chest heaves rapidly.

'It's okay, Mary. You're safe. You can tell the truth.' I squeeze her hand gently.

Wee Mary mumbles something into her mask. We lean in closer.

Ellen raises her hand. 'She's obviously distressed.'

Mr Singh speaks to a nurse. He asks us to step aside so he can pull the curtains around wee Mary's bed. Not wanting to be in the way, Da, Gran and I walk out to the corridor.

'Do they think wee Mary's too scared to talk in front of us, is that it?' Da paces up and down. Gran tugs my arm. 'What do you know, hen?'

'I promised wee Mary not to tell.'

Da shoots me a look. 'Well, you better start speaking now, young lady! *Where did those bruises come from?*'

My stomach lurches. 'I can't, Da. I promised.'

Hanging my head, I shuffle over to slump onto a chair. I didn't think things could get any worse. But they just have. I've promised my little sister that I'll keep her secret, and at the same time, I promised that I'd sort out her bullies. So far, I've kept only the first promise. Silent and brooding, Gran and Da join me. The air between us hangs heavy.

Nurses and orderlies swish past us. A cleaner dumps her mop and bucket, and, wiping her brow, begins to rhythmically work the mop from side to side down the corridor floor. As she nears, we lift our feet without being asked. She doesn't acknowledge us as she continues to mechanically mop the floor, left to right, right to left, all the way down the corridor to the next set of double doors.

Mr Singh steps into the corridor from the ward. 'We're ready.' He tells us as we follow him to wee Mary's bedside: 'I've given her some adrenaline to help her breathe. She's ready to talk now.'

My heart lightens a little at the sight of my little sister, who now has some colour in her cheeks, and her breathing seems more comfortable.

'So, Mary. What do you wish to tell us?' Ellen Terrence rearranges her headscarf while she waits on her reply.

Wee Mary's oxygen mask mists as she rasps. 'My family would never hurt me.'

'Then you need to explain the bruises.'

Wee Mary turns her head away from us, her wheezy breathing now interspersed with sniffles.

'Tell her, please.' I stroke the side of my little sister's face, but she shoves her head further along the pillow, away from my touch.

Stunned and hurt by her rejection of me, I shout. 'So you're not going to tell them the truth then, Mary? Shall I tell them for you?'

Eyes wide and gasping for air, Wee Mary flicks her face back towards me to hiss: 'You promised!'

'Tell us!' Da thunders, visibly shaking.

Gran's face crumples, wee Mary wails.

'She's been getting beaten up by a gang of older lassies – women, really!' I throw my hands in the air.

'You promised!' Wee Mary tears her mask off, gasping.

'Sometimes promises have to be broken.'

Da glares at me. '*You knew?* You knew that this wee slip of a lassie's been getting beaten?'

The vice of guilt tightens around my heart. I whisper. 'I had no idea it had gotten this bad. She made me promise not to tell.'

Mr Singh and Ellen Terrence watch us, silent. Da and Gran stand grim-faced while my little sister sobs.

Surveying the scene around me, I now deeply regret that I haven't said anything sooner.

Ellen Terrence, her voice softer, leans over to wee Mary. 'Is what Aileen told us true?'

'Yes.'

'These women sound like they could be classed as adults, Mary, and if so, what has been happening to you can be called assault and should be reported to the police.'

'Police?' I didn't think the situation could get any worse. Police involvement will take things to a whole new level if wee Mary admits she knows the names of those who have been beating her. I shudder at the thought of JoJo and Lorraine and the rest of the Pollocks marching to our front door again to give me and wee Mary a leathering in public for being police snitches.

My sister seems to sense my unease. 'No police. I don't know who they are.'

Ellen Terrence sniffs.

'Are you sure you don't know them?' Da addresses wee Mary as he sits beside her bed. Her chest heaves, and she puts her face mask back on.

'I don't know the women. No need for police.'

Ellen Terrence clears her throat. 'Without a complainant, the police won't make a case.' The social worker is undeterred, though. 'Mary, we can't allow this to continue. Can you tell us anything which might help us help you?'

Wee Mary closes her eyes and purses her lips. Only the sound of her wheezing can be heard.

Mr Singh shakes his head. 'Listening to this, I'm not surprised now by the symptoms Mary's been presenting.'

'Why haven't you told us?' Gran perches on the bed to take wee Mary's bandaged hand.

'I didn't ... want to be ... a bother.'

'Taking after your big sister, then.' Da scowls at me. More regret and shame for me. 'Please, Mary. You must remember something that the police could use to have them arrested?'

Wee Mary shakes her head, her eyes wide.

The social worker snaps her notebook closed. 'What I don't understand is why these women beat you, Mary. Why?'

'Because I'm a Catholic.'

'I don't understand.'

Mr Singh steps forward. 'I do. In this part of Scotland, it really can matter whether you're a Protestant or Catholic. I'm still trying to figure it out. Christians fighting Christians.'

Ellen Terrence raises her eyebrows. 'Really? Where I come from, it doesn't matter which religion you follow.'

'It never ceases to amaze me, Mrs Terrence. As part of my training, I worked in A&E in Glasgow, and the number of injuries I saw inflicted in the name of religion astounded me. I once had a young drunken lad turn up, his foot and leg badly torn and bleeding. When I asked what had happened, he told me that in a fit of rage, he'd kicked in the screen of

his television after his football team, Celtic –
that's the Catholic team, lost to Rangers – the
Protestant team.'

As we listen to this exchange between two
strangers, not from our area, on the intricacies
of our culture, Gran, Da, wee Mary and I smile
at each other.

'So, it was self-inflicted?' Ellen Terrence fusses
with her headscarf some more.

'Yes, but he wasn't worried about the stitches
or scars he'd have – he was more worried
about his mother's reaction when she found
out what he'd done. Not because he'd destroyed
the television set, but the fact that they didn't
own it – it was rented from Rediffusion.'

Chapter 34

Saturday, 6 October 1984

'Here. These might cheer you up.' Steve tosses me a pair of red boxing gloves. 'I bought these in Glasgow for you. They're second-hand, but the best-smelling pair I could find.'

Confused but grateful, I slip the boxing gloves on over my bandaged knuckles.

Steve smiles. 'These are your gloves now. I've given them a good clean. So no more moaning about how much the gloves stink – any smell after this is your own.' He straps my gloves on a little tighter.

I grin at him, surprised at how happy I am to be given a pair of second-hand boxing gloves.

'Now for the moment of truth.' Steve taps my boxing gloves with his own. 'Sparring practice allows you to test out the punches you've been learning, on a real opponent, on someone who wants to beat you badly, to win.'

Layered in sweatshirts and jogging pants, our breath comes out in white wisps as we face each other in the centre of the ring in the chilly gym. Even though it's October, Mister Mac refuses to put the heating on any earlier for us. Steve smiled when he told me Mister Mac's exact words were that we 'should be working up a sweat anyway.'

We assume our boxing stances. Steve regards me over the top of his gloves.

'Boxing is chess with gloves. It's just as strategic. While you'll learn to anticipate what your opponent's next moves might be – you'll also be training your body to be more intuitive – to have already made a move before you've consciously thought of it. You'll read your opponent in the moment, and you'll be ready to deploy the boxing combinations you've been practising on the bag and pads. It becomes second nature.'

Butterflies collide in my stomach as I contemplate throwing punches at Steve – they flutter harder when I think about Steve throwing punches back at me.

As if reading my mind, Steve sends a slow-motion jab that falls just short of my face. 'Normally, we'd wear gum shields to spar, but as I don't have any for you, it'd be unfair of me to wear one. Now, I'll throw real punches at you, but I'll whip my arms away just before I connect with you. I'll quicken the speed of my punches but still not physically hit you. Your goal is to block these punches, and when you can, land a punch on me – hit me hard.'

'I don't want to hurt you.'

'You won't because I'll be defending myself – just the same as I've taught you.' Steve grins. 'And anyway, you're a girl ....'

I swing a left hook into his ribs before he can finish his sentence. 'Is that right?'

'Ooft!' Steve bounces back, holding his side. 'Okay, I take that back about you punching like a girl. Of course you do, and it was a proper punch, too. Truce?' Steve's bright blue eyes twinkle as he resumes his stance.

I nod, gloves by my chin, arms tucked in to protect my ribs. We circle in the centre, and Steve throws punches while I block and parry as best I can. His eyes widen in surprise as he picks up his boxing speed, and I respond by testing some of the new boxing combinations he's taught me. 'Atta girl!'

We keep sparring, getting into a rhythm as we duck, defend, or attack with our punches. Quicker and quicker, we spar with each other until sweat trickles down our faces. 'Turns out we're working up a sweat, after all.' Steve chuckles as he comes to a halt. He prises off his gloves to strip the clothes from the top half of his body.

He stands in front of me, his bare chest glistening, his breathing rapid. 'Is this okay? I'm too hot.'

I can only nod. *Dear Lord, how am I supposed to concentrate?*

Steve drops his arms by his side, his face and voice serious: 'I've been thinking about this next thing I'm going to teach you. It's very, very important. If you get knocked down, you must always get back up!' He grips my arms. 'No matter how hurt you are. When you're back on your feet, you either take another shot or run away. But never, ever, stay on the ground!'

Steve demonstrates this by dropping his body onto the canvas and rolling away from me. 'As your fight won't take place in a ring, there won't be any ropes to help you to your feet if you get knocked down. What you do have, though, are strong core and leg muscles which you can use to roll away to a safer distance from your opponent.'

Next, Steve gets into a sitting position on the canvas and tucks his knees to his chest. 'You rise, like this.' He rocks back onto his shoulders, hands on either side of his head. Pushing off with his hands, he then rolls forward on his back and kicks his legs out to propel himself upwards into a standing position.

'Okay, now you're teaching me gymnastics, or kung fu, or something!' I laugh nervously, trying not to stare at his body as he unfastens the ties on my gloves. His fingers brush mine, sending my pulse rate higher.

'We'll break it down. Keep practising each stage. Now – fall!'

Dubious, I drop onto the canvas. I manage the 'rolling away' part fine but struggle with the 'jumping straight onto my feet' thing. Sitting beside me on the canvas, Steve breaks this second move down even more for me. I try. I fail. He demonstrates over and over. At one point, I question myself if I'm deliberately messing this up so that I can re-watch the constriction of the muscles on Steve's naked torso as he shows me how to make the move.

Whatever the reason, I keep practising but can't seem to get that 'final spring on to my feet' ending. Finally, frustrated, I cry out, punching the air. I get to my feet, the old-fashioned way, swiping at the sweat trickling down my face.

Steve readily springs to his feet, grinning, just to rub it in. 'Don't worry. We'll practice this at every session from now on. Are you too warm?'

My heart pounds as he steps closer to me. *Please don't let him notice the effect he's having on me. I'm trying hard to act cool, but my goodness, look at him!*

Steve gently takes hold of the bottom of my sweatshirt. His eyes search mine. I nod even though I'm uncertain about what he's about to do. Very carefully, he lifts the sweatshirt up and over my head and drops it to the side. I step closer to him, barely able to breathe. He pauses. His eyes lock on mine, his lips part slightly, and then, gently, he brushes his cool fingertips across my clavicle and over my vest top.

Such a thrill explodes through me that I gasp in surprise.

Steve misreads my response and promptly steps away from me. 'Sorry, I don't know what I was thinking. You have a boyfriend.'

Remembering that he has a girlfriend, and not wishing to lose face myself, I say nothing, which Steve reads as my agreement with what he's just said.

He clears his throat. 'Let's just pretend that that didn't happen. Start again?'

Now that we've stopped moving, the icy air bites at my skin, making me quiver. I put my sweatshirt back on, and Steve does the same. My mind whirls. *What just happened?*

His face is now solemn as he hands me my boxing gloves and holds the ropes so that I can step out of the ring. Wordless, I follow him to the mirror, and he helps put my boxing gloves back on. Facing his reflection in the mirror, I wait for instructions. I bring my breathing back under control; my heartbeat slows.

Steve stares back at me and doesn't move. Silence. Waiting, I tap my gloves together and kick my legs out.

Finally, Steve speaks. 'This next combination I have is the final one I will teach you. I hope you won't need it. I hope the other punch combinations I've taught you will do the trick.' He seems to be finding it difficult to talk. I reach my glove across to tap him on the arm and smile a little at him. He looks so sad.

'Everything's okay.'

'Sure?'

'Definitely.' I reach to hug him and to help lighten the atmosphere, 'Now are you going to teach me this punch combo, or what?'

This does the trick. Steve's face brightens as he gets into his boxing position. 'Okay. This combo is called the *Left-Right, Goodnight!*'

'Tell me more.'

Demonstrating the punches for me, Steve huffs, 'If you're in a situation where you're taking blows, and maybe you're hunched over defending yourself. Choose your moment to step back from your opponent, and with as much strength as you can muster, land a left and a right body hook into the ribs.

'When they drop their arms to defend themselves, you launch as powerful an uppercut punch as you can with your right fist, up and under their chin. If you don't knock them out, you'll at least knock them flying! Hence, its nickname – *Left-Right, Goodnight!*'

This sounds like a serious punch combination and one I might need for the next time I see Lorraine. My thoughts immediately go to my little sister recovering from wounds that may never heal. 'Wee Mary's in the hospital!' I blurt before I can stop myself. 'She's been in since Monday. I haven't said anything because – well – that's what I do with everything. Keep it to myself.'

Steve turns me around to face him. 'What happened?'

My lip trembles. I swallow hard. 'Wee Mary's asthma and eczema have gotten bad. The doctor sent for an ambulance to take her to hospital. That's when they discovered the bruises....'

'Bruises?' Steve's face tightens.

'Aye, turns out that Lorraine Pollock and JoJo have still been bullying her. Those twisted women find it fun to knock nine bells out of a wee lassie! The consultant had Social Services in; there was even talk of bringing in the police – can you imagine?'

'Get the police onto them! That's assault, and on a minor too!' Steve bangs his gloves together.

I shake my head. 'She's too afraid. Doesn't want to get our family in trouble with the

Pollocks. It doesn't matter what me, Da, or Gran say to her. She won't budge. She's stubborn.'

Steve scowls. 'I wonder who she takes after? How is she now?'

'Her breathing's a lot better, and her skin's clearing up. Should get out in the next few days. But she's enjoying the sweets and comics while she's there.' I notice that Steve has edged closer as he's been listening to me.

'Thanks for asking,' I add, now finding it a little difficult to breathe myself. When he's this close, I find it hard to focus. He extends his arms out and gently guides me to him for a hug.

Into my ear, he murmurs, 'I'm so sorry about what's happened to wee Mary, and what's been happening to you.'

At his firm and reassuring hold, warmth spreads through my body, and I realise my face is wet with tears. 'Thank you.' I mumble into his chest. We stand locked like that for a moment, and as much as I'm enjoying this closeness with Steve, I don't wish to make a fool of myself. Stupidly, I half-joke: 'Careful. Your girlfriend might get jealous.'

Steve steps back. 'She might do. If she was still my girlfriend.'

Before I can react, Steve takes up position beside me to show me the shadow boxing moves for the *Left-Right, Goodnight!* punches combination. Working hard to bury my surprise about him now being single, I watch us in the mirror, standing side by side. On Steve's commands, we throw out the punches in unison, like a well-choreographed and brutal ballet. We speed up, throwing the punches harder and faster. Steve then has me practice on the pads until, finally, we're facing the boxing bag with the blue crosses.

Steve calls out the various punch combinations, including the new *Left-Right, Goodnight!* ones. He urges me on, to punch faster and harder and move around the bag. At one point, though, I'm moving so fast that I trip over my own feet, but Steve catches me before I fall. Safe in his arms, I look up into his eyes. Neither of us moves; I don't even think I'm breathing.

Just then, heavy footsteps sound close by. Maybe I'm expecting Mr Mac, but I almost faint as Da strides into the gym.

'Hands off her, son!' Da bounds down the gym towards us, his face set.

I scramble out of Steve's arms, my mind whirling. 'Da, what are you doing here?'

'I could ask the same of you, young lady!' I've never seen Da look so angry.

Fear seeps into my pores. 'I'm learning to box, Da.'

'Looked like something else to me!'

Steve raises his gloves. 'Cross my heart, Mr Murphy. Aileen tripped. I caught her. I've only been teaching her to box.'

'Home. Now, kid!' As Da steps towards me, Steve puts his arm around my trembling shoulders. Glaring at both of us, Da loosens and removes my gloves.

With a sinking heart, I unfurl the bandages binding my knuckles. 'How did you know I was here?'

Da throws his hands in the air. 'Last night in the pub. Colin Mackenzie takes me aside for a quiet word. Said he's surprised that I'm allowing my girl to box. You could have knocked me over with a feather, Aileen. I didn't believe it. Not until now.'

I keep my head down, wringing my bare hands together. 'What's the big deal, Da? You boxed in the Navy.'

'I'm a bloke!'

'That's sexist.'

Da glares at me. 'It's practical! Boxing's a brutal sport!'

'And women can't box?'

Da leans towards me. 'Women *don't* box, not in this country. Isn't it enough wee Mary's lying battered and bruised right now in the hospital without you signing yourself up to get beaten?'

I work hard to hold back the tears pushing against the back of my eyes.

His voice softens. 'I don't mean to sound old-fashioned, but you're a girl ... it's too dangerous, physically.'

I move out from under Steve's arm. 'I know, Da, and I haven't forgotten where wee Mary is. I ended up in A&E, too, remember? That's why I'm here now, learning how to box. After what happened to me, would you not rather that I'm able to defend myself if I need to?'

The memory of the beating on the twelfth of July creeps into my mind. I shudder when I think of what could have happened if Steve hadn't saved me, and the reality that he may not be there next time Lorraine finds me. 'I should be able to stand up for myself. What if a man tried to attack me?'

Da winces. 'I'd rather not think about that, thanks.'

'You have to. I'm only training with Steve. I won't ever fight in a ring. You did the same in the Navy, didn't you? Why?'

'Because I enjoyed it.'

'Exactly. I'm loving it, Da. The discipline. That powerful feeling of delivering punches, connecting with something that matters.'

'And lying all this time to Gran and me doesn't matter?'

Cut by Da's disappointment, I gulp down tears as I toss my gloves and bandages into my training bag. I don't know how I thought Da would react when he found out that I was boxing. Perhaps I've been hoping that he'd never find out. I've been so focused on the possibility of finally being able to stand up for myself and wee Mary. Now, looking at the anger and disbelief on Da's face, I can see that it was a stupid dream.

'I didn't know how to tell you. I'm so sorry.' Guilt wells up inside me that I've been lying to Da all these months and tears leak from my eyes.

Stony-faced, Da points to the door. 'Home, now. And we best not tell Gran. She'd have a fit if she knew!'

'Mr Murphy.' Steve crosses his arms. 'Aileen's getting really good at boxing.'

Da's face tightens. 'What are you doing? Taking advantage of a young girl like this?'

Now it's my turn to be angry. 'Da, I'm seventeen next month! I can take care of myself. And Steve's been nothing but kind to me! Giving me his time to help me learn how to defend myself! That's it, nothing else!'

His eyebrows knitted, Da rubs his chin. 'What are you talking about? Defending yourself – against who?'

I purse my lips. Do I tell Da the truth or not? It's now or never. 'Lorraine Pollock. Her pal, JoJo. The other bullies.'

'I thought Tony Pollock had put a stop to that?'

'So did I, Da.'

'And what's this about other bullies?'

More of my lies and half-truths are about to be exposed. 'When I got beaten by Lorraine and Billy on the twelfth of July – that wasn't the first time.'

'What do you mean?'

Taking a deep breath, I pull myself up tall to look directly into Da's eyes. 'What happened then wasn't a one-off. I've been getting battered for years.'

Da gasps and looks from me to Steve and back to me again.

Then I tell Da about it all: the bullying in South Africa and here in Scotland, my home country. With my head bowed, I describe the taunts, the gang and individual beatings and how I sometimes have to sneak across people's back gardens, like a criminal, just to be safe.

Although I manage not to cry while telling my story, I shake uncontrollably – I realise through fear. I'm afraid of what Da will think about me and how weak I am. But my story has started and needs to come out. On and on, it comes pouring out of me – all the fear, anxiety, hurt, pain, and the belief that I must somehow deserve all this.

Finally, my words spent, I look up at him. 'I'm so sorry.'

Tears glisten in Da's eyes. *'Why didn't you tell Gran and me?'*

My chin wobbles. 'I hoped it'd all get better when we came back to Scotland – but it didn't – just got worse. Then Mammie wasn't well, and she was dying, and so it was just never the right time. You were too busy with Mammie, and that's the way it should have been. I never wanted to worry anyone about my troubles. I've just kept hoping it'd all go away. But it never has.'

I swallow hard so that I can say this next thing to Da. 'And that Lorraine Pollock and her pal are the women who've been hitting wee Mary.'

Da exhales through gritted teeth. 'And you've known this all along? How could you not trust me with this? I could have made this better for you both.'

I shrug. 'I don't know. It's what I do, what I've always done. I say nothing and try to sort it myself.'

'And, how's that going?' Da sounds bitter as he swipes at the tears on his face. 'And wee Mary? She's also supposed to endure what you've been putting up with?'

'No! Of course not! That's why I've been learning boxing, Da – so that I can defend myself, and wee Mary.'

'But boxing, Aileen – really?' Da shakes his head.

'I need something. I've got to make a stand. It's the only way.'

'It's not the only way. I know people ....'

'No, Da, you'll start a war. It's me against Lorraine and JoJo.'

Da rubs his hands, a dark shadow crossing his face. 'Sounds like I need to pay Tony Pollock another visit.'

'No, Da, please.'

'I'll take care of this,' Da growls. He reaches across for my hand, but I snatch it away.

'I want to stay. I want to keep learning boxing. Please don't stop me.'

'No more boxing, Aileen. I'll sort this.'

'Go with your father.' Steve places his hand on my shoulder.

Stung by his betrayal, I shrug his hand away and snatch up my bag.

As Da's leading me out of the gym, I glance back over my shoulder. I take one last mournful look at the room, deep sadness filling me as I gaze at the bar with the photos on the wall, to the boxing ring, and over to my punching bag with the blue crosses on it. I will miss this place.

In the mirror, I see the reflection of Steve standing with his back to us, arms folded across his chest.

I will miss him.

Chapter 35

Wednesday, 10 October 1984

Wee Mary's sitting on her bed, her back against Cornflake, her giant teddy bear, as I step into her bedroom. 'Welcome home!'

She grins as she cradles Gran's statue of Our Lady. Seeing the statue in wee Mary's arms reminds me of the night after I was savagely beaten when she woke me to witness Our Lady making an appearance in her room. The memory brings me comfort, and, strangely, a glimmer of hope. 'Did you miss me?'

'Of course!' I sit beside wee Mary to give her a gentle hug. 'How are you?'

'Better, and Mr Singh's pleased with my progress.' Wee Mary frowns. 'He didn't give up, though, trying to persuade me to 'remember' the names of the women who've been beating me up.'

'You could still do that, you know. Maybe, it's what they need?'

Wee Mary shakes her head, her eyes wide and her face pale. 'I couldn't. It would make things ten times worse. I just want peace.'

I tug at some fluff on Cornflake's leg. 'So, what will you do?'

Wee Mary brightens. 'Da's promised he'll not do anything to upset the Pollocks – so that'll help.'

It's the first I learn of Da changing his mind about getting in touch with Tony Pollock. The tension that I've been carrying around in my shoulders loosens.

'And Gran's promised to walk me to and from school. Other than that, I'll just stay in the house, keep out of Lorraine and JoJo's way.'

Heartened by the sight of her looking better, I confide to wee Mary: 'I've been working on something secret that will help me stand up to them – maybe stop them once and for all.'

'I'm very good at keeping secrets.' Wee Mary eyes me as she sets Our Lady aside.

'I can't tell you – not yet.' *Maybe not ever*, I think, as I remember that I'm not allowed to train with Steve anymore. A heavy sadness descends upon me. It's only been four days, but I miss him so much.

'Does the secret involve Steve?'

'No.' I lie. 'What makes you ask that?'

'Just that you've been spending a lot of time with him, and you always come back looking happy. Those are the best kind of secrets.' She nods her head sagely.

'I run with Steve, and running makes me happy.' Then I remember to correct myself. 'Except that now Da doesn't want me to train with him.' I'm getting nearer to the truth, using the word 'training' instead of boxing.

'Why? What's Steve done?'

'It's nothing that Steve's done. It's just that I'm not to train with him.'

'I don't understand.' Wee Mary's brow furrows.

'Me, neither, to be honest. But Da's made it clear that he doesn't want me to train with Steve.'

'But you're a great runner. That must make you sad.'

'It does. But Da made me promise.'

'Made you promise not to train with Steve, or not see Steve?

'Just not to train with him.' I smile at her. 'You know, Mary? Sometimes, I think you're wise beyond your years.'

'Nah, I just spend too much time with Gran.' Wee Mary settles further back into Cornflake. 'Why don't you train on your own? You don't need Steve. Maybe go for runs when Da's working? Then he doesn't know, and you're not breaking any rules anyway.'

I stare at her. She's right – I can still train without Steve. I can go running and keep up my conditioning exercises, practice my footwork and I can shadow box anywhere. I can also keep practising that 'springing onto my feet' thing in my bedroom. I don't need to be in the gym.

The only thing missing is the punch bag because I'd like to practice hitting something, just for the connection. While my mind's mulling this over, my eyes fall onto my grinning wee sister, sitting so cosy against Cornflake.

That's it! It won't be as good as a punch bag suspended from a ceiling, but an overstuffed, giant teddy bear will do very nicely for practising my punches, and I have the boxing gloves Steve gave me.

To wee Mary's confusion and delight, I plant a smacker on her cheek. 'You are a genius!'

Chapter 36

Saturday, 13 October 1984

The day has finally arrived for Doll, Sandy, and I to have our hair permed at Steve's mum's salon. Nerves knot my stomach. Steve won't be there, but it'll be lovely to see Queenie and my pals.

I miss Steve so much. Just being in his company, hearing his voice, his laugh, watching his face while he teaches me or tells me stories. I have an ache inside of me that won't go away, no matter how hard I train or try to forget him.

My mind frequently wanders to the moment he took off my sweatshirt and the mesmerising look on his face when he brushed his fingertips across my collar bone. I relive the thrill of his cool touch. Try as I might though, I can't match the Steve in that moment with the stony-faced Steve who told me to leave with Da. When I try to make sense of it, I reason that maybe I had a bit of fluff on my shoulder that he was shifting away? But it did feel more than that.

'Aileen!' Gran roars up the stairs. 'What are you doing? It sounds like you're going to come through the living room ceiling!'

'Sorry! I'm just practising some dancing, ready for Doll's wedding.'

'Well, you sound more like a fairy elephant than a ballerina! I'm away to Moira's – you've got the house to yourself. Looking forward to getting your hair done?'

'Nervous. I'm sure it'll be fine.' I call down.

'Well, I'll see the finished result later. Cheerio!' The front door bangs, and the clicking of Gran's heels fade as she heads to her best friend's house.

The truth is, every time Da's been out, I've been boxing and practising that leaping-onto-my-feet thing Steve was teaching me.

Using Da's cloth measuring tapes, I've marked out a cross shape on my bedroom floor to practice my footwork and shadow boxing. While I'm chuffed that I've worked out this alternative way to train, it's bittersweet without Steve.

Now that the coast's clear, I fish out the bag with my gloves and bandages from under my bed. I quickly bind my fists and slip on my red boxing gloves.

'Now, for the moment of truth.' I giggle as I line my body and fists up with Cornflake, who I've perched on top of my waist-high chest of drawers, wedged in the corner between two walls.

Feeling guilty about using Cornflake as a punch bag, I switch my mind to pretend it's Lorraine. 'Take that, you cow!' Throwing out some jab combinations, I land left and right-hand body hooks and follow with some head hooks.

The only thing, though, is that a boxing bag is anonymous. It has no face. So, while I feel bad punching Cornflake, my body tingles as my fists connect with something. I focus all my anger and frustration through my fists and my sadness at losing Steve. At never having had Steve. He was never mine to lose. On and on, I punch, only stopping when I knock Cornflake to the floor and notice the time.

⇒⇒ ⋅⋅♦⋅⋅ ⇐⇐

A bell tinkles above the door of the hairdresser's as I enter, and I squeeze my eyes to soothe the stinging sensation of the cigarette smoke hanging in the air. All around, ladies are seated, facing a mirror, puffing away on cigarettes as they gossip. Just above the chatter and laughter, the lively voice of a radio DJ announces that the next song is "Eye of the Tiger" by Survivor, which cheers me because I know it's the theme tune from *Rocky III*.

Queenie waves to me from an open room at the foot of some steps at the back of the salon. When I join her, I'm relieved to find that it's less smoky down there. Four client stations line one wall, with the backwash area opposite. Queenie hugs me. 'Steve told me what happened with your dad last week. Sorry, love.'

'That's okay.'

'Steve's been acting a bit sad, too. Not that he'd admit it. Just been grumpy around the house.'

'Really?'

'Yes. He enjoyed training you, I think. Don't tell him I told you this, but I think he looked forward to it.' Queenie winks at me.

My heart gladdens on hearing this. Then it saddens me as I remember that I won't be training with him anymore. 'Will you tell him I said hello?

'Of course, love. Now, I'll just fetch my YTS girl. HEATHER!'

The girl called Heather has short, blonde spiky hair and oozes confidence as she makes her way into our area of the salon. She's wearing a figure-hugging black mini-dress, fishnet tights and boots. Her face is pale, her lips painted red, and as she approaches us, she re-positions her black-framed glasses on her nose.

I'm obviously not being subtle enough in staring at the girl because she gazes back at me, breaking into a big smile. 'Aileen?' Heather, strides towards me, holding out her hand.

'Do I know you?'

Heather takes off her glasses as though this will give me more of a clue. I blink at her. 'I've no idea who you are, sorry.'

'Heather Sneddon. We went to school together.'

It can't be. 'Heather? I haven't seen you since ...'

'The fight with Trisha Gallagher? I know.'

'What a surprise! I heard you'd taken a YTS job, but I didn't know where it was! How are you?'

Heather laughs. 'Doing great. I'm loving learning hairdressing.'

'Do you still do your art?'

She nudges her glasses up her nose. 'Well, I still draw and paint at home – and hairdressing is art when you think about it!' She grins as she spreads her arms wide to encompass the array of hairstyles in the salon.

I shake my head in wonder, trying to marry up my previous memory of Heather: the bloodied face with muddy hair stuck to it, with the self-assured and trendy lassie standing in front of me. 'You look amazing! What a transformation!'

Heather blushes as she wheels a hairdressing trolley over to Queenie.

'You sit here, Aileen. I'm starting your hair first because it's the longest, and spiral perms are trickier to do. Doll and Sandy should be here in an hour or so.'

Heather takes my jacket while I sit in the chair to face the mirror. She returns to drape a towel, a cape, and another towel over my shoulders.

As I watch Heather work, curiosity creeps through me. 'Why were you and Trisha Gallagher fighting that day?'

She cocks her head back, a smile tugging on her lips. 'I think she was afraid of me.'

'Afraid of you? Why?'

'Because I had a crush on her.'

Heather giggles as she sees my surprised expression in the mirror.

Queenie is rolling my hair into sections when the voices in the salon hush and the hairdryers are switched off. The sombre voice of the newsreader on the radio sounds out across the speakers. The main news story is about yesterday's attempted assassination of Margaret Thatcher and her cabinet when a bomb was set off in a Brighton hotel. The IRA has claimed responsibility.

Chatter erupts around us as the newscaster finishes. One lady, cigarette in hand, stands to address everyone else. 'Bloody IRA! Fenian bastards! Three dead and thirty injured! What were they thinking?'

There's a pause; then another shouts: 'It's one way to get rid of the evil witch!'

Embarrassed silence.

Another lady rises to her feet, black cape on, and with her perm rollers in, looks like a judge. 'There's no need to bomb her, or innocent bystanders. We just need to vote her and her Tory cronies out!'

Mutters of agreement fill the salon, hairdryers are switched back on, and the next song comes on the radio.

'Best to steer away from politics and religion,' Queenie mutters and smiles at me.

Then, out of the corner of my eye, I spot Sandy and Doll entering the top of the salon. Unable to move my head, I grin at my reflection.

My heart almost stops when a familiar voice pipes up at my side. 'You look fetching.' It's Steve, striding in behind Doll and Sandy. My heart explodes into a million happy pieces. It's so good to see him, but I try to act calmly while I call out greetings to them.

Heather, smiling, stands patiently by the trolley to hand Queenie each rod and piece of tissue paper. 'Shouldn't be too much longer with this part. Have a seat.' Queenie motions to the empty client chairs on either side of me. Doll takes the chair to my left and Sandy the chair to my right.

U2's "New Year's Day" plays next on the radio. Watching us from his mirror, Sandy flicks his hair. 'I've got some good news.' He pauses. 'Our Shakey's got us all tickets for the U2 concert on the seventh of November!'

'Your seventeenth birthday, Aileen!' Doll squeals.

Stunned, I can only grin from ear to ear. 'What a present! I can't wait!'

Steve touches my shoulder, his eyes twinkling. Tinkles of electricity course through my veins.

'Man, I'm nervous!' Sandy runs his fingers through his long straight hair.

'Me too!' Doll chimes in.

'It's your wedding hair, and it's going to be fine. Besides, you've placed yourselves in the capable hands of Liverpool's finest hairdresser, trained under the famous Herbert Howe!' Queenie throws her hands in the air with a flourish, a lit cigarette clenched between her teeth.

'I'm nervous too – my first ever visit to a hairdresser.' In my reflection, I look so odd. Gone is the tumble of dark hair around my face – and instead, rows and rows of blue plastic rod rollers are lined up with military precision on about two-thirds of my head. I look like an extra in *Star Trek*.

Much as I love Steve's company, I'm hoping that maybe in a parallel universe, there might be a minuscule chance that he'll want to go out with me in the future. I don't want him to hang around and see me all rollered up, like an old granny, with cotton wool lining the edge of my scalp, like some of the other ladies in the salon. That's not an attractive look. 'Haven't you somewhere more interesting to be?' I ask him, pointing in the direction of the door. Sandy and Doll nod their agreement, grinning.

'And miss all the fun here?'

Queenie makes a shooing motion with her hands. 'Off you go, lad. Their hair won't be finished for another few hours or so.'

Steve looks across the three faces in the mirror and sees we're serious. 'Okay, guess I'll go punch a bag or something. I'm coming back, though. I'm not missing the sight of Sandy in rollers!' He chuckles as he nudges my arm. 'See you later. *Good luck!*'

Once Steve leaves, Sandy seems to get lost in the music being played over the speakers, and Doll and I catch up with what's happened since the last time we saw each other, ending with Da catching me in the gym with Steve and banning me from boxing.

Doll knows me too well. 'So, as well as losing your chance to be coached by Steve, you also miss being with him? Am I right?'

I look at Sandy, but he seems to be in his own world, tapping his hands to the music on the radio. I nod quickly. 'It's so wrong that I miss him. From his point of view, he's only been training me. From mine, well, I've just loved being with him.' My face falls. 'I definitely have a crush on him.'

Doll reaches for my hand and winks at me. 'I'd already guessed that.'

I groan.

'To be fair, he'd set most lassies' hearts racing.' Doll glances at Sandy and smiles. 'All except me, of course.'

Heather leads Sandy and Doll off to shampoo their hair while Queenie finishes rolling my hair and applies the perm solution. 'That smells like rotten eggs!' I splutter, my eyes stinging again.

Queenie laughs. 'We all have to make sacrifices to be beautiful! I don't notice the smell anymore because I do that many perms. Ritchie says I stink of it when I get home, though.'

Next, Queenie rollers up Doll, telling her that she'll give her a regular perm which will look different to my spiral perm. After assessing Sandy, Queenie decides that she'll put a demi wave through his hair so that it has more of a wave than a curl. She tells him his hair will look like rock stars such as Jon Bon Jovi or David Lee Roth. Sandy's satisfied with that.

Later, Queenie partly unrolls a section of my hair to check the curl, and satisfied that the perm has taken, she instructs Heather to rinse the perm solution from my head. In between rolling Doll's hair, Queenie's blotted my hair dry with a towel. Then using a sponge, she dabbed the bleachy-smelling neutraliser solution to the plastic rods holding my hair.

Now, sitting in the backwash chair, my head laid back into the sink, Heather works quickly to release each of the rods, deftly removing the tissue papers at the same time. She applies neutraliser and then rinses and re-rinses the neutraliser solution from my hair. The rods chink as they hit the sink.

'Do you still have a crush on Trisha Gallagher?' I ask Heather, noticing the herbal smell of the conditioner she's massaging into my hair.

'Nah. I've met a nice lassie from Glasgow now.' I hear the smile in Heather's voice as she rinses off the conditioner and towel dries my hair.

'I'm glad for you.' I beam at Heather.

'It's great to finally be me.' She grins as she bundles my hair into a black towel and leads me back to my chair.

Doll's hair has been rollered, and I can smell the perm solution. Queenie's now working fast to roll Sandy's hair into thicker black rods. To the left of me, I have the pale, elfin face of Doll framed by rows and rows of little white rollers, and to the right, the larger, unshaven face of Sandy, framed by large black rollers. Just as Queenie's finished applying the perm solution to Sandy's hair, I spot Steve coming through the salon door, carrying something.

'Check you three out!' Steve laughs. We exchange glances in the mirror and chuckle too. We do look funny sat together – like three versions of Hilda Ogden from *Coronation Street*, minus the house pinafores.

Steve's brought a Polaroid camera with him, which he's now pointing at us. 'Smile!' He commands, as he takes snap after snap of us dutifully grinning or pulling funny faces and making rude hand gestures. I'm having so much fun.

In the mirror, I watch him smiling as he removes each Polaroid picture from the camera and shakes them off before placing them on a shelf nearby to dry.

Having finished applying perm solution to Sandy's hair, and Doll now over by the backwash having her hair rinsed, Queenie approaches my chair, grinning. 'Now for the moment of truth!'

I bite my lip as Queenie deftly swipes the towel from my hair to reveal a mass of limp, dark curls. We all gasp. I stare.

'What do you think?' Queenie teases and tousles my damp hair into a style using an Afro comb.

'I think it'll take a bit of getting used to!' I scrutinise my reflection. I can see that it's me, but I look so different.

'Looks great, Aileen.' Steve whistles softly as he takes another photo. Sandy grins at me.

'Gorgeous!' Doll calls to me as she's led back to her chair by Heather. 'I hope my hair turns out lovely, too.'

As Queenie and Heather work through the various stages of doing our hair, we chat and laugh and tell stories. I love watching everyone as they move and smile. Sandy can't help but tap his hands and feet to the drum rhythms playing on the radio. He and Doll exchange adoring looks, and occasionally, I catch Steve locking eyes with me, a smile on his lips. I sigh. I so miss training with him. And it turns out that we're now both single – not that that matters, as Steve thinks I'm not – and if he did know the truth, why would he be interested in me?

'Is your dad asking for me?' A shy smile flickers across Steve's face.

My face burns brighter as I remember how Steve caught me when I lost balance, how he held me there, and how the spell was only broken by the interruption from Da. Of course, I remind myself, Steve's not talking about that moment, but about Da banning me from boxing with him.

'He doesn't have anything against you. He just doesn't want me to box with you in the gym.' I pause to consider if I should tell him about my new home workout, but then the moment is broken.

'Oh my God!' Sandy shrieks, leaping to his feet. 'My hair's on fire!' Wisps of smoke rise from Sandy's head.

'Backwash, now!' Queenie's already switched on the water and quickly rinses the neutraliser solution from Sandy's head. 'Have you used any product on your hair?'

'Product? No.' Sandy mumbles.

'Henna, or maybe Sun-In?'

Sandy's voice lowers, 'Maybe a bit of Sun-In in the summer.'

Doll gasps. 'You told me that was natural – just the sun bleaching your hair!'

Sandy tries to raise his head to reply to Doll, but Queenie presses it firmly back to continue rinsing the solution from his hair. 'That's why your hair was smoking. The Sun-In's reacted with the neutraliser solution.'

'Sorry, I didn't think to say! Will my hair fall out?'

'We'll know more when we dry your hair. Heather – Doll's due to be rinsed now. Bring her over to the backwash too.'

Doll sits on the chair beside Sandy and settles her head back into the sink. We laugh as she says seriously to Sandy: 'I'll still marry you, even if you're bald.'

Queenie leaves Heather to finish rinsing Doll's hair and take the rollers from hers and Sandy's heads.

'Now, young lady, time to finish your hair.' Queenie's eyes sparkle as she scoots some styling mousse into her palm and works it through my roots. Choosing a hairdryer, she fixes what she calls a diffuser head onto it and begins to dry my hair. Steve continues to watch everybody. I close my eyes, afraid of how I'll look when Queenie's finished my hair. *What if I end up looking like a poodle? Or worse?* I've already decided that I can tie my hair back or wear a hat or just get it all chopped off if needs be.

The chinking sound of the rods being dropped into the backwash sink ring out to the background noise of the chatter between Heather, Doll and Sandy. Then I hear their voices beside me again and the high-pitched noise of other hairdryers being switched on.

Behind my closed eyes, I'm daydreaming about Steve, even though he's sitting only a few feet away from me. In my daydream, he has taken me in his arms and is staring deeply into my eyes, about to kiss me. I crane my neck to receive his kiss.

'Open your eyes, Aileen.' Queenie's voice snaps me back from my reverie.

I gasp. Instead of seeing the usual scruffy-looking lassie, a young woman stares back at me. My head is full of dark, shiny, tumbling curls, and it's so much shorter. From being below waist length when down, my hair now falls just below my shoulder blades.

Steve wolf whistles. Heat rises in my cheeks, and I cast my eyes to the floor.

'I knew you would suit this hairstyle!' Queenie exclaims, beaming at me in the mirror.

'Who's the one who's been transformed now?' Heather winks at me.

I smile shyly, unused to the attention and compliments from everyone.

Doll sits under a hairdryer stand while Queenie moves on to finish Sandy's hair. Steve takes another photo of me. 'This is one for the album, your first visit to a hairdresser.'

I dutifully smile at him, but inside, the ache of just wanting to be with him, not as a friend, but as a proper girlfriend, grows stronger. I want to be back in his arms in that moment in the gym. *Jeez, which planet am I living on? This guy's never going to be my boyfriend!* I grin at my silly self in the mirror.

'That's going to make a perfect photo!' Steve waves the new Polaroid picture around to dry before setting it on the shelf beside the others.

Heather finishes Doll's hair with a flourish. She looks stunning, with loose blonde curls perfectly framing her pretty face. We smile at each other, then turn our attention to Sandy, who frowns at his reflection as Queenie fusses around his hair.

'What's the verdict?' Sandy asks.

Queenie combs a section of hair forward at the front of Sandy's head and gently tugs at it. Part of the hair breaks off in her hands. 'We'll need to cut this off.'

Sandy's mouth drops open. 'Am I going to be bald on my wedding day?'

Queenie smiles reassuringly. 'No. We managed to catch your hair on time – not too much damage was done. I just need to cut this front section into a fringe.'

Sandy squirms in his chair, his eyes wide.

'Get your hair like mine.' Steve laughs as he points to his short blonde spiky hair.

'No danger! Why do you think me and Shakey have long hair?'

Steve and I shrug our shoulders.

'Cos our dad is ex-army, and he never stops nagging us to join up! If our hair's long, we have a case not to join any of Her Majesty's forces.' Sandy grins at his own logic, then turns to Queenie, 'So you see, I need to keep my long hair. And it has to look decent.'

'Don't worry – it's going to look great.' And Queenie was right. When she's finished cutting and drying Sandy's hair, he looks like a rock star.

Steve takes 'after' photos of the three of us, then one of Doll and Sandy together, and then I take one of him and Sandy pulling a pop band pose.

'Come on. One of you two together.' Queenie prods me in the back to go stand by Steve. As I take my place beside him, Steve places his arm across my shoulder and nudges me into his side. My heart sings when he asks, 'You coming to McCoy's tomorrow?'

Chapter 37

Sunday, 14 October 1984

'I can't believe it's less than two weeks to your wedding!' Doll and I are sitting at our usual table in McCoy's, waiting on the Clyde Alloys to come on stage. Gas has been playing a steady stream of Wham, Spandau Ballet, Duran Duran, and Madonna tracks, to keep the lassies dancing and the guys hanging around to watch them.

With her hands clasped across her tummy, Doll smiles, twirling her engagement ring around her finger. Then, she frowns. 'We'll get the keys to view our flat the week of the wedding. My mum and dad are insisting on viewing it with us.'

'That's exciting, isn't it?'

'Nope. My parents will just complain about everything. Why don't you come at the same time?'

I hesitate. 'Your mum's not a big fan of mine.'

'Steve's coming.' Doll dangles this last piece of information.

I laugh, 'That's called bribery! I'd love to come, but I don't want Steve to think I'm following him around.'

'Don't be silly. You're coming to see your best pal's new home.' Now grinning, Doll swigs her Irn Bru. 'Plus, my parents will have to curb their snobbery in front of you and Steve. So you'd be doing me a huge favour.'

'A new baby. A new husband. A new home. Wow, Doll McLintock – you don't do things by halves.' Smiling, I raise my drink in salute.

Doll twirls one of her curls. 'I'm feeling nervous now. Not about marrying Sandy, but about the day itself. What if I do something wrong – you know – with everyone watching me.'

'You're the bride. Nothing you will do will be wrong.' I take Doll's hand. 'Have to say though, that it's a mind bend to think of you as a married woman, with a baby on the way. Doesn't seem that long ago that we were hiding behind the community centre so we could share a stolen can of your dad's lager!'

Doll chuckles. 'And you – convinced you were steaming because you'd had two sips!'

'I was a bit queasy!' I protest, laughing.

Doll's face becomes serious again. 'It's definitely a time of change ahead – and for you – not just Sandy and me. Any gossip you want to share about you and Steve?' She eyes me mischievously.

'Nope. Not a thing. I'm just a girl he trained to box, who's the best friend of the drummer's soon-to-be-wife. That's it.' I shrug as though it doesn't matter, but try as I might, I just can't seem to get Steve out of my mind.

My gloom deepens as I spy some eager lassies who've already claimed their spot in front of the stage, ready for when the band comes on. I nod over in their direction. 'I mean. Even if Steve was a little interested – what chance would I stand with these lassies? They've got the looks, the charm and the money.'

'Aye, aye.' Doll's face lights up as Sandy takes a seat beside us, followed by Steve.

Steve casts me an appreciative glance. 'You look nice.'

Heat rises in my cheeks, and my mind goes blank. Perhaps sensing my embarrassment, Doll suggests to Sandy that they go to the bar to order some drinks, leaving us alone.

Steve twists a beer mat over his fingers and flicks me a shy smile. 'You still being a good girl?'

The memory of my earlier boxing session using Cornflake as a punch bag pops into my mind. Suppressing a grin, I nod.

He leans into me, a cheeky look on his handsome face. I notice that we've caught the girls' attention by the stage, and so I enjoy my time, even more, with having Steve's full attention.

I cup my hand to whisper directly into his ear, the intoxicating smell of his aftershave wafting over to me. 'Uh huh. But,' I pause for some effect, enjoying Steve's interest in what I'm about to tell him, 'I'm still training.'

He leans away from me, a large smile plastered across his face. 'Atta girl! But how?'

I quickly explain how I secretly train at home and in the Country Park, doing the conditioning exercises, practising my shadow boxing, and using Cornflake as a makeshift punch bag.

Steve's eyes glisten. 'I love that! You have the makings of a great boxer. I know your dad doesn't want you boxing, but you have natural skills. You've shown a lot of know-how in your tactics and responses.'

My breath catches as he takes my hands. 'You've no idea how happy I am to hear that you're still doing it. The more you train, the better prepared you'll be for the next time Lorraine or JoJo square up to you!'

A shadow falls across Steve's face. 'It's been strange, though. Not seeing you for the training.' Still holding my hands, he drops his head to mumble, 'I've missed you.'

'Drinks all round!' Sandy sets the drinks tray on the table. Doll eyes me in a way that asks if everything is okay. I grin in response. I'm still not sure what's happening, but it feels great to hear Steve say that he misses me.

'Come on! Time for us to get moving!' Sandy tugs Steve's T-shirt.

Clutching their drinks, Steve and Sandy head off to join the rest of the Clyde Alloys to get ready for the gig.

By the time the band files on the stage, McCoy's is packed. The crowd cheers as the Clyde Alloys play song after song. At the end of a cover of Big Country's "Fields of Fire", Steve announces that the next song is a brand-new song called "Heart Attack". The crowd bounces to the beat and joins in the chorus with their own made-up words, which go something like:

When she walks away and stares
There's nothing you can do
You just want to love her
When she comes for you
All the way to your heart
When the girl comes for you
It's like she's giving you a heart attack
Like an exploding crackerjack
All the way to your heart and back
Heart Attack

'I love this song!' Doll shouts in my ear.

The crowd reacts more enthusiastically with each track the Clyde Alloys play. An out-of-breath Steve announces that the band needs a minute or two. He strolls to the side of the stage to wipe the sweat from his face and takes a quick swig of beer. The rest of the band follows suit, some light cigarettes.

Steve gives the signal when they're ready, the lights are dimmed, and the band begins to play Cyndi Lauper's "Time after Time". Pleasantly surprised by the song choice, I stare transfixed at Steve as he sings this slow song, his soothing tones making it sound so different. His eyes closed, he brings the mood and the energy in the room right down.

Entranced, I watch him, wishing that he's thinking of me when he's singing this song. Glad that the lights are dimmed and he has his eyes closed, I drink in his every facial expression. I glance around at the mainly female faces and recognise that they must be wishing the same as me. I return my gaze to

Steve, who gently opens his eyes and searches in the semi-darkness until his eyes fall on my face. He holds my gaze while he sings, a small smile tugging on his lips. My heart soars. I cannot think. The world stands still. As Steve continues to sing, I stand there mesmerised, vaguely aware of the girls' jealous stares around me, and then, just like that, the song is over.

The spell broken, I turn to find Doll beaming at me. 'Well, look at you!'

My mind whirs, and I know I'm grinning like an idiot. I work to put a more serious, nonchalant look on my face. I'm just someone Steve knows in the crowd, his secret former boxing pal.

But it sure felt wonderful to be such a public object of his attention.

Chapter 38

Sunday, 21 October 1984

It's a blue-skied, chilly day, and wee Mary and I happily scuffle through some dried autumn leaves as we walk in the woods with Bruno. To the left, just below us, the sunshine twinkles on the River Clyde, and up ahead, a red brick railway bridge spans the wooded valley. Wee Mary's clutching a collection of her favourite leaf shapes and colours that she's planning to place in her scrapbook when we get home. Smiling, she hums a wee song to herself, her cheeks rosy.

It's been three weeks since wee Mary got out of the hospital, and her skin and asthma have improved. I believe that she hasn't met Lorraine and JoJo again because she seems so much happier and healthier.

'It was great seeing Da weeding and digging Mammie's garden today.' Wee Mary sighs as we walk arm in arm.

'I never thought I'd see the day, Mary. He was even whistling! He was all embarrassed

though when we asked him what he was doing.'
I chuckle at the memory of Da earlier, trying
to play down the fact that for the first time
since Mammie died, he was now tending to her
beloved flower beds.

Wee Mary beams. 'I love that he's planted
tulip bulbs – can't wait until they flower.
Mammie would have been so pleased.'

'Aye. Finally, Da's gardening endeavours will
look more pretty than tattie plants!'

'Feels like a fresh start.' Wee Mary says,
reaching across for the dog's lead while
handing me her leaf collection. 'Let me take the
dog.'

'Are you remembering how strong Bruno is?'

'Aye, aye.' Wee Mary waves her hand in the
air, already being dragged forward by Bruno,
who has his nose to the ground, on the trail of
something.

'Be careful!'

'He's just excited! He's found a scent.'

Bruno speeds up, yanking on his lead and
wee Mary's hand. He strains his head and neck
forward, yelping, desperate to be free of the
lead. With a final push, he lurches, and the
chains of his lead clink as they loose from wee
Mary's hand.

'Bruno! Heel!'

Oblivious to my calls, Bruno hurtles towards
the entrance to the railway bridge, his lead
trailing in the leaves behind him. We give
chase, but our shouts to Bruno are drowned
by the noise of an express train flying across
the top of the bridge. Bruno bounds under the
bridge and disappears to the right.

The noise of the express train fades into the distance, and Bruno growls and barks like he's found something. Tossing wee Mary's leaves behind me, I sprint away from her toward where I think Bruno is. My head spins. Has Bruno been hurt? No, he's not whimpering; he's snarling.

As I round the corner, my breath catches as I behold the surreal sight of Bruno pinning a half-naked Billy against a wall, snapping his teeth close to his private parts. Billy is standing in front of a girl, who gingerly steps out to reveal herself.

JoJo. Not Lorraine.

His trousers around his ankles, Billy visibly shakes as he clasps his hands together to protect his genital area. White as a sheet, JoJo slowly edges her knickers up her pink thighs and nudges her skirt down.

'Bruno never forgets the smell of a rat – a lying, cheating rat at that.'

Billy's voice trembles. 'Git yir devil dug aff me!'

Out of the side of my eye, I spot wee Mary approaching and not wishing to risk her witnessing Billy's crown jewels on display; I call Bruno off.

Bruno snarls and yelps in protest.

I repeat my command. 'Heel!' Bruno drops his tail and crawls back to me, just as Billy manages to whip up his trousers before wee Mary rounds the corner. As soon as she spots JoJo, she dashes to my side.

My cheeks burn. I'm more embarrassed that we've stumbled upon Billy and JoJo having a shag than I am about being afraid of them. My plan now is to simply walk away while burning the image of Billy's scraggy nether regions from my brain.

It's not to be, though.

'You stole ma pals fae me! You and yir scouse boyfriend!' Billy swaggers forward, waving his fist in the air.

'He's not my boyfriend. And no one took any pals away from you. You managed that all on your own.'

Billy takes a few more steps towards me.

Bruno growls, shifting on the ground, keeping his eyes locked on Billy. 'Stay!' I warn Bruno.

Wee Mary quivers against my side. 'It's okay. You stay here. Bruno will protect you.' I feel her nod as she lets me go, and I step towards Billy. JoJo scurries to his side to take his arm.

Bruno snarls behind me.

It's a week until Doll and Sandy's wedding, and I don't want any cuts or bruises, but it looks like I may be about to get into a fight.

I address JoJo. 'Do you know? Lorraine will be really interested when she finds out that you've been shagging her man. You'll no batter my wee sister ever again.'

'Whit dae ye mean? Ah kin batter the shite oot i' yir wee scabby sister, any time I like!' She smiles smugly at Billy.

My fists clench, my jaw tightens. I am so close to losing my cool.

Billy drops JoJo's arm, strides right up to me, and leans his face into mine. 'If you know whit's guid fir ye, you'll no' breathe a word to Lorraine about this. *Ya Fenian hoor*!'

'Fucking *liar*!' I respond. Incensed, remembering how much wee Mary's suffered, adrenaline pumps through me. It's taking all my strength not to react.

Bruno responds to my raised voice and catches Billy's attention when he jumps to his paws to snap and snarl at him.

Not missing a beat, I take the opportunity to drive as hard a left and right hook as I can into Billy's ribs. He crumples onto the path. JoJo's jaw drops, and she stumbles backwards.

Trembling, and now not caring how I'll look next week, I challenge JoJo, 'Do you want some too?'

JoJo shakes her head, wide-eyed at the sight of Billy holding his sides, moaning on the ground.

I twist away from them and walk back to wee Mary and Bruno.

My knuckles smart as I take wee Mary's hand. 'Now I know what it feels like to punch a real person! It felt great. And even better, my first time was Billy McIntyre! Lying, cheating shite!'

Wee Mary beams and Bruno trots beside us, wagging his tail.

Chapter 39

Wednesday, 24 October 1984

'Home, sweet home!' Sandy shoves the front door open. Steve and I follow him and Doll into their new council flat, almost tripping over the piles of old post and newspapers on the way in.

I zip my jacket up against the chill nipping at my skin. A sour smell makes me cough.

Doll catches me covering my nose. 'Dampness. Nobody's lived here for months.'

'It's our gain, though.' Sandy tries to sound cheerful as he gives us a tour of the flat, which takes less than two minutes. There is a small lounge, a kitchen, a bathroom, and two bedrooms. The wallpaper in each room is either well-worn or has fallen off in sections, presumably because of the black damp patches growing on most of the walls. There are no carpets, no curtains, not even a light bulb.

In the bathroom, the dampness is especially dark and lumpy around the perimeter of the bath, sink and toilet. Various tiles lie smashed on the ragged linoleum floor. A deep crack runs the length of the bathroom window. The mould in the kitchen is just as bad, with cupboard doors missing and exposed wiring on the plug points.

'It must be freezing in here in the winter.' I remark without thinking.

Doll frowns. 'Aye, the Council's coming out next week to see what needs to be repaired, and then it's up to us to do the rest. Of all the rooms, we need to make sure that the baby's room is cosy and finished by February.'

Sandy rubs Doll's baby bump. 'I can't wait for then. Although this place is a shit tip now, we'll soon have it looking lovely.'

'I'll give you a hand with what needs to be fixed and painted. Beer works as payment.' Steve winks at Sandy, who smiles back gratefully.

'And I'll help with the tidying and cleaning, Doll.' I hug her. 'Can't believe you have your own place. So grown up!'

Doll laughs. 'It's not ideal, but it'll do us until we can get on our feet.'

A loud rap on the front door makes us jump. 'Doll and Sandy?' A man's voice roars.

'It's my mum and dad.' Doll rolls her eyes as she leaves to let her parents in.

As soon as they enter the living room, the pinched faces of the McLintocks say it all as they scan the tatty, neglected interior of their daughter's new home.

'Has your father viewed this flat?' Mr McLintock addresses Sandy.

'No, we're the first to view it. My mum and dad wanted us to see it first, and then you decided to come too. We would have fixed some of it ....'

Mr McLintock's moustache twitches. 'Son, the place is not even fit for rats to live in. We cannot allow our daughter to live here, never mind with our grandchild. They'd be in the Law Hospital in no time. Is this really how you intend to look after our daughter? Is this the standard of what we can expect of you as a husband and a father?'

Sandy flicks his hair out of his eyes and shoves his hands in his pockets. 'It might not be brilliant, but we'll fix it up with a bit of time.'

'You need to earn a proper living. Tell us again how you intend to support our daughter and grandchild?'

'Mr McLintock, you know how hard it is to get a job around here, especially when you're my age. There are only crap jobs with crap wages. My dream's to make it with my band – '

'We all had dreams, son. But you soon put them aside when you get married and have a family.'

'Simon!' Mrs McLintock places her hand on her husband's shoulder and shakes her head.

Mr McLintock shrugs off his wife's hand. 'The laddie has to know the truth of how we feel!'

Sandy pulls himself up tall. 'I might be signing on, Mr McLintock, but I'm still making some cash on the side.'

'What? By stealing coal from the Craig? Do you think I don't know? Do you think we want a son-in-law who's a common thief? And what happens when you get arrested and charged? What happens to our daughter and grandchild then, eh?' Mr McLintock visibly shakes, his face purple. 'And then there's me – your father-in-law – a policeman!'

Doll puts her arm around Sandy's waist. 'We'll get by, Dad. We don't need either of you to come here and tell us how to live!'

Uncomfortable with witnessing a personal family disagreement, I suggest to Steve that we wait outside. In the lobby, we lean against the wall, facing each other. The noise of the voices inside the house becomes louder, more animated, and angrier.

'Not a good sign, and only three days from the wedding.' Steve whispers.

'Poor Doll and Sandy! This is all they need!' I wring my hands and wince as I catch a scab on my right knuckle.

'Training injury?' Steve reaches across to examine my hand.

'Not exactly. I decked Billy McIntyre on Sunday.'

Steve whistles softly, and grins. 'Atta girl.'

Chapter 40

Saturday, 27 October 1984

The living room of Doll's parents' home is festooned with various ribbons, bows, and balloons on this, her wedding day. She's seated on a wooden chair across from me, wearing a towelling dressing gown, with her hair in rollers and Queenie applying her make-up. Doll's wedding dress and my bridesmaid dress hang from the wall unit. Her mum and aunts filter in and out of the living room to fuss over Doll.

Heather's just finished putting rollers in my hair. I smile across at Doll, whose hands are resting on her bump.

'Special delivery for the bride-to-be!' Mrs McLintock sails into the living room, enjoying the attention of being the Mother-of-the-Bride, to present Doll with a gift-wrapped package and a bunch of red roses. 'A ginger-haired laddie chapped the door. Said these are from Sandy, and to make sure you got them right away.'

I join the ladies in gathering around Doll as she unwraps the package to reveal a red, heart-shaped jewellery box. When she opens the clasp, a white card falls out, and her voice breaks as she reads it aloud: 'For my beautiful bride. I love you now and forever. Sandy. Kiss.' We sigh as Doll shows us the beautiful pearl necklace with matching earrings displayed inside the box.

'He's bought me my wedding jewellery. I told him about the cheap jewellery I'd bought in the market and how I wasn't pleased with it.' She smiles at us, a tear in her eye.

Mrs McLintock brushes her daughter's cheek, and murmurs, 'I wonder where he got the money to buy these.' She unhooks the wedding dress from the wall unit and, smiling, says, 'Time to get dressed.' Doll follows her mum out of the room, their differences put aside for the day, with her aunts trailing behind her. The sight gladdens my heart.

Tugging at the tail of my happiness for Doll is a sad regret that I won't have Mammie fussing over me on my wedding day.

Sat back on my chair again, Queenie applies my make-up and styles my hair into a French twist at the back, with loose curls on top. She slips a silver tiara into the top of my hair and fastens a silver bracelet onto each of my wrists. Queenie looks at me approvingly. 'We'll leave so you can get dressed.'

Alone, I gently pull on the figure-hugging bridesmaid dress and breathe a sigh of relief as it zips smoothly. Despite the rigorous boxing training, I was worried that I might have put on weight since the last dress fitting. I slip on the delicate silver high heels that Doll chose to match the dress. Curious to see how I look. I wander over to the mirror hanging above the fireplace. I like the result. The lady staring back at me from my reflection looks older – elegant even – like one of those ladies in the perfume adverts.

The bridesmaid dress's sweetheart neckline sits snugly across my bust, the midnight blue silk fabric complementing my pale skin. As I turn, a glint catches the light from the centre of the sweetheart neckline, at the bottom of the V shape. I smile as I touch Mammie's crystal bead that Mrs Hooper kindly added to my dress.

A gentle knock at the door and Queenie and Heather re-enter the living room. Queenie nods at me approvingly. 'My, you look beautiful.'

Squeals and giggles alert us that the other ladies are approaching. Doll glides in – a vision in white in her wedding dress, carrying a pink-flowered head garland.

She beams at me. 'You can't see my bump, can you?' Doll turns to the side. She's naturally slim, and the small bump she does have, has been expertly disguised by Mrs Hooper, who's created a few extra folds of fabric to drape delicately around Doll's tummy area.

'No. Besides, no one is going to be looking at your stomach. They'll all be mesmerised by the sight of you in this stunning wedding dress and jewellery, with your beautiful hair and face.' I hug her gently.

'You don't scrub up so bad yourself, Aileen.'

I chuckle: 'I suppose it makes a change from us wearing muddy cross-country clothes!' A touch of sadness casts a shadow over my heart saying this, as today marks a whole new chapter in our friendship. Gone are the giggly, girlish days; Doll will soon be a married woman and a mother.

Queenie guides Doll to sit. Using clear comb slides, Queenie expertly sweeps up the hair on either side of Doll's ears, leaving the crown and back of her head a mass of soft curls. Next, she carefully places the circular garland of fresh flowers on Doll's head and pins her long veil to the back of this. Doll rises to face us.

Tears spring to my eyes. 'You look like an angel. You'll take Sandy's breath away when he sees you.'

Sniffles break out around us, and Doll's mum and aunts whip out hankies, smiling through their tears.

'Come on, you lot! Everyone's make-up is going to be running!' Queenie shoos us out of the room. 'The cars are ready. Time to go!'

I lift Doll's wedding bouquet and my own from the hall table before I step out into the dry and chilly October day, and take my place on the path, facing the front door.

Doll's father waits to greet his daughter as she comes out of the front door. He's stood proudly to attention, wearing a green and blue kilt in his family's tartan. A sporran hangs on a leather and silver chain. The colours of the family tartan contrast vividly with his black dress jacket and waistcoat with silver buttons. A tie that matches the tartan of his kilt is knotted against a crisp white shirt. His black brogues have been polished to such a shine that they stand out against the matt black of his knee-length socks. The hilt of his *sgian dubh*, the traditional single-edged knife in a cover, sticks out the top of his right sock.

Neighbours gather on the other side of the garden fence to wish the bride well as she leaves her family home for the last time as a single woman. The heads of small children bob around just above the hedge line, itching to get a better look at the 'princess', and as she steps outside to take her dad's arm, Doll waves to the small crowd who clap and cheer.

With a camera hanging from her neck, one of Doll's aunts snaps the scene as the chauffeur opens the door to Doll's wedding car and her dad kisses her on the cheek before helping her inside.

Just like I've done on countless occasions, the children here are waiting for the traditional 'scramble'. Doll's father tosses handfuls of coins for the shrieking children to catch, a tradition meant to bring good luck and fortune to the happy couple. I scoot to enter the wedding car on the other side. Neighbours and onlookers gather around, clapping and cheering.

Once inside, I rearrange Doll's dress and veil for her. 'Happy?'

'Never happier.' Doll's eyes shine.

Mrs McLintock and the rest of the wedding party disappear into various cars, and then our vehicle moves off. The church is only a ten-minute drive away, but we do two loops of the route to allow the guests to get into the church on time. Our wedding car with the white bow on the front draws many admiring glances from passers-by on the street, who peer intently into the windows to catch a glimpse of the bride. Doll giggles and waves at some of them, enjoying the attention. When we finally arrive at the church, our car is met by the red-kilted Shakey. He opens the car door for Mr McLintock, who offers his hand to help his daughter exit the vehicle.

'Great to see you didn't change your mind, my soon-to-be sister-in-law.' Shakey grins through his bushy beard at Doll. 'Our Sandy's been convinced you'd change your mind or something!'

Doll laughs as she steps out of the car and stops to pose for more photographs with her dad and then just inside the church.

Rearranging Doll's dress, veil, and hair one last time, I kiss her on the cheek and hand her the bridal bouquet. I do my best to ignore the butterflies working overtime in my tummy so that I can help Doll and her dad, who both look nervous. The opening bars of the "Wedding March" sound out across the church. Shakey offers his arm to me, which I take, grateful for something substantial to hold on to as I'm trembling so badly. We're first to make an entrance. He gives my arm a reassuring squeeze with his hand and escorts me up the aisle, nodding and grinning at the wedding guests as we pass by them. I know Da, Gran and wee Mary are in the congregation somewhere, but the sea of smiling faces is just a blur as I concentrate on not tripping and getting to the altar in one piece.

Sensing how calm Shakey is, helps me to relax, too, so that by the time we reach the front pews, I'm able to fully focus on the smiling face of Steve. I blush as he mouths 'wow' at me as I pass him. Shakey kisses me on the cheek and walks to the right of the altar to stand by his brother's side. I walk to the left and turn to face the bottom of the aisle.

Sandy looks so handsome. He's wearing the same red kilt as his brother and his father, but his jacket is longer and fancier. As well as a tartan tie, he's also wearing a plaid over one of his shoulders which matches his kilt. His sporran is more ornate and distinctive too. As he turns his head to look down the aisle, I spot that he's tied his hair back with a thin, black velvet bow. The congregation stands as Doll, escorted by her dad, glides up the aisle, clutching her bouquet and smiling at her friends and family on either side of the church. She looks radiant and relaxed.

I watch Sandy's face as he catches the first glimpse of Doll approaching the front of the church. His eyes shine. They exchange smiles as Doll offers her cheek to her father to kiss. Sandy holds his hand out to Mr McLintock, who pauses, then, smiling at Doll, shakes Sandy's hand before he takes his seat beside Mrs McLintock in the front row. Sandy leads Doll to the altar, and the Minister opens his bible. Shakey stands beside Sandy, and I take my position behind Doll, fixing her veil and dress one last time.

The wedding ceremony passes by in a blur except for the amusing moment when Sandy and Doll are making their wedding vows and placing the rings on each other's fingers. 'Do you, Alexander Dunphy Ross take Dora Alice McLintock to be your lawful wedded wife?' *Dunphy?* What kind of a middle name is *Dunphy?* I glance at Steve, who's twisting his face to suppress a grin. I, too, do my best to keep my face straight through what's supposed to be a very serious section of the service. I duck my head, blushing.

When it's safe to look up, I find Steve grinning at me. I smile in return, my cheeks burning. He may not be my boyfriend, but it's safe to say that we're friends.

And I'm good with that – for now.

Chapter 41

Saturday, 27 October 1984

It's dark when we arrive at McCoy's, where the wedding reception's being held. Shakey disappears inside, leaving me to stand outside on the pavement with Doll's and Sandy's parents. The wedding guests are already inside, being entertained by Gas's stellar music selection as they wait for the happy couple.

Shakey returns with a bagpiper in full highland dress, including a tall, black feathery hat I've only seen on drawings on the front of whisky bottles. As the piper approaches us, grinning, I realise that it's Ruaridh. 'Surprise!' He bellows, laughing.

'You play the bagpipes too?'

Ruaridh shrugs. 'Guy of many talents.'

The wedding car approaches, and the chauffeur holds the door open for Sandy and Doll. Radiant, they step out into the streetlight.

'Congratulations, and welcome, Mr and Mrs Ross! I'm your piper for the evening.' Ruaridh bows, laughing as they recognise him. 'This is your wedding present from me.'

Ruaridh addresses Shakey. 'Tell Gas to announce that the newlyweds are about to enter. I want happy people with clappy hands as I lead Sandy and Doll in. I'll play "Scotland the Brave". That should get their toes tapping!' He points at the parents and me. 'You lovely folks follow behind Doll and Sandy.'

Shakey disappears into McCoy's. The music inside stops, and we hear the muffled voice of Gas as he makes an announcement. Shakey comes back out to escort me into the wedding procession. A thrill of excitement courses through me as Ruaridh sounds out the first skirling notes on his bagpipes. The noise is loud and commanding, making my heart thunder in my chest. Ruaridh stands in front of Doll and Sandy and twirls round to face the door, his kilt and piper's plaid swinging majestically with his movement.

Pride swells inside me as the doors to McCoy's are held open by the bouncers, and Mr and Mrs Ross enter to the sound of enthusiastic clapping and loud cheering. Shakey and I hold back for a minute or so, and followed by the parents, we enter the reception room to take our place at the top table near the stage. Da, Gran and wee Mary are stood about a third of the way down the pub, and I blow them a kiss as I'm escorted past them.

The dinner courses come and go, and the speeches are made. The noise of chatter and laughter fills the room. The more whisky and wine that's poured, the friendlier Doll and

Sandy's parents become with each other. The sight gladdens my heart.

Later, Gas stops the music to announce the first dance of the newly married couple. With the wedding guests lining the dance floor, Sandy leads Doll on a waltz to one of their favourite love songs, "Can't Fight This Feeling" by REO Speedwagon.

The next song is "Time After Time" by Cyndi Lauper, which makes me think of Steve. My heart skips a beat as, across the dance floor, I find him watching me, a small smile playing on his lips.

Mr McLintock taps Sandy on the shoulder to take Doll away on the traditional Dad and Daughter dance. He looks so proud, waltzing his beautiful daughter around the dance floor, their differences set aside. As I'm watching Sandy ask Doll's mum to dance, someone taps me on my shoulder. It's Shakey. He bends in a mock bow. 'Would you care to dance, Chief Bridesmaid? It's another wedding tradition.'

I hesitate. I didn't know about this one. I wouldn't be comfortable dancing in front of all these people. But Shakey's face falls a little, and I feel bad.

'Of course. I'd be delighted.' I give a little pretend curtsy, and he laughs.

Shakey's surprisingly light on his feet for a big man as he twirls me around the dance floor, weaving us expertly around Doll and her dad, and Sandy with Doll's mum. Feeling great, I ask Shakey: 'Now that we're better acquainted, will you tell me your real name?'

'It's Hugh.' He tickles my ear with his beard.

'So, why 'Shakey'?'

He smiles and twirls me around some more. 'Oh, for that, I'll need to get to know you a lot better!'

I make a sad face, and he chuckles, clearly delighted that I'm itching to know. All too soon, the song ends, and Shakey releases me with another mock bow. I pretend to spread the back of my dress and curtsy in return. We both laugh, and he pats me on the head as he leads me back to my table, with Sandy and Doll following.

Doll's cheeks glow as she snuggles into Sandy. 'Are you having a good time?'

I nod, squishing my cheeks into a grin. 'All your wedding plans are working out perfectly, eh?'

'I know. I wasn't expecting it to turn out this well. And that Ruaridh was an amazing surprise!' Doll clasps her hands together, beaming as she looks around at her guests dancing, enjoying themselves.

Sandy leans into both of us. 'And we have another surprise!' He slides the velvet bow from his hair and shakes his curls across his shoulders. He gives Doll a lingering kiss, 'See you soon, Mrs Ross,' and walks out of the front door of McCoy's. We are all left puzzled. Ruaridh seems to have disappeared, too, while Gas continues playing pop tunes.

The evening reception guests have been filtering in, filling the room some more. A swishing noise catches our attention, and the red curtains covering the stage behind us separate as Gas lowers the music. On stage are the Clyde Alloys, and Sandy runs on from the side to take his place behind the drums. The full band are dressed in the Ross Red tartan kilts, black jackets and waistcoats. I almost faint at the sight of Steve in a kilt. Boy, does he have great legs! I hadn't noticed what he was wearing in the church because I was so busy looking at his face.

'Good evening, ladies and gentlemen. Welcome to the wedding reception of Mr and Mrs Ross!' Steve extends his arm towards Sandy, who rises from behind his drum kit, and Doll's parents coax her to stand. The guests cheer loudly. Steve continues, 'The Clyde Alloys are Sandy's band, and so it wouldn't be a wedding without a little set from us!'

Sandy taps his drumsticks together, and the band launches into "Fields of Fire". Doll and I join the rest of the wedding guests on the floor to dance to the rallying guitars, which sound a lot like bagpipes being played. The Clyde Alloys are enjoying themselves on stage, swinging their kilts in time to the music. The band's set tonight is perfect with songs by U2, Lloyd Cole and the Commotions, Simple Minds, and then, a wee bit cheekily, Steve announces that the next song is for the chief bridesmaid – me. My cheeks burn as the band launches into the JoBoxers song, "Boxerbeat". Confused but amused, the guests grin at me as Steve belts out the catchy lyrics. I smile sheepishly.

The band and the crowd chant 'boxerbeat', stamping their feet in time to the bass drum's double beat each time that's sung. I have never been in a room packed with people so intent on having a great time; my cheeks are sore from smiling. All too soon, the Clyde Alloys finish their set with a flourish, leaving the crowd breathless and happy.

Gas softens the room's energy with easier-paced pop songs. I go find my family.

'You look beautiful, just like your mammie.' Da says. 'I'm afraid to crumple you!'

'Just like a movie star, Aileen!' Gran beams, and wee Mary gazes up at me adoringly.

Gas plays a mix of songs from the fifties, sixties, and seventies, encouraging all the age groups up to dance. When he puts on a medley of Beatles songs, Da invites the three of us to dance. He bats off my refusals and swings the three of us onto the dance floor. I look around at my family's smiling faces and realise that we've never danced together like this at an event since before Mammie died. The thought gladdens my heart, and I hug each of them.

It's then that I sense someone watching me. It's Marie. Ruaridh has his arm around her while he chats to Frankie Fingers and Rab from the band.

Marie walks towards me, smiling. 'You look stunning!'

I tap the tiara. 'I don't know how Princess Diana wears these. They fair dig into your head!' We giggle as we stroll over to Ruaridh, Rab and Frankie Fingers.

While we're chatting, I peer around the semi-darkness and multi-coloured flashing disco lights.. Through a gap in the dancing crowd, I can see the side of Steve's face as he chats and laughs with Queenie and Ritchie. I smile at the sight. Not only have I been so lucky to have met Steve, but also his family, whom I've grown fond of. Steve senses me looking and beckons me to come over. Marie encouragingly shoos me off, but not before she gives me another hug.

Steve stands as I approach their table. He puts his hand on my back and says wickedly: 'Did you like your song?'

'I did, but I'm not sure Da did.' I jab him in the arm.

Steve chuckles. 'Couldn't resist, sorry.' Then, with a more serious look, he says: 'I thought you'd be with your boyfriend – is he coming later?'

'We split up.'

Steve frowns. 'You didn't mention it ....'

'I didn't think you'd be interested.' I drop my head to watch the colours of the disco lights twirl on the dance floor. But consumed with curiosity, I dare to look up to gauge his reaction.

His eyes hold mine. He smiles as he bends his head towards me. 'In that case, I can tell you this.' His mouth brushes my ear, my heart races. 'You take my breath away.' I'm stunned, unsure of how to respond, except to smile across at Queenie and Ritchie as a greeting.

Inside, I'm bursting with joy. I want nothing more than to be standing here with Steve's hand on my back and the sound of his voice in my ear as he tells me that he likes me. The spell's broken, though, when Queenie ushers me to sit beside her to compare notes on what's happened so far at the wedding. I huddle in to speak with Queenie and Ritchie, aware of Steve's eyes on me.

'Ok, ladies and gentlemen!' Gas's voice booms across the speakers as he lowers the music. 'It's time for a wee ceilidh! Please welcome back our new resident piper, our very own Ruaridh McDonald! Go grab your partner and take your place on the dance floor for the Gay Gordons!'

There's a lot of chair scraping and chatter as coupled dancers take their positions in a big circle. I love Scottish country dancing; it's always great fun to watch as well as take part in.

'Come on, kid! Time for another dance with your old da!' Before I know it, Da's led me away from Steve onto the dance floor to take up the start position for the Gay Gordons. Ruaridh's standing on the stage, back in full Highland regalia, sounding the dance's opening notes on his bagpipes. The anticipation and excitement in the room grow as we pause, waiting for the point to begin the dance.

In time with everyone on the dance floor, we step forward for four counts and back for four counts, repeat, then Da holds his hand above my head, and I twirl underneath for four counts. We finish that set with a waltz and keep repeating the sequence. Some couples ahead and behind get the dance wrong, and pileups are happening around the floor, with people laughing good-naturedly as they crash into each other. By the end of the dance, we are all doing our own thing, and wheeze with laughter as we collide around the floor in any old way which suits us. Da and I flump back on our chairs, out of breath.

'Ok, you crazy lot! You need me as a caller. Luckily, I also learned how to do this at DJ school!' Gas, smart in a suit, shirt and tie and no eyeliner for a change, takes the mic and announces each dance's name and calls out step-by-step directions.

I enjoy watching Doll, Sandy, and their families have so much fun on the dance floor. Feeling a little left out and mischievous, I skip back over to Steve and ask him to dance. I can tell that his first reaction is to decline, but a warning look from Queenie has him shaking his head in disbelief. 'All right – I'll have a go at this Jock dancing!'

Next thing, we take our places for Strip the Willow alongside three other couples. Steve is hilarious as he tries to follow what he's supposed to be doing in the dances. He turns the wrong way, he turns me the wrong way, and at various times, we're bent over double, laughing our heads off. 'Listen and learn those combinations!' I shout at him, mocking what he's been saying to me for the last few months. We dance the room's length and breadth; Steve's brow furrows as he concentrates on following Gas's instructions. After the fourth dance, Steve is getting better so that by a third of the way through each dance, he has the steps.

'I never knew this Jock dancing could be so much fun! The skirt helps!' Steve jokes, twirling his kilt a little more than necessary and attracting the attention of some lassies nearby.

I decide to be brazen. 'The big question is – are you a true Scotsman?'

'Well, I did start off wearing boxer shorts, but the lads said they wouldn't play tonight unless I went commando!' He winks at me, and I blush.

Gas is on the mike again. 'That's the ceilidh finished now.' There's a collective moan from the wedding guests. 'I know, but poor Ruaridh could do with a pint, and I need to rest my voice. More importantly, though – we need to wish Mr and Mrs Ross well as they'll be leaving soon for their honeymoon on Loch Lomond!'

Later, when Gas lowers the music to announce that it's time for Sandy and Doll to cut the wedding cake, Steve takes my hand. 'Come with me.'

I follow him through the crowd to stand in a semi-circle as we applaud the moment Sandy unsheathes a ceremonial sword, and he and Doll, with their hands on its hilt, make the first cut in the wedding cake. They twist around to face their guests and blink in the flash of camera bulbs. It's then that Steve puts his arm around my waist. This feels more intimate than a friendly arm across my shoulder. I turn to him in the semi-darkness. His eyes are soft.

Oh my. Is he going to kiss me? Steve's hand gently presses on my hip as he guides me around to face him. Inclining his head towards mine, he places his forefinger under my chin to tilt my face up to his. I've lost all sense of where we are and who we're with. All that matters is this moment, right here, right now. I close my eyes. My heart explodes as his soft lips brush mine.

A cheer erupts behind us, and startled, we break our kiss to watch as the newlyweds leave the room to change into their honeymoon clothes. A little later, Doll, in a pink dress and jacket and Sandy, in a grey suit, appear holding hands, ready for their honeymoon.

Gas plays Runrig's jolly version of "Loch Lomond", which has everyone breathless with excitement as they sing, dance and link arms to form a great circle around Doll and Sandy in the middle. As far as I can tell, there are no rules to this dance other than the dancers holding each other's hands while they encircle the newlyweds. The circle becomes an oblong shape as the dancers step forward into the centre, their faces bright with mischief as they squash the couple in the middle. Da, Gran and wee Mary are opposite us and take great delight in running towards Steve and me. The farewell dance finishes with loud clapping, cheering and whistling. Group hugs erupt around the room. I'm so enjoying my first time at a wedding.

Sandy and Doll have made their way to the top of the room again to collect their honeymoon bags. The wedding guests throng around them.

Smiling, Steve takes my hand to lead me towards the bar. 'Let's get a drink. It'll take them another half an hour just to get to the front door with all the well-wishing.'

A big grin spreads across my face. I didn't think this day could get any better, but it just has.

Chapter 42

Saturday, 27 October 1984

'Great wedding, but time for us to go.' Gran bustles over to me, smiling, with wee Mary in tow, both dressed in their coats. She waves over to Da, chatting to some old pals at the bar.

Gesturing to Steve, who has his back to us while he's waiting to be served at the bar, Gran nudges me. 'Looks like you've been having lots of fun with that laddie.' She cocks her head, a wicked smile on her face. 'Do you know if he's a Catholic or a Protestant yet?'

'Gran!' I smile as I kiss her and wee Mary goodbye.

I watch them as they stop along with some other people to wish Doll and Sandy well on their way out. The newlyweds are still completing the round of hugs that is like an obstacle course they have to make their way through before they can leave for their honeymoon.

Steve notices I'm standing on my own and pulls me into the space beside him at the bar. I watch our reflections in the mirror behind the bar. The tiara glints under the bar spotlights. It's still digging into my head, but as it's not every day I wear one, I'm putting up with the discomfort. Behind me, the reception is in full swing. Multi-coloured disco lights strobe through the darkness, lighting the cheerful faces of the guests as good-natured chatter and laughter bubble underneath the beat of the music. About halfway down the room, Marie, Ruaridh and the rest of the band are spaced across several tables, chatting and laughing. I'm so glad that Marie and I have made up. We smile at each other, and she makes an approving face to indicate that she's noticed who I'm standing beside.

Feeling pleased, I allow myself to sneak another look at the side profile of Steve's handsome face as he makes our drinks order. I sigh. What would I give to have this guy as my boyfriend? I touch my fingers to my lips as I remember our earlier kiss. The one that was interrupted by the announcement that Doll and Sandy were about to leave. Except they're still here, speaking to Sandy's parents, trying their best to exit out the front door. Will Steve kiss me again tonight? I smile ruefully at my reflection.

'What are you thinking about?' Steve cuts through my daydream to hand me my drink.

I tell a half-truth. 'Poor Doll and Sandy must be champing at the bit to get away.' We look in their direction. Mr McLintock stands beside them, dressed in his coat, pulling on black leather gloves, getting ready to drive them to their hotel on Loch Lomond tonight.

Although people have been leaving, it seems like the wedding reception is still full, as if extras have filled in for them. No one I recognise from earlier. And they're dressed more casually than you would be for a wedding reception.

At the same time as I notice this, a lull descends on the party, like someone has lowered a volume switch somewhere. I turn around to Steve – almost in slow motion – something shiny sails through the space between our faces and smashes against the bar mirror behind us. I stare stupidly at the broken pint glass shattered across the drinks shelf and spin back to register the shock on Steve's face.

Out of the speakers, there's a sharp, scratching sound of the record needle being hastily lifted, and the dance music abruptly stops.

Silence.

Everything and everyone seems to stand still – just for a heartbeat.

Then out of the gloom emerges Billy McIntyre, running full tilt at us, his face twisted. He roars at Steve: 'Ya scouse bastard! You stole ma best pal, and you stole ma fuckin' band!'

I scream.

Steve shoves me to one side so that he can punch Billy square in the face. As Billy's knocked off his feet, I sprint to the side of the room to hide under the buffet tables with other ladies seeking safety as fighting amongst the men breaks out all around us. The strangers must be part of Billy's gang.

Gas ducks behind the transparent screen of his DJ booth as glasses are hurled through the air. Guys lurch at each other from every direction, cracking the ends off beer bottles to use as weapons and throwing punches. I can't believe my eyes. Why has the good-natured, happy wedding atmosphere been replaced so quickly with a full-on fistfight?

Sandy shields a dazed-looking Doll behind his back and unsheathes the sword he's just cut his wedding cake with. Brandishing this at anyone who comes near them, he quickly backs him and Doll towards the open front door.

Past the chaos of chairs being tossed, tables overturned, and bodies clashing, Mr McLintock yells at the bouncers to call the police before sprinting to get into the driver's side of the car waiting outside. My heart sinks at the sight of Doll's face, pale and miserable, as she slumps into the back seat.

A small crowd who've innocently gathered to wish the newlyweds well watch on in horror as the groom comes flying towards them while sheathing a sword, his long hair flying behind him as he jumps into the car. Mr McLintock pulls away with a high-pitched screech, the words 'Just Married' written in shaving foam on the back window peel away to land on the onlookers. Empty Tennents Lager cans tied with string to the back bumper clank noisily on the road as the car speeds off.

Back in McCoy's, my body trembles as chaos unfolds before me. The figure of Billy lies prostrate on the floor. Standing head and shoulders above the scrapping crowd, I spot Shakey, Steve's dad, and the bouncers in the middle of the fight, trying to stop it, but pretty soon, they give up and start punching the faces of guys that, hopefully, they don't recognise. Steve is also out there hitting anyone who comes near him.

A lone guy staggers to his feet. He's clutching a knife and heading toward Steve, who has his back to him, defending himself against two other guys. My heart drops – it's Billy McIntyre again! Fumbling, I shove the heels off my feet and stagger out from under the table, knocking it sideways, intending to stop Billy from reaching Steve, but with absolutely no idea how I'm going to do it.

I've dislodged the tiara and yank it free from my hair, and as I bolt forward, I launch it like a frisbee towards Billy. The tiara sparkles in the silent disco lights as it strikes Billy on the head.

He stops in his tracks.

He twists around and shakes his head at me, as he spots the tiara lying on the floor. He leers as he pretends to draw the knife across his neck. Fear floods through me.

Then everything happens in slow motion again. I'm on a forward momentum towards Billy and his knife. Steve is further away with his back to both of us, still fighting the two guys, when out of nowhere, Da appears, arms raised, his face etched with pure rage. I gawp as he seems to fly through the air to take Billy down, 'You fecking bastard!'

Da grabs Billy's wrist to shake the knife out of his hand, wrestling him to the ground at the same time. 'I know what you did to my lassie!' Da has Billy pinned to the ground on his back, punching him.

Billy, defiant, sneers: 'Yir lassie's a hoor!' The veins on his neck stand out as he raises his shaven head. 'She loves giein' heid, by the way!'

Da smacks Billy so hard that even in the noise and confusion of the fighting, I hear the crack of his head as it bounces off the floor.

A glint catches my eye in the flashing disco lights. It's Billy's knife, and it's lying too close for my comfort to the skinhead's hand. I must protect Da.

The figure-hugging bridesmaid dress I'm wearing is fine for a wedding but not much use in a bar brawl. Getting ready to fight, I shimmy the dress fabric up my thighs, and as I use my foot to kick the knife away, I'm knocked off my feet to land with an agonising crunch on my side.

'Aw no, you don't, ya *durty hoor!*' To my horror, Lorraine Pollock's standing over me, clutching the knife in her chubby hand, 'Ah'm gonna cut yir ugly, hoory face!'

Not again. My mind reels. What was it that Steve taught me? *Jeez. What are the rules if you're about to be slashed by a crazy, knife-wielding lassie?*

Lorraine licks her lips, flicks a strand of her sweaty fringe out of her eyes as she advances closer, the knife pointed towards my face.

I freeze.

Move! My mind screams, but I'm paralysed by fear, capable only of lying here on the floor, useless and vulnerable.

'On! Your! Feet!' Steve roars so loudly that it snaps me into action.

I propel my body away from Lorraine and, in one move, kick my legs out and spring to my feet.

'Now that was a skoosh!' Steve cheers somewhere behind me which fills me with much-needed courage.

Instinctively, as he taught me, I immediately assume my boxing stance, clenching my fists on either side of my head. Tucking my elbows in, I keep my chin down and pray that Lorraine can't tell that I'm shaking from head to toe. I lock eyes with her. My breath comes in short gasps as I work hard to relax. Now, for the first time, I want her to come to me. For once, I want to, and am going to, take control of this fight. The thought both surprises and terrifies me.

Lorraine throws her half-shaven head back and laughs. *'Whit the fuck ur ye doin'? Yir a mile oot! Ur ye goanna box me?'*

I don't flinch. I eyeball her. In the end, it's not about who's stronger physically; it's about who's stronger mentally.

Chess with gloves.

Taking a few more steps towards me, Lorraine smirks, circling the knife in the air.

I focus, blocking out the noise and confusion of the others fighting around us. 'Why?' I hear myself ask. 'Why do you hate me?'

'Cos yir an ugly, durty, Fenian cow!' She edges closer.

'That can't just be it – my religion?' Now I'm facing her again; my newfound courage is making me ask her questions that I didn't know that I wanted answers to. I stand still, locked in my position.

Lorraine hesitates, glances over to where Da and Billy are still fighting. *'You tried to take ma man aff i' me! Naebody takes ma man! Ah'm goanna cut you ugly – you'll no' be stealing anybody's man after this!'*

Teeth bared; she comes flying for me like a banshee. In two swift moves, I've swung my left fist into her wrist to knock the knife out of her hand, and I've followed through with a right punch straight to her nose. Her hand flies to her face, and she gawps in disbelief at the blood dripping through her fingers.

I step back into position and wait. I can tell from Lorraine's face that she's not going to give up. She's working out the best way to get me back. She swipes at her nose again and flicks the blood from her hand as she locks eyes with me. She sways from side to side, inching nearer to me. As her eyes slide to my left, a small smile forms on her face, and I realise too late that I'm about to be ambushed from behind.

Someone yanks my hair which makes me trip backwards, but I manage not to lose my balance. Instead, I pivot around and land a left jab onto the surprised face of JoJo. Wordless, her eyes widen as she drops to the ground.

Encouraged that I managed to foil that ambush attempt, I twist to face Lorraine again. It's then that I notice that the fighting around us has stopped, and everyone is stood in a cautious circle around us. The silent strobing of the disco lights picks out faces in the darkness. Ritchie has his arm around Queenie, looking sombre. Da's leaning forward, his face bloody and etched with concern. Steve and Ruaridh stand on either side of him, their arms in front of Da's upper body like they're holding him back.

Sensing I've been distracted, Lorraine charges for me, grabbing my hair so that she can yank my head to the ground. My mind whirls. *How do I get out of this head hold? If she gets me back on the ground, who knows what damage she'll do.*

'*That wis ma wee sister ye just punched!*' She swings me back and forth by the hair.

I laugh through the pain. Of course. That explains a few things. JoJo is Lorraine's sister. 'Now you know how it feels!'

Lorraine screeches. She keeps pulling me by my hair, forcing my head further to the ground. My focus now is to keep her away from the knife which glints nearby. Blocking out the pain, I quiet my mind to think of a plan. My only option to get upright and closer to her is to dig my nails as hard as I can into the underside of her wrists. She squeals, releasing her grip on my hair and dashes to reclaim the knife lying on the floor.

'Yir getting it noo!' Her eyes are fiery as she stands with her hands on her ample hips. '*No' so much Miss Snooty Drawers noo, ur we?*'

Chess with gloves. Throw her off guard.

'Speaking of 'drawers' – I caught your *wee sister* shagging your 'man' last weekend!'

Lorraine's jaw drops. *'Yir a fuckin' liar!'*

'Am I?' I turn to JoJo, who's holding her face. She scrambles backwards as Lorraine lurches for her. JoJo spins on her feet and runs for the door.

'JoJo!' Billy chases after her.

'Not a liar!' I grin triumphantly.

Then, with her head down, Lorraine barrels towards me with the knife.

I've heard the expression 'see red' before but never really understood what it meant until now. My mind shuts down like someone is running around it, flipping off all the lights except one – the one which is focused on making a stand for myself and wee Mary.

Lorraine launches at me. I send a left hook into her side, winding her.

The knife drops from her hand and being careful to trap only the handle with my bare foot, I boot it across the floor. I get back into my boxing position and scowl at her between clenched fists, locked into place by my chin.

My stomach tight and fuelled by adrenaline, I spit: *'Nou bliksem ek vir jou pimpel en pers, jou teef!'* And right now, I'm fully intent on beating this bitch black and blue.

Taking the bait, she swaggers back towards me slowly. *'Wull ye quit wi' that voodoo shite?'* She circles me, presumably looking for a chink in my defences.

As we're facing off, just beyond Lorraine, Da cries out my name.

I lose concentration and Lorraine lunges for me, pulling me down, this time, by my shoulders. I hook alternate blows to the side of her body, and she staggers away from me, clutching her sides.

'*Fuck sake! That's no' fair!*'

We're both taken by surprise as the crowd around us laughs.

Lorraine's indignant, pointing a red fingernail at me. '*It's no funny! She's a hoor! Her mammie's a hoor! Her sister's a hoor!*'

Into my mind pops the memory of Lorraine's mother cruelly slapping my sick Mammie and the pain and the shame on Mammie's face afterwards. 'Don't you dare bring my mammie into this! You are scum! Keep the feck away from my family and me!'

Releasing her arms from her sides, she cackles. '*As long as ye breathe, hen, ah'm here tae make yir life miserable!*'

Instinctively, looking for comfort and strength, I touch Mammie's crystal bead sewn into my dress. It's then that I hurtle towards Lorraine, and rain punch after punch on her.

She has her arms up, doing her best to defend herself, but I'm too strong, and I'm too angry. Blood sprays from her mouth – but it's not enough – I need to hurt her. I need her to know my pain. I will get justice for Mammie, and wee Mary.

On and on, I punch, until a voice inside my head tells me to stop. I take a step back and scowl at her bloodied face, waiting for a reaction. I don't know what I'm expecting. Maybe an apology from her for inflicting years of misery on me? A declaration of surrender?

But she's not apologising, and she's not going down. *'Yur scum.'* She leers, as she begins to circle me again.

Bringing my breathing back under control, I drop my arms to my sides. Leaning forward, I jut my chin defiantly at her. 'Come on! Hit me with your best shot!'

Her eyes flicker. She's trying to work out if this is a trick or not.

Of course, it is. Because as soon as she swings for me, I've blocked it and throw a rapid combination of punches at her, finishing with as powerful an uppercut as I can muster, straight under and up her jaw.

Left-Right, Goodnight!

I knock her off her feet, and she sails backwards onto the floor, unconscious. The crowd cheers. I stare, stunned by their smiling faces.

Breathless and empty, I turn back to Lorraine. She's still lying on the floor; her bloodied face flopped to one side. Her eyes are swelling, and blood trickles from her nose. Her cronies gather around her, but she doesn't seem to stir.

What have I done?

The triumph I expected to enjoy isn't there, and neither is there relief.

Panic seeps into my pores. I've gone too far.

Numb and dazed, I stumble for the exit, to escape. Da approaches me, but I throw his hand off. As I reach the door, one of the bouncers whistles, 'You're some fighter, hen! You ever want a job on the doors, you let me know!'

I nod and step outside. The cold pavement stings my bare feet. The icy chill of the wind nips at my face. I break into a run.

I run harder. I don't want to think. I don't want to feel.

I only want to run ... away.

Chapter 43

Sunday, 28 October 1984

It's dark when I open my eyes. The stiffness in my back, arms and shoulders makes it difficult for me to adjust my body in bed. I'm not ready to think yet. I fall into a dreamless sleep.

The sharp rat-a-tat of hailstones chipping against my bedroom window wakens me. I lie there, comforted by the sound. It's like: *your world may be about to fall apart – but this world – the other world outside – is still carrying on as usual.*

Memories of last night come flooding back. Images turn over in my mind of Billy's fury as he ran after JoJo and Lorraine's bloodied face lying on the floor after I'd knocked her out. I had no idea I was capable of such violence. And I don't feel proud of that. Dread, fear and shame run through me. Did I really fight Lorraine Pollock in front of a crowd, and at Doll's wedding, no less?

There's movement downstairs in the kitchen: cupboard doors being opened and closed, and the noise of the kettle boiling. I think it's Gran because of the rapid-fire precision of the noises. She's making breakfast, her usual Sunday morning fry-up for the family.

When I walk into the living room, Da's sitting alone in the armchair, facing me. 'About last night, kid.' Da runs his hand through his hair as he's speaking; he seems to be as uneasy as I am.

'What about it?' I tug on the sleeves of my jumper and wrap it around me a little more, as I sit on the couch.

Da laughs a little self-consciously as he moves over to join me on the couch. 'I don't know where to start. They say it's not a good wedding until a fight breaks out!' He visibly shudders. 'I'm sorry that you saw me fighting – I had to stop that Billy stabbing you.'

I pick at some balls of fluff from my jumper and add them to a little pile I'm making to the side of me on the sofa. Clearing my throat: 'I'm sorry you had to see me with Lorraine.'

'She's a vile piece of work, isn't she?' Da growls. 'I wanted to stop the fight – tried to. I didn't want you to get hurt, to end up in the state you did last time she battered you. But Steve wouldn't let me - he said that you needed this fight, that you needed to prove yourself against her.' Da joins in with plucking the fluff balls off my sleeve.

I line the little balls of fluff into a circle, then put two balls in the centre. 'At first, I wondered why everyone was just watching me. I felt like I did that night in July when Lorraine and Billy were beating me to a pulp, and none of the neighbours did anything. Then, last night, I knew it was up to me to take care of myself, so I focused. I got calm. It was like tunnel vision; all I could see and hear was Lorraine. And all I could think about was knocking her out.'

Da chuckles. 'Well, you certainly did that! If it weren't for the hair and the dress, I would have thought I was watching a bloke in a boxing match. You looked impressive! And I mean bloody scary!'

I laugh. 'Oh, Da. Did I?'

'Only you could worry about what you looked like in a fight for your life!'

'Don't be dramatic!'

'She had a knife, remember. She meant you harm. Make no mistake about that.'

I stop picking at the fluff on my jumper and look Da in the eye. 'I scared myself last night. I didn't know I could be that violent.'

Da gathers me in for a hug. 'You did what you had to do, kid. She was the aggressor, making your life miserable for years – you only defended yourself.' Hearing Da say this makes me feel better.

He leans back and smiles. 'Let's get some brekkie before your Gran eats all the square sausage!'

When we come into the kitchen, wee Mary's already seated, and Gran finishes putting the last of the breakfast dishes on the table.

Nothing seems different on the face of it, but we sense the undercurrent of unspoken things, all except wee Mary.

'Wasn't yesterday wonderful, Aileen?' Her eyes sparkle as she butters her toast. 'You looked like a princess, and I felt very proud of you.'

I laugh at the unexpected compliment. 'Aw, thanks. I didn't act much like a princess at the end of the night!' I spot the confused look on wee Mary's face just in time. 'I mean – because I was so tired after the long day.'

Da and Gran relax on either side of me. I know Gran well enough to know that Da's told her about last night's events after her and wee Mary left.

'What happened to your hands?' Wee Mary lightly touches my bloody, scabbed knuckles.

'I ... eh ... fell! Tripped up on my heels and landed on my knuckles.' Wow, this is such a bad lie, but wee Mary nods as she picks up a sausage to dip into some tomato sauce on her plate.

Da and Gran seem to be concentrating on eating their breakfasts.

'By the way, Mary, that Lorraine turned up last night. Along with her *sister*, JoJo.' I announce as casually as I can. Gran drops her knife onto her plate with a clatter.

'Sisters? That makes sense. Although they don't look much like each other.' Wee Mary takes a slurp of milky tea.

'Different fathers.' Gran eyes me as she sips her mug of tea. 'Bound to be.'

Wee Mary pauses, now mid-munch of her toast. 'Did they cause trouble?'

'Oh, you could say that.' I ignore the warning look from Da. 'A lot of trouble.' I stab a piece of bacon with my fork and pop it into my mouth.

'Was there a fight?'

'Aye. I decked JoJo, and then I knocked Lorraine out. That's the real reason my knuckles look like this.' The words coming out of my mouth sound flat, like someone else is saying them.

Wee Mary gasps while Gran frowns at me. Da remains quiet.

Gran breaks the silence. 'After everything I've taught you about being a lady, Aileen Murphy! Your da told me what happened. And he told me about Steve teaching you to box.' She glances at my hands. 'My granddaughter bare-knuckle fighting – and at her best pal's wedding of all places!'

'Sorry, Gran. I had to defend myself – she came at me with a knife.'

Wee Mary clutches Gran's arm.

'I had to stand up to her and her sister. They deserved all they got after wee Mary ended up in hospital.'

A half-smile tugs on Gran's lips. 'So, that's why your arms have gotten so muscular. And all the racket in your bedroom when you said you were practising dancing?'

Wee Mary's eyes light up. 'You didn't look like a princess last night – you looked like Wonder Woman! You beat Lorraine and her sister, wearing a tiara and bracelets!'

'I've finally got a superpower.' I smile as I split the yolk on my soft fried egg to pour it over my bacon. I sprinkle a little salt on top. 'I used my superpower to make a stand for both of us.'

Wee Mary springs from her chair to come around the table to hug me. 'Thank you.'

I hug her back, unexpected tears welling in my eyes. 'I'm only sorry it took me this long. That I had to learn boxing first.'

'Can I learn boxing, too?' Wee Mary pouts as the three of us laugh.

There's a loud knock at the front door. Gran ushers the visitor into our kitchen.

I recognise the rain jacket. It's Steve. He's pulled his hood down, a serious look on his face. 'Didn't mean to disturb your breakfast; I just wanted to check on Aileen. And return these.' Steve hands me my silver shoes.

There's a pause in the room, and I realise that I'm afraid of how Da is going to react to Steve's arrival.

I needn't have worried, though, because Da stands to shake Steve's hand. 'You're as welcome as the flowers in May, kid. You know I wasn't happy about you training my daughter how to box – but I'm saying to you now – I'm glad you did.' He points to the empty chair vacated by Gran. 'Have a seat.' Da takes Steve's jacket away to hang it on the stair bannister to dry.

'Would you like some breakfast? We've got plenty left over?' Gran's already filling a plate with assorted breakfast items.

'Okay, then.' Steve laughs, accepting the plate of food Gran's just handed him.

Smiling, I begin to pour myself a mug of tea but am forced to promptly pull away from the handle, as pain sears through my knuckles.

'You'll need to cool the drink with cold water first. Then use the side of your hands to lift the mug. Your knuckles will take a while to heal.'

Steve butters some toast, then chuckles. 'Us lads pee on our hands to help the wounds toughen up! Don't we, Mr Murphy?'

'Oops!' Gran covers wee Mary's ears and indicates that she should go upstairs. Puzzled, wee Mary grabs the last piece of toast from her plate and takes her leave. Gran immediately sits in the chair that wee Mary's just left. While Steve's eating and Gran and Da are making small talk with him, I move the dirty dishes over to the sink. Even through the rubber gloves, the heat of the dishwater makes my knuckles sting, and I gasp.

'Leave them. I'll do them,' Gran commands. She has her bright blue eyes fixed on Steve. 'I believe our Aileen would have given Jim Watt a run for his money last night?'

Steve grins, 'Or Tom Conteh!' He looks across at me: 'I know you weren't in a boxing match. But you pulled some quick-thinking moves out on Lorraine! I was very impressed – especially by your *Left-Right, Goodnight!* combo!' He demonstrates, using his fists.

'What happened after we left?' Da motions his hand over in my direction.

'Lorraine's mates helped her limp out of the door. Billy's mates had enough, too, in the end. They knew they were beaten. They scarpered, not long after Billy went running after JoJo. Gas was already packing his equipment, so the rest of the stragglers left too. I think they had a night to remember! There was broken glass everywhere. I've never seen so much! Then the police arrived – a bit late – but they took a statement from Alan and gave him a crime number to claim off the insurance.

'Shakey got glassed on the head, so we went to the hospital. Your pal, Angela, was working on reception – she was asking for you.' Steve smiles over at me. 'She recognised me as soon as I walked in, joked that I'm always bringing in trouble.

'A few of the other lads got stitches too. Not me. Once we'd all been checked over, we decided to go back to McCoy's for a lock-in. We went in, and Alan and the bar staff were drinking coffee around the bar.'

Steve's eyes shine as he recalls more of the story. He puts on his best Scottish accent. 'Shakey asked, *'Whit's aw this? Where's the beer?'* And Alan said, *'There isnae a whole glass left in the bar! We're drinking beer oot i' these mugs.'* Imagine that, eh? Not a single glass left. So, we pulled up our bar stools and joined them!'

The four of us laugh. Gran places her knife and fork to the side of her plate.

'Sounds like it was definitely a wedding to remember!' Gran rises to finish clearing the rest of the breakfast things.

Steve stands too. 'Anyway, I need to go. Mum wants some help moving stuff in the hairdressers. Just wanted to check on you, Aileen.'

When I open the front door to let Steve out, he gently cups the side of my face. 'You, okay?'

I nod, placing my hand on his, and watch his face while I whisper, 'Thank you for everything. You have no idea what you've done for me.'

Steve kisses the back of my hand. 'No bother, *Sassy Lassie*.'

Sadness steals through me as he uses his boxing nickname for me. I so miss boxing training with Steve. When it's just us, and I have his undivided attention.

Then, as Steve makes his way down the front steps, he turns to me with a cheeky grin, 'Can I take you out sometime?'

Taken by surprise, heat blooms in my cheeks and I can only nod as I close the door behind me. With a huge grin on my face, I punch the air with joy.

When I return to the living room, Gran is standing by the window, watching Steve's car disappear into the rain. 'He's a Protestant, isn't he?'

'Yes, I think so.' Panic rises in me. Oh, my God. Gran's going to tell me that I'm not allowed to see Steve.

'He's a nice laddie.' Gran turns to smile at me.

Shocked, I manage to smile back at her.

'He's done an amazing thing for you – teaching you that boxing. Are you winching him?'

'No!' My defensiveness melts when I spot the twinkle in Gran's eyes.

'Because if you are, I approve. I take back everything I ever said about Protestant men. He's a keeper.' Gran winks at me, and leaving me speechless, heads upstairs.

·》··◆··《·

Outside, the weather is clearing, so I pop on my winter coat to take Bruno for a walk. I've no particular destination in mind. I'm just walking on whichever street I want to.

Splashing through puddles, I'm soon lost in thought. At first, I think about my almost-kiss with Steve. Well, I suppose it was a kiss. And it was certainly sweet. One of the best kisses I've ever had. But it was just a short one that was interrupted. My thoughts turn next to Lorraine and JoJo, who it turns out are sisters, like me and wee Mary. Except we don't pick on people for the enjoyment of it.

Still mulling things over in my mind, I don't notice the gang on the street corner until it's too late. My first instinct is to cross the road or turn around, but Bruno pulls me forward. The gang members stare. My heart sinks as I recognise some of them as people who've bullied me in the past. The chilly air nips at the scabbed skin of my knuckles as I take my hands out of my pockets.

Then, baffled, I watch in disbelief as the gang members divide to make space for me to pass through. My heart thudding in my chest, one of them hisses as I pass, 'That's the lassie that knocked out Lorraine Pollock last night! Did you see her knuckles?'

I flex my fists as I walk on, a slow grin spreading across my face, relishing this moment I never dreamed would happen.

Bruno tugs at his lead, his nose to the ground, and I trot to keep up with him. I could walk forever; I have so many thoughts colliding in my head. Through an open window, the sound of Radio 1's Top Forty countdown plays. I'd normally be in Marie's house with Geraldine, enjoying this. Regret hits me as I realise that I miss my pal. Maybe in time, I can forgive Geraldine and move on.

Up ahead, a girl with short messy hair speed marches towards me. She's dressed in leggings, flat shoes and a baggy black coat. I know now that I don't need to cross any more streets to avoid people. I keep walking towards her.

Nevertheless, I keep my eyes on the ground, wishing just to walk, undisturbed.

'Aileen?'

Surprised, I look up into the girl's make-up-less, pale face. At the same time, as I register the fear in her eyes, I realise that I'm looking at Geraldine. A very plain, stripped-back version of Geraldine.

'Didn't recognise me, eh?' She pulls her coat sleeves over her hands, hopping from one foot to the other.

'I was coming to see you. To tell you how sorry I am. Even if you don't ever talk to me again, I had to say that to your face.' Geraldine speaks rapidly, bowing her head. 'I've been too afraid to see you. I'm a coward.'

'I think we all are, somewhere, deep down.' Bruno whines and sits at my feet.

'I was just in Marie's house, listening to the Top Forty. She told me all about last night. And you taking up boxing?' Geraldine shakes her head and gazes at my fists.

I nod.

'I just said to her that I have to go find you, to apologise, right now. And here you are.' Her eyes glisten with tears. 'I am so sorry. I was a jealous cow. I let you down.' Her face crumples.

Exhausted from all the recent drama, I say nothing.

'Can you ever forgive me?'

I bite my lip and take a step towards her. 'Yes. You did me a favour in the end. I should have split with Paul a long time ago.'

Geraldine raises her eyebrows.

'But maybe you'll think twice about nicking someone else's boyfriend in the future?'

Geraldine chuckles, wiping her eyes. 'Have you noticed my new 'nun' look? I've been doing my own form of penance. Plain clothes, no make-up, no boys and only soft drinks when I go out.'

I'm not sure I can get used to this toned-down, subdued version of Geraldine. Tugging on her oversized shabby coat, I tell her: 'The world's not right unless you're glammed up.'

Geraldine chuckles. 'You know, when I saw you from a distance, I didn't recognise you either with your curly hair and bruised knuckles. I almost crossed the road.'

Chapter 44

Wednesday, 7 November 1984

'How lucky are you, Aileen, to be going to a U2 concert for your birthday?'

I grin at Marie and Geraldine as we're stood shivering under a bus shelter, waiting on a minibus to take us to the concert at the Glasgow Barrowlands.

Being our first proper concert, we've no idea what to expect, but just the thought of Bono and the rest of U2 being in the same room as us, playing our favourite songs, has us giddy with excitement. And, as if that isn't enough, Steve's coming along with Marie and Geraldine's boyfriends, and Doll and Sandy, just back from their honeymoon. This is going to be the best birthday ever.

The girls have chosen a rock-chick look for me, teaming a black denim jacket with a grey second-hand U2 T-shirt that I bought in the market from their last *War* tour and a pair of bleached jeans and black high-heeled boots. My curly hair falls loose down my shoulders and inspired by Geraldine, I've put on eye make-up and bright red lipstick. Despite it being early November, Marie and Geraldine have dressed in thin tops, mini-skirts, and little jackets. Neither wears tights, and both stamp their feet to keep warm.

We're dazzled by the headlights of an approaching minibus as it comes to a smooth halt alongside us.

'Three to Glasgow Barrowlands?' Steve jumps out to hold the door open for us. 'Happy birthday!' I blush as he pecks me on the cheek.

Sandy grins at us from behind the steering wheel. Inside, there are seats on either side of the minibus, facing each other.

Geraldine wiggles past me to sit beside a beaming Shakey, and Marie hurries to take a seat beside Ruaridh. Doll's sitting immediately behind Sandy, and there's a spare seat beside her which I take. I haven't spoken properly to my best pal in nearly a fortnight.

Doll hands me a birthday card. 'Finally seventeen, eh?'

This prompts the rest of the minibus to erupt into an uproarious rendition of "Happy Birthday". Grinning, I try to shush everyone.

Snuggled against Ruaridh, Marie calls to Doll, 'How was your honeymoon?'

'Gorgeous, thanks! And that's all the details you're getting.' Doll chuckles. 'But tell us more about the rammy at our wedding.'

This starts a conversation with everyone's take on what happened and who did and said what. I cover my face, embarrassed, as Steve, Shakey, Ruaridh, and Marie are full of praise for how I fought JoJo and Lorraine and 'sent them packing'.

'Big shock for that Lorraine when Aileen revealed that Billy had been shagging her sister.' Shakey laughs at the memory. 'He's a wee skitter pretending to be a gangster. I bet he scarred his own face.'

'There's something not right about him, though.' Sandy calls out, his eyes fixed on the motorway in front of him. 'I know he used to be my best pal. But he's turned ... nasty, bitter.'

The minibus turns into a car park near the Barrowlands. As we assemble outside, Steve takes my hand. I don't know what this means, but I'm not objecting.

Doll raises an eyebrow at me as Sandy puts his arm around her, and we walk out of the car park towards the Barrowlands.

As we near the venue, the animated chatter of the crowd drifts towards us. The queue's already long, snaking back from the entrance and down the street. The multi-coloured flashing lights of the Barrowlands neon sign are reflected on a huge puddle in the middle of the road. With Steve holding my hand and walking with my pals to my first-ever concert, I could explode with joy. I smile up at Steve; he grins back at me. Even if nothing else happens, I'm happy to enjoy the warmth and strength of his hand on mine.

Shakey speeds up and ushers us to follow him and Geraldine past the crowd. When we arrive at the entrance, he has a word with the security guys, and the next thing, we're being counted in.

Steve realises before me what's just happened. 'Nice one!'

Shakey shrugs his shoulders and winks at me. 'It's the least I can do for the birthday girl.'

'Have you just got us in first?'

'Aye. I work the doors with these guys in Glasgow through the week. They know they've got unlimited free entry to McCoy's in return!' We all laugh. I'm delighted we didn't have to stand at the back of the long queue to get in.

'It also means that we get to the front of the stage too.' Shakey's eyes shine as he leads us through the wooden doors into the former ballroom, now turned concert venue. I don't know what I was expecting, but the inside is much bigger than I imagined. Feeling the same wonder that I feel when I walk into a new church, we stride across the empty dance floor towards the stage.

Shivers tingle up and down my spine as I drink in the atmosphere. I turn to look at Steve. He is the view that I'd also never tire of gazing at.

'It's like a dream.' I murmur. 'Do you think the band are backstage right now?' I'm giddy with excitement. Along with my pals, we take our place in a line along the edge of the stage.

Steve and I stand in silence, staring at the stage in front of us where guitars sit on stands and the drum kit and keyboards are laid out. He leans into me, his eyes bright as he whispers, 'I have a secret to confess.'

I turn to face him, chuckling. 'No secrets – they only get me into trouble!'

He takes both my hands. 'Do you remember our new song? The one called "Heart Attack"?'

'Yes, the one you played at your last gig in McCoy's. What of it?'

'I wrote that song about you.'

I grin with delight as Steve puts his arm around me.

Doll taps me on my shoulder, making me jump. 'Sandy and I are moving to the back of the gig – don't want the baby squashed – great view of U2 or not,' she says, then, almost as an afterthought, adds, 'You two look *great* together.'

Steve watches me, smiling, 'Are we together?'

I hesitate.

'Looks like it to me!' Doll winks, kisses my cheek quickly and grins at Steve as she and Sandy make their way back through the throngs.

Still reeling from Steve's secret, I watch with him as the stage lights dim. Whistles and cheers rise from the crowd behind us. He grins at me as some guys come onto the stage. I turn to him, confused. 'That's not U2.'

Steve laughs and shouts in my ear. There's always a warm-up act at every concert. This band is called The Waterboys.'

I hop up and down. 'Aw, I just want to see U2!'

'They won't play long. Besides, I've heard that they're pretty good.' And The Waterboys are good, but everyone's come to see U2.

In the break between bands, the crowd stamp their feet and clap their hands rhythmically. Some roadies come onto the stage to test the equipment to the sound of fresh cheers from the crowd. When they leave, the lights dim again, and I stare, starstruck, as U2 bound onto the stage to a deafening roar.

Steve and I and our gang grin at each other and turn back to watch as the black-clad figure of Bono launches into "11 O'Clock Tick Tock". The crowd surges forward, and I thrill as Steve stands behind me to act as a buffer against them. With his arms linked around my waist at the front, he strains his body against the forward pressure of the fans standing behind us. Now ecstatic, I watch each of the band as they play their instruments and sing. I want to pinch myself. I cannot believe that U2 is right there, just a few feet away from me, playing all my favourite songs, live. And the man of my dreams has just declared that he has a crush on me.

In between songs, Bono talks to us. 'Do you know who I want to be president of the United States? Bruce Springsteen!' The crowd roars their approval.

'Wouldn't that be something?' Steve's breath is warm on my ear. 'I don't think he'd put up with any snash from Maggie Thatcher, though, like that Ronald Reagan does!'

Later, when U2 play the opening notes of "Bad", I reach up to tell Steve that this is my favourite U2 song. He hugs me tighter, and then something miraculous happens. Bono crouches in front of me, takes my hand and sings to me.

All too soon, though, Bono moves to a different part of the crowd. Further along the edge of the stage, Geraldine and Marie, Shakey and Ruaridh wave their arms, cheering for me. I'm on cloud nine. I've made up with my pals, Steve is holding me, and the guy on the popstar poster on my wall has just sung one of my favourite songs to me.

I lean back into Steve. 'My seventeenth birthday couldn't be any better.'

He beams and tugs gently on my hand to turn me around to face him. Now, I'm oblivious to U2 playing behind me and the noise and movement of the crowd in front of me. All I can do is stare into Steve's beautiful blue eyes, which are the softest and brightest I have ever seen them. My stomach tightens; I can hardly breathe.

And then it happens. The moment I've been dreaming of – our next kiss. Very gently, Steve inclines his head towards me, and his lips find mine. He kisses me softly, sweetly. I close my eyes. Joy surges through me as I kiss him back, hesitantly at first. Steve slides one arm across my shoulder, the other around my waist, as he pulls me closer to his body. He kisses me more deeply. My body thrills as I press myself against him, pulling him tighter towards me. Every fibre in my body lights up.

Time seems to stand still. As we kiss, I feel the energy of the crowd around us, the music ringing in my ears. Reluctantly, I break the kiss. Steve slowly opens his eyes and smiles at me.

Complete contentment washes over me as Steve hugs me against him. I sigh and snuggle against his chest and shoulder, closing my eyes. My heart soars when Steve murmurs into my ear, 'You make me feel amazing.' He holds me close as we turn to watch the band again.

I tease him: 'Imagine what it'll be like when you play big concerts like this.'

He laughs. 'The Clyde Alloys have a lot more work to do. I could only dream of owning a stage like him!' We watch Bono as he prowls around the stage, standing high, crouching low, singing to different sections of the crowd – lifting the tempo and bringing the mood back down. 'He has the audience eating out of his hand!'

After a few encores, too soon, the concert ends. We wait for the crowd behind us to disperse towards the exit before we do the same and catch up with the others. Outside, it's pouring with rain, but nothing can dampen our spirits.

Doll grins as Steve puts his arm across my shoulder.

'So, wishes on engagement rings really do come true, eh? Even in the darkness, I can spot you blushing, Aileen Murphy! About time you two, is all I can say!' Doll tenderly rubs her baby bump, which has become more prominent since her wedding day.

Back in the minibus on the way home, the chat is all about the concert. I'm cuddled against Steve, and Doll has her feet across two seats, leaning with her back against Sandy's driving seat, hands across her tummy. I smile over at her as the streak of a streetlight passes us in the darkness. I feel so high, and my ears are still ringing from the concert.

'Life's good.' Ruaridh remarks, stroking Marie's hair.

I snuggle some more into Steve. 'I don't think I could be any happier.'

'Thanks so much for the free U2 tickets, Shakey!' I call out, and the rest of the minibus joins in.

'No bother!' Shakey calls back, his arm draped around Geraldine's shoulder. Shakey's big hairy frame really contrasts with the petite, well-turned-out figure of my pal. They look so opposite that I would never in a million years have put them together as a couple, but somehow, they suit each other.

Another thought occurs to me. 'Now, will you tell me why you're called 'Shakey'? He's dodged the question every time I've asked, and everyone else seems to be in the know except me.

Shakey laughs his deep-throated laugh. 'Shall I show her?'

'Aye, for feck sake – put her out of her misery! I'm fed up with her asking me!' Sandy calls from the driving seat.

'Get your kit off!' Doll giggles, her eyes bright with mischief.

'Okay.' Shakey grumbles as he starts to unbutton his shirt. Everyone begins to sing '"The Stripper".

'Shut it!' Shakey growls, standing to take his shirt off. The first thing I notice is how hairy he is.

'What?' Confused, I peer at his naked upper body, which, apart from being hairy, is covered in tattoos.

Shakey sighs. He extends his arms out like Jesus on the Cross.

'What?' I'm struggling to see when suddenly the streetlights illuminate his body. Then the answer to one of life's mysteries is revealed to me.

There's a portrait of a man with a ruffle collar on the inside of Shakey's right arm. I laugh, a little nervously. 'Is that Shakespeare?'

'Aye, what of it?' Shakey says, sounding defensive.

'I'm just ... surprised!'

'Don't judge a book by its cover, Aileen Murphy. I might be a big, hairy biker, but I love Shakespeare. The man knew his stuff. And he knew about us eejits – how we all operate – the lies, the love, the deceit, the loyalty ....'

Geraldine pulls Shakey back onto his seat. 'Sit back down, ya big teddy bear!'

He looks at her, about to speak. She kisses him before he can.

Chapter 45

Saturday, 10 November 1984

The door to the ladies bathroom creaks open, and the noise from a packed McCoy's drifts in. Gas is spinning the records tonight, getting the crowd warm for the Clyde Alloys as the headline act. Steve, Sandy, and the lads are especially excited as Gas has hinted that there may be an Edinburgh record producer he knows coming through to watch the band.

I've locked myself into a toilet cubicle to stretch my stiff arms and shoulders out in private following yesterday's boxing training session with Steve. I adjust the spaghetti straps of my black dress while I finish the upper body stretches.

From the left, just outside my toilet cubicle, a couple of women giggle. 'Oh my God! What does she look like? Has no one told her?'

I stop what I'm doing, straining to hear better. Are they talking about me? I double-check the gap between the door and the floor and overhead, and no, there are no faces gawping at me, or secret mirrors slid under or over to spy on me. The women on the other side of the door must be talking about someone else.

A voice hisses, 'Halloween was last month! Look at the state of her!' They erupt into fresh peels of stifled laughter.

Another voice muses: 'Do you think she even looked in a mirror before she left her house?'

Eager to get back to Doll, Marie and Geraldine and be ready for the Clyde Alloys' entrance, I finish my stretches. I clear my throat and turn the handle of the cubicle door to step out. Three women with big hair, too much make-up and expensive-looking clothes glance back at me. They shuffle further to the left, still staring at whoever is at the sink area, which is out of my sight. Judging by the noises, I'm guessing the woman at the sink is rifling through her handbag for make-up.

'Haw, you!' One of the three women shouts, 'Yir gi'in me the boak!' Another pretends to vomit. The others laugh.

'Whit dae ye mean?' The girl at the sink's voice falters.

One of the women, I'm guessing the ringleader, changes tack. 'Ah heard you called me a cow.'

My stomach tightens. Fighting talk. A familiar challenge, usually to get beaten, but this time, not directed at me – yet!

The woman by the sink's voice shakes. 'How can I call you a cow when I don't even know who you are?'

'Ur you callin' me a liar?' The same script. The ringleader folds her arms.

My fists clench. I stand still, unsure of what to do next. I can wait it out here or just walk past the women. *Nothing to see here. Move on.* I know, though, that I'm inserting myself into this fight as soon as I walk forward.

And all I want is to enjoy a night out with my best pals, watching my boyfriend play in our favourite band. Perhaps, I can reason with them? Gulping, I step forward. 'Ladies. There's no need for this. We're all here to enjoy a night out. Leave the lassie alone.'

'And who the fuck are you?' The ringleader snorts.

She clickety-clacks over to the door of the women's bathroom, and her two friends join her. The ringleader lifts the door handle, clicks something which sounds like a lock.

Great. Now we're trapped.

I take a few steps towards the women; they take a few steps backwards, forming a tighter line across the exit. The lassie by the sink sighs, and when I turn, JoJo Pollock is gawping back at me, clearly as surprised as I am – at this – our unexpected next meeting.

Jeez, if I'd known it was her, I wouldn't have bothered getting involved! At the same time, another part of me is aware of how vulnerable and wretched she looks, her make-up smeared across her face, her eyes red and puffy, as though she's been crying.

'Answer me! Who the fuck are you?' The ringleader rolls up the sleeves of her suit jacket.

My nerves jangle. I could just push past these women and leave that JoJo to fight her own corner. She and her rotten relatives have made my family suffer, but another part of me knows that this isn't right. It doesn't *feel* right. JoJo's outnumbered. Despite their well-dressed appearances, these women want a fight – an ugly fight.

I take a few more steps towards the gang, pulling myself up tall. 'I don't answer to you. Get the fuck out, or I'll make you!'

They look uncertain, and one of them asks, 'Do you even know this sad case!' She gestures over to JoJo, who's still stood by the sink, eyes cast downwards, her knuckles white from clutching her handbag.

'I know *her.*' I step forward some more until I'm within punching distance of them. I spread my feet, clench my fists by my side.

'Aye, she knows me.' JoJo calls. 'She's a great boxer.'

I'm self-conscious of how muscly I've become, but I flex my arm and shoulder muscles for effect as a warning sign to the women.

JoJo continues, 'She's knocked me oot, ma big sister, and even a hard man like Billy McIntyre!'

The ringleader holds her ground. 'You don't scare me. Ah'll have a square go with ye!'

'Fine.' I only tap the ringleader with a left and right body hook. She drops to the floor, groaning.

'Now, fuck off! The lot of you!' I unlock and swing the bathroom door open to shove the three women out into the packed pub. Shaking, I slam the bathroom door behind me and lock it again.

I turn to JoJo. Only the sound of a dripping tap can be heard.

Wide-eyed, JoJo heaves a sigh of relief. Then she frowns. 'Why did you help me?'

'Good question.' I pause.

It comes to me as I search her pale face. 'Because everyone deserves to feel safe.'

Black mascara-stained tears roll down her cheeks. 'Thank you.'

I nod an acknowledgement, and, leaving JoJo in the bathroom, I stride out into the crowd. Doll, Marie, and Geraldine greet me as I claim the spot they've saved for me in front of the stage.

When the lights dim, I make out Steve, my Steve, and the rest of the Clyde Alloys emerge onto the stage. In the semi-darkness, he finds my face and winks at me. I smile and wave back. My knuckles smart, reminding me that only a few minutes ago, I had doled out a one-two body blow to a bully back in the bathroom. I flex my hands, feeling the strength and power within them, the strength that's always been within me.

How times have changed. *How I've changed.*

Steve's voice booms. 'We're the Clyde Alloys!' The band immediately launches into the opening of Depeche Mode's "New Life". Beams of light move around the stage and over the crowd as it surges forward. The girls squeal. I love the band's more punked-out version of the song. Doll blows Sandy a kiss as she and the girls dance and sway next to me.

Caught up in the excitement, I raise my arms in the air. Steve grins at me, but instead of blowing him a kiss, I ball my hands into fists and pantomime *Left-Right, Goodnight!* Microphone in hand, Steve stumbles back, pretending to receive my air punches. The crowd eats it up.

Then the keyboard and guitars drop out of the song, with only the beat of Sandy's drums and Steve's vocals booming across McCoy's. Fervent voices from the crowd join Steve and the Clyde Alloys as they chant "*New Life, New Life*".

My voice sings loudest.

Acknowledgments

I'm grateful to everyone who has helped and supported me in writing *Real Gone Kid*. Please forgive me if I've forgotten to list you here: know that my gratitude remains for your contribution.

My warm thanks and love to my mother, Margaret, and my siblings Gerry, Frank, Maggie and Wendy for their wholehearted support and enthusiastic contributions. I'm also grateful to my Icelandic relatives, especially Árni, Thor, Sverrir and Elísabet. I'm lucky to have such an amazing family!

For her kind support, I'm deeply grateful to Jane Couch MBE, former five times world boxing champion and pioneer of women's professional boxing in the UK; and to Colin McAuley, a three-weight Royal Air Force Boxing Champion and Combined Services Featherweight Boxing Champion, who generously offered his knowledge and experience about all things boxing in the 1980s.

I also wish to acknowledge my high school English teacher, Mr William Duddy, who, along with my father, nurtured my love of reading and literature. And to Jack Black from MindStore; and Senga from Senga Cree Coaching, who helped me believe what could be possible.

Special mentions go to my book coach and friend, the lovely Nicole Johnston; my wonderful editor, Andy Moseley and Lynne Walker, a more perfect proofreader I could not have found! And to acknowledge Julie Adams from New Leaf Book Design for the beautiful cover, Fiona Morear for the business support and David Elder for the social media designs.

I would like to thank James Lees, Jim Nicholas and Harry Morton for answering my questions about Ravenscraig. For their input on bands of the 1980s, my thanks go to Paul and Alan from Liverpool band Candy Opera. I'm also grateful to Emma, Lynn, and Ilker and Kathryn. Thanks to Letitia Boshoff who kindly reviewed the Afrikaans sections for me, and to Amy Simpson, who taught me the *Left-Right! Goodnight!* punch combo.

Massive thanks to my critique partners, Liv and Lissa-Rae, and my beta readers whose honest feedback helped shape the book into what it is now: Tracey, Karen, Elise, Caitlhan, Julie, Richard, Angela Cullen, Angela Travis, Kat, Kevin and Dorothy.

And finally, my huge love and gratitude go to my husband, Jón, and my son, Daníel, for being so understanding, patient, and thoughtful when I'd disappear off to work on *Real Gone Kid.*

About Author

KATE FRIDRIKS is a Scottish writer from Wishaw and Motherwell. She spent her early years in a South African steel town and her later childhood and teenage years within sight of the Ravenscraig steelworks.

Her debut novel, *Real Gone Kid*, is inspired by her experiences.

For further information about the author and news of her next novel, visit www.katefridriks.com

Printed in Great Britain
by Amazon